W9-CCV-377

THE COLLECTED STORIES OF WILLIAM GOYEN

Books by William Goyen

THE COLLECTED STORIES

THE HOUSE OF BREATH, 25TH ANNIVERSARY EDITION

COME, THE RESTORER

SELECTED WRITINGS

A BOOK OF JESUS

THE FAIR SISTER

THE FACES OF BLOOD KINDRED

IN A FARTHER COUNTRY

GHOST AND FLESH

THE HOUSE OF BREATH

THE COLLECTED STORIES OF WILLIAM GOYEN

1975

DOUBLEDAY & COMPANY, INC., GARDEN CITY, NEW YORK

Loving gratitude, as always, to my special spirit, my wife, Doris.

And I feel special gratitude to Robert Phillips for his help in bringing this book together and for his loyalty in general.

Some of the stories in this book were previously published in GHOST AND FLESH and THE FACES OF BLOOD KINDRED published by Random House, Inc. Other stories were first published in the following publications: *The Saturday Evening Post*, THE FIGURE OVER THE TOWN, Copyright © 1963 by The Curtis Publishing Company; *Transatlantic Review*, TENANTS as TENANT IN THE GARDEN; *The Atlantic Monthly*, BRIDGE OF MUSIC, RIVER OF SAND, Copyright © 1975 by The Atlantic Monthly Company; *The Bicentennial Collection of Texas Short Stories*, TAPIOCA SURPRISE, Copyright © 1974 by James P. White; *The Southwest Review*, The Southern Methodist University Press (Dallas) publisher, THE ENCHANTED NURSE, THE RESCUE, THE THIEF COYOTE, Copyright © 1953, 1954, 1971, respectively, by The Southern Methodist University Press.

The author wishes to acknowledge the following publications which first published some of his stories: *Best American Short Stories*, *Botteghe Oscure*, *Transition*, *Kenyon Review*, *Mademoiselle*, *Harper's Magazine*, *New Story*, and *Partisan Review*.

Library of Congress Cataloging in Publication Data

Goyen, William.
The collected stories of William Goyen.

I. Title.
PZ3.G7484Ck [PS3513.097] 813'.5'4
ISBN 0-385-00734-5
Library of Congress Catalog Card Number 75-6157

Printed in the United States of America
First Edition

For
Margaret Hartley and Allen Maxwell.
With me through all this,
through all the years.

CONTENTS

Preface

Of the twenty-six stories in this volume, nineteen were originally published in two volumes under the titles *Ghost and Flesh* and *The Faces of Blood Kindred,* and the remaining seven in American and European magazines. Some of the uncollected stories have enjoyed a long-time popularity in Europe and have only recently been published in America ("Tenants," "Tapioca Surprise," "The Thief Coyote"), years after they were written. The stories cover a span of nearly thirty years: "The White Rooster" was first published in 1947 in *Mademoiselle;* "Bridge of Music, River of Sand" was published in 1975 in *The Atlantic Monthly.*

A number of these stories were written in the fifties, which now turns out to have been a kind of Golden Age of the short story in America. In those days we were all publishing in several magazines, large and small. *Mademoiselle,* with high enthusiasm, published many of us young story writers, including James Purdy, Truman Capote, Jean Stafford, Shirley Jackson and Tennessee Williams. This was because of two women, Cyrilly Abels and Margarita Smith, the editors. Many serious American writers owe a debt to these two women of taste, courage and belief.

But no matter where these stories of mine were published, a small but enduring and distinguished magazine has played the most prominent part in my writing over the years. This is *The Southwest Review.* Through the years, since 1946, the editors, Allen Maxwell and Margaret Hartley, fervently and faithfully published my stories. I cannot imagine my life and its work of writing, from the very beginning, without Allen and Margaret and *The Southwest Review*. Whatever its meaning, the progress of my work is documented in its pages and issues, year after year. It is a calendar, a diary. And Margaret Hartley and Allen Maxwell have been a presence in the life of my writing.

For what it is worth to those who want to write stories or simply to know something of one writer's insight in the writing of short fiction, I have felt the short-story form as some vitality, some force that begins (and not necessarily at the *beginning*), grows in force, reaches a point beyond which it cannot go without losing force, loses force and declines; stops. For me, story telling is a rhythm, a charged movement, a chain of pulses or beats. To write out of life is to catch, in pace, this pulse that beats in the material of life. If one misses this rhythm, his story does not seem to "work"; is mysteriously dead; seems to imitate life but has not joined life. The story is therefore uninteresting to the reader (and truly to the writer himself), or not clear. I believe this is a good principle to consider.

But for me, as I have written, I've been mainly interested in the teller-listener situation. Somebody is telling something to somebody: an event! Who's listening to this telling? Where is the listener? I've not been interested in simply reproducing a big section of life off the streets or from the Stock Exchange or Congress. I've cared most about the world in one person's head. Mostly, then, I've cared about the buried song in somebody, and sought it passionately; or the music in what happened. And so I have thought of my stories as folk song, as ballad, or rhapsody. This led me to be concerned with speech, lyric speech—my heritage. Since the people of the region where most of my stories start—or end (they do, I believe, move in and through the great world) are natural talkers and use their speech with gusto and often with the air and bravura of singers; and since the language of their place is rich with phrases and expressions out of the King James Bible, from the Negro imagination and the Mexican fantasy, from Deep South Evangelism, from cottonfield and cotton gin, oil field, railroad and sawmill, I had at my ears a glorious sound. A marvelous instrument of language was *given* to me. I worked with this instrument as though it were a fiddle or a cello, to get its true music out of it; and I was finally able to detach myself from this speech so as to be able to hear it almost as a foreign language; and in several of my stories (most notably "Ghost and Flesh, Water and Dirt"), I have wanted to record as closely as possible the speech as *heard*—as though I were notating music.

The landscape of my stories, generally East Texas, is pastoral, river-haunted, tree-shaded, mysterious and bewitched. Spirits and ghosts inhabit it: the generations have not doubted their presence, their doings. Here there exists the local splendor of simple people who "wonder" and "imagine." Some heartbreak is here, too; and something of doom. The landscape of these folk, and mine, is more like Poussin or Claude or Manet than Grant Wood or Norman Rockwell or Rosa Bonheur.

Landscape and language and folk, I seized it all, early, as mine to work with and to make some manner of art out of. It truly was, early, my absolute life's work and my dedication. In Europe, in nearly a dozen states of the United States, this was my work. Living in Rome, it was never more urgent, this faraway haunting landscape, this ringing speech, this tender and yearning, rollicking people, this notion, this vision of "home," this ache of "homesickness." It seems to me that I was always homesick. Standing before great paintings in Venice or Paris, I saw my own people in Rembrandt's, my own countryside in Corot's. Europa was my fat cousin in Trinity, Texas (pop. 900) and the bull that was "raping" her was our own, named Roma. I wrote quite a bit about them both.

When I was two-thirds through my first novel, *The House of Breath,* I announced to my editor, Robert Linscott, that I was going to live in Europe for a while. He was astonished that I would make such a radical move and seriously concerned that the book would lose focus and vitality. I went, and the immense experience disturbed my concentration not at all: what I saw in Europe I put right into my novel: it fit very well—ancient frescoes, grand avenues, plazas, noble ruins—into the little town of "Charity" that I was creating out of my own home town of Trinity, Texas. Ernst Robert Curtius, the distinguished German translator of this novel wrote in his Preface:[1] " 'The House of Breath', to be

[1] "Haus aus Hauch," *Verlag Der Arche*. Zurich, 1952. (English translation by Michael Kowal, in *Essays on European Literature,* E. R. Curtius, Princeton University Press, 1973.)

sure, tells us about Charity and East Texas; yet when it does extend itself, it reaches only as far as neighboring Louisiana. And for all that, this book is different from a regional novel. No regionalism is offered here. The language and the landscape of East Texas are only foils to a fabric, in which vital and neighborly human beings talk and move about. In the kitchen of the house near Charity hangs a map of the world. To the boy, whose story is being told, the outlines of countries and continents seem to be the organs of the human body. The organization and formation of the earth has imprinted itself upon the child's consciousness, and in the most perceptual form. In sleepy Charity he had sensed the quality of the whole world and realized that he belonged to it. So it is that this novel of a childhood has become a book of universal scope."

So, I could hope, for these stories that came out of that same childhood, that same town, that same breath.

William Goyen

New York City
January 1975

THE COLLECTED STORIES OF WILLIAM GOYEN

The White Rooster

[Walter's Story]

There were two disturbances in Mrs. Marcy Samuels' life that were worrying her nearly insane. First, it was, and had been for two years now, Grandpa Samuels, who should have long ago been dead but kept wheeling around her house in his wheel chair, alive as ever. The first year he came to live with them it was plain that he was in good health and would probably live long. But during the middle of the second year he fell thin and coughing and after that there were some weeks when Mrs. Samuels and her husband, Watson, were sure on Monday that he would die and relieve them of him before Saturday. Yet he wheeled on and on, not ever dying at all.

The second thing that was about to drive Marcy Samuels crazy was a recent disturbance which grew and grew until it became a terror. It was a stray white rooster that crowed at her window all day long and, worst of all, in the early mornings. No one knew where he came from, but there he was, crowing to all the other roosters far and near—and they answering back in a whole choir of crowings. His shrieking was bad enough, but then he had to outrage her further by digging in her pansy bed. Since he first appeared to harass her, Mrs. Samuels had spent most of her day chasing him out of the flowers or throwing objects at him where he was, under her window, his neck stretched and strained in a perfectly blatant crow. After a week of this, she was almost frantic, as she told her many friends on the telephone or in town or from her back yard.

It seemed that Mrs. Samuels had been cursed with problems all her life and everyone said she had the unluckiest time of it. That a woman sociable and busy as Marcy Samuels should have her father-in-law, helpless in a wheel chair, in her house to keep and take care of was just a shame. And Watson, her husband, was no help at all, even though it was his very father who was so much trouble. He was a slow, patient little man, not easily ruffled. Marcy Samuels was certain that he was not aware that her life was so hard and full of trouble.

She could not stand at her stove, for instance, but what Grandpa Samuels was there, asking what was in the pot and smelling of it. She could not even have several of the women over without him riding in and out among them, weak as he was, as they chatted in confidence about this or that town happening, and making bright or ugly remarks about women and what they said, their own affairs. Marcy, as she often told Watson, simply could not stop Grandpa's mouth, could not stop his wheels, could not get him out of her way. And she was busy. If she was hurrying across a room to get some washing in the sink or to get the broom, Grandpa Samuels would make a surprise run out at her from the hall or some door and streak across in front of her, laughing fiendishly or shouting boo! and then she would leap as high as her bulbous ankles would lift her and scream, for she was a nervous woman and had so many things on her mind. Grandpa had a way of sneaking into things Marcy did, as a weevil slips into a bin of meal and bores around in it. He had a way of objecting to Marcy, which she sensed everywhere. He haunted her, pestered her. If she would be bending down to find a thing in her cupboard, she would suddenly sense some shadow over her and then it would be Grandpa Samuels, he would be there, touch her like a ghost in the ribs and frighten her so that she would bounce up and let out a scream. Then he would just sit and grin at her with an owlish face. All these things he did, added to the trouble it was for her to keep him, made Marcy Samuels sometimes want to kill Grandpa Samuels. He was everywhere upon her, like an evil spirit following her; and indeed there was a thing in him which scared her often, as if he was losing his mind or trying to kill her.

As for Grandpa, it was hard to tell whether he really had a wicked face or was deliberately trying to look mean, to keep

Marcy troubled and to pay her back for the way she treated him. It may have been that his days were dull and he wanted something to happen, or that he remembered how he heard her fight with his son, her husband, at night in their room because Watson would not put him in a Home and get the house and Marcy free of him. "You work all day and you're not here with him like I am," she would whine. "And you're not man enough to put him where he belongs." He had been wicked in his day, as men are wicked, had drunk always and in all drinking places, had gambled and had got mixed up in some scrapes. But that was because he had been young and ready. He had never had a household, and the wife he finally got had long since faded away so that she might have been only a shadow from which this son, Watson, emerged, parentless. Then Grandpa had become an old wanderer, lo here lo there, until it all ended in this chair in which he was still a wanderer through the rooms of this house. He had a face which, although mischievous lines were scratched upon it and gave it a kind of devilish look, showed that somewhere there was abundant untouched kindness in him, a life which his life had never been able to use.

Marcy could not make her husband see that this house was cursed and tormented; and then to have a scarecrow rooster annoying her the length of the day and half the early morning was too much for Marcy Samuels. She had nuisances in her house and nuisances in her yard.

It was on a certain morning that Mrs. Samuels first looked out her kitchen window to see this gaunt rooster strutting white on the ground. It took her only a second to know that this was the rooster that crowed and scratched in her flowers and so the whole thing started. The first thing she did was to poke her blowsy head out her window and puff her lips into a ring and wheeze shooooooo! through it, fiercely. The white rooster simply did a pert leap, erected his flamboyantly combed head sharp into the air, chopped it about for a moment, and then started scratching vigorously in the lush bed of pansies, his comb slapping like a girl's pigtails.

Since her hands were wet in the morning sink full of dishes, Mrs. Samuels stopped to dry them imperfectly and then hurried out the back door, still drying her hands in her apron. Now she would get him, she would utterly destroy him if she could get her hands on him. She flounced out the door and down the steps and threw her great self wildly in the direction of the pansy bed, screaming shoo! shoo! go 'way! go 'way! and then cursed the rooster. Marcy Samuels must have been a terrible sight to any barnyard creature, her hair like a big bush and her terrible bosom heaving and falling, her hands thrashing the air. But the white rooster was not dismayed at all. Again he did a small quick hop, stuck his beak into the air, and stood firmly on his ground, his yellow claw spread over the face of a purple pansy and holding it to the ground imprisoned as a cat holds down a mouse. And then a sound, a clear melodious measure, which Mrs. Samuels thought was the most awful noise in the world, burst from his straggly throat.

He was plainly a poorly rooster, thin as some sparrow, his white feathers drooping and without lustre, his comb of extravagant growth but pale and flaccid, hanging like a wrinkled glove over his eye. It was clear that he had been run from many a yard and that in fleeing he had torn his feathers and so tired himself that whatever he found to eat in random places was not enough to keep any flesh on his carcass. He would not be a good eating chicken, Mrs. Samuels thought, running at him, for he has no meat on him at all. Anyway, he was not like a chicken but like some nightmare rooster from Hades sent to trouble her. Yet he was most vividly alive in some courageous way.

She threw a stone at him and at this he leaped and screamed in fright and hurdled the shrubbery into a vacant lot. Mrs. Samuels dashed to her violated pansy bed and began throwing up loose dirt about the stems, making reparations. This was no ordinary rooster in her mind. Since she had a very good imagination and was, actually, a little afraid of roosters anyway, the white rooster took on a shape of terror in her mind. This was because he was so indestructible. Something seemed to protect him. He seemed to dare her to capture him, and if she threw a shoe out her window at him, he was not challenged, but just let out another startling crow at her. And in the early morning in a snug bed, such a crowing is like the cry of fire! or an explosion in the brain.

It was around noon of that day that Mrs. Samuels, at her clothesline, sighted Mrs. Doran across the hedge, at her line, her long fingers fluttering over the clothespins like butterflies trying to light there.

"That your rooster that's been in my pansy bed and crows all the time, Mrs. Doran?"

"Marcy, it must be. You know we had two of them intending to eat them for Christmas, but they both broke out of the coop and went running away into the neighborhood. My husband Carl just gave them up because he says he's not going to be chasing any chickens like some farmer."

"Well then I tell you we can't have him here disturbing us. If I catch him do you want him back?"

"Heavens no, honey. If you catch him, do what you want to with him, we don't want him any more. Lord knows where the other one is." And then she unfolded from her tub a long limp outing gown and pinned it to the line by its shoulders to let it hang down like an effigy of herself.

Mrs. Samuels noticed that Mrs. Doran was as casual about the whole affair as she was the day she brought back her water pitcher in several pieces, borrowed for a party and broken by the cat. It made her even madder with the white rooster. This simply means killing that white rooster, she told herself as she went from her line. It means wringing his neck until it is twisted clean from his breastbone—if we can catch him; and I'll try—catch him and throw him in the chickenyard and hold him there until Watson comes home from work and then Watson will do the wringing, not me. When she came in the back door she was already preparing herself in her mind for the killing of the white rooster, how she would catch him and then wait for Watson to wring his neck—if Watson actually could get up enough courage to do anything at all for her.

In the afternoon around two, just as she was resting, she heard a cawing and it was the rooster back again. Marcy bounded from her bed and raced to the window. "Now I will get him," she said severely.

She moved herself quietly to a bush and concealed herself behind it, her full-blown buttocks protruding like a monstrous flower in bud. Around the bush in a smiling innocent circle were the pansies, all purple and yellow faces, bright in the wind. When he comes scratching here, she told herself, and when he gets all interested in the dirt, I'll leap upon him and catch him sure.

Behind the bush she waited; her eyes watched the white rooster moving towards the pansy bed, pecking here and there in the grass at whatever was there and might be eaten. As she prepared herself to leap, Mrs. Samuels noticed the white hated face of Grandpa at the window. He had rolled his wheel chair there to watch the maneuvers in the yard. She knew at a glance that he was against her catching the white rooster. But because she hated him, she did not care what he thought. In fact she secretly suspected Grandpa and the rooster to be partners in a plot to worry her out of her mind, one in the house, the other in the yard, tantalizing her outside and inside; she wouldn't put it past them. And if she could destroy the rooster that was a terror in the yard she had a feeling that she would be in a way destroying a part of Grandpa that was a trouble in her house. She wished she were hiding behind a bush to leap out upon *him* to wring *his* neck. He would not die, only wheel through her house day after day, asking for this and that, meddling in everything she did.

The rooster came to the pansy bed so serene, even in rags of feathers, like a beggar-saint, sure in his head of something, something unalterable, although food was unsure, even life. He came as if he knew suffering and terror, as if he were all alone in the world of fowls, far away from his flock, alien and far away from any golden grain thrown by caring hands, stealing a wretched worm or cricket from a foreign yard. What made him so alive, what did he know? Perhaps as he thrust the horned nails of his toes in the easy earth of the flower bed he dreamed of the fields on a May morning, the jeweled dew upon their grasses and the sun coming up like the yolk of an egg swimming in an albuminous sky. And the roseate freshness of his month when he was a tight-fleshed slender-thighed cockerel, alert on his hill and the pristine morning breaking all around him. To greet it with cascading trills of crowings, tremulous in his throat, was to quiver his thin red tongue in trebles. What a joy he felt to be of the world of wordless creatures, where crowing or whirring of wings or the brush of legs together said everything, said praise, we live. To be of the grassy world where things blow and bend and rustle; of the insect world so close to it that it was known when the most insignificant mite would turn in its minute course or an ant haul an imperceptible grain of sand from its tiny cave.

And to wonder at the world and to be able to articulate the fowl-wonder in the sweetest song. He knew time as the seasons know it, being of time. He was tuned to the mechanism of dusk and dawn, it may have been in his mind as simple as the dropping of a curtain to close out the light or the lifting of it to let light in upon a place. All he knew, perhaps, was that there is a going round, and first light comes ever so tinily and speck-like, as through the opening of a stalk, when it is time. Yet the thing that is light breaking on the world is morning breaking open, unfolding within him and he feels it and it makes him chime, like a clock, at his hour. And this is daybreak for him and he feels the daybreak in his throat, and tells of it, rhapsodically, not knowing a single word to say.

And once he knew the delight of wearing red-blooded wattles hanging folded from his throat and a comb climbing up his forehead all in crimson horns to rise from him as a star, pointed. To be rooster was to have a beak hard and brittle as shell, formed just as he would have chosen a thing for fowls to pick grain or insect from their place. To be bird was to be of feathers and shuffle and preen them and to carry wings and arch and fold them, or float them on the wind, to be wafted, to be moved a space by them.

But Marcy Samuels was behind the bush, waiting, and while she waited her mind said over and over, "If he would die!" If he would die, by himself. How I could leap upon him, choke the life out of him. The rooster moved toward the pansies, tail feathers drooped and frayed. If he would die, she thought, clenching her fists. If I could leap upon him and twist his old wrinkled throat and keep out the breath.

At the window, Grandpa Samuels knew something terrible was about to happen. He watched silently. He saw the formidable figure of Mrs. Samuels crouching behind the bush, waiting to pounce upon the rooster.

In a great bounce-like movement, Mrs. Samuels suddenly fell upon the rooster, screaming, "If he would die!" And caught him. The rooster did not struggle, although he cawed out for a second and then meekly gave himself up to Mrs. Samuels. She ran with him to the chickenyard and stopped at the fence. But before throwing him over, she first tightened her strong hands around his neck and gritted her teeth, just to stop the breathing for a moment, to crush the crowing part of him, as if it were a little waxen whistle she could smash. Then she threw him over the fence. The white rooster lay over on his back, very tired and dazed, his yellow legs straight in the air, his claws clenched like fists and not moving, only trembling a little. The Samuels' own splendid golden cock approached the shape of feathers to see what this was, what had come over into his domain, and thought surely it was dead. He leaped upon the limp fuss of feathers and drove his fine spurs into the white rooster just to be sure he was dead. And all the fat pampered hens stood around gazing and casual in a kind of fowlish elegance, not really disturbed, only a bit curious, while the golden cock bristled his fine feathers and, feeling in himself what a thing of price and intrepidity he was, posed for a second like a statue imitating some splendid ancestor cock in his memory, to comment upon this intrusion and to show himself unquestionable master, his beady eyes all crimson as glass hat pins. It was apparent that his hens were proud of him and that in their eyes he had lost none of his prowess by not having himself captured the rooster, instead of Mrs. Samuels. And Marcy Samuels, so relieved, stood by the fence a minute showing something of the same thing in her that the hens showed, very viciously proud. Then she brushed her hands clean of the white rooster and marched victoriously to the house.

Grandpa Samuels was waiting for her at the door, a dare in his face, and said, "Did you get him?"

"He's in the yard waiting until Watson comes home to kill him. I mashed the breath out of the scoundrel and he may be dead the way he's lying on his back in the chickenyard. No more crowing at my window, no more scratching in my pansy bed, I'll tell you. I've got one thing off my mind."

"Marcy," Grandpa said calmly and with power, "that rooster's not dead that easily. Don't you know there's something in a rooster that won't be downed? Don't you know there's some creatures won't be dead easily?" And wheeled into the living room.

But Mrs. Samuels yelled back from the kitchen,

"All you have to do is wring their necks."

All afternoon the big wire wheels of Grandpa Samuels' chair

whirled through room and room. Sometimes Mrs. Samuels thought she would pull out her mass of wiry hair, she got so nervous with the cracking of the floor under the wheels. The wheels whirled around in her head just as the crow of the rooster had burst in her brain all week. And then Grandpa's coughing: he would, in a siege of cough, dig away down in his throat for something troubling him there, and, finally, seizing it as if the cough were a little hand reaching for it, catch it and bring it up, the old man's phlegm, and spit it quivering into a can which rode around with him on the chair's footrest.

"This is as bad as the crowing of the white rooster," Mrs. Samuels said to herself as she tried to rest. "This is driving me crazy." And just when she was dozing off, she heard a horrid gurgling sound from the front bedroom where Grandpa was. She ran there and found him blue in his face and gasping.

"I'm choking to death with a cough, get me some water, quick!" he murmured hoarsely. As she ran to the kitchen faucet, Marcy had the picture of the white rooster in her mind, lying breathless on his back in the chickenyard, his thin yellow legs in the air and his claws closed and drooped like a wilted flower. "If he would die," she thought. "If he would strangle to death."

When she poured the water down his throat, Marcy Samuels put her fat hand there and pressed it quite desperately as if the breath were a little bellows and she could perhaps stop it still just for a moment. Grandpa was unconscious and breathing laboriously. She heaved him out of his chair and to his bed, where he lay crumpled and exhausted. Then was when she went to the telephone and called Watson, her husband.

"Grandpa is very sick and unconscious and the stray rooster is caught and in the chickenyard to be killed by you," she told him. "Hurry home, for everything is just terrible."

When Marcy went back to Grandpa's room with her hopeful heart already giving him extreme unction, she had the shock of her life to find him not dying at all but sitting up in his bed with a face like a caught rabbit, pitiful yet daredevilish.

"I'm all right now, Marcy, you don't have to worry about *me*. You couldn't *kill* an old crippled man like me," he said firmly.

Marcy was absolutely spellbound and speechless, but when she looked out Grandpa's window to see the white rooster walking in the leaves, like a resurrection, she thought she would faint with astonishment. Everything was suddenly like a haunted house; there was death and then a bringing to life again all around her and she felt so superstitious that she couldn't trust anything or anybody. Just when she was sure she was going to lose her breath in a fainting spell, Watson arrived home. Marcy looked wild. Instead of asking about Grandpa, whether he was dead, he said, "There's no stray rooster in my chickenyard like you said, because I just looked." And when he looked to see Grandpa all right and perfectly conscious he was in a quandary and said they were playing a trick on a worried man.

"This place is haunted, I tell you," Marcy said, terrorized, "and you've got to do something for once in your life." She took him in the back room where she laid out the horror and the strangeness of the day before him. Watson, who was always calm and a little underspoken, said, "All right, pet, all right. There's only one thing to do. That's lay a trap. Then kill him. Leave it to me, and calm your nerves." And then he went to Grandpa's room and sat and talked to him to find out if he was all right.

For an hour, at dusk, Watson Samuels was scrambling in a lumber pile in the garage like a possum trying to dig out. Several times Mrs. Samuels inquired through the window by signs what he was about. She also warned him, by signs, of her fruit-jars stored on a shelf behind the lumber pile and to be careful. But at a certain time during the hour of building, as she was hectically frying supper, she heard a crash of glass and knew it was her Mason jars all over the ground, and cursed Watson.

When finally Mr. Samuels came in, with the air of having done something grand in the yard, they ate supper. There was the sense of having something special waiting afterwards, like a fancy dessert.

"I'll take you out in awhile and show you the good trap I built," Watson said. "That'll catch anything."

Grandpa, who had been silent and eating sadly as an old man eats (always as if remembering something heartbreaking), felt sure how glad they would be if they could catch *him* in the trap.

"Going to kill that white rooster, son?" he asked.

"It's the only thing to do to keep from making a crazy woman out of Marcy."

"Can't you put him in the yard with the rest of the chickens when you catch him?" He asked this mercifully. "That white rooster won't hurt anybody."

"You've seen we can't keep him in there, Papa. Anyway, he's probably sick or got some disease."

"His legs are scaly. I saw that," Mrs. Samuels put in.

"And then he'd give it to my good chickens," said Mr. Samuels. "Only thing for an old tramp like that is to wring his neck and throw him away for something useless and troublesome."

When supper was eaten, Watson and Marcy Samuels hurried out to look at the trap. Grandpa rolled to the window and watched through the curtain. He watched how the trap lay in the moonlight, a small dark object like a box with one end open for something to run in, something seeking a thing needed, like food or a cup of gold beyond a rainbow, and hoping to find it here within this cornered space. "It's just a box with one side kicked out," he said to himself. "But it is a trap and built to snare and to hold." It looked lethal under the moon; it cast a shadow longer than itself and the open end was like a big mouth, open to swallow down. He saw his son and his son's wife—how they moved about the trap, his son making terrifying gestures to show how it would work, how the guillotine end would slide down fast when the cord was released from inside the house, and close in the white rooster, close him in and lock him there, to wait to have his neck wrung off. He was afraid, for Mrs. Samuels looked strong as a lion in the night, and how cunning his son seemed! He could not hear what they spoke, only see their gestures. But he heard when Mrs. Samuels pulled the string once, trying out the trap, and the top came sliding down with a swift clap when she let go. And then he knew how adroitly they could kill a thing and with what craftiness. He was sure he was no longer safe in this house, for after the rooster then certainly he would be trapped.

The next morning early the white rooster was there, crowing in a glittering scale. Grandpa heard Marcy screaming at him, threatening, throwing little objects through the window at him. His son Watson did not seem disturbed at all; always it was Marcy. But still the rooster crowed. Grandpa went cold and trembling in his bed. He had not slept.

It was a rainy day, ashen and cold. By eight o'clock it had settled down to a steady gray pour. Mrs. Samuels did not bother with the morning dishes. She told Grandpa to answer all phone calls and tell them she was out in town. She took her place at the window and held the cord in her hand.

Grandpa was so quiet. He rolled himself about ever so gently and tried not to cough, frozen in his throat with fear and a feeling of havoc. All through the house, in every room, there was darkness and doom, the air of horror, slaughter and utter finish. He was so full of terror he could not breathe, only gasp, and he sat leaden in his terror. He thought he heard footsteps creeping upon him to choke his life out, or a hand to release some cord that would close down a heavy door before him and lock him out of his life forever. But he would not keep his eyes off Marcy. He sat in the doorway, half obscured, and peeked at her; he watched her like a hawk.

Mrs. Samuels sat by the window in a kind of ecstatic readiness. Everywhere in her was the urge to release the cord—even before the time to let it go, she was so passionately anxious. Sometimes she thought she could not trust her wrist, her fingers, they were so ready to let go, and then she changed the cord to the other hand. But her hands were so charged with their mission that they could have easily thrust a blade into a heart to kill it, or brought down mightily a hammer upon a head to shatter the skull in. Her hands had well and wantonly learned slaughter from her heart, had been thoroughly taught by it, as the heart whispers to its agents—hands, tongue, eyes—to do their action in their turn.

Once Grandpa saw her body start and tighten. She was poised like a huge cat, watching. He looked, mortified, through the window. It was a bird on the ground in the slate rain. Another time, because a dog ran across the yard, Mrs. Samuels jerked herself straight and thought, something comes, it is time.

And then it seemed there was a soft ringing in Grandpa's ears, almost like a delicate little jingle of bells or of thin glasses struck, and some secret thing told him in his heart that it was time. He saw Mrs. Samuels sure and powerful as a great beast, making certain, making ready without flinching. The white rooster was coming upon the grass.

He strode upon the watered grass all dripping with the rain, a tinkling sound all about him, the rain twinkling upon his feathers, forlorn and tortured. Yet even now there was a blaze of courage about him. He was meager and bedraggled. But he had a splendor in him. For now his glory came by being alone and lustreless in a beggar's world, and there is a time for every species to know lacklustre and loneliness where there was brightness and a flocking together, since there is a change in the way creatures must go to find their ultimate station, whether they fall old and lose blitheness, ragged and lose elegance, lonely and lose love; and since there is a shifting in the levels of understanding. But there is something in each level for all creatures, pain or wisdom or despair, and never nothing. The white rooster was coming upon the grass.

Grandpa wheeled so slowly and so smoothly towards Mrs. Samuels that she could not tell he was moving, that not one board cracked in the floor. And the white rooster moved toward the trap, closer and closer he moved. When he saw the open door leading to a dry place strewn with grain, he went straight for it, a haven suddenly thrown up before his eye, a warm dry place with grain. When he got to the threshold of the trap and lifted his yellow claw to make the final step, Grandpa Samuels was so close to Mrs. Samuels that he could hear her passionate breath drawn in a kind of lust-panting. And when her heart must have said, "Let go!" to her fingers, and they tightened spasmodically so that the veins stood turgid blue in her arm, Grandpa Samuels struck at the top of her spine where the head flares down into the neck and there is a little stalk of bone, with a hunting knife he had kept for many years. There was no sound, only the sudden sliding of the cord as it made a dip and hung loose in Marcy Samuels' limp hand. Then Grandpa heard the quick clap of the door hitting the wooden floor of the trap outside, and a faint crumpling sound as of a dress dropped to the floor when Mrs. Samuels' blowsy head fell limp on her breast. Through the window Grandpa Samuels saw the white rooster leap pertly back from the trap when the door came down, a little frightened. And then he let out a peal of crowings in the rain and went away.

Grandpa sat silent for a moment and then said to Mrs. Samuels, "You will never die any other way, Marcy Samuels, my son's wife, you are meant to be done away with like this. With a hunting knife."

And then he wheeled wildly away through the rooms of Marcy Samuels' house, feeling a madness all within him, being liberated, running free. He howled with laughter and rumbled like a runaway carriage through room and room, sometimes coughing in paroxysms. He rolled here and there in every room, destroying everything he could reach, he threw up pots and pans in the kitchen, was in the flour and sugar like a whirlwind, overturned chairs and ripped the upholstery in the living room until the stuffing flew in the air; and covered with straw and flour, white like a demented ghost, he flayed the bedroom wallpaper into hanging shreds; coughing and howling, he lashed and wrecked and razed until he thought he was bringing the very house down upon himself.

When Watson came home some minutes later to check on the success of his engine to trap the rooster and fully expecting to have to wring his neck, he saw at one look his house in such devastation that he thought a tornado had struck and demolished it inside, or that robbers had broken in. "Marcy! Marcy!" he called.

He found out why she did not call back when he discovered her by the window, cord in hand as though she had fallen asleep fishing.

"Papa! Papa!" he called.

But there was no calling back. In Grandpa's room Watson found the wheel chair with his father's wild dead body in it, his life stopped by some desperate struggle. There had obviously been a fierce spasm of coughing, for the big artery in his neck had burst and was still bubbling blood like a little red spring.

Then the neighbors all started coming in, having heard the uproar and gathered in the yard; and there was a dumbfoundedness in all their faces when they saw the ruins in Watson Samuels' house, and Watson Samuels standing there in the ruins unable to say a word to any of them to explain what had happened.

The Letter in the Cedarchest

Now this is about the lives of Old Mrs. Woman, Sister Sammye, and Little Pigeon, and how they formed a household; but first, about Old Mrs. Woman.

Her early name, and rightful one, was Lucille Purdy; and she had had a pretty good life until she started getting fat. Lucille's husband, a tall, good-looking man, with no stomach, a good chest and a deep voice, but he had evil lips—and whose mother had lived with him and Lucille from the day they married until the day she died in Lucille's arms—had begun to hurrah her some two or three years back, especially when he saw her in her nightgown. He had said, "Lucille one thing I cannot stand and that is a fat woman; I'll leave you, swear to God, if ever you get fat. . . ." At first Lucille had laughed and said, "Don't worry, Mr. Purdy (no one ever heard her call him anything but Mr. Purdy—when his name was Duke), I won't; I have already given up bread and potatoes."

Yet Lucille kept on putting on weight, there seemed nothing she could do to stop the fat acoming; and with the constant increase in stoutness came a more and more nervousness. Naturally. Mr. Purdy's threat seemed to produce as much fat on Lucille as bread and potatoes. She noticed Mr. Purdy had begun to wear a moustache, which made him look younger and devilish, what with those lips, now with fringe on top.

When Mr. Purdy moved into a room to himself, Lucille cried

alone in the master bedroom at night. Finally, one night she went into hysterics and accused Mr. Purdy of no longer caring about her. Mr. Purdy lost his temper and said, "You ought to kill yourself Lucille, because you're slobby and no longer any good to anybody, and you're nervous and going crazy"; and he laid a revolver on the table by the side of Lucille's bed. She lay all night crying and thinking seriously of taking Mr. Purdy up on his suggestion to blow out her brains. But she prayed and remembered the sweet Christian memory of old Mother Purdy who had suffered out her life to the end and then died in her arms; and did not use the gun.

Then Lucille found out Mr. Purdy was carrying on with his stenographer. A voice advised her this on the telephone, and then Lucille called on the phone, made certain investigations, and found it all out to be true. She had hysterics and ordered Mr. Purdy out of the house. He gladly went, admitting everything, said he wanted a divorce, Lucille said she would not give him one to her dying day, he said that he was going to be married to the woman in question (who was twenty-one). And he reminded Lucille of the revolver, to take her out of her misery.

Lucille had a very hard time. She read books from the Normal for the dreams she was having, about white and black horses pulling her up mountains, and about her pulling the same horses up mountains. She was also riding the horses sometimes. The books helped her some (yet they didn't stop the dreams); but it was the minister of her church that really helped her—for awhile. Helped her so much that she begun to have giggling and crying spells when she was in his office counseling with him. The minister was stumped as to what to do. The minister suggested that Lucille go into Sunday School work with children, and Lucille added that she loved working with children; so she did this. But other Sunday School teachers complained that Lucille was too fussy with the children, that she would humor them, then pinch them and even slap them, then cry over them. They asked her to take a rest.

It was while she was taking a rest, and crying most of the time, that she decided to go on with the divorce which she had so stubbornly opposed up to now. She took it to court, got the divorce, Mr. Purdy (still not married) left her the big house but took all the furniture out which was his by rights, he said, since it had been his mother's. This left Lucille's house completely bare except for the cedarchest which she had married Duke with, from her girlhood—she had been raised by two old women cousins, and an orphan since she was twelve.

Now Lucille was alone in her big empty house, and still putting on poundage. Her minister advised her to put her house up for sale and move into just a little board cottage somewhere, but the house was all Lucille had and she wanted to cling to it. She made her a cat pallet in the master bedroom and cooked on a gas burner she bought. She barely lived on the monthly allowance Mr. Purdy was compelled by law to send—and when he pleased, sometimes on time, most of the time not. She cried nearly all the time; and the neighbors who had known her all these years naturally began to turn from her and to suspicion her because she acted so funny. If they asked her questions about herself or her husband, she was quick to snap at them, "Ask me no questions I'll tell you no lies," and walk away. Therefore, one by one they let her alone; politely but firmly.

When she went back to her church they would not have her in the Sunday School and so she cried and said she knew it was because she was too fat, the minister couldn't do much with her, she went into a red rage with the woman in the Sunday School, and this is when she asked to have her church Letter out. She got it, read it carefully to see that there were no mistakes in it: 'This is to certify that Lucille Marie Purdy is a member of the Lord's Household in good standing and full fellowship and to recommend her as a faithful servant to all those present. . . .' She put it in her cedarchest.

It was then that Lucille decided to take on boarders. She furnished two bedrooms when she found out three young men from the Normal would rent the rooms. The three young men moved in, two in the big room—these were the gentle one and the outspoken one—where Mr. Purdy had gone off to sleep and live when Lucille had got so stout, and one in the corner bedroom next to Lucille's—this one was the young wild one who had worked his way to Spain on a freighter and had gone crazy over bullfights, bringing back from Spain a long black whip which he practiced cracking, even late at night you could hear the stinging hot crackling of it in his room. Lucille's room continued to be the master bedroom, just furnished with a pallet and a cedarchest.

These three young men are a story in themselves, and it is peculiar how life arranged to bring them into Lucille's house, and at such a time in Lucille's life. Often Lucille said, "I know the Lord sent you all here; it is His Divine Hand; there is more love in this household than in any church, I am glad I have moved my Letter into this house." But anyway, these three young men were a nice thing for Lucille to have in her house and Lucille became very nice with them in her house. They wondered about the state of the house, why it was not furnished, and so on, but they did not ask questions. Mostly they were at the Normal all day, and at nights they studied in their rooms or met in one another's room to have their talk and laughter, which Lucille would overhear if she stood against the wall and listened; until one night Lucille knocked on their door at late night and said, "Listen here, since you are still up and talking would you like to move your conversation on down to the kitchen and have you some hot cocoa with it?" and in a little while they had formed the pleasant habit of meeting in the kitchen for hot cocoa every night about eleven. Naturally some talk ensued. The young men told of their work at the Normal and told of their lives and interests, the gentle one told how he wanted to be a poet (Lucille said she often wrote poems and would show him hers); the outspoken one disagreed with most of Lucille's philosophy about life, but in a friendly way that made Lucille feel intellectually stimulated; and the wild one said he only wanted to wander and to travel, free on the road. Lucille responded that her father himself had been a sea captain and roamed and that that was why she was part gypsy, her two cousins raised her but never understood her, she had always had a gypsy heart. Then Lucille had something in common with each of the roomers, she declared; and it wasn't long before Lucille had told the roomers all about her husband leaving her, explaining that he had taken the furniture; and as she told her story she broke out crying. The roomers were very sympathetic and tried to comfort Lucille.

After awhile you had this nice household of Lucille and the three comforting young men. They began to wait on her hand and foot, and Lucille wore fresh dresses and kept the house clean.

They refused to allow her to sleep on a pallet and all bought her a daybed. They went through the winter this way. When it snowed so heavily that one time, some of the neighbors were surprised to hear Lucille's voice squealing outdoors and looked out to see her shooting down the slope of her snow-covered lawn on a sled pushed by the three roomers. Life had changed for Lucille, she had a regular household, the roomers had built furniture of tables and bookcases and things and they had chipped in and helped buy other things to make the big living room nice, there was fire in the fireplace, often singing (the wild roomer played a guitar), and Lucille fixed supper every night for the household; they were all around the table like a family.

When spring came, the young wild roomer quit the Normal, he was too restless; and Lucille let him stay on free of charge until he could determine what to do, whether to get a job and study castanets, or what; and they all worked together in the yard and planted flowers in the beds. This is where Little Pigeon comes in.

Being for the most of the time alone over in her house across Lucille's back yard, she lots of the time just stood at her window and watched across to see the life and lights of Lucille's big changed house; all the shades were raised, now. She heard singing and she heard laughing and she saw figures busy in the lighted rooms of the house that had been dark so long. She heard guitars and she heard castanets and she heard the snapping of the bullwhip. Finally, one time when she could not find her purse and had called long distance to Rodunda to ask her widow sister Sammye where she had hidden it but Sister Sammye had just hung up in her face, Little Pigeon thought of the bright and living house of Lucille's across the yard. She decided to knock on the door of this house. She did, and when Lucille came to the door, Little Pigeon said, "Mrs. Woman (for she did not know her name), I have lost my purse."

Now Lucille had had a few experiences with Little Pigeon before, and with Little Pigeon's sister Sammye, too; and she knew about the trouble and disorder of that household over across the yard and wanted nothing to do with it. Earlier, and just after Mr. Purdy had left Lucille, Sammye had come over and asked her please to keep an eye out after Little Pigeon while she was away, and Lucille had tried but it didn't work out—mainly because of Sammye. Lucille wanted nothing to do with the two sisters, and she very quickly said to Little Pigeon, "You better go on back home and look for your purse again, or call your sister Sammye, because I am sure it is not here," and was going to close the door, when one of the roomers, the gentle one, came up and began to make friends with Little Pigeon. He had seen her at her window and he had heard Lucille speak of the crazy woman next door. He invited Little Pigeon in before the fire. Little Pigeon came in timidly, looked all around, and said, "You all have a nice household here. Is it a party?" And they all said no and to sit down. They gave her some cocoa, Little Pigeon told a story about a place she and Selmus, her husband, had gone to when they used to travel around; and then the gentle roomer saw her home (having to stay in Little Pigeon's house for her to show him all her things and tell him the story of them). Little Pigeon kept her new discovery of the party across the yard a secret from her sister Sammye, among other secrets she kept.

This started all the trouble. Constantly Little Pigeon's voice at her back door would call out, "Mrs. Woman! Mrs. Woman!" And when Lucille would answer at her back door, Little Pigeon would have nothing to say but, "Can you come over?" quietly. Lucille would give some excuse and not go; but finally she weakened and went over. Usually it was for nothing and Little Pigeon would have nothing to say, except to show her things and ask about the party in Lucille's house. When Lucille would turn around and leave, Little Pigeon would weep very quietly and this would hurt Lucille, for she knew enough about tears. Finally, Lucille found herself over at Little Pigeon's most every day, at one time or another, looking at Little Pigeon's things, which Little Pigeon would count and tell about. Lucille would complain that she had her work to do in her house, to look after her roomers, they were such a handful, and Little Pigeon then began to appear every night at Lucille's house, her face would be at the window or her knock on the door, and they would have to let her in to join them.

When Little Pigeon's sister Sammye would come in from the next town of Rodunda and find that Little Pigeon had been neighborly with Lucille and over visiting in her house, she would be angry and order Little Pigeon to stop ever calling Lucille again.

For Sammye had heard the stories in the neighborhood about Lucille; she, in fact, knew the *whole* story, and would have nothing to do with her. In turn, the neighbors would have nothing to do with Little Pigeon *or* Sammye because of Little Pigeon's antics in the neighborhood, her wandering about and her calling the fire department and the police for the slightest thing, and then just to talk with them. Some of the neighbors tried to get Little Pigeon ordered to a Home, but Sammye stopped that and told them to mind their own business; and fell out with the neighbors.

So you had this complicated neighborhood, all enemies to Lucille and to Little Pigeon, having nothing whatsoever to do with either of them; and Lucille and Little Pigeon divided against each other by Sammye, but coming together when she was away.

Then things began to wear in Lucille's household. Lucille began to pick on and pester the roomers, or humor and coddle them, much in the same way as she had treated the Sunday School children. She would fuss at them when they wouldn't eat, she would order them around, she would criticize their habits, she would have spells of temper or poutishness; and sometimes she would suddenly change into such wildness, like doing a gypsy dance—even as fat as she still was (she seemed to have forgotten that)—while the wild roomer played his guitar or cracked his long black bullwhip. The outspoken roomer did not like what he saw, and the gentle roomer suffered most of all, for he had to return the clothes of Mr. Purdy which Mr. Purdy had left behind and which Lucille had given to him, and they fit perfectly, when she suddenly asked for them back. The roomers were more and more unsettled in Lucille's house. They could not predict what she would break out and do, without any warning. The household was like a troubled mind, with tormenting ideas, desires and suspicions. The outspoken roomer got fed up with Lucille's talk and tantrums and just stayed out of her way. The gentle one tried to reason with her but he could get no farther with her than the minister had been able to. So he withdrew. The young wild roomer tried to make light of her misery, to liven her up, of course, by cracking his whip suddenly behind her; but this only made Lucille scream into hysterics. Even Little Pigeon deviled Lucille by playing a kind of hide-and-seek with her: face at the window, voice at the back door, vanishing and appearing.

The first thing to go was the hot cocoa at night; no one would come down—just to go through all Lucille's story and spells again. The next was supper; the roomers wouldn't come down to that, either. So Lucille stopped cooking. Her bad crying spells started again.

Well, this situation grew and grew, the roomers were all in their rooms with doors shut; Lucille was shut out and left alone again. Lucille took it out on Little Pigeon and was mean to her, abusing her and teasing her and confusing her. Little Pigeon could not understand and did not know what to do, but she fought back gamely and seemed to have a good time doing it. Finally, when the roomers notified Lucille that they were leaving, Little Pigeon invited them to move over into her house, where the party, as she called it, could go on; but the roomers packed up and left, taking their furniture with them. Lucille remembered the revolver Mr. Purdy had given her, and his words with it, except that now it seemed to her that the roomers had left the revolver, and in the same way. She was on the point of using it upon herself. Why did everything spoil in her household? It was because she was so fat. She would stand for minutes before the mirror and look at herself, turning round and round. She would do this nude, too; and beat herself in the fattest places, she hated them so. She ran up and down the stairs nude, either to reduce herself or because she was going crazy, who knows. It was this way, running naked up and down the stairs in her empty house, that Little Pigeon found her once, and laughed until she cried. Whereupon Lucille covered herself and began to cry with Little Pigeon, there on the stairs. There was this sympathy between the two poor women. Then is when they became very close; and then is when Sammye enters the picture.

When Sammye came in from Rodunda and found Little Pigeon turned over in the hedge like a toy bird with its spindly legs kicking as if they were unwinding, she picked Little Pigeon out and what do you think Little Pigeon did for thanks? Sassed Sammye and said *she'd* pushed her in the hedge, all to run and get her purse. But Sammye didn't care, she didn't get mad or anything, she just picked Little Pigeon out and took her in the house and washed her off. And said, "You are my sweet sister that I love and adore."

Then Little Pigeon said, "I can't figure it all out. Old Mrs. Woman pushed me in the bush and went back to her house across the yard and the ghost of Sister Sammye come and pulled me out."

Sammye said, "Forget the ghost of Sister Sammye and leave Old Mrs. Woman to her own house. It is all over, your playparty, and I am back here to look after you and to tend to you and I am no ghost either, I am your fleshandblood Sister Sammye. Sweet Little Pigeon." And everything seemed all right.

Now that Little Pigeon and Sammye were old, both their husbands dead, Sammye came up from Rodunda as often as she could to stay with her as long as she could suffer it. Because Little Pigeon was no longer accountable to herself; and, besides, she had to have someone to give her her insulin every morning, no practical nurse would do it, no practical nurse would stay in the same house with Little Pigeon, Sammye had tried it, don't worry, because Little Pigeon thought a nurse was trying to take her money, which was in a bank, and safe there, but that didn't make no difference to Little Pigeon; she worried about it anyway. "Besides, Little Pigeon loves me and I love and adore her," Sammye would say. "She is my sweet sister that I love and adore. She fights me a lot (*I* don't want her Irish linens and her bone china), but that's all right, that don't make me no difference. She's my sweet sister that I love and adore, truly do."

Once Sammye missed her and called through all the house, through all the yard, went up and down the sidewalk calling through the neighborhood, but no Little Pigeon. Then she came back in the house and wondered whether to call the police again. Then Sammye heard a ruckus upstairs. Up she went and there was the kicking legs of Little Pigeon with the rest of her under the bed. Sammye said, "What on earth are you doing under there, Little Pigeon? Come out"; and Little Pigeon said, "Hush up, I'm looking for my lost black purse."

"Oh have you lost that again?" Sammye said.

And Little Pigeon said, "You hush it because you have stolen it anyway"; and out she came fast as lightning. They had it all to go over again, the black purse. They spent half the day looking for it, and of course they found it, Little Pigeon had thrown it in the trashcan. Then said Sammye had done it. And was as mad as all outdoors.

Little Pigeon's life was never hard, she was spoilt from the beginning. She was very beautiful, you could still tell it if you looked at her complexion; she still was, hair real fine and naturally curly, a set of flashing lashy eyes like Miss Maybelline, and a little sweetheart mouth. She was always prettier than Sammye, she was the flighty one, cute as a thimble, had all the boy friends, Sunday beau, Candy beau, every one; Sammye was the practical one, and had nothing. "And what does it matter if she was ugly to me then?" Sammye would declare. "I am sweet to her now and I will be till she dies, I don't care if they say it's for her money, that is a Satanish lie, I am here to look after her when I can be, for she is my sweet sister that I love and adore."

Little Pigeon's husband wedded her when he was twenty and she was eighteen, and they had lots of trips all their life, to Cuba and every place. He knew a lot about horses, bred his own, and Little Pigeon swore he brought his finest horse in the kitchen one morning to have breakfast with them. "But don't pay any 'tention to her when she says that, it's the effect of the insulin," Sammye would say. "Makes her tell the wildest tales. But oh she is so sweet, that sweet sister."

They never had chick nor child, Little Pigeon and her husband Selmus, just all they wanted, big cars and chinaware, Persian rugs and fine furniture. Sammye said she remembers coming to visit them when they were flourishing, and wanting to touch the pretty things, but Little Pigeon would say, "Take your hands off my crystal candy jar," or, "Don't smut up my Dresden compote made of Dresden." Selmus would be down in the basement listening to the radio. He died there, of a sudden, in the basement listening to the horse races. But Little Pigeon was already weakening by then, in her notions of things. She needed insulin then but they didn't know it. She was a sweet thing and cried at Selmus's funeral. When Sammye and Little Pigeon came home from the funeral, Little Pigeon counted her silver that Selmus had given to her, and cried again; but not a tear fell on the silver to smutten it up, you understand; she was careful of that. "Oh now she's sweet and I love and adore her, but I know her bad points, and I know her good points, too, of which they are bountiful," Sammye would say.

"Pity Little Pigeon," Sammye would say. "She's got nothing in this wide world but me and a house full of fine things. (*I* don't want any of them.) Her days run away in a dream. She dusts her porcelain, cleans her pretty Persian rugs, counts her linens and counts her silver. If an ant had crawled over one little spoon of that sterling in the night, Little Pigeon would know it the next morning. Yet she can't see to find her purse."

Well, Sammye stayed as long as she could with Little Pigeon, until she had to go back up to Rodunda to see after her own house. "After all," she said, "I have my own house. Pigeon thinks I can just close that house up and run to her whenever she needs me, but she don't reckon that *I* have a house, too, with my life in it and all my things, not so fine as hers, but my house; and all my responsibilities." Once when Sammye had to leave Little Pigeon, she asked that old Mrs. Whatchamacallit next door please to look after Little Pigeon and not let her catch the house afire or leave the garage lights burning all night and then wake up and call the fire department because she thinks the garage is burning down and it the middle of the night. Now Old Mrs. Whatsername was in a bad fix, too; but she agreed to watch out after Little Pigeon after hemming and hawing that she had her hands full already. "How come?" Sammye said. "She has nothing to do—her husband's just left her and she's all alone in a big two-storied house in which she cries all day and half the night, I've seen her. Once I said, 'What's the trouble, Mrs.—Thing?' And she said, 'Because I'm the fattest woman in church.' Then said she had taken her Letter out because the church showed favoritism. Said she had her Letter in her cedarchest and was going to keep it there, said that even that cedarchest was a better church than most; and cried and cried. I didn't know what to say to humor her, but I finally said, 'Well I'm sure there are fatter women than you in church,' but guess this was the wrong thing to say." Anyway, she sure was the wrong thing for Little Pigeon, the same devilment in both of them and they fought like dog and cat when they came upon each other outdoors. Sammye said she knew for a fact that Old Mrs. Woman hit Little Pigeon because Little Pigeon showed her where and showed her the blue place it left. Oh well, they was a-pulling stunts right and left, they spit and they spat, and then Sammye had *two* of them on her hands. Then Old Mrs. Woman and Sammye had it good and proper, and Old Mrs. Woman ended up by saying, "Mrs. Johnson, your sister ought to be in an institution." And Sammye said, "This strikes me as real funny, why don't you let it strike you thataway. If anybody's going to be sent to an institution it ought to be *you*." For a long time after, Old Mrs. Woman did not speak to Sammye and Little Pigeon once, kept all her shades pulled down on the side of the house facing Little Pigeon's, what she did in that big house no one knew, but it was guessed she went on crying and crying. Sammye told Little Pigeon time and time again not to call her any more, but when Sammye was not watching, Little Pigeon would go to the back steps and call out before Sammye could catch her, "Mrs. Woman! Mrs. Woman!"—until Sammye would go out and shut her up and bring her in. There was this devilish attraction between Little Pigeon and Old Mrs. Woman.

Well, one time Little Pigeon and Sammye had a real frickus, all over the lost purse again, nobody could find it anywhere; and Sammye just couldn't stand it any longer so just walked out the front door and went back to Rodunda, tired of it all. She stayed a few weeks, and no long distance calls came from Little Pigeon, no sound or sign of her; and Sammye said just let her stew and learn her lesson. Finally, though, Sammye got worried and was in a stew herself—that's the way Little Pigeon did her: always turned things back onto *her*, and double—so took the bus and came on to Little Pigeon's. She went in the house, unlocked as usual, and couldn't find her anywhere. She called and she called, but no Little Pigeon. Then she looked out the window and what did she spy but the two of them, Little Pigeon, her sweet sister, and Old Mrs. Woman, prissing arm in arm down the sidewalk like two Queen of Shebas. Old Mrs. Woman and Little Pigeon had made friends! Sammye saw Little Pigeon all dressed up and all fixed up like she had never seen her before, her hair waved and set, lipstick on and rouge on, her ruby earbobs on, her good shoes on, and the right shoe on the right foot, and in her lovely fur coat. Glued onto her and just as prissy was Old Mrs. Woman, fat as ever but primped up, too, and they were going along like this. Sammye raised the window and called "Little Pigeon! Little Pigeon! This is Sister Sammye come to visit her sweet sister, come on in and let me kiss you hello!" But know what Little Pigeon did? Prissed at Sammye and raised her nose, turned her head away and walked on, Old Mrs. Woman clamped onto her and walking straight along without moving her eyes from ahead. This hurt Sammye to the core. But she pulled down the window and sat down in Little Pigeon's living room to think about it. She thought, well I'll leave; and then she thought, no, I'll just stay, that's what I'll do.

Then they came home, after they had had their beauty walk and seen a show, they came in the house and began ignoring Sammye. Sammye could have been a ghost for all she knew. They went into the kitchen, whispering and cooing, and Sammye came in and said, "It's time for your insulin, Little Pigeon," just to see. Little Pigeon turned and declared that only Mrs. Woman gave her her insulin any more. Then they fixed supper and invited Sammye to sit down and eat, oh they offered her some supper, but they never talked to her at all, they talked about the picture show they had seen, Old Mrs. Woman saying in her baby-talk, "What did the man in the picture show do, Sweetest Thing in This World?" and Sweetest Thing in This World answering, "Killed the woman!" And Old Mrs. Woman spoke back so smart, "Tha-a-a-s right!" It was plain to Sammye that Old Mrs. Woman had taken over Little Pigeon and had made a kindergarten out of Little Pigeon's house, for she saw those tissue paper snow crystals pasted on the sun porch windows. Old Mrs. Woman would coo, "Now drink your milk, Sweet Thing"; and Little Pigeon would drink it right down. Then she said, "Now Sweet Thing it's time for bed, let's go on upstairs." And up they went without a whimper from Little Pigeon. What is this new Little Pigeon, my sweet sister? Sammye thought. She just stood up and said, mad as the mischief at the bottom of the staircase, "Well how do you do!" Then she got her things and went straight back to Rodunda where she wrote a letter to Old Mrs. Woman at Little Pigeon's address. "I demand to know," her letter stated, "what have you caused to come over my sister, what have you done to turn her against me?" Said, "If you think you will get her to give you some of her pretty things you are just sadly mistaken, because you won't." Said, "I want you to stop taking her around, and I want you to stop prissing her up and I want you to stop humoring her, right this very minute. She's not *your* sister." Sammye sent the letter.

In a few days a call came for Sammye and it was Old Mrs.

Woman on the telephone, long distance, in her creamiest voice, as if she was a receptionist or something—and had never received the letter. "Your sister has lost her purse and says to call you because you have hidden it." Sammye said, "I certainly have not and you will do me the favor of stopping ever calling me about my sister's purse or about any other thing that goes on in my sister's house, I am through. You have done something or said something to lowrate me in the eyes of my sister. You old crazy, you have lost your marbles. You have turned my sweet sister against me and if you are not careful I will take out action against you." She told her upside down, crossways and crooked; then she hung up in Old Mrs. Woman's face and began to think: now use your head, Sammye Johnson, and take aholt of the situation, now that you have told Old Mrs. Woman off. You have fussed and nearly pulled your hair out because of the worry of Little Pigeon, now here is somebody to look after her if you handle it right. Make out a list of what she must do for Little Pigeon, tell her you will pay her by the week, and you have got the practical nurse for Little Pigeon and one she apparently will let stay in the house.

A few days passed and Sammye could find nothing to do with herself. Rodunda was small and there were only a handful of people she would have anything to do with, and they were all busy with their husbands and housekeeping. Sammye begun to realize that she had nothing in her life to do or take her mind and interest because she had centered everything around worrying over Little Pigeon. She suddenly felt how alone she would be not to have to worry or look after Little Pigeon. What did she have? She looked around her house one night and got scared. She put on her things next morning and went to go see Little Pigeon.

But when she got there it was too late. They wouldn't let her in because they shouted out the window that she had hidden Little Pigeon's purse. That settles it, Sammye said; and went back to Rodunda. She kept saying to herself, But Sammye why are you so upset? You ought to be relieved. Take this good thing while you can. You are free of all that worry that was driving you to your grave.

Some nights in her house Sammye got unnerved because she was so all alone. She tried to fix up her house, to have some company, to visit around; but she was so all alone. Often she dreamt of

Little Pigeon. Why didn't she think of her sister, why didn't she have the telephone operator call her sister? Finally she said to herself, This is too much of a good thing; and she got on the bus and went to go see Little Pigeon.

But when she got there they wouldn't let her in again, even after three weeks. In fact, Little Pigeon's face at the window looked like she thought Sammye was a stranger or a ghost. She didn't care about her at all. And Old Mrs. Woman wouldn't come to the window at all or unlock the door. Well, Sammye felt like some dream was going on inside that house, that she was left outside some dream. She cried, "I have to get in to see you Little Pigeon, I have to talk to you, I am your Sister Sammye, have you lost your mind?" What could she do? Night was falling and she left and went down to the drug store and ate her a sandwich, to let things settle. She walked on back to Little Pigeon's in the dark, wondering whether she would have her in, this time; and thinking, well, maybe I am a ghost, I've been by myself so long I don't know whether I'm live or dead.

But the drapes were drawn almost to, and when she peeked in between them she saw the two of them by the fire, Little Pigeon just dreaming and purring, Old Mrs. Woman lumped and rolled up into herself whispering some story to herself. But what kind of a room was this? The room was so full of decorations and stuff that there wasn't enough space left in it to cuss a cat in. There were hanging paper lanterns, paper streamers streaming from the ceiling, paper balls and paper stars. They had made a fairyland playhouse out of Little Pigeon's spotless living room. Then Sammye saw Old Mrs. Woman moving around through all the waving shapes and strands of colored paper. She saw her go to the mirror and look in it at herself and say, "I'm not so fat, am I, Sweet Thing?" And heard Little Pigeon answer back, "No, Mrs. Woman."

Sammye said to herself outside the window, "I know one thing and that is that Old Mrs. Woman is crazy. I'll break up *this* playparty." She began to beat on the sides of the house calling, "Little Pigeon! Little Pigeon! Let me in. I am your sweet sister who loves and adores you!" But she could not disturb the dream of this playhouse. She walked round and round the house, trying to understand it and decide what to do. She saw across the yard Old

Mrs. Woman's big dark empty house, wrapped in a dream, too. She felt so left out. Then she thought of what to do. She tried the basement door and it was unlocked. She went down there quietly and sat under them to see what else she could hear. Suddenly she heard the music begin, it was "Whispering," and she heard their feet adancing, just like ghost feet. They danced and they danced, then the music stopped and Sammye heard their feet going up the staircase to bed. Then it was all quiet. Sammye went to sleep on the basement divan, cold and peeved, down among the pipes and storage like a mouse or a lonesome cricket.

The next morning they were up there, in the kitchen, over Sammye. She heard them fix their breakfast and eat it, she heard Little Pigeon getting her insulin. Then they went into the dining room and they were in the china and the silverware. Sammye heard Little Pigeon say where each piece came from, how her husband had given her this and that, not to smutten up the Dresden compote made of Dresden, Sammye heard her ghostly voice counting the table service of pure silver, one two three four five—and heard Old Mrs. Woman say softly, "Tha-a-a-s right!"

After awhile Little Pigeon suddenly came into the basement without a word of warning. She saw Sammye sitting there and did not pay her any mind. Finally Sammye spoke out and said, "Hello Little Pigeon!" and Little Pigeon said, "Hush up, ghost of Sister Sammye." She was looking for her purse, very seriously, going through everything in the basement. Then she said, "Well, I guess it's not down here, guess Sister Sammye's stolen it," and went on up and out in her dream that Old Mrs. Woman had put her into.

This gave Sammye an idea. For then she knew that Old Mrs. Woman had told Little Pigeon that she had passed on, or something, and that her face at the window and around the house had been her ghost and not to worry about it. Sammye made her a plan. "If that's the way they want it, I'll just *be* a ghost, and a good one at that!" she declared. She decided to make her home in the basement for awhile, and started making it nice down there where poor Selmus had come to live when Little Pigeon abused him so, by making him go down there to listen to the horse races, which he adored.

Then when Sammye heard Old Mrs. Woman go out the back door, she watched her through the basement window and saw her going over to her big empty house across the yard. When Old Mrs. Woman was inside her big house, Sammye rapped on the basement ceiling and called out very mournfully, "Little Pigeon! Little Pigeon!" Sammye heard Little Pigeon's feet acoming down the basement stairs. Little Pigeon came in the basement. The two stood looking at each other. Then Little Pigeon said, "You are Sister Sammye's ghost, and go away." Sammye said, "Now looka here, I am *not* my ghost, I am your real Sister Sammye and you are looking straight at me. I am live as a coal of fire, and want to know what's going on in this house that I have to bang on the sides of it and at the windows to try to get in to see my own sister. What has Old Mrs. Woman done to you to change you? Now tell your sweet sister."

Little Pigeon just swanked and said, "Go 'way, ghost of Sister Sammye."

Sammye waited a minute and then said, in a ghost's voice, "Put out something you treasure for a ghost and he will go away."

"But what?" Little Pigeon asked. "You are trying to get my things, just like Old Mrs. Woman said."

Sammye said, "I don't care about your things, put out the ghost some supper. And never tell a soul."

Well, this is the way Sammye got her supper, for awhile.

Then Sammye started working her plan. Sammye thought, I'll wart them to death, I'll be a regular Jonah to those two, I'll give them what they asked for and deserve. When Little Pigeon and Old Mrs. Woman would be out walking, Sammye would steal up into the house and touch her fingers on the silver or on the crystal. When they would come back Little Pigeon would find the prints and smuts of fingers on her things and say, "Somebody's fingers been on my things. The ghost has been here." And Old Mrs. Woman would look with big eyes and not know what to think. Or, again, Sammye would sneak Little Pigeon's purse from where she had it and put it in another place. Sammye would hear the two of them tearing the house down looking for it.

Well, you don't have to hear any more, you can see how it all ended up: Old Mrs. Woman began to get the blame from Little Pigeon for all the stunts Sammye pulled. She tried then to say there was no ghost and to blame Little Pigeon for trying to devil *her,* Little Pigeon was all mixed up but said there most assuredly *was* one, for she had seen it, etc. etc.; and it was the end of their happy honeymoon when Little Pigeon and Old Mrs. Woman had a knock-down-drag-out in the driveway and Old Mrs. Woman pushed Little Pigeon over into the hedge. Then is when Sammye appeared from the basement and picked Little Pigeon out.

Old Mrs. Woman went back over to her big empty house, back to crying; and everything was like it started out, except that Little Pigeon couldn't get *ghost* out of her mind and still thought Sammye was Sammye's ghost and Sammye could not change her mind. So Sammye stayed a ghost; anything to humor Little Pigeon. But otherwise everything was just the same, Sammye had Little Pigeon back, worrying her to death, calling her long distance at Rodunda when she was not with her, mistreating her and fussing at her when she was with her, and accusing her of stealing her purse or of touching her things—Sammye got the blame for everything that was wrong—Sammye was about to pull her hair out with Little Pigeon, said she had no life of her own, said she had nothing, was just a ghost of herself. "But she is my sweet sister that I love and adore," Sammye would still say.

Yet it was peculiar how there seemed to be a real ghost in Little Pigeon's house, just as Little Pigeon had said; for very often they would hear commotions in the basement, and on many mornings they would come down to find the prints of fingers that had touched all over Little Pigeon's things. Sammye would go down to the basement to look around for signs, but there seemed nothing. Once in awhile she caught Little Pigeon still going faithfully down the basement stairs with some hot supper for the basement ghost and would have to stop her and try to reason with her that the ghost that used to be down there had gone away and would never come again. But this was difficult, since Little Pigeon was so far gone in her dream of things by that time; so often Sammye would just let her go and play with the ghost she thought was living in the basement. Sweet Little Pigeon.

But when Sammye went down to the basement one day, and just to get something this time, not to investigate or spy, what should she find but Old Mrs. Woman! Sammye smelled a rat and said, looking at her out of the corner of her eye, "Go 'way ghost of Old Mrs. Woman!" Old Mrs. Woman prissed and flaunted and said, "Put out something you treasure for a ghost and she will go away. Ha!"

Then Sammye, who had always been the practical one, decided to use her head. She sat down on the divan that used to be her bed when she was a ghost in the basement herself, and said, "Well, Mrs. Woman, this is foolishness, a ghost pestering a ghost, we'll drive each other into insanity and all end up in the Home. I'm not going to give up and you're not either. We mind as well be ghosts together. I've got no household anymore and you've got none, nor Little Pigeon either, except for what we make for her, by hook or crook; we mind as well make one whole household out of three pieces of households. Why don't you move on in the basement, move your cedarchest with the Letter in it on over here and I'll move my things in from Rodunda—and we'll all three have us a household, us two old ghosts and the sweet Little Pigeon. She can't get us out of her head anyway, thinks we're here when we aren't and we aren't when we are. Everybody's everywhere, so far as I can make out, and I'm beginning to not be sure where I am, myself—and I don't believe you know. This shuttling from house to house is killing us both and will make ghosts of us before we know it. Come on over, Mrs. Woman." And then Sammye said something which if she had said it much earlier in the game would have changed the whole story from the beginning; and saved a lot of traffic. She said it in a quiet tone that she used in talking to herself, "All we want, I guess, is a household that will let us be the way we are."

The two women shook hands, here were the two ghosts down in the basement making covenant, bargaining to make the ghost story come true for Little Pigeon upstairs—who already believed in it anyway and had more or less made it come true, will or nill.

But Sammye and Old Mrs. Woman had a few things to settle first. Old Mrs. Woman said, "This basement is as much your house as it is mine, you seemed to like it well enough to live down here once. Why don't *you* move in the basement, Sammye Johnson?" Sammye did not argue and suggested that they take turns living in the basement, adding that the divan was uncomfortable, though, even for a ghost to sleep on. Old Mrs. Woman said she would move in her daybed that the roomers had bought for her; and it was agreed upon. "One last thing," Mrs. Woman said, "and that is please to note that my name is Lucille Purdy and you will do me the favor of please calling me the same."

So Lucille moved her cedarchest with the Letter in it into the basement, and the daybed, too; and the household flourished. In a few years the life of the town all shifted in another direction and moved there, towards the new development of what had been just a no-good thicket, something was suddenly there—oil or mineral or better land or something—that the town craved or thought it did, the way towns do, sometimes; change their shape and size and way, trying to form something—what?—and trying to find something to gather round. It was a time when everything shifted and changed, swarmed and clustered around an idea or a craving, used it up or wearied of it, then scattered to pieces again, it was a time of clashes of cravings, it was like a bunch of sheep moving and wandering, shepherd or no—he only followed when he was supposed to lead and could not summon them all together, or there was no shepherd (maybe that was the trouble), he was lost under the hill.

People of this section followed the town into the thicket where the town became so changed; politicians fought, money came from another part of the country; the town thrived. The old houses in the left-behind section were torn down or simply just abandoned, almost as if in a hurry because of a plague or a flood, this left-behind section became a kind of ghost town—almost as if the whole living town had turned away from Little Pigeon and Sammye and Lucille and would have nothing to do with them. But they stayed behind, and did not even know they stayed behind, they did not even know there was another place to want to go to, their shuttling was through. For the shape of the household in Little Pigeon's house was fixed forever, and it never changed again, it went on aflourishing—it had found something to hold it together, and that was a covenant of ghosts.

In a few years Little Pigeon died, still believing her house had two ghosts living in it, one above and one below, one stealing her purse and the other dancing with her in the paper room; and both of them giving her her insulin, listening to her count her things and tell about them.

After Little Pigeon was buried, the two women Sammye and Lucille had several good years together in Little Pigeon's house;

you could see them swanking down the sidewalk on many a sunshiny afternoon, arm in arm, hair all set and good clothes on, strolling through the neighborhood of empty houses and down deserted streets, Sammye in Little Pigeon's ruby earbobs and in her good fur coat, Lucille fat as ever; and few people will ever know what had brought them together to be such friends, who had been such enemies.

Those who know the story to the end say the ghost of Little Pigeon came regularly and counted and touched all her things, but no more to devil the household or to cause it trouble, only just to join it and keep it whole, and that the basement room was always kept nice for her—it was her turn down there, now—until Sammye finally died and left Lucille with too many ghosts for flesh to bear; and so she opened her cedarchest and took out the Letter and put it in her bosom and then took out the revolver Mr. Purdy had given her years ago and ended the last life of the household—joining ghost to ghost, the best household and the longest lasting.

People of the town, the kind who always know mysterious stories about this old house or that dead person, say the ghosts of two old women walk arm in arm through this ruined section when the sun shines in winter. That you can occasionally still see the three ghosts moving through the house. That one of the women was crazy and another committed suicide, and that the house was a household of violence and hatred and jealousy.

It is true that the house of Little Pigeon still stands, closed up and passed by, as it had always been even when the town was living close around it; so go and look at it if you don't believe it. Go and look through the side windows at the faded paper streamers in the paper room, go around and find the withered tissue snow crystals peeling from the sunporch windows in the back. It has not been sold or rented or tampered with until this day, that anybody knows of, but has grown along in some dream of its own. The trees have grown up high around it and locked branches over it as if to roof it away from the world, and the hedges are uncropped and rank, high and thick as a wall. This makes it seem ghosthouse enough, and it is true that the house is known only as the house where three old evil women lived, a crazy woman and her sister and a woman who shot herself. But that's one story. And if you know the whole story, as now you do, you can come stand at the window and hear a ghostly voice counting out the silverware and linens, or the riffle of ghost feet to the music of "Whispering"; and then you can have it all straight and can understand the household that was covenanted for there. And can understand the town, too; and can have your own story, ghost story or flesh story, out of the whole thing.

Anyway, that is the story about the lives of Old Mrs. Woman, Sister Sammye and Little Pigeon, and how they formed a household in a town that passed them by.

Pore Perrie

For James McAllen

"Tell me the story of pore Perrie. Tell how she lived all her life till she died."

"Hush asking me 'cause I don't want to tell it. 'Twas buried with pore Perrie in her grave. . . ."

"The flesh of it is buried, but we have the ghost of it again. Pore Perrie's grave holds only half the story—the other's yet to come."

"Then let me bring the half to the half myself. When Perrie and I join in the Polk plot in the cemetery, laid side by side, we'll settle it all, ghost and flesh, under the dirt. Dirt takes everything back again, in the end. Now let us alone. Leave us to dirt."

"But this is a good time to tell, while I'm here and you're here—and we may never be again. For soon (tonight) I moan be on my way; I cain't stay. So tell it to me because I want to get it all straight. Let me have it from your mouth now, and for the last time, and then I can have it again from my memory as I go on, on the road."

"Some one of you always passing through and stopping by, asking my stories, asking my time, asking my grief, won't let a life be. Worse than a bed of red ants. Be glad when my life's story settles down into the ground, a fallen message to be told out no more, locked in the box of my bones: message and bone go back into dirt. (Blood kin buried together settle their *own* stories, a family graveyard plot is a mailbox of messages all reading each other—who ever thought they lie quiet together and in peace at last, gladly beyond?)

"But go get me something to fan with, my cardboard fan from the church is done fanned out; the newspaper will do. . . ."

2.

"Well if you see yonder at those bunch of houses by the boxy churchhouse and see the little squatty one huddling next to it like a chick to a hen, then that's the house where we all lived during the story of pore Perrie. And if I tell you about it one more time, about Aunt Perrie and Uncle Ace (when he was home) and Son, man and boy, then I want you to hush ever asking me about it again. Because you know good and well that I've told it to you, chapter and book, time and time over, and this will be the last, until I go to my grave. Pore Perrie."

3.

The thing of it is, Son was over in Benburnett County working for awhile with a rigging outfit when suddenly Aunt Linsie began to have his letters. Son wrote and said Aunt Linsie can you tell me about Aunt Perrie, all how she was when I wasn't there to see, all how she lived and how she died. This gave Aunt Linsie a chance to write one of her long good letters that was like a story she was telling (when you can get her to tell one); and she wrote back, "Son to begin with why don't you stop keeping me in a tumult, I should think you'd have seen for yourself, your pore Aunt Perrie's ghost is haunting you and I'm glad, this is because you ought to have been here with her when she needed you (and not just skimming and skirting round the place here the way you did, like a ghost of yourself), not everywhere you were during those days, there's plenty of ghosts will tell you that, won't let you rest pretty soon, it's your conscience, thas all, Son," etc. etc. . . .

Son wrote back and said, "All right Aunt Linsie, I know I've led you and Aunt Perrie a life, but none of that ghost stuff, this is no ghost, I just want to know about Aunt Perrie and am asking you."

Aunt Linsie wrote back and said, "Well, Son, if this is some other stunt of yours I'll cherish it against you the rest of my life, for pore Perrie was my own sister and your only mother in this world and gave a goodly part of her life to raising and tending to you when you was a boy; but anyways you remember how she was such a stout woman when you left? She fell off so you wouldn't have recognized her as the same pore Perrie after you and Ace left, and when she died (that death's part yours and you know it) we buried her as small as a Cheedee. If you're hurrawing about pore Perrie I can't stand it, that pore suffering thang Perrie."

Son wrote a letter back that said, "No, Aunt Linsie, I'm not making light of Aunt Perrie, how could I? So write me back and tell me what I ask, then I'll tell you why I'm asking."

Aunt Linsie's answer said, "Son don't you know by now there's no room anywheres in the world, no quarters in any house or billin, that can hide you from your own folks, they live in your memory and blood, you bring them in a room when you move in. You can build a house against weather, but you can't build it against your own conscience. Get right, face your life, all what's in it, and that includes pore Perrie, was like your own mother, called you her own, and then you treated her like you did, *when are you going to settle down?* That's all right, you're coming outa the little end of the horn now, and I know it and you know it; but I'll help you outa your trouble, will do it till I'm dead and gone (and then who'll do it then, oh who, I wonder?)"

Son's answer said, "Aunt Linsie, hush lecturing me. I'm not perfect and I know it; and Uncle Ace was not perfect. But there was only one man in this wide world who was perfect and He was crucified. Just don't devil me. I expect you're right on most of what you say. The thing of it is, I all of a sudden see Aunt Perrie's life so plain, plainer than I could ever see when I was looking, and I can see her rooms in our house, the one with the machine she pumped and sewed at, with the wooden drawers full of spools and bias tape. *I want to get something straight.*"

(Aunt Linsie did not answer, and the next thing she knew, Son was on the place.)

4.

"Now listen to me while I tell you the story of pore Perrie, because it'll be the last and enough. Then hush ever asking me about it.

"Well, as you know, because I've told you, they called us the

Polk Sisters in this town of Crecy Texas. We were the seamstresses of the town. Our mother and father died young and Perrie took me and brought me up. Our house was a good house—'cept for the 'shackley steps in back—built next to the Campbellite church (now a Presbyterian one); cool in summer and then with a vine on every string that strung the porch like a harp, and cold in winter; but good lives found a home in it. Pore Perrie sat on the porch in summer and sang the hymns along with the congregation next door despite they was Campbellites, for hymns are the same in all Houses of God, she said. She had her own church there behind the vines. In the front flowerbeds was a duke's mixture of Rainlillies after it rained, Touchmenots, Old Flags and Calico, with always a grasshopper on the Calico. There was a frail Huisache tree on the side of the house, brought there from a West Texas place by a cousin long ago who said it might live, she couldn't say, in this damper climate; but it did, grew up pretty as a tree on a calendar, spraying out its yellow insect blooms and so limber that even a bird would bend it to light there, and scatter the blossoms. On one side was the churchhouse and in the afternoons the shadow of the churchhouse lay on the grass and Son played in the shadow; and on the other side was the patch. In back was the clothesyard where there lived several White Leghorn hens that left enough eggs for us to eat and bake with, and there was a few Golden Seabright Bantams just for ornament and for Son to have. Back of that was the grove of little pinetrees.

"Perrie and me were both cut out by the Lord, who has his designs for all of us, to be missionaries; but I gave my life to Perrie and Perrie had a lame foot, to begin with, and then she spoiled the Lord's design by marrying—against all wishes—and so late. . . . And there my story commences. Or ends . . . 'cause I don't want to tell it anymore. Hush making me."

"Tell it out, this is the time to tell."

5.

"When Perrie Polk married—so late (she was thirty-eight and I was twenty-eight)—Ace Wanger, a traveling lumber salesman living in hotels and all that kind of boarding-house life, she adopted a child, little Son, through the Methodist Church Orphanage, because she could have none of her own. The Church was this orphan child's parentage, and that's the way Perrie wanted it.

"Now Uncle Ace had been an orphan too, a foundling of some kind, nobody knows or ever knew who his folks were; and he would never talk about it. He took our home when he came into it as Perrie's husband and he took little Son as his son, as you will see; but this so late and after so much misery.

"Son grew along, in the house and in the yard, me and Perrie doing our sewing, Ace away on the road three weeks out of four all over Texas and Arkansas with his lumber, and little Son playing around the sewing machine that Perrie was pumping. When he could call a name he said Aunt Perrie and Aunt Linsie and Uncle Ace. So there was this household. All in the little house you can see right chonder, that nobody lives in since I moved, just a shell of a house.

"Son was the best child in this world, then; never put his fingers in the sewing-machine pedal, never took the bobbins or the needles, sat very quiet—whose child? As he grew along he never gave any trouble, not even to switch his legs, and when he was old enough in the summertimes—we never even had to send him to Bible School in the summertime—but he went of his own choosing—nor give him a real blistering. Pore Perrie and I would watch him through the window where he played in the woodpile and wonder where Son came from.

"By the time he was twelve he had turned real dark complected and very very nervious. His nerviousness so worried Perrie that she took him to Doctor Browder for it. Perrie said Doctor Browder said this is the most nervious child ever I saw in my practice, but think he'll outgrow it—Perrie said Doctor Browder said—*if* he has his tonsils and adenoids out. Son had these out, and then we got him glasses. But we had to take him out of school.

"Then we trained him ourselves, with the Bible, Stories of the Bible, Children of Faraway Lands—put out by the Missionary Society; and had him count eggs and tomatoes. He planted and pruned and toted round the place; and grew along.

"By the time he was seventeen his distress began, finding him dark and lean and beginning to be very different. He was so nervious that if he'd be sitting by the washhouse studying something on his mind—oh I wonder what?—and the Leghorn rooster would crow in his face, Son would startle up and chunk a rock at him. Once he did this; and hit the Leghorn rooster in the head and killed it—to give you a notion of how Son was in those days. We didn't know what to do with Son, and pore Perrie worried and worried. I worried too. Uncle Ace was no help, as he should have been, for he was always off traveling. So what could we do, so what could pore Perrie do? We tried to quieten Son down. We read him out of the Bible—*My mother and my brethren are these* . . . Saint Luke eight twenty-one.

"The thing of it is he had never had it told to him that he was an orphan. People who knew it kept it quiet; but they tried to tell him about it in ways that people have about a stranger—as you will later see. Some came to Perrie and said Son probably had some foreign blood in him, did he have nigra blood in him maybe? Did he have any papers? These things hurt pore Perrie, and hurt me; but Perrie said Son was Child of the Church and any parentage beyond that was unbeknownst to her. Once I said, 'Perrie regg'n it is the time to tell, do you think Son is of the age to have it told him'; but Perrie said, 'Not yet.'

"Something had happened between Perrie and Ace, as it was bound to. One day in July he wrote a letter from Memphis and said he had a new job that would keep him there and he was going to take it and stay. Perrie would not quarrel with him and sent him all his things. There had never been a whole minute's talk between Son and Ace, but suddenly when it was known that Ace was gone, and to stay, Son's change happened. He was gone from his room one July morning soon after and there was a message left saying, 'I have gone to Memphis to see Uncle Ace.'

"A long terrible time and no word. Perrie was ailing most of the time now, her lame foot had caused her hip to ache so that she could scarcely pump the sewing machine. I said a mite, not much; but I was grieving. We ate supper together quietly. There was a medicine show come through, but we didn't go. A Preacher Healer from the 'Postolics came to town and the town filled his tent and several were healed by the Miracle; but Perrie said that if the Lord had taken her one side it was for His uses and that he had strengthened the other for her own; it was His Design; she pumped left-footed and would not go to the Healer. Now that's enough; quit asking me. My mouth is shut."

"But tell how the letters started. Tell about the letters."

6.

"Well, then the letters started. First Son wrote and said, 'Aunt Perrie why did you have to let me find it out for myself that I am somebody's son we never knew, probably a bastard'—he wrote that word. 'Uncle Ace has told me again what was first told to me on the Church Hike the Fourtha July.'

"Perrie wrote back and said, 'Son I never wanted to hurt you and you were too young to know, besides. If you hadn't run off I'd have told you, or had Brother Riley at the church to tell you. But I have been your mother as good as any mother could have been; and your Aunt Linsie, too. If you had no mother then think how you had *two* mothers showering all their love and care on you, count your blessings Son, and don't make light of me. For I done the best I could.'

"Son wrote a letter back that said, 'Aunt Perrie I am working in a lumbermill out of Memphis and like it; and if I had two mothers in Crecy Texas then I have three in all, but one to begin with and that one to end with, will you please do me the favor of telling me who my mother was, and where; and I'll be much oblige.'

"Perrie wrote back an answer that Son was to please not change his nature and his ways, that he was please not to hurraw about three mothers, that she would tell him now that who or where his mother and father were never would be known, and to send his things on home and come on with them. To just count her, Aunt Perrie, as his mother and go on with his life. 'For I have raised you,' Perrie's letter said, 'In this house and yard in Crecy Texas to the best of my gumption, under the shadow of the Church and in the name of God. You was a good child and now can be a good young man. I ask you to abide in the Lord who is our only Father.'

"No answer.

7.

"On the Fourtha July on account of the celebration at the Picnic Grounds all the heavens was aglow for two hours, just one solid blast, shook us all up, you'd have thought the world was coming to an end; and about nine o'clock I looked out and here was Son coming from the to-do and we could see something was wrong, that he had been hurt. He looked so hurt. Perrie said, 'Son commere to me and tell me who or what it is that's hurt you; I can tell when something has hurt you, and come and tell me.' But Son wouldn't say. And I thought, because he was so peculiar and so changed, *what child is this?* And I thought child o child what is ever going to happen to you in this world I wonder, oh what will your life be, if we could just put it into the right hands, see that it goes right and good and doesn't get hurt or astray—who will ever look after you, you little thing. But I know we can't help, no one can do that for nobody, have to go this way and that, find our ground and try to stand our ground, learn our wisdom and then try to be strong enough to bear our wisdom, O hep this little boy, child a mine, is what I thought.

"Well, Son wouldn't tell and so Perrie didn't press him, he went to bed and I said, 'Perrie regg'n what's the matter with him?' and Perrie said, 'Let him alone, Linsie, he'll tell dreckly.'

"The next day he was so peculiar, we was so far apart, wouldn't say much, face right peaked, until that afternoon Perrie said he come to her with the wildest face and said, 'Aunt Perrie I've hurt myself and I'm scared, maybe we ought to call Doctor Browder.' Perrie said, 'Son what have you done to yourself, come talk to me, come let me see.' Son said, 'Aunt Perrie I can't tell you or show you, 'cause you see I was climbing over a bobwire fence at the Fourtha July fireworks and I slipped and fell upon the bobwire. I didn't look until we got in the light of the fireworks and then I saw blood on myself.'

"Oh, I said, this is when he needs his Uncle Ace, but let Ace stay on away on the road, let him stay until Doomsday, we can get along without him (this boy was always trying to run away from where he was or from people he was with to be by himself, as if to still something rankling in him, as if to put something to rest within him or for some reason we could never know. But everytime he broke and ran away, and mind you this, he harmed or wounded himself in some way: it was the harm and the wound that brought him back, then, time and time again, so as to heal harm and hurt, it seemed). 'Come let *me* see,' I said, 'Son.'

"'Nome,' he said, 'you can't see, either, just call Doctor Browder.'

"Doctor Browder come and he and Son went in the back room and closed the door, and we heard Doctor Browder say, 'Son let me see you, let me see what have you done to yourself.'

"After that we scarcely knew Son any more, he was a stranger in the house. It was just a little after this that the letter came from Ace saying he was staying in Memphis and then Son left his message and left. (*Child a mine, child a mine, something touched you and changed you all over. I know some hand touched that good boy Son and left him never the same again. Some hand led him away from pore Perrie (Lord hep me forget his face, his head of hair, let me forget him all over, the way he was all over, bless his hide, he was the only thing I ever had. I remember him in the garden counting the tomatoes for arithmetic, I remember him in the clothesyard bumping like a ghost through the wet sheets, I remember him in the pinegrove; child a mine.*))

"And that's the end of this story. Don't ask me no more. Because I'm old, poor Perrie's buried in her grave, and Ace, too—you know this—and Son is out somewhere in the world on the road like his Uncle Ace before him. There is no more to tell."

"But tell it all, Aunt Linsie, tell about the two Sons, the ghost and the flesh of Son. This is the time. Go on to the end, and then we'll let it alone, the sad story, forever. By telling it true we'll keep it straight and never tell it again. We'll let it go.

"Pore Perrie."

8.

"One summertime something made a ghost out of the Huisache tree—spun a web around the top of it—some treedevil that lime wouldn't drive away; it seemed the touch of Satan. It was so hot and no Gulf hurricane would come, to bring a norther, the whole world stood still, trees hot and tired with their limp leaves hanging like a panting animal's tongue, flowers in a trance; and us all fanning ourselves. At dark in the evenings a ghost would come. He would linger at the edge of the yard just when Perrie would be feeding the chickens or bringing in the clothes, and Perrie would come in the house white yet her calm prayerful self, but not to mention a ghost. Finally she told me one evening at the supper-table. 'He is at the window,' she said. 'The ghost of Son. And next he will be in the house. He comes closer and closer.' I sat still and told no lie by opening my mouth.

"(Oh don't ask me no more, 'cause I'm uneasy to tell it; don't ask me no more. You've heard it—don't beg me no more.)"

"Tell how it wasn't the ghost of Son, Aunt Linsie, tell how it was the flesh and blood Son. Go on, go ahead, make haste and tell it . . ."

"It was no ghost atall but the genuine flesh of Son. I had known it for some time, had met him in the grove. He was dressed like a tramp and he said, 'Aunt Linsie commere and don't be afraid of me, I'm Son and I'm all right. I've come back to see you all, to see the house, to see the place, if everything and everybody is all right.'

" 'Well come on home, come on in the house,' I said, 'Son, pore Perrie's waiting for you, in her sickness, in her quiet Christian sorrow.'

" 'Nome Aunt Linsie,' Son said. 'Never tell her I've been here. I'm going away again, after a little while. Just come to see everything for myself, and not in dreams or imagination, but everything the way it really is and was. Look by the Huisache tree and find some money I've left for you and Aunt Perrie. And cross your heart you'll never tell her I was here.'

" 'All right, Son,' I said, 'if that's the way you want it, that's the way it has to be. Except I wish you'd come on through the yard and into the house and have yew some supper with us.'

"Then Son went away. I watched him go. He had that same walk.

"But he'd be back again, I'd see him here and there on the place, got to looking for him, would see him behind the barn, in the field, and at the Huisache tree on a moonlight night—he was leaving his money again—and sometime by the chimney window, eyes between the green fringe of the velveteen curtains in the living room. Pore Son, Lord hep this boy; *what child is this?* I thought and prayed; he can't stay and he can't go away. Pore Perrie. Perrie would see him and say in a low voice her prayer, '*Go away, ghost of Son, go 'way and let me be.*'

"Then he'd be gone again for awhile, no sign of Son, I'd look and look for him, but he'd have disappeared, and for a long time sometime, no sight of Son. I'd wait for the flesh of Son and Perrie would wait for his ghost.

"Perrie got weaker and weaker, and sweeter, like a lovely angel. She took to her bed. We had this ghost and this flesh between us, but we never mentioned it, never broached the subject, but it was between us, living and real. It bound us together and broke us apart—we'll settle it one day.

"One night at the end of this hottest summer in our memory, the saving storm came. The trees were nervious and jumpy, but all in the house was green and still. Then it hit. I was in my bed in my front room, next to Perrie's middle one; and I said Lord let it come, it has been trying to come for so long, it has been so slow, let it come, our salvation. Son had not been around the place for some time, but I knew he was there, somehow I knew it. Then in a brightness of white lightning I saw him at my window, and I spoke out, 'Hello Son, please to come in out of the storm.' But the blackness of the night flashed on again, like black lightning, and took away his face. I knew pore Perrie would see him, her ghost, at her window, for he would be there next; so I got up and put on my kimona and using the lightning like a lamp, went to her room. I stood in the doorway and saw this in the lightning: Perrie was standing before her window, beautiful and white as a Saint, naked, the white voile curtains waving and falling and rising round her like the garments of an angel. She seemed young, like a vision of herself, frail and fleshly, and this vision was burned upon my sight, and upon the sight of Son, whose face was there at the window like a lantern; and it will be there till we both of us die, Son and me, I know to God.

"That was the last of the life of pore Perrie, for I picked her up when she folded on to the floor and put her in her bed, a little bundle. I sat the rest of the night through by her side, both of us quiet, Perrie quiet forever—so small and so beautiful in her corpse, the storm raving round the house in great boots, sloshing in the muddy yard and road, and the trees wild and hysterical, Son somewhere outdoors in the storm, me saying, *'Son, Son come on in, come on in and join us now'*; and the night passed. When Doctor Browder came the next morning I said Perrie has passed away, into God's Kingdom; and Doctor Browder said rest her weary Christian soul.

"Pore Perrie was buried in her grave, you know it well, where it tis and what grave will hold her eternal neighbor, room for me, when I will come. And that Uncle Ace is not there beside her but over alone in a corner of the Crecy graveyard—how Son brought him back to bury him, how they had wandered all over three States together, two pore homeless thangs, Son writing me the letters to tell him again all about pore Perrie; he never could seem to get it all straight. This Noah's bird that went forth from the ark kept coming back to us, coming back, with no place to rest his foot; until the last time he came with his burden, his pore homeless, childless, wifeless father; and then he went away for good, in peace, and never returned. He must have been put on this earth to rove about and nurse the wandering homeless, to find them graves to rest in, to bring them to *that* home again, yet he was homeless too and I wonder who will go out to find *him* and bring *him* back? He is aloose forever and in what world and on what way I wonder? The world is too big; we lose people in it. This weatherbird flies into all the four corners of the wind, Lord pity pore little suffering children, oh come on home Son and let's cry together like we use to, even when you were little we would cry together . . . even if you were playing in the clothesyard I'd just run out to you under the shadetree and grab you and cry and you would cry with me. You little trembling thing you already knew (how *did* you know?) what breaks a heart; nobody ever had to tell you a thing you just knew. That's your purpose you were placed in the world to cry with people, you were sent for grief, called to the grieving world. But I know you're a gay little thing, too, and that's why I know you're meant for grief because you are so gay and are so good to laugh with, oh we've had our laughs, laughed until we cried . . . *why don't you send your clothes on home you said you would where are your things?*

"Go on now. *That is all I will tell and I will never tell it again.* Now I've told you it and I never will again. Go on now and hush ever thinking about it.

"Pore Perrie."

9.

(The thing of it is, they say Son still comes to Crecy once in awhile. That Linsie would see him at the edge of the grove and go out to meet him, after Perrie passed away, speak his name, 'Son,' and say, 'Commere Son,' only to find him not there at all. She would see him and then she wouldn't. Had he come, or hadn't he? Sometimes she would see a lantern going over the ground or hanging in a tree in the grove; sometimes it was just the light in the brooder. Was he there or wasn't he? They say a Peeping Tom with a flashlight has been seen at windows of Crecy houses. That the 'Postolics say the Devil was seen walking in the pastures at night with a torch. That somebody has been living with the Gypsies up on the hill. That a Negro on the road saw Son and Linsie dancing naked in the pinegrove one night. And that Linsie's seen Son all through the house, behind the beaded curtains between the hall and middle bedroom, his face at the frosted pane on the front door and called, *'Son Son commere to me and tell me what is in your craw.'*

The thing of it is (and then I'm through, this story is done), when Linsie is buried in the family plot next to pore Perrie, these two sister-mothers will have this to settle between themselves there under the dirt. Linsie has a message for pore Perrie, and it won't be long, now, before she takes it to her. They have this Son between them, until Doomsday, ghost and flesh.

And now I'm moving on (oh hear my song); this is the story as it was told to me; and as I go on, on the road, with a message to deliver, *I* want to get it all straight. There is this Son's pain to understand and tell about and I look for tongue to tell it with.

Pore Perrie.)

Ghost and Flesh, Water and Dirt

Was somebody here while ago acallin for you. . .

O don't say that, don't tell me who . . . was he fair and had a wrinkle in his chin? I wonder was he the one . . . describe me his look, whether the eyes were pale light-colored and swimmin and wild and shifty; did he bend a little at the shoulders was his face agrievin what did he say where did he go, whichaway, hush don't tell me; wish I could keep him but I cain't, so go, go (but come back).

Cause you know honey there's a time to go roun and tell and there's a time to set still (and let a ghost grieve ya); so listen to me while I tell, cause I'm in my time a tellin and you better run fast if you don wanna hear what I tell, cause I'm goin ta tell . . .

Dreamt last night again I saw pore Raymon Emmons, all last night seen im plain as day. There uz tears in iz glassy eyes and iz face uz all meltin away. O I was broken of my sleep and of my night disturbed, for I dreamt of pore Raymon Emmons live as ever.

He came on the sleepin porch where I was sleepin (and he's there to stay) ridin a purple horse (like King was), and then he got off and tied im to the bedstead and come and stood over me and commenced iz talkin. All night long he uz talkin and talkin, his speech (whatever he uz sayin) uz like steam streamin outa the mouth of a kettle, streamin and streamin and streamin. At first I said in my dream, 'Will you do me the favor of tellin me just who in the world you can be, will you please show the kindness to tell me who you can be, breakin my sleep and disturbin my rest?' 'I'm Raymon Emmons,' the steamin voice said, 'and I'm here to stay; putt out my things that you've putt away, putt out my oatmeal bowl and putt hot oatmeal in it, get out my rubberboots when it rains, iron my clothes and fix my supper . . . I never died and I'm here to stay.'

(*Oh go way ole ghost of Raymon Emmons, whisperin in my ear on the pilla at night; go way ole ghost and lemme be! Quit standin over me like that, all night standin there sayin somethin to me . . . behave ghost of Raymon Emmons, behave yoself and lemme be! Lemme get out and go roun, lemme put on those big ole rubberboots and go clompin. . . .*)

Now you shoulda known that Raymon Emmons. *There* was *somebody*, I'm tellin you. Oh he uz a bright thang, quick 'n fair, tall, about six feet, real lean and a devlish face full of snappin eyes, he had eyes all over his face, didn't miss a thang, that man, saw everthang; and a clean brow. He was a rayroad man, worked for the Guff Coast Lines all iz life, our house always smelt like a train.

When I first knew of him he was livin at the Boardinhouse acrost from the depot (oh that uz years and years ago), and I uz in town and wearin my first pumps when he stopped me on the corner and ast me to do him the favor of tellin him the size a my foot. I was not afraid atall to look at him and say the size a my foot uz my own affair and would he show the kindness to not be so fresh. But when he said I only want to know because there's somebody livin up in New Waverley about your size and age and I want to send a birthday present of some houseshoes to, I said that's different; and we went into Richardson's store, to the back where the shoes were, and tried on shoes till he found the kind and size to fit me and this person in New Waverley. I didn't tell im that the pumps I'uz wearin were Sistah's and not my size (when I got home and Mama said why'd it take you so long? I said it uz because I had to walk so slow in Sistah's pumps).

Next time I saw im in town (and I made it a point to look for im, was why I come to town), I went up to im and said do you want to measure my foot again Raymon Emmons, ha! And he said any day in the week I'd measure that pretty foot; and we went into Richardson's and he bought *me* a pair of white summer pumps with a pink tie (and I gave Sistah's pumps back to her). Miz Richardson said my lands Margy you buyin lotsa shoes lately, are you goin to take a trip (O I took a trip, and one I come back from, too).

We had other meetins and was plainly in love; and when we married, runnin off to Groveton to do it, everbody in town said things about the marriage because he uz thirty and I uz seventeen.

We moved to this house owned by the Picketts, with a good big clothesyard and a swing on the porch, and I made it real nice for me and Raymon Emmons, made curtains with fringe, putt jardinears on the front bannisters and painted the fern buckets. We furnished those unfurnished rooms with our brand new lives, and started goin along.

Between those years and this one I'm tellin about them in, there seems a space as wide and vacant and silent as the Neches River, with my life *then* standin on one bank and my life *now* standin on the other, lookin acrost at each other like two diffrent people wonderin who the other can really be.

How did Raymon Emmons die? Walked right through a winda and tore hisself all to smithereens. Walked right through a second-story winda at the depot and fell broken on the tracks—nothin much left a Raymon Emmons after he walked through that winda —broken his crown, hon, broken his crown. But he lingered for three days in Victry Hospital and then passed, sayin just before he passed away, turnin towards me, 'I hope you're satisfied. . . .'

Why did he die? From grievin over his daughter and mine, Chitta was her name, that fell off a horse they uz both ridin on the Emmonses' farm. Horse's name was King and we had im shot.

Buried im next to Chitta's grave with iz insurance, two funerals in as many weeks, then set aroun blue in our house, cryin all day and cryin half the night, sleep all broken and disturbed of my rest, thinkin oh if he'd come knockin at that door right now I'd let him in, oh I'd let Raymon Emmons in! After he died, I set aroun sayin who's gonna meet all the hours in a day with me, whatever is in each one—*all those hours*—who's gonna be with me in the mornin, in the ashy afternoons that we always have here, in the nights of lightnin who's goan be lyin there, seen in the flashes and makin me feel as safe as if he uz a lightnin rod (and honey he *wuz*); who's gonna be like a light turned on in a dark room when I go in, who's gonna be at the door when I open it, who's goin to be there when I wake up or when I go to sleep, who's goin to call my name? I cain't stand a life of just me and our furniture in a room, who's gonna *be* with me?' Honey it's true that you never miss water till the well runs dry, tiz truly true.

Went to talk to the preacher, but he uz no earthly help, regalin me with iz pretty talk, he's got a tongue that will trill out a story pretty as a bird on a bobwire fence—but meanin what?—sayin 'the wicked walk on every hand when the vilest men are exalted'—now what uz that mean?—; went to set and talk with Fursta Evans in her Millinary Shop (who's had her share of tumult in her sad life, but never shows it) but she uz no good, sayin 'Girl pick up the pieces and go on . . . here try on this real cute hat' (that woman had nothin but hats on her mind—even though she taught me *my* life, grant cha *that*—for brains she's got hats). Went to the graves on Sundays carryin potplants and cryin over the mounds, one long wide one and one little un—how sad are the little graves a childrun, childrun ought not to have to die it's not right to bring death to childrun, they're just little toys grownups play with or neglect (thas how some of em die, too, honey, but won't say no more bout that); but all childrun go to Heaven so guess it's best—the grasshoppers flyin all roun me (they say graveyard grasshoppers spit tobacco juice and if it gets in your eye it'll putt your eye out) and an armadilla diggin in the crepemyrtle bushes—sayin 'dirt lay light on Raymon Emmons and iz child,' and thinkin 'all my life is dirt I've got a famly of dirt.' And then I come back to set and scratch aroun like an armadilla myself in these rooms, alone; but honey that uz no good either.

And then one day, I guess it uz a year after my famly died, there uz a knock on my door and it uz Fursta Evans knockin when I opened it to see. And she said 'honey now listen I've come to visit with you and to try to tell you somethin: why are you so glued to Raymon Emmonses memry when you never cared a hoot bout him while he was on earth, you despised all the Emmonses, said they was just trash, wouldn't go to the farm on Christmas or Thanksgivin, wouldn't set next to em in church, broke pore Raymon Emmons's heart because you'd never let Chitta stay with her grandparents and when you finely did the Lord purnished you for bein so hateful by takin Chitta. Then you blamed it on Raymon Emmons, hounded im night and day, said he killed Chitta, drove im stark ravin mad. While Raymon Emmons was live you'd never even give him the time a day, wouldn't lift a hand for im, you never would cross the street for im, to you he uz just a dog in the yard, and you know it, and now that he's dead you grieve yo life away and suddenly fall in love with im.' Oh she tole me good and proper—said, 'you never loved im till you lost im, till it uz too late, said now set up and listen to me and get some brains in yo head, chile.' Said, 'cause listen honey, I've had four husbands in my time, two of em died and two of em quit me, but each one of em I thought was goin to be the *only* one, and I took each one for that, then let im go when he uz gone, kept goin roun, kept ready, we got to honey, left the gate wide open for anybody to come through, friend or stranger, ran with the hare and hunted with the hound, honey we got to *greet* life not grieve life,' is what she said.

'Well,' I said, 'I guess that's the way life is, you don't know what you have till you don't have it any longer, till you've lost it, till it's too late.'

'Anyway,' Fursta said, 'little cattle little care—you're beginnin again now, fresh and empty handed, it's later and it's shorter, yo life, but go on from *here* not *there,*' she said. 'You've had one kind of a life, had a husband, putt im in iz grave (now leave im there!), had a child and putt her away, too; start over, hon, the world don't know it, the world's fresh as ever—it's a new day, putt some powder on yo face and start goin roun. Get you a job, and try that; or take you a trip. . . .'

'But I got to stay in this house,' I said. 'Feel like I cain't budge. Raymon Emmons is here, live as ever, and I cain't get away from im. He keeps me fastened to this house.'

'Oh poot,' Fursta said, lightin a cigarette. 'Honey you're losin ya mine. Now listen here, put on those big ole rubberboots and go clompin, go steppin high and wide—cause listen here, if ya don't they'll have ya up in the Asylum at Rusk sure's as shootin, specially if you go on talkin about this ghost of Raymon Emmons the way you do.'

'But if I started goin roun, what would people say?'

'You can tell em it's none of their beeswax. Cause listen honey, the years uv passed and are passin and you in ever one of em, passin too, and not gettin any younger—yo hair's gettin bunchy and the lines clawed roun yo mouth and eyes by the glassy claws of cryin sharp tears. We got to paint ourselves up and go on, young *outside,* anyway—cause listen honey the sun comes up and the sun crosses over and *goes down*—and while the sun's up we got to get on that fence and crow. Cause night muss fall—and then thas all. Come on, les go roun; have us a Sataday night weddin ever Sataday night; forget this ole patched-faced ghost I hear you talkin about. . . .'

'In this town?' I said. 'I hate this ole town, always rain fallin—'cept this ain't rain it's rainin, Fursta, it's rainin mildew. . . .'

'O deliver me!' Fursta shouted out, and putt out her cigarette, 'you won't do. Are you afraid you'll *melt?*'

'I wish I'd melt—and run down the drains. Wish I uz rain, fallin on the dirt of certain graves I know and seepin down into the dirt, could lie in the dirt with Raymon Emmons on one side and Chitta on the other. Wish I uz dirt. . . .'

'I wish you are just crazy,' Fursta said. 'Come on, you're gonna take a trip. You're gonna get on a train and take a nonstop trip and get off at the end a the line and start all over again new as a New Year's Baby, baby. I'm gonna see to that.'

'Not on no train, all the king's men couldn't get me to ride a train again, no siree. . . .'

'Oh no train my foot,' said Fursta.

'But what'll I use for money please tell me,' I said.

'With Raymon Emmons's insurance of course—it didn't take all of it to bury im, I know. Put some acreage tween you and yo past life, and maybe some new friends and scenery too, and pull down the shade on all the water that's gone under the bridge; and come back here a new woman. Then if ya want tew you can come into my millinary shop with me.'

'Oh,' I said, 'is the world still there? Since Raymon Emmons walked through that winda seems the whole world's gone, the whole world went out through that winda when he walked through it.'

Closed the house, sayin 'goodbye ghost of Raymon Emmons,' bought my ticket at the depot, deafenin my ears to the sound of the tickin telegraph machine, got on a train and headed west to California. Day and night the trainwheels on the traintracks said *Raymon Emmons Raymon Emmons Raymon Emmons,* and I looked through the winda at dirt and desert, miles and miles of dirt, thinkin I wish I uz dirt I wish I uz dirt. O I uz vile with grief.

In California the sun was out, wide, and everbody and everthing lighted up; and oh honey the world *was* still there. I decided to stay awhile. I started my new life with Raymon Emmons's insurance money. It uz in San Diego, by the ocean and with mountains of dirt standin gold in the blue waters. A war had come. I was alone for awhile, but not for long. Got me a job in an airplane factory, met a lotta girls, met a lotta men. I worked in fusilodges.

There uz this Nick Natowski, a brown clean Pollock from Chicargo, real wile, real Satanish. What kind of a life did he start me into? I don't know how it started, but it did, and in a flash we uz everwhere together, dancin and swimmin and *everthing*. He uz in the war and in the U.S. Navy, but we didn't think of the war or of water. I just liked him tight as a glove in iz uniform, I just liked him laughin, honey, I just liked him *ever* way he was, and that uz all I knew. And then one night he said, 'Margy I'm goin to tell you somethin, goin on a boat, be gone a long long time, goin in a week.' Oh I cried and had a nervous fit and said, 'Why do you have to go when there's these thousands of others all aroun San Diego that could go?' and he said, 'We're goin away to Coronada for that week, you and me, and what happens there will be enough to keep and save for the whole time we're apart.' We went, honey, Nick and me, to Coronada, I mean we really *went*. Lived like a king and queen—where uz my life behind me that I thought of onct and a while like a story somebody was whisperin to me?—laughed and loved and I cried; and after that week at Coronada, Nick left for sea on his boat, to the war, sayin I want you to know baby I'm leavin you my allotment.

I was blue, so blue, all over again, but this time it uz diffrent someway, guess cause I uz blue for somethin live this time and not dead under dirt, I don't know; anyway I kept goin roun, kept my job in fusilodges and kept goin roun. There was this friend of Nick Natowski's called George, and we went together some. 'But why doesn't Nick Natowski write me, George?' I said. 'Because he cain't yet,' George said, 'but just wait and he'll write.' I kept waitin but no letter ever came, and the reason he didn't write when he could of, finely, was because his boat was sunk and Nick Natowski in it.

Oh what have I ever done in this world, I said, to send my soul to torment? Lost one to dirt and one to water, makes my life a life of mud, why was I ever put to such a test as this O Lord, I said. I'm goin back home to where I started, gonna get on that train and backtrack to where I started from, want to look at dirt awhile, can't stand to look at water. I rode the train back. Somethin drew me back like I'd been pastured on a rope in California.

Come back to this house, opened it up and aired it all out, and when I got back you know who was there in that house? That ole faithful ghost of Raymon Emmons. He'd been there, waitin, while I went aroun, in my goin roun time, and was there to have me back. While I uz gone he'd covered everythin in our house with the breath a ghosts, fine ghost dust over the tables and chairs and a curtain of ghost lace over my bed on the sleepinporch.

Took me this job in Richardson's Shoe Shop (this town's big now and got money in it, the war 'n oil made it rich, ud never know it as the same if you hadn't known it before; and Fursta Evans married to a rich widower), set there fittin shoes on measured feet all day—it all started in a shoestore measurin feet and it ended that way—can you feature that? Went home at night to my you-know-what.

Comes ridin onto the sleepinporch ever night regular as clockwork, ties iz horse to the bedstead and I say hello Raymon Emmons and we start our conversation. Don't ask me what he says or what I say, but ever night is a night full of talkin, and it lasts the whole night through. Oh onct in a while I get real blue and want to hide away and just set with Raymon Emmons in my house, cain't budge, don't see daylight nor dark, putt away my wearin clothes, couldn't walk outa that door if my life depended on it. But I set real still and let it all be, claimed by that ghost until he unclaims me—and then I get up and go roun, free, and that's why I'm here, settin with you here in the Pass Time Club, drinkin this beer and tellin you all I've told.

Honey, why am I tellin all this? Oh all our lives! So many things to tell. And I keep em to myself a long long time, tight as a drum, won't open my mouth, just set in my blue house with that ole ghost agrievin me, until there comes a time of tellin, a time to tell, a time to putt on those big ole rubberboots.

Now I believe in *tellin,* while we're live and goin roun; when the tellin time comes I say spew it out, we just got to tell things, things in our lives, things that've happened, things we've fancied and things we dream about or are haunted by. Cause you know honey the time to shut you mouth and set moultin and mildewed in yo room, grieved by a ghost and fastened to a chair, comes back roun again, don't worry honey, it comes roun again. There's a time ta tell and a time ta set still ta let a ghost grieve ya. So listen to me while I tell, cause I'm in my time atellin, and you better run fast if you don wanna hear what I tell, cause I'm goin ta tell. . . .

The world is changed, let's drink ower beer and have us a time, tell and tell and tell, let's get that hot bird in a cole bottle tonight. Cause next time you think you'll see me and hear me tell, you won't: I'll be flat where I cain't budge again, like I wuz all that year, settin and hidin way . . . until the time comes roun again when I can say oh go way ole ghost of Raymon Emmons, go way ole ghost and lemme be!

Cause I've learned this and I'm gonna tell ya: there's a time for live things and a time for dead, for ghosts and for flesh 'n bones: all life is just a sharin of ghosts and flesh. Us humans are part ghost and part flesh—part fire and part ash—but I think maybe the ghost part is the longest lastin, the fire blazes but the ashes last forever. I had fire in California (and water putt it out) and ash in Texis (and it went to dirt); but I say now, while I'm tellin you, there's a world both places, a world where there's ghosts and a world where there's flesh, and I believe the real right way is to take our worlds, of ghosts or of flesh, take each one as they come and take what comes in em: take a ghost and grieve with im, settin still; and take the flesh 'n bones and go roun; and even run out to meet what worlds come in to our lives, strangers (like you), and ghosts (like Raymon Emmons) and lovers (like Nick Natowski) . . . and be what each world wants us to be.

And I think that ghosts, if you set still with em long enough, can give you over to flesh 'n bones; and that flesh 'n bones, if you go roun when it's time, can send you back to a faithful ghost. One provides the other.

Saw pore Raymon Emmons all last night, all last night seen im plain as day.

The Grasshopper's Burden

Here was this school building in the town, holding young and old, this stone building that looked from the front like a great big head with flat skull of asphalt and gravel and face of an insect that might be eating up the young through its opening and closing mouth of doors; and across its forehead were written the words: "Dedicated to all high emprise, the building of good citizens of the world, the establishment of a community of minds and hearts, free men and women."

In this building and in its surrounding yards were many people, children and teachers—it was a world:

This was a rainy afternoon in Social Studies and Quella could not stand hearing again the story of Sam Houston read out by different people in the class. She was just waiting for two-thirty when she would get her pass to go to the auditorium where the May Fete in which she was a Royal Princess (and one of two elected by the whole school) would be practiced.

Miss Morris, who would never at any time in her life have been a Royal Princess, she was so ordinary, was the Social Studies teacher and listening as she sat in good posture at her desk to the story of Sam Houston as if it were a brand-new tale just being told for the first time. She did not like to sign a pass—for anything, May Fetes included. Miss Morris had a puckered mouth just like a purse drawn up. She knew everything about children, whether they told a story about undone homework; and especially about boys, if they had been smoking or had a jawbreaker hidden over their last tooth, or a beanshooter in their blouse—she surmised a beanshooter so dreadfully that it might have been a revolver concealed there. And when she fussed at a boy who was mean by stealing a girl's purse and going through it, showing all a girl's things to other boys in the class, Miss Morris would draw her pursey mouth so tight that she seemed to have no lips at all and stitches would crack the powder around it. Then she would shake this boy hard, often causing bubblegum or jawbreakers to fall from him everywhere and roll hard on the floor under all the seats. She did not like to sign a pass.

But Quella must have an early pass, not only to keep from having to read her turn at Sam Houston but to give her time to go get her hair ready for the May Fete practice. She thought what an early pass might be for—not to go to the Nurse to see if she had mumps because it felt sore by her ear, because yesterday she had said this and caused a lot of attention, but all the M's in her row and the L's and N's on both sides of her row shrank away from her and even Helena McWorthy had not wanted to go around with her between classes, the way they did, seeing what was in the halls together, or let her use her powder puff or blue woman's comb, just to get mumps. And she could not have something in her eye because not long ago she had got an easy pass from Miss Stover in Math for this and the Nurse, a little mean woman that smelled like white, had said, "I find nothing whatsomever in your eye that does not naturally belong there," and wrote this on a note to Miss Stover and then glared at her with the whites of her eyes.

Quella sneaked a good black jawbreaker into her mouth, acting like she was just brushing her hand across her mouth, and Miss Morris never knew. Then she sat, waiting for a reason to get an early pass to dawn upon her. She could hear the voices of this one and that one reading out about Sam Houston—forever Sam Houston! They had had him in the Third Grade and they had had him in the Fifth. And now, even in the Seventh and as far as Junior High School they had to have him again. It was Mabel Sampson, the biggest girl, reading now. If she would say *thee—ee,* Miss Morris would stop her and make her say it *thuh;* and she could not even pronounce the word that clearly spelled *Puritan* but said it

Prutan. Mabel Sampson was so dumb. Because Mabel Sampson was bigger than the rest in the class, she deviled them and snooted them whenever and wherever she could, to make it plain that she had somewhere (and Quella was going to find out) passed all the rest of them on her way to something and would get there first.

And then it was Billy Mangus reading. He was fat and white and whined a lot, and the worst boy to sit in front of if you were a girl and an M. She and Helena McWorthy just hated him for what he would do with redhots. He would plant these little dots of sticky candy in Helena McWorthy's beautiful hair and she would not even know it or feel them there and go all through the halls between classes having redhots in her hair until someone laughed at her and made fun of her and picked them out to eat them. Or Billy Mangus would bore a sharpened pencil into Helena's back right through an Angora sweater or even her Mexican bolero which her aunt brought her back from Tijuana Mexico. Helena was a very quiet girl. She would let Quella stroke her, huddled blinking in her seat, keep her always right and everything about her straight, plait and unplait and plait again her hair, arrange her ribbons. Helena would go anywhere holding Quella's hand, submissive to be with her. She had little chinkapin eyes fixed close to the bridge of her nose like a cheap doll's, dull and with scant white eyebrows. Her almost white hair, which was long and divided down her back, was infested with lures like sometimes two red plastic butterflies lighted there, or a green Spanish comb staked over one ear, and always red or blue knitting yarn wound through a spliced hawser of it, which arched over the top of her head from ear to ear. Helena had discovered that a pencil, too, might be stuck there and stolen often by Billy Mangus, who sat behind her alphabetically, and have to be fussed for.

Billy Mangus was reading and Quella wondered if his false tooth in front was wiggling, and she stretched over to see. No. It must be locked in place now. But if he wanted to, Billy could, by unlocking this false tooth some way with his tongue, cause it to wiggle like a loose picket in a fence. This tooth was his special thing in a class or anywhere if he wanted to unlock it. Suddenly she just had to see it wiggle and she did not know why but she shouted, right in the middle of the reading, "Wiggle us your tooth, Billy!" This made Miss Morris very outdone and Billy

Mangus giggled and the whole class tittered. Miss Morris made everything quiet, then stared so hard at Quella and all the class sat very still to watch Miss Morris do one of her stares, hold her rocky eyes, never even breathing or blinking, right on a pupil until he had to look down first. Quella did not know whether to try to outstare Miss Morris by doing just the same to her until *she* put her eyes down, or to look to see if Billy Mangus was wiggling his tooth. But she decided she would rather see the tooth and turned to look; and so Miss Morris won. "Sit up straight, Quella, and do not talk one more time out of turn!" Miss Morris said, very proud because she had won a staring contest.

Quella sat up in her seat and there seemed nothing to do, so she remembered her lips, if they had enough lipstick on them. Very carefully she opened her nice black patent-leather purse and got out her lady's mirror which was of red-skinned leather and had some redhots sticking to it. She cleaned them off into her purse to save them and held out the mirror for her lips to see themselves. She put her lips in a round soft circle. She saw them in her mirror, red enough, sweetheart lips, so beautiful. Then she made different shapes with them, some kissing shapes, some like "OOOOO!"; and one like being prissy, or a word like "really!"; or like the Nurse saying, "I find nothing whatsomever in your eye that does not naturally belong there." But she would not do her lips like Miss Morris at a mean boy, for then it would spoil the lipstick. Last, she gently kissed a piece of composition paper to leave her lips there. Liz her sister kissed letters at the end and all over, she mailed her lips to boys, and she would, too, when she began to write letters to somebody besides her Grandmother in Yreka, who would certainly not be thrilled with kissing lips in a letter.

Then she put her mirror back in her purse and spied her big blue comb in there. She scraped some redhots off it and brought it out and raked her hair with it. It was a good feeling. She thought of Helena's bunch of hair and how she wanted right now to be behind her plaiting it and fixing it as she did in Science where they did not have to sit alphabetically. She seined her hair again through the net of her comb, right in back this time, being very careful not to comb down the red ribbon which was pinned there like an award for something. If a boy pulled at it, this would make her mad and stamp her foot and have to slap him. She lolled the black jawbreaker around in her mouth and devoured the sweet juice from it.

Then suddenly there was something being unwrapped cunningly in the L's across from her. She looked to see Charlotte Langendorf, the ugliest girl, holding something sticky and blue in her lap. It had been wrapped in wax paper. "What is that stuff?" she whispered across to Charlotte. "A thing we cooked today in cooking and I am going to eat it when the eating period comes," Charlotte whispered, glad someone had noticed it. "Let me see it," Quella whispered again. "I won't eat it, cross my heart. I have Cooking next period and I need to know what we will cook." Charlotte passed it secretly across and Quella looked at this peculiar thing which they would cook next period. She examined it, smelled of it, and wanted right then to taste some of it. "What is it?" she asked. "It smells funny." "I don't know," Charlotte whispered back, "but it's something we made out of ingredients. Miss Starnes told us how." Quella tasted it. It was not good to eat at all, not even cooked; but she had another taste. "Let me have it!" Charlotte whispered severely. "Give me back my cooking!" Quella gave it back. "It smells tacky," she said. Then she looked ahead of her in the front of the S's and watched Bobby Sandro's broken arm in a cast, how he was writing tattoos on it, in a cast and a sling from breaking it in Gym and he did not have to write because of it. And then at Suzanne Prince's bandaged-up finger, so she couldn't write, too, saying it was bitten by their cat that went insane.

And then she surveyed the whole row of mean boys, every one of them mean, not a one cute, whose names began with B as though all the meanest were named alike, and she thought how they would step on your saddle shoes to dirty them. Then she thought of several things in a row: horses and their good gentle one named Beauty they used to have; of a fight in the rain before school by Joe and Sandy and how all the girls stood purposely to get their hair wet and be so worried about it; of Liz and her boy friend Luke Shimmens who owned a hot-rod and took them riding around town and up and down dragging Main blowing the horn and backfiring and seeing different kids walking along and waving out at them.

Then there seemed nothing else going on to see or do, and Quella wanted to have an early pass again. Wayne Jinks was just finishing his paragraph. When it was over she raised her hand and popped it to jingle the jingles round her wrist. Miss Morris said, "Do you want to read next, Quella?" "Nome," Quella said, and prissed, "it is time to go to May Fete practice."

Miss Morris said a surprise. "All right, take a pass and go ahead." And she took a pad of passes from her drawer and wrote on one. She tore it off and gave it to Quella, looking for a moment as if she were going to stare at her. But Quella went out of the room quickly.

She was in the hall with a pass in her hand, going down the very quiet hall that did not have another single person in it. She passed all the rooms, sometimes seeing through a door pane some teacher writing on a blackboard or standing talking to a class. She noticed as she went along that without any other kids, alone in the hall (and this same thing was true when she was by herself with a teacher) she was no more than somebody quiet and courteous. But when the others were around, she could be all the things they were, shouting and slapping boys and eating at the wrong time, provoked with the way things were or excited about them. She stopped by the closed door to the Teachers' Room where all their mailboxes were, like pigeons' holes. No one was in there. She remembered seeing the teachers gathered in front of their boxes before the first class began, fumbling, dipping and rising like homing pigeons. She came by Mrs. Purlow's room where the Stuttering Class was—in there was George Kurunus and she spied him through the glass pane of the door, sitting like some kind of an animal. She heard Mrs. Purlow's perfect words, like "lit-tle," like "yel-low" floating across the room, how she would say every word right. And next was Mrs. Stanford, who would treat you so very nice when you met her in the grocery store after school or on Saturdays, with her hand on your head, saying, "How's little Quella?" and patting you, but mean in class and acting as though she never had seen you in a grocery store in her life, or anywhere. Then here was the typing class. It was like a heavy rain in there. And old Miss Cross, who had been teaching how to type for thirty years, standing at the front of the class pointing with a long stick at the letters on a chart and saying "A" and then an enormous clack! to make an A, then "B" and another clack to make this letter. Then faster, and it was like a slow gallop of a horse on pavement and Miss Cross with her stick like a circus trainer, "A - S - D - F - G." And next was Miss Winnie's room where this teacher cried a lot and for this was called Weeping Winnie and spoke in a soft cooing voice and seemed so sad. She always lost her voice the Ninth Period and said, "Cheeldrin you will have to write today, my voice is gone."

As she went along she would walk like different kinds of people, or in different ways, very quickly and hopping; or as she had seen Miss McMurray, the English teacher and very pretty, going down the halls—as though she were carrying a bag of eggs, afraid to break them, or a sleeping baby that might be waked; and like the Royal Princess with a train that she had been voted to be in the May Fete. Then she meandered in big S's or in zig-zags from one side of the hall to the other; or smeared one finger along the wall, loitering, browsing, lolling at every drinking fountain to sip a long time or spew the water back. She saw some faded redhots and the little stone of a jawbreaker in one fountain.

Once she thought of Helena and wished Helena could be with her. Helena was such a beautiful name. She came to her sister Liz's room and peeked in. The good-looking Mr. Forbes was teaching them some important senior subject and they were all listening as if what he was saying had to be learned to take out in the world when they would soon go. She looked to see what color his tie was today. Liz had counted seventeen different ties in seventeen days on Mr. Forbes and he wore so many different kinds of coats and trousers that they said he changed sometimes between classes. Yes, he had his saddle shoes on, too. Then she saw Mr. Forbes looking towards the door where she was. She ducked down quickly to wait until he turned and she could look again for Liz, to see how she looked sitting up in class.

As she crouched there she suddenly heard someone coming down the hall and looked to see who could it be. It was the awful deformity George Kurunus writhing and slobbering and skulking towards her. She was afraid of him and thought she would scream as all the girls did when he came to them; but she knew if you went up to him not afraid of his twisted face and said George to him and talked to him he would not do anything to you. Together, all the kids played with him, at him, as though he was some crazy and funny thing like a bent toy on a string; but no one ever wanted to be with him alone. Often a class would hear a scratching at the door and would see his hoodlum face at a door pane like Hallowe'en and be frightened until they saw it was just George Kurunus. Then the class would laugh and make faces back at him and the teacher would go to the door and say "Now, George . . ." and shoo him away; and the class would titter. The boys all went around with him as if he was something they owned, something they could use for some stunt or trick on somebody, their arms around his shoulder; and they talked and laughed with him and told him ugly jokes and things about girls and sicked him on certain girls. Why did this deformity George have to be in a school? He couldn't even hold a word still in his mouth when he said it, for it rattled or hopped away—this was why he was in Stuttering Class, but it did him no good, he still broke a word when he said it, as if it were a twig, he still said ruined words.

He could not speak a word right and whole no matter how hard he tried or how carefully. But if you live among breakage, he may have reasoned, you finally see the wisdom in pieces; and no one can keep you from the pasting and joining together of bits to make the mind's own whole. What can break anything set back whole upon a shelf in the mind, like a mended dish? His mind, then, was full of mended words, broken by his own speech but repaired by his silences and put back into his mind. The wisdom in all things, in time, tells a meaning to those things, even to parcels of things that seem to mean disuse and no use, like scraps in a mending basket that are tokens and remnants of many splendid dresses and robes each with a whole to tell about.

Whenever the Twirling Class for girls in the Black and Gold Battalion practiced on the football field, here was this George on the field, too, like some old stray dog that had to be shooed away. And in a marching line of some class to somewhere, the library or a program in the auditorium, he ruined any straight marching line and so was put last to keep the line straight. But at the end of a straight marching line he twisted and wavered like the raveling out of a line and ruined it, even then; he was the capricious conclusion and mocking collapse of something all ordered and precise right up to the tag end. When he walked, it seemed he always ran upon himself like someone in the way—or like a wounded insect. He was a flaw in the school, as if he were a crack in the building.

This day he had sat in his row by the window and the sun was coming in upon him. It warmed his vestigial hand, lay upon a page of his book. It touched some leaves of a begonia on the teacher's desk and showed their white lines and illuminated the blooms to like glass flowers. *Flower* was a word, but he could not say it. The sun came in and lay upon Miss Purlow's face and showed where the round spot of rouge ended and her face's real skin began. The sun made, also, between Miss Purlow and the blackboard, a little transparent ladder leading up and out through the window. Specks of golden dust were popping in it, dancing and whirling on out the window. Then suddenly Miss Purlow walked through it and broke it, but it joined together again, in spite of Miss Purlow, and made him glad. Miss Purlow went to the blackboard and wrote upon it some perfectly shaped words in her pretty curlimacue handwriting that said:

"Come into the garden, Maud,
For the black bat, night, has flown . . ."

Then she read them aloud, musically and perfectly, and he so wanted to have these words in his mouth. Miss Purlow asked him to say them after her but he could not, they fell away from him, they were all hers; yet he had it perfect, the little melodious collection of words, in his mind from Miss Purlow's mouth, a small tune of sounds that hung clear and warbling in his ears like birdsong. He turned and shuffled away, to leave the room. Miss Purlow called at him that she would report him to the Principal again as soon as the class was over, but he did not care, he opened the door and went away from this room where he could not speak and where words tormented him.

Then here he was, ruining a quiet hall for Quella. Although with other children she laughed at him and thought him a funny thing, alone she was afraid of him and detested him. Where was this George going? He was shuffling closer. She stood up and pressed against the wall and watched him, hating him. It was said that if he ever fell down he could never get up unless somebody helped him, but just lie there scrambling and waving his arms and legs, like a bug on its back, and muttering. His little withered left arm was folded like a plucked bird's wing and its bleached and shriveled hand, looking as though it had been too long in water, was bent over and it hung limp like a dead fowl's neck and dangling head. But he could use this piece of hand, this scrap of arm quickly and he could snap it like a little quirt and pop girls as they passed him in the hall. Here he came, this crazy George Kurunus, a piece of wreckage in the school. What did *he* want? She looked to see if *he* had a pass in his hand. No. Certainly he was not going to practice for any May Fete. Why should *he* be in the halls and without a pass?

She shrank close to the wall, but did not want to be caught there by him. She decided to run fast past him, not looking at his goblin face and not going close enough to him to be popped by his whip of an arm. She darted and fled past him, wanting to push him down and leave him wriggling there in the hall. He said some sound, all drunken and gargled, to her as she passed him; but he did not try to pop her. She ran looking back at him and when she came to the turn of the hall that led to the lavatory, she ran around it fast, then crept back to peek around and see if he was still going on or coming after her. George Kurunus was staggering along, his knees scraping each other, sounding like a little puffing train in the hall, without ever looking back. This made her furious and she was going to yell, "Stuck u-up!" until she remembered she would be heard and was supposed to be going to the auditorium.

She ran in to the girls' lavatory and was dramatically hiding from him there, panting faster than she really had to. She stopped to listen and heard his *sh-sh-sh-sh* down the hall away from her. This was another narrow escape she would tell Helena McWorthy about.

Then it was time for the May Fete practice and she went to the auditorium that always seemed so cool when the whole school wasn't in it. There were the royalty, already assembled: Joe Wright, the handsome King, also the Chief Yell Leader; Marveen Soames, the beautiful Queen, the other Princess, Hazel May Young, not pretty but with personality, and all the Dukes and

Duchesses. Miss McMurray, the perfect-walking English teacher, was there to take charge.

They all marched down the aisle, very proud, and the King and Queen mounted the throne, the Princesses and Princes, Dukes and Duchesses swaggered to their places around the throne. The King had on his silver crown and was holding his tinfoil wand. When it was time to crown the Queen, the biggest moment of all, and everything was real quiet, all the empty seats in the auditorium hushed and watching, she spied in the glass frame of the auditorium door the terrible face of George Kurunus, like a grasshopper's face. He was watching the May Fete and had it all in his eye. This George Kurunus was everywhere, why did he have to be everywhere she was? But she turned her eyes away from him, upon all the beautiful royalty, and they went on with the practice. Then suddenly it was the bell for the next class, which was Homemaking—a dreary place for a Princess to go: to a cookstove after a coronation.

The Homemaking teacher was Miss Starnes and there she was, waiting for the girls at the door, smiling and standing straight. Miss Starnes would stand before her class reading from some book. Each day she had a fresh rose or some other flower from her own garden stuck to her strict dress, and the way she maneuvered her mouth and bowed and leaned her head towards the girls sitting before her made them know that she knew she was saying something good, as though she were smacking her lips and gollopping something like a dessert. Yet Miss Starnes was very serious and meant what she would say or read and paused often, sticking out her chin (which had hairs on it) for emphasis.

The girls in Homemaking class who sat before her were not sure at all what these words meant, but they sat there, among the linen dresses and the fancy aprons hanging on hangers, which last year's class had made with its own hands and left the prices pinned on to show that they were good enough to be bought in any store. Then there was a manikin on a stand—in a corner by the American flag which the manikin seemed to need to drape around itself to hide its nakedness, headless and with a pole running right up through her to be her one leg; and in an adjoining room—the kitchen—there were rows of little stoves where Miss Starnes told the girls things to cook.

The bell had rung and all the girls were in their seats—any chosen seat and not alphabetically—and "responsibility" was a word Miss Starnes was already smacking off her lips to the girls in Homemaking. "Domestic re-spon-si-bi-li-ty." These were words Miss Starnes started right in telling to the class, things they should be or do in the good home they would have or make—and which lay off somewhere in the vague unknown and which they could not quite see as something of theirs but just imagine and did not even particularly want, now. But whatever or wherever or however this place "The Home," they would be there, all these girls, going industriously around in aprons, there would be a lot of busy sewing and a difficult cooking, and . . . "Domestic re-spon-si-bi-li-ty" . . . these words Miss Starnes was saying.

Quella was going to start in plaiting and unplaiting Helena McWorthy's hair when Miss Starnes kneaded and worked her lips and they were getting ready to say another careful word to the class. "E-con-o-my." The manikin was standing there in the corner trying to be that word, which was a good thing to be. The manikin was a pitiful thing, undressed, or something headless like a fowl, or something deformed, but proud and seeming to want to help Miss Starnes with the lecture by standing there as though it, too, were teaching Homemaking. It was about the size of her mother in her short slip in the summertime, Quella observed.

And then Miss Starnes led them in the kitchen and they were going to cook their lesson. "I know what it will be," Quella told the others. "Like some stuff Charlotte Langendorf cooked first period and carried in wax paper to Social Studies—of potatoes or something." But Miss Starnes was saying that in this class today there would be cooked pudding and to light the stoves and listen to some things she would say about the making of pudding, and to put on their white cook aprons. "Ingredients" was a word about pudding which Miss Starnes was saying, and it seemed just the word for what milk and sugar, which they were already mixing, looked like together. There was a gregarious stirring. Then Miss Starnes told about the soft ball that the mixture would make in a cup of cold water to show it was ready. Here and there already a soft ball was found in a cup and a girl would raise her hand to tell it to Miss Starnes.

Just as Quella's and Helena's mixture made a soft ball for them in their cup of cold water, a staccato bell-ringing that was certainly not the regular bell resounded in the school building, and it was fire drill. Although the mixture was ready and showed its undeniable sign, all the Homemaking girls had to leave it and line up in two's and march behind Miss Starnes through the hall smelling of their mixture which even then, though it was not yet anything but ingredients, made them feel important because they had caused this smell to move all in the corridors just as they were moving now, and even reach around as far as the algebra room, where there were no good smells, and hang under the noses of the class doing unknowns. The girls marched and fretted.

When the Homemaking class got outside under the trees where the school busses were waiting for school to be out, and stood in their right place under the cottonwood trees, Miss Starnes suddenly thought about the windows in Homemaking and remembered she had not closed and locked them according to fire drill instructions. "Quella," she said carefully as though she were saying "do-mes-tic" or "e-con-o-my," "please to run back to Homemaking and close all the windows tight and see that no stoves are burning."

"Don't I need a pass?" Quella asked.

"No, Quella. Run."

She was alone in the hall again. The pudding will be ruined, she thought. If the school burns, they will have to save the pudding and the May Fete pretties. She could smell smoke, and then once she was sure she saw a flame lick out of Boys' Lavatory, but she would never go in *there* to put it out. She went very fast to Homemaking and in the room she went right to her and Helena's cup with the soft ball in it. She felt it. It was still soft. She went around looking at other cups. Margy Reynolds' was not ready but was still just ingredients in a cup of water. But some hand or finger had been in it all, in all the cups and pans, who had been meddling in Homemaking? She thought she heard the crackling of flames above her, so she rushed to close the windows, and as she ran out, she swiped her finger through her and Helena's ready mixture and strung it along the stove and floor and on her dress; but she licked it up quick and slammed the door.

Then she ran through the hall, not liking the halls this way, with no pass, without classes in the rooms, no different teachers standing or sitting there as she passed them. How scarey the school seemed now, full of the echoes of her clapping feet and her panting. She passed Miss Purlow's room and looked in through the door. On the blackboard were written the lines in beautiful penmanship:

> *"Come into the garden, Maud,*
> *For the black bat, night, has flown . . ."*

and under the lines was—what? Was it a joke or what? There was a curious disheveled chaos of giant and dwarf runaway shapes, tumbled and humped and crazy . . . like the Devil's writing or like a ghost's. She ran.

Then she was by the auditorium and stopped to make sure there was no flame in there to eat up all the May Fete pretties—the dresses and the paper flowers, the paper wand and all the paper streamers. She could feel something in there! There was some live thing in there! She listened. No sound. She looked through the pane of the auditorium door and what should she spy but George Kurunus sitting on the King's Throne like a crazy king in a burning building. On his head was the silver crown and in his ruined hand the silver wand. He was into everything, who would keep him out of all the things at school; he was a disturbance in this world of school and in her own world, touching and tampering with everything she did. She thought she saw him rise and come down from the throne and down the aisle towards her, after her; and she ran away and down the hall, now full of smoke she was sure, hearing him after her—*sh-sh-sh-sh*—and seeing rags of flame waving out from alcoves and recesses at her. She ran out the door and into the open, without looking back. If the school house burned it would burn him like a cricket in it. She would not tell.

She was thrilled to see all the boys and all the girls lined under the trees and gladly joined them. She stood shivering under the trees in her place in line, waiting to see what was going to happen, in the unearthly quiet that lay over all the school people, over all the school building. Suddenly at a window on the second floor she saw his face, as if her fear of fire had a face and it was George Kurunus'. No one else seemed to see it—was she imagining it? for she now had the insect-headed and devil-bodied image of him in her head. No, there it was, his face, looking down at her, she was sure. And then she thought she saw him crying! If he was crying she wanted to save him from the burning building, to call out that he was in there, or to run in and save him herself; hurry! hurry! hurry! But suddenly the all-clear bell that would bring them all back to where he was, separate and waiting, but never back to him whirred out, convulsing through her whole body and through his own tilted body like electric shock . . . it was all a nightmare: if there had been no fire then there had been no George in the empty building, she thought.

Now they all began to move, in their colors like a field of flowers jostling in the wind; and she saw again, for sure, his grasshopper face at the window, watching them coming back to the skulled building of stone that held him like an appetite or a desire that would surely, one day, get them every one: all the beautiful schoolchildren gathered and moving like the chosen through the heavenly amber afternoon light and under the golden leaves—the lean ball-players, the agile jitterbuggers, the leaping perch of yell leaders, the golden-tongued winners of the declamation contests, Princes and Princesses, Duchesses and Kings, and she, Quella, among them, no safer than the rest but knowing, at least, one thing more than the rest.

Children of Old Somebody

For Katherine Anne

Her nis non hoom, her nis but wildernesse:
Forth, pilgrim, forth! Forth, beste, out of thy stal!
Know thy contree, look up, thank God of al;
Hold the hye wey, and lat thy gost thee lede:
And trouthe shal delivere, hit is no drede.

—Chaucer, *Trouthe.*

On the road, the dust at his feet, where was he bound, where was he to go, our Old Ancestry? He seemed to find no rest for the sole of his foot. For he knew another country that had a landscape he could not wink or water out of his eye; and he had another language in his ears.

Where was the leader, whom to follow, shall we follow a follower? was the thought that hissed like a snake in the brake of the brain of his times and led to confusion in the flock, for a thought can destroy. It was a time when everything shifted and changed, swarmed around and clustered on an idea or a craving, used idea and craving up, or wearied of them, then scattered to pieces again; it was a time of confusion of cravings, it was like a bunch of sheep dispersed and broken, shepherd or no . . . he only followed when he was supposed to lead, another sheep, one of the broken flock, and could not summon them all together; or there was no shepherd (maybe that was the trouble), he was lost under the hill.

Yet the permanent gesture was passing up and down, hovering, vanishing.

Fallen to the grasshopper, the plague year at hand; brother against brother, the community broken into Real Estate, a price on the head; flesh sealed up, men in a male prisonhouse, the women gone mad—where was the road, the wayfarer's flower, the bird in the air, the roadside spring? It was out of this broken flock that he broke, free and loose, to keep the idea of himself uneaten in his brain. Preserve my image of myself, he thought; set my skull over this image like a glass cover. Losing this, befouling this image is whoring all our hope, the fiendish betrayal of Satan, the destruction of our Old Ancestor.

So he was a shape of dust—and if all things return to dust, fall back into it, dust was his great pile, he the dust-grubber, himself formed of the dust of the ground, from which he would find the first things formed out of the ground and bring them to himself and to us all to see what would we call them. Breathed out of dust, he was yet the enemy of all dust-eaters; he would save the dust from the appetite, from the blind voracious driving bite of hunger: the grasshopper and the worm. Then, before it all is eaten, he would have his hands in it, on it, to touch it to smut it with his fingermarks—but even more: to shape it, out of its own dust and with the miraculous light of his own dust, and thus set it away, preserved. Shaped from no more than the small and agitated dust of dancers' feet on the side of the hill, all his aim and all his desire was to return to the dust to prospect in it and to save the grubbings. Consider this old road-runner: he is shuttler, hoverer: face at windows, fingers at panes, stick-knuckles on doors. But the dust is at his heels and his feet are on the road that he thinks to lead him for a little while to the blood beginnings of himself.

So the figure of Old Somebody comes to mind; this is to consider Old Somebody, who had no more of a name than what people gave him when he was not there to hear it.

Once, in another house, in another country, there passed on the road by the side of the house an old stranger who sometimes turned off to come to the back door and knock upon it with a stick he always carried. We of the house would know his knock on the house and though we seldom went to answer him with fear, unless it was after dark and a convict had escaped, we always felt a vague unearthly question in us as we went to answer his knock, as though some great unnamable phenomenon, like weather or like love, knocked on our house to call us away or to tell us something. This old stranger would knock and call out, "Somebody! Somebody! Hello-o-o!"; and for this we came to call him Old Somebody. What fears or visions the children of the house might have had of him no elder would ever know, for children's images sink into nameless depths of themselves—there is this loss to recapture, to salvage up from the fathoms, hovering over the depths to rescue the shape when it rises. We came, then, people of the house he knocked on, to the back door to see this old knocker covered with dust. Given a begging—some momentary mercy: a biscuit or a cold potato or a dipper of well water—he would turn away and we would watch him through the window as he took his road again and went on.

To threaten children in the house against the repetition of any mischief they had it in their minds to commit, the elders warned them that they should be given to Old Somebody to take away next time he came, as any begging, unless they corrected their ugliness in advance or dried up and straightened their face right that very minute. "Old Somebody's goan come get you and carry you off down the road if you don't hush it right up." So they used Old Somebody for a threat: we would be delivered into the hands of a passing figure of dust if we did not behave. And what we had to grow into was the knowledge that, behave or no, his hands would have us, this old haunting threat, this old vagrant intimidation.

And so we learned that the dust trembles at the touch of dust, agitates its own kind, rouses it, bestirs it, recruits its gratuitous army of it, dust, that becomes a choir of dust; and everything is taken, behave or no, by Old Somebody. For in the winter the ghostly fruit that clove to the unleafed branches would crumble at the touch and fall to the ground, fruit of dust. We dug holes in the ground and cupped our hands around our mouth and cried into the dirtholes "Old Somebody! Old Somebody!" and covered up our cry with dirt, while elders thought it was a warning to a doodle-bug that his house was on fire.

Tales told of him tried to create him in the minds of us listeners. It was told how when the boardinghouse where Old Somebody once lived burnt to the ground, how he appeared suddenly as if risen up out of ash and was seen fingering the ash—and how he found something and disappeared with it. Was it some old ashen vanity of his past that he grubbed for and found, some object his flesh had loved, some locket or letter or picture frame with the face once in it vanished?

And it was also told how he lolled and haunted about in the winter orchards touching and gathering the ghosts of summer fruit that hung like balls of dust on the bare branches. Was it to save them? How moss was Old Somebody's beard, how the Devil's Snuffbox, sifting to rusty powder in the hand that picked it from the ground, was Old Somebody's dippingsnuff; how the urchins of dust in corners that the broom could not snare were the restless children of Old Somebody. He belonged to all ghostly, elusive, vanishing things. All vanishing things! We would not give our life, our heart, our soul to the Devil of all vanishing things. Yet how they haunted and begged the heart and how one grieved after them. We knew that it was said to us that we must cleave to the permanent things and let all vanity pass; but think how because a life was given, haunted and called after by all vanishing things from the first, to vanishing things that appear and then slip away so suddenly, passing through the hands and on away, think how a life so given therefore suffered and was cursed and set on evil ground, unstable in unstable things. But what else could be done but to claim unto oneself, *passager* himself, what was his, all passing things. We pass with them and in them . . . they do not leave us behind but pull us on down and away with them. But to leave something of us both behind, a shape of dust in the dust, was the task, so early taken, of Old Somebody's children.

We grew into the kind of men who wished only that our life might be often enough in our own hands—something that arrives, knocks, announces itself, is looked upon in a clear, still moment, goes away, and appears again—to give us a feeling, and a sense of its shape, so that we could describe it and get that joy of recognition from it that comes from handling something one wants to *know*, all over, as a lover, though later lost. For such children made up their mind that in their time all their purpose and all their desire would be to discover and establish, for themselves, at least—and, they hoped, for many men—a sense of self as related to this coming and going that asked to be shaped; and if we could set down a line, a chain, a continuity to keep a touch between men before us and ourselves, all linked together through what happened, burst living again and into new being out of dust, then we might leave figures of dust in our time and out of our time, and go into the dust that was ours, waiting for other hands to shape us, and joined there. We grew into the kind of men who kept, by nature and as if we had made them and named them, a restless, loving watch on things—there was some shape to this roving watch of ours. Beyond this, indeed all around this, lay a huge, roiled and anxious shapelessness, the impulsive and unquiet and suspicious doings of men, hunts to kill, plots to gain, plans to trick to glory or increase. But we knew where the exquisite and delicate morsels of dust were given to us: the sweet glaze on trees called rawsum, the little bled and crystalline droplet of gum on a fallen plum, the tiny single sup of nectar at the end of a shoot of sweetgrass. Exhalations, musks, juices, gums and icings, we knew them as well as any bee or hummingbird or butterfly that fell into insect of dust at the end of any summer. These were there, then, for us to come and see, come and get, for us to admire and touch, our own discovered shape of things.

One time in the afternoon when Old Somebody knocked, the elders went to the door and the children followed. We saw him with eyes like dusturchins in his face, a clayey face white in the cheek hollows, blue ridge along the corona of the lips, blue at the mouth's corners, and hoods of flesh over the dust-shot eyes: a figure clothed in dust: he had been walking a dry country. Who was his mother, who was his father, what was his race? Did he want an answer—what answer could we give him? The beggings were given him, and after he went away, the children threatened, the elders gathered in the kitchen and built their story of him so as to make another accounting of him and so answer away his call. He was the child of the Summer Hill people who had long since passed away. The elders as children had known his old folks. Bright Andrews had finally married his little housekeeper, Cora, and at an old age this accident of a child was born. The child grew up on the place, so far behind all the rest of the people of Summer Hill, the only small one, the rest all old and past him, a kind of unpossessed foundling. When he became a young man he had suddenly disappeared, gone to where, nobody knew . . . but to get his world. Years passed; he passed out of the minds of his people and might, to their minds, never have been born, only a passing fiction. One day he returned, so changed by whatever had happened to him that he was not even recognized. He was turned away from the door of his own people's house—his half-sisters and brothers and their married children. He began to wander up and down, appearing, vanishing, hovering. It was said that he wanted the graves of his mother and father, Cora and Bright Andrews. It was said that he lived in a cave in the hills beyond the cotton gin; it was said he lived under a broken bridge. But his was a life never told; there was no tongue that could tell it. That was his life, that was his accounting.

Yet surely Cora Andrews remembered how she kept him quiet in her shell of flesh, like my own image of him in my mind, Bright Andrews stiff abed with his stroke and knocking on the wall with his stick when he wanted something. And surely she could not forget how when she felt the pain of her child she went quietly into the woods and brought him into this world with her own hands and hid him in a hollow log. One day he, this secret child, would have his own truth as one day I would have his truth, and mine in his. Our search and our waiting were, then, the same. It all went into the mind of a child, listener, this accounting of the elders who shaped Old Somebody's life with their guessing tongues; and something closed up around it there in my mind, a soft shell to hold it. This mind would shape it all again one day, all its own, when something would touch the shell that kept it and it would open and the life within it would come out.

A knock opened it. Long later on the midnight watch at sea, I heard suddenly from the deck, after unconsolable loss, the knocking of the masts in the quiet midnight, and his image came back to me. "Somebody! Somebody! Hello-o-o!" the soft voice called with the knocking. He was back, Old Somebody. Walking the road of the waters, knocking on this riding house of men, this sleeping and watching family with whom I watched or among whose mysterious breathing beings I walked at night, shining my flashlight on their nameless faces; he had come back. Something of mine so precious, another vanishing beautiful thing, had been lost to sea; but something, too, was restored. This old man of dust had settled the dust with the waters, knocking on the waters of the grave of my loss, "Hello! Hello-o-o!" his stick on the waters. Dust of my loss was a pilgrim gone in peace to the waters, O waters hold him, settled forever, while I and you, Old Somebody, dust-bound, shore-bound, walk the shore and the waters, knocking and calling "Hello! Hello-o-o!" where no door opened. Far away from the borrowed house and the road that once brought him past it, but he still upon it, I upon that road now, borrowed child, I with his help saw my truth of him: the buried shell opened at his knock, he had called up his own buried image left years ago with me, and the figure of dust rose to its life and meaning out of the deeps and took its everlasting shape.

For they had lately put me down from the ship into the waters in a little leaf of a boat and sent me to wait upon the spot where a plane had fallen into the sea, to hover at the rim of the broken waters to watch when a body would rise from the depths, and capture it. I waited on the leaf, at the spot of this destruction, and behold he came rising up like a weed, the drowned sailor. I, whose hands had named and shaped and blessed this sunken shape, dipped my hands into the water and lifted it from it and brought back the salvaged shape lying across my knees, sea-boy lie light on my body, to the ship; welcome us back to the ship that enchanted us, so back we rode to the enchantress in our sorrow, welcome with garlands and vows to the temple; sleep in soft bosoms forever and dream of the surge and the sea-maids. Back we rode back to the ship in our grief, see how I found him I who shaped him, see how I returned him—tumbleweed of dust on the desert sea, the sea's dust which I, rover upon water, must settle, unquiet dust that blows in the deserts of the mind; dust can settle dust—back to the ship of our beginning. In the days and nights that followed, one a burial day, and with the help of Old Somebody who had returned, knocking, to take this begging away, I made my accounting.

When she had him she had him in the woods, alone, and then she put him in a hollow log and never told a soul. She came back several times a day to nourish him, and at night she kept a watch on him through her window. He was, then, a little woods animal nested in the hollow tube of this old log on Summer Hill; and he lived like this for quite a while. When he first got his sight he watched at the nether end of the log the little speck of light that was his daytime and in his unmothered nights he saw there sometimes the spangle of a star or the horn of a moon. This little druid never complained of his log life, it was only another hollow for him to curl in; and his first sounds, not counting the gurgles to his mother's milk as he took it from her when she came to give it, sitting on the log, were the tap and scrape of creatures' feet over his wooden dome and heaven. What was this little knocking?

This little tree spirit, could you believe it, lay unmolested by the life of the ground or by gypsies, never an ant stung it or snake bit it, there was no hostility between its world and the creatures' world, that hostility is learnt; he slept, little camper, right among the leaves and grass, a little seed dropped and left in the soil; can you believe it; waking to find a beak of horn over it or the adoring fierce eye of something of the woods hung over it. Its sky was the roof of a log and its moon the eye of a creature.

Now in old histories we can read of such, like of Childe Percival and like of little princes, secret folk, kept in secret woods places by charmers or enchanters. But would you believe it that this child could be put there in our sensible time, so far along later after old fables have faded away into just stories to be told for want of fable, after all the fancies had perished, and that it flourished, this child, and thrived; and that its mother, an old woman startled by a child out of her, could keep it all so quiet and in her heart and never tell a soul. This little pipping never doubted its beginning just as it never doubted the womb it came from while it was in it, but accepted it as right and took the nourishment that was piped into it from the veins and ducts it never thought to question. So with this new life of this little sprout within this hollow log.

Can you wonder, then, that when Cora, its mother, finally fetched it from its hollow and brought it out into the light of day, for good, it might have thought it was being born again, and that its eyes, with so much light after so much gloom, squinted into long bushy caterpillar shapes with a green fleck shining in the middle; and wouldn't you wonder, then, that there was before its eyes eternally a speck of light; it could not blink it out, the speck of light was singed into its vision as the blast of the sun itself is when you look long enough at it: you will see this ball of light wherever you look, as though your eyeballs were the burning globe of a sun in your head. Another thing about this child was that its hide was speckled with moles and spots, and that its hide was downy with hair, even on its back. So when its mother Cora Andrews took it out for good she had a kind of little animal that she had robbed from the summer woods; and the day she took it away it is said that the woods began to faint away and die into an autumn.

There is a lot of traffic in our life because we are unhoused. This rough, uncosseted, uncircumcised, spotted and downy being, put into the world beyond his beginnings, never knew, of course, of its deliverance from the log in the woods, nor why it had the speck of light in its eyes or the knocking in its ears; but its life was one long and incessant searching for the meaning of its own household and to name its blood.

That day Bright Andrews rose from his bed and came on good legs through the woods and saw ahead of him the young man's vision and the meaning of manhood, the whole tormented striving: his woman suckling his child, sitting on the log, was all the beginning. His little creature was curled upon her breast and joined to her in a connection that he had known with her, a suckling coupling. He watched, behind a tree, his child at his woman's breast, here was this woods family; but he would not join them, yet. He lingered on the edge of this woods household and filled his eye with it, then he crept away.

He came, later at night and by the light of a lantern, to be by himself with it, to take his own child to his arms and look at it all over, yearning to suckle it but knowing he could reach the child only through the woman, no other way, rocking it in his cradled arms, crying with an unutterable new pride at it, loving it more than anything he had ever known in this world, his lantern hanging in a tree, bringing the little being to the light like a moth to see its marks and features, to find its eyes' color, to see the look on its face. Is it a boy, he whispered, and found its tiny unharming and untormenting boy's sex and fingered its precious hide.

Standing under the light with his armful bundle, Cora found him like her vision of womanhood. She thought, now I have given it to him, this child, for him to come and see, to come and get, to come and adore. She stood longer, quiet, watching the creator adoring its begotten. It was made in the grass of the woods, she thought, it is a little animal. She could bear it no longer and she called out "Bright!" and when he saw her he could not speak but only looked darkly at her. She came to them under the light, the family was complete; and without a word they placed the child in its nest. Then they stood for a moment looking upon each other until they met against each other and fell down into the grass together, he lowering her gently and descending over her like a falling tree, terrible; and then he was upon her, sweet and soft, and his wide wing-like folding in of her clapped her in to him up against his loins. He smelled the grass around her nested head and smelled her juices that oozed from her to greet him. Flesh onto flesh by the light of the lantern in the trees, they threshed and harrowed the grass, their bed of earth, grinding gently and clapping swelling against swelling, worming in the grass; he beating her with his body and the one body of them flipping in the leaves like a dying fowl until they lay still in the leaves. Thus they adored their child that lay, ghost of their passion, in the log, chastening themselves.

"But what will we name it?" he asked softly, lying upon his narrow pallet of her. She could not think; it seemed so nameless.

"Just Little Somebody," she finally said, "until it names itself."

He fell back to his bed, an old stiff man again, and he did not judge his dream. Cora kept the dream and never told it, even to the dreamer.

Where it went when it left, this vision of their flesh, this dream of an old man stiff abed and a woman who hid it in a log, where it went in the years that followed was to all places that would join it to its own flesh's vision and bring it its own time; and in the end it joined itself to dust and loved it more than the world or any creature, and got its name—who will tell or whisper or knock it out?—and saw its own flesh fall away from it into dust and cast unsettled upon the water and the road.

Where its parents, Cora and Bright Andrews, went was into dust, into all elusive, ghostly and vanishing things, a handful of dust and a clasp of bones in a country graveyard, marked by tilted gravestones, the end of all wandering, peace we are home, pilgrims come in peace, we wait for a pilgrim.

So we learned that there is no house he does not knock on, no room in which to hide away from him. And the rapping on the side of any house we are ever housed in builds for a second that old sudden vision of Old Somebody. What is it he knocked the dust with his stick for, what was it he rapped out on the dust? Say it, say it, whisper it out, stick-message, knock it out in the dust, a bird's foot knocking on the ground, say it, say it, do not be afraid. If we build the bridge of flesh we must cross over, over it, into the land of dust, and burn the bridge of burning flesh behind us: *cross over flesh to reach ghost.* The dust yearns for dust, but dust will have its flesh and, having it, deliver it over with its own hands, into dust.

Where is he, Old Somebody, where has he gone? Into the heart, into the spirit, where we must settle him; and out of the heart, out of the spirit, he rises, the dust that blows, his ghost, our Old Ancestry. He is the ghost of fruit on winter fruit trees, he is the snuffbox that crumbles in the hand, he is the ash of houses, he is the dusty hound on the road, a ladder of dust in the light of a lantern in the trees.

And on he goes, on the road, the dust at his heels; there is no rest for the soles of his feet. Think how in the towns he passes through they are electing mayors, raising funds for churches where there will be christenings and marriages, funerals and soul-savings; where there are halls for town meetings, jails for correction, fines for punishment and awards for deeds. Or how in the cities he rings around with his circle of dust there is all this ten times over—causes, codes, contests, beliefs. He is passing on the road, he is the gesture, the connection of dust, the old simplicity, the old common particle, our old ingredient, carrying our truth on the nap of his back.

I give him my accounting and his, and hope he will take it to his disturbed dust and that it will settle his dust as he has settled mine. See how an old Shape hidden in the depths and folds of the mind can appear, knocked for, when it is time, and show its meaning, salvage the dust of the truth, give a biscuit of courage and a dipper of faith and put us on the road again to who knows where?

For our feet have been broken by the ways we have gone, we have walked the waters and cinders; and the blood of our feet stains the wave and the dust. There is no balm for the soles of our feet.

Nests in a Stone Image

Now this was in San Francisco, on the eve of Easter, in a hotel where he was nested for a little while like a wild passing bird in the stone mouth of some image whose builder had vanished, waiting, in such wildness, for the time of hush when something might be put to rest and definition in him. Thighs spanning an anonymous bed, arms out like rays from him, spread-fingered hands like stars, the listener lay like a five-point star in the sky of this city hotel world. The eve of Easter seemed so sad, this hotel was so sad, sitting there in the Easter world in all that winter weather, this tall, lean, dingy, forlorn city building where he hung, anxious burning tormented star, in this stone sky tonight.

Yet the celled, stone skull of this hotel held him, too: tenant in it like a captured and entombed idea. In its eyes, windows, he had stood like the hotel's vision of himself in the street, uncared for, caring. His tenancy had been a search through all the rooms for himself, to liberate an image of it, a constant self-regarding. For he thought how he would contain all his own life and have it clear and as it existed, regardless of the consequences. What matter what else he had gained, if he did not possess, as it existed, the shape of his own life, finding it out again and again, what human use had done to it? What could he do for others, what could he create, of what use was he if he did not know his own wholeness—falling to fragment, forming again, scattering again—if he did not make his attempts to get plain to himself the meaning of his own experience, rising up erect and firm and fullest expanded into it to define what hovers and rises and falls, what arrives and vanishes, what stays? Now this seemed the only story to try to tell.

Now, for awhile, he wanted to hold still this turning and rousing inside him, this agitation that was like insects coming alive in the spring. What would hush it, what would bring the time of hush that would press all turmoil back away from him and leave a center of silence within which he could hold still and listen? He thought what a frail reservoir the skull is; yet it must hold back all the torrent and flood of the world to keep within its little cove that quiet pool where all things rest and root and show themselves clearly and calmly. Not to betray the meaning! To ride into the territory where what he followed had led him, into the darkness, and to stay there, in that terrible region until he had had his conversation with what had led him there or with what he had found there, on its own terms, and to leave, when it was time, bringing something out into the light again. To be like a good word, uncorrupted and umlauted by the daily usage of one's human life. To use incessant care! That men might reach each other, reconciling themselves with their intentions and get clarity, get understanding between themselves, being good and honest words!

It seemed that at the end of a long long darkness of wandering and shifting there was finally only this hotel room holding him upon his back on a rented bed, ungiven to it, alone and turned into himself—what would deliver him beyond this self-devouring to which he had consigned himself? To listen? To stop speech and listen? Yet it might be that this old agony might die in this very room and rise up to something beyond agony. Between him and the life he came from, there seemed to exist such distances that he could only hear across them sometimes forlorn and dying calls calling him back to confront them, to listen. For there had happened in him a slow breakdown and falling away of all he had tried and been, some enormous change was at work within him; and there was going on within him a speaking, in a language that created the speakers as it spoke, that seemed yet to be his own voice and his own speech, so that all seemed one.

He thought how he had always wanted to belong to a landscape, yet it seemed his destiny to be only a figure riding through many landscapes, drawn to places and faces, bodies and minds, drawing these to him, disappearing and vanishing. Sitting in public places in his own country, returned, listening, he had thought how strange and outlandish he was, as though he were a ghost that was revisiting his native place and was never seen, never spoken to. He listened; something in him, so warm, responded immediately to the language; but then there moved into him a moment of terrible aloofness and the most painful sense of dismemberment occurred in him, a feeling of mutilation, even; and he thought, I have cut my Self away, they can never graft me back, for I will not grow green to this parent root though it be buried in the very dirt I have tasted and which holds the bones of my bloodkin. He had cast himself out, but he had come back and the coming back was hard, hard, full of tears and pain; but it did show so much. Nor was it a falling back to childhood, only a turning back to rediscover there and keep for himself what were the best beginnings of himself, what was the most lucid and the most terrible and did not ever vanish, even in the purity of maturity, but would go on and on into his life, year by year, like a thread. Whatever keeps me from my beginnings, whatever chops me off and isolates me from my whole life is to the harm of my spirit; it unmothers me; it dispossesses me of my heritage and of my truth, and how can I pass on what is mine if I have not received what was others' and passed on to me? he thought.

Once, at dusk, returned to his own country, he had followed a river a little ways and had suddenly come upon a little place where the river turned. There was a deep purple pool and round it there sat on the banks four very still and quiet men, fishing. In that lovely luminous time before nightfall the lightningbugs were twinkling and here sat these delicate fishermen, holding themselves so still. Something broke in him and he thought, "To be still! To be made still!" Old trees bent and crooked, as if in the gentlest tenderness, almost as if to be stroked like some animal that brushes and curls round the legs to be caressed. He remembered the night that followed, one of terrible labor and wrestling with voices calling to him and his own calling to the voices; of his roving through the twilight among the lightningbugs and on through the deepest darkness like someone in deep pain; and how, the long night labored through, he found the morning crystalline and splendid with sunlight, the water flowing and refreshed, as though by his own agony in the night; and lo! the water-hyacinths had bloomed in the night and were freed and floating down the river: even in his despair which was the celebration of some death there had been a blooming.

So, here in this hotel room, something was laboring to come *through* to him, through him *to* him, to take its death and get its permanent life through its death and rise to its place, fixed and steadfast and clear, defined.

The world around him ground on its greased haunch upon the very ground; hunched and thrust its smooth sprocket and pumped on its pelvic axle towards a terrible mechanical collapse. How could such a world help him struggle with the delicate robber vision suddenly at the door? It could not, it had murdered and buried too many visions; but they had risen, notwithstanding, in their time and from whatever grave.

He thought: to sink down to that unlighted place, spaceless and primordial and slimy, where seeds, roots, sprouts originate . . . where the life in us has its genesis, is honest, pure, unmuddied and unsuspicious, moving among the eternal gestures of men, in the great, permanent ooze; and here to find connections between that life and the life above, to reclaim for oneself the deepest, imperishable meanings of his human life! The life above these depths seemed to him a conspiracy to obscure this gesture. Below, he thought, is all our purity, is all our reality, all our truth. This is what we rise from.

Then here he was, this being, in his time and of his life's wholeness. He had come here out of some loss and bereavement and to sit to have back again, as it wanted to come back to him, with whatever face or feature, shape or name, what he had lost; to turn back into what had happened and let it speak to him and, out of his listening, make it all over again, this time, at least, to control it and keep it from chaos again, to give it its meaning that it waited for. . . . This was what claimed him.

All night in this hotel he was wrestling with it, to put it to order, across the slate of the darkness of his room, across the giant crumpled page of the sheet of his bed, across his very body's flesh: chest, thigh, belly: with his fostering fingers, speaking to the ghost in his flesh. For what defense against ghost but his own flesh? He featured all the rooms that had possessed him and to which he had so utterly given himself while he was tenant in them—what good had they been but mere shelter from wind and rain?—rooms where he had failed and where failure still must hang like very air (listen! is there anyone on the stairs?): a little room where the smell of bacon he cooked hung in the air all day and cloyed his clothes in the streets at night; the long, windowed upstairs room in a large house, with her coming home to him at nightfall—always, it seemed in memory, through softly falling rain.

"Have you worked?"

"No, not again today. I told you not to ask me that."

"Oh I would do anything, *anything* to help you back to your work again!" (she weeping).

"Then leave me, turn away and go out that door, *now,* and do not come back."

But all night the rain fell softly around their room and they turned in the night, not touching, captive in solitary traps of themselves, to hear rain, and fell to sleep again, waking in the dark mornings with rain still falling—and no change. They moved towards chaos and crisis, for their ground was precarious ground.

"Put the pillow over your head, the way you sleep at night, and do not watch me when I go out the door." There was the click of the door lock, even under the pillow heard (listen! is there a knock on the door? Do not move, lie perfectly perfectly still; do not call her back, for you will only turn her to stone again).

From this room he went out alone, left alone, to walk under dripping trees—not even her going had stopped the rain—and across a bridge where there stood a high wall of trembling sodden-leaved poplars; and standing on the bridge he thought he saw a vision in the trees. He walked, day after day—how much of his life had been a walking, his feet on the pavements, through parks that seemed full of terror, along dismal back streets, waterfront streets and main streets; and twice, because he thought he was going to perish of his loneliness, he went in through a crooked door over which hung a dimly lighted painted ball of glass and written on it MECCA ROOMS, up dark stairs to women, and was touched yet was not less lonely because of it, nor relieved of this ghost in his flesh.

Then there was the little basement in another town, swept round by leaves of one remembered autumn; and in a frosted and glistering western winter that followed he saw the sparkling net of frozen dew spread to thaw and dry outside his windows; and in the cold clear mornings the brindled sun strayed through his glass door and sprawled on the floor at his feet like a friendly animal in the room as he worked at the kitchen table.

One more room—the little mud one that held him like some egg an insect had left in the dried mud. There in the evenings he sat in such a quietness, smelling the odor of mountains and piñon and sage, that he thought all wildness might now be stilled in him forever. Outside and all around him were the faraway calls of mountain and valley animals and the soft cries of desert creatures; and through a great window hung the glittering huge balls and chains of stars that knew steadfastness—and yet he saw among them plagued Orion in his pestilence of swarming ghosts of stars.

What good had it all been, what did it all mean? It must mean something, for he could not see, in all honesty and humility, how these lives could not finally mean something, they had taken up so very much of his best mind and his best heart. If they had taken so many tears from eyes, so much ache from heart, surely they must not mean *nothing* . . . or he must find out.

So he brought all the ghosts of these rooms, boxes of light and darkness that had captured him for a time and from which he had escaped, to this room where he lay, flesh, upon this bed.

Suddenly there were words, spoken words. Was he forming them himself, were they rising up from him, at last, to free him of himself? He lay listening. There were two women in conversation not far off, somewhere below. It must be early morning, for the voices had the mysterious metallic timbre of speech in early hours.

"I tell you Finney is a liar. . . ."

"But he said this. I heard him say this. He said this to me."

"So you've talked it over!"

"I tell you Finney is a sweet liar."

"And you *have* talked it over. . . ."

"I like Finney a lot. But I don't *love* him. I love my husband Jack."

"Finney's a liar."

"My neighbor said to me, 'That Finney is so nice!'"

"Oh everybody likes Finney Robinson. But he's a damned liar."

"And me standing there, with my husband Jack sick in the back room for three solid months and Finney saying this to me. . . ."

"I *knew* you'd talked it over. . . ."

"Oh I like Finney a *lot,* I mean a lot. But that's not like loving a man, which I do my husband the sick Jack."

"There's very little difference, I can tell you, between loving a man and liking one a lot." (He heard her laugh hysterically.)

"I tell you Finney's a goddamned liar!"

And then silence. It is a party, he thought. They are all drinking in a room.

Then from somewhere there sounded the clear delicate singing language of two Orientals, filling the silence: *lalalalolula.* It blew into his room through the window, floated in almost like petals of an exotic flower or their sweet scent . . . just for a moment. Just for a moment they had said something to each other in the night, in the world; just for a moment they had turned to each other in the night and exchanged a kind of music, maybe only something insignificant or trivial as their unseen bodies brushed each other, turning, swimmers in the dark gently stroking off into a distance, greeting, brushing arms, legs, then on away. And then no more, they fell into the silence out of which they had for a moment risen. Who were they? Where, in the world?

Then there was the noise of some running around and some loud laughter from below. He must see what this was. He got up and went to his door, opened it very quietly and peeped through the crack. It was in the lobby, this commotion.

A foxy little old man whom he recognized as the hotel night clerk was cavorting mechanically before two women who were sitting in the lobby chairs. Suddenly the old man pulled to him the face of one of the women, the younger of the two, and kissed it demonstratively.

"Look, Mrs. Fisher!" he cried, dancing, and he did it again. The kissed woman laughed wildly and threw her head back.

"For a man old as you, Mr. Johnson!" he heard Mrs. Fisher say. "Well nigh sixty."

"The older the better," Mr. Johnson said and laughed. The hysterical kissed woman spun out discs of wild laughter.

Then there was quiet among them again, almost as if they were actors in a blackout and had finished their scene. But the little old night clerk was saying something again, this time in a whisper. He could hear only the whistle of a whispering voice. The night clerk was telling the women something that should be whispered, probably some lewdity. . . .

Then the hysterical laughter of the woman rose again in the night. Her laughter was terrifying; it was like the cry of a woman in childbirth. He closed his door finally and went back to his bed and lay there. He was drugged half-asleep and all this seemed like the theatricality or credible fantasia of dream. In the room above there was suddenly the noise of love. He listened—it was like a bed breathing. The night was so quiet now, except for the hastening pant of the lovers' bed above him. He grew suddenly tense and fixed and ashamed, not wanting to hear, not wanting to be forced to participate in this. Then suddenly the shrieking voice of one of the women below in the lobby rose and called, "I tell you Finney is a lousy liar!" No response—utter quiet again, except for the low panting of the bed above, now like the breathing of a chased thief hiding in a dark place.

He looked at his watch. It was two in the morning. Now it was Easter. He was getting a headache. He did not want to listen, but he was listening hard. He decided he would have to call down to the desk and tell the little night clerk that their noise, which had stopped now, but for how long?, would have to stop, and he could not listen for listening. But the two up above him. He did not want to disturb them—yet.

It was over. It had happened. Everything was quiet. They had calmed each other, they had made each other still. Then there was a little low measure of note-like words, and an answer like harmony; then the steps of bare feet on the floor which was his ceiling; and silence again. The bridegroom had come forth of his chamber.

Suddenly he knew he was wretched. He was choking at the throat, and he discovered himself lying diagonally across the bed with his mouth on the sheet, biting into the mattress. He raised his fist and came down with it on the bed and pounded it. He was weeping. Why? He was supposed to be damned mad at the party in the lobby, but he had wept. And then he knew, for a quick second of clarity—he had to face it now that it was clearly before him

—how lonely and like stone he really was, had always been, right through all of it, this room in this stone world, this stony Easter world, this struggle above and this mysterious and idiot variation below. He spoke to the mattress, which still gagged his clenching, dripping mouth, "To not always be wanting to call it back, the vanishment; not to grieve the loss of what one later knows had to be only an ephemeral, fleeting parcel of a greater, steadier and unchangeable whole. What vanishes returns, again and again in any room at any hour; there is no room in the wide world will shelter you from it, no place to go into out of it, no refuge, no asylum. Stand and face it and endure it, the vision; but tell of it, in its multifarious ways and changes and appearances, its hundred faces and cries and sounds, its infinitely elaborate wardrobe of masks and costumes: everything contributes to the whole image, there is the total contribution, there is the listening and the speaking."

He featured another time. They sat on a dry white drift-log back on the beach against the low hill. The light of the moon showed everything, even the features of the face, and it lay over the sea that seemed soft as flesh.

"I'm cold," she said, and shivered, but not so much with cold as with an enormous tenderness for him.

He did not move, neither his arms to warm her nor his mouth to comment.

She was trembling violently now, and when she could bear it no longer, she turned to him and said, tremblingly, "Please hold me."

He did not answer.

What was it he did not want in her, she wondered. Yet he was trembling, too. She leaned against him, then she put her arms around him, to feel his shaking body. With one movement she pulled him down off the log and into the sand. He lay there, immobile. She began to nuzzle over him, panting and kissing him, his cheek, his eye, his hair, his neck. She unbuttoned his shirt and put her lips to his chest. But he lay out flat, unmoving. Then she moved the muzzle of her tenderness down his body, past his belt, and she buried her head in his loins. Her feet were digging in the dry sand. He did not squirm or shift his position. She felt the tender kerneled bundle of his genitals like a soft sack of something, caressed them with her eyes, her lips, her forehead, her hair, then lay still on this still soft place of him.

Then she heard a cry from him, at first it was like a bird's cry out over the water, and she raised her head, slid up his length, feeling so delicious, for the cry increased her delicious longing, and she lay fully upon him, seeing his tears. His tears were only something else of his to put her lips upon, and then she lay her mouth over his and took his cry into her throat.

"Why? Why?" she whispered, gasping.

Her question broke his low cry and gave him courage to let go the sob clotted in his chest, and he groaned and exploded into bitter sobbing, catching his breath and letting it go again, rolling and rocking in the sand. She drew away from him and sat up in the sand on her folded legs under her, suddenly quelled.

Free of her, he leapt to his feet and ran towards the sea. She rose and fled after him, thinking surely he would run into the sea, and caught him at the edge of the water. Holding him here by the elbows of his long arms dangling limply from him, she felt his body convulsing with his pain that she could not name or understand, and saw his wild-haired head sway and roll and fall back. They stood huddled in the wet sand in the shallows, the sliding ends of waves drowning their feet to the ankles, the sand clinging to their clothes, and she caught his head between her hands and saw his wet light eyes, pale glaucous in the moonlight and said again, softly, "What has happened to you?"

He could not say a word.

Then she embraced him and folded him against her and he rested his head in the little hollow between her shoulder and her neck, and she rocked him there, in the shallows. He quietened to a low sobbing. "Let's walk down the beach," she said.

They walked apart, she on the ocean's side to keep him from it, he some distance from her on the shore's side. He kept looking back over his shoulder at the dark house on the cliff where Wallace and the girl were and saw, still, no light on.

"I am dismembered and unmanned," he said. "Oh when will this ghost rise out of my flesh and let me be still?"

"I *knew* you'd talked it over!" The voice came back again from below.

He got up, turned on the light, and went to the phone on the wall. He called the lobby. He heard the buzz down in the lobby, and then the old night clerk answered. He told him. He was trembling a little. He wanted to be angry.

After he hung up the receiver, he heard the dead silence of the below. The fiends had been quietened. . . . Then the sibilant whispers of the old man who was telling the women what happened.

Now all three were whispering.

In a few minutes he heard the women going out of the hotel. It fell very quiet. He went to the street window of his room and stood, naked, as he slept, in the strange flashing light of an electric sign across the street, to see the figures of the women fleeing, like hellshades, down the sidewalk and into the early morning. For one moment they turned to look back and they saw him in the window and turned and fled, as though he were a vision of evil.

Lying across the bed again, he waited. A tiny child's voice cried out, delicate and small and sorrowful, from some other room, "Go 'way, Leo; go 'way!" Its mother said something to it. "Go 'way, Leo; go 'way Leo." The child cried in a plaintive, croupy voice, "Mommy, tell Leo to go 'way!" Leo laughed in a low husky voice. Then the mother chuckled and pacified the child, and it hushed. Silence.

He lay in his bed and all the human dialogues went round and round in his head, though all was quiet now . . . *"Finney is a liar . . ."; "Go 'way, Leo!"; lalalalolula:* whatever the beautiful Oriental voices said, just for a moment and never said again all that night that he would never never know; the bellows sound of the love bed above, breathing now in his head like longing; *"What has happened to you, tell me; tell me what has happened to you. . . ."*

He thought how all things glow, glimmer out and fade and fall away and how we must let ourselves be claimed by all passing things, vanishing bit by bit in them, but flourishing in them, too, flaring up in them as light passes over them like motes of dust: this is the slow giving away of oneself, the slow sacrifice, bit by bit. No, he thought, I belong to all things that glow and glimmer out, I am in their life and in their death, I live and die with and in them. I pass in seasons, blow in and out in weathers. I must suffer the death of living lonely things. I blow over my landscape like a wind. I am a part of everything that arrives, announces itself, flourishes, and passes. What, then, shall I proclaim? It is my moral struggle as what I am, then, that shapes me, gives me my meaning and my meanings; it is my moral responsibility to this image of myself that is my life, and this moral struggle is the making of my death.

He had had, again, his pain; and now something had lifted out of him and risen up out of stone to where it would have its long long meaning. And then the tenant thought spoke itself what he had been trying to shape all this mysterious night, as though a stone image, carved by whom, when? were speaking, in whose mouth the nests of these passing lives' moments were left, the stone image his brain, the hotel, too; built and the builders vanished. Let us be tender, let us be loving and gentlehearted, handling each other, touching; bring love into all the dark lonely rooms and strike love like a match to light a candle and in the light see each other's generous grateful faces . . . to touch it all with light! To touch everything with light as with a wand to glitter and shine upon it and show it, there, in the world, as our life passes over it! For we are like sun that rises and sheds light upon things, and then falls and leaves them in darkness again. We come in like a robber in a dark room and shine our flashlight across and upon the faces, their eyes like gems, their cheek radiant, beloved faces of men, and over all the details and objects and study them ever so carefully, then go out. . . . Where to find the light to go with? In the still, central listening darkness of one's self. It is what the flesh does with its ghost, the vision and the beholder, that matters. It is a falling and fallen world, but there is the rising from what falls. Find us the light to go into the darkness with!

The morning sun was abroad, now, and within the walls and window casements of this room there began a low moaning and wailing—the winter-slept insects were coming to life and rousing their wings. Soon they would rise and fly away. And he thought, let the blood of the image rise and the wings of it soar. When the little dry sleeping wings hidden in all our inner winter turn, tremble, unfold in that long eventual day, rise, beat and soar away, let them go let them go: a Lamb, a Son, a Message, a Sacrifice.

And he thought, *Because you were youth and bright-eyedness and I could never be young with you, because I was ancient and full of too many days, what I knew I did not want to teach you because it was of darkness and shadow and I did not want to corrupt your mirth, your glee, your brightness, no gloom, no tempests, no witchcraft, no sorrow, no doubt, no confusion, all clear all clear all clear. I did not want to teach you all that, to lead you into the shadow; I wanted to keep you in the sun, walking and singing and leaping down the road in the sun, bright and bright of flesh and blood, all color, no darkness: and so I betrayed you. I am unconnected who was most profoundly joined. Salute me! I hear you but I cannot see you, hearing the fire, hearing the greeting, I salute you!*

He lay like star, in a kind of new curious steadfastness, feeling himself calm purity, deep clarity, clear cold star, as though he had been lifted through violence into pure anonymity, pure uncraving, untouching and untouchable *being,* removed and uncaring, unrestive and unanxious, calm and still and clear as a star, quiet and sweet and fast, in a speechless tenderness.

Now he knew that something was all over, that through all the little hotel, in every room, something was finished, and that another long beginning had begun.

A Shape of Light

So it was there that, long ago, in that town, the message was sent and lost; and it is here, many years later, in this city and in this time, that the lost message is risen and reclaimed and fixed forever in the light of so much darkness and of so many meanings.

1. *The Record*

The words he wrote down on paper, shaped in long thin skeletal characters, with a bony forefinger maneuvering his pencil, even as though the characters themselves were ghosts of the alphabet, are ghosts of a page—the page is haunted. But on this haunted page he comes back to us, his face and his look and all about him; he comes back like an old sad age yellow on a page. It is a dim ghostly line of words, his words on the page; bring a light to it: see how the words flare up to light, answering to what put them there. The page is lighted.

So the record reads: "If on an evening of a good moon you will see a lighted shape, much like a scrap of light rising like a ghost from the ground, then saddle your horse and follow it where it will go. It will lead you here and yonder, all night long until daybreak. Then you will see it vanish into the ground. Some old-timers here call this Bailey's Light and say that it is the lantern of a risen ghost of an old pioneer, Bailey was his name; and that old Bailey is risen to search for something he has lost in his lifetime, something, even as ghost, he wants to get back or to get straight, riding on his horse to find it. So he is flashing his lantern through the night, for this. Others have said it is a farmer's lantern, glowing as the farmer swings it down to the river to see its tide and whether it will flood his crops. Still others say it is a ghostly hunter hunting. At any rate, there is a ghost in my night here, and I have studied him and finally thought to watch for him and to follow his light if he should rise up and go abroad."

"Oh where you agoing Boney Benson, and it nightfall? Why are you leaving the supper table so suddenly; you have golloped your food; your supper will get cold and I will get cold. Where you agoing so suddenly, Boney Benson?"

Because he followed the light, lo here! lo there! time and time again, every time he saw it, he knew where the light went, he found its secret territory. Something was there for him to find out and he had to endure, wait, study and study it until its buried, difficult meaning came to him. But it didn't finally come, when it came, like an easy vision. He had to *follow,* hard and in hardship and torment, he had to give himself wholly, unafraid, surrendered to it. He had to leave things behind. When he left the territory of his meaning, his burden was to bear, understanding the meaning at last, what he had found out, and to pass it on—and this was his life, bearing, suffering the found-out meaning of what he was involved in, haunted by it, grieved by it, but possessing it—and watching it continue to grow, on and on, into deeper and larger meaning. This, only, was all his pain.

Well, then, let me see here how to tell it, for I tell you this man had seen a strange and most marvelous passing thing and now has made me see it; and to fasten it in a telling and hold it recorded that way, though it itself run on, is all my aim and craving, find I tongue to tell it. I will want to tell you how, after seeing this light rise up and glide, a man got up to leave whatever he was doing to follow; and how the following of this light came to be the one gesture of his life—not to catch the light or disturb it or claim it for himself, how could he? It belonged to all the others before him, too, and to those after him, to whom this is told, but just to see what he could see, shown up in the shed light of this light where it went; and to keep himself out of it, he didn't matter, it was the light that mattered: he passed away, the light remained and went on.

Yet one must acknowledge how he loved, *required,* respected the *idea,* the *image* of himself as alone after the light and tormented by it, wandering sometimes weeping in a cold place, anonymous, alien, free. The times he raced through the freezing and windy spaces, desperate, full of strange fears—*what* was he looking for?—were often terrible; yet the idea, later in his mind, the image of himself: that wild and terrible shape riding the land, makes us both weep for him, as though he were some pitiful begging stranger; and silently rejoice, because we know he was free in his suffering and that he was surrendered to and claimed utterly by the truth of himself, belonging to that mysteriously beautiful and often cruel Force that wanted to use him for something. Then what did the light want to use him for? His only aim was to find out.

So this man made covenant with himself not to ally himself with any pattern of life or form of human activity that would keep him from his suffering after the lighted shape in which he sought the truth he was after. He would use this light to shine it over all things, live and dead, to see what they were, to touch them with light so that he could give them a name, as though they were the first things and he the first man, to keep taking inventory of it all, to hold it all straight and named and preserved in the light. This task, this pursuit, seemed the best he could do in his time, having found the light or having had the light passed on to him by those before him and so keep it alive and so pass it on.

For what other task was there in the world to give oneself to? All around him roiled a giant and anxious watchlessness, the blind conquests of men engaged in hunts to kill, plots to gain, plans to trick to glory or increase. The little light! Sometimes only like a speck in the eye; sometimes only a tiny bright spot at the end of a long and dark corridor. Often he thought of all the places to be or go, of the people in places, kin and comrades and lovers, of their faces, the light in eyes, of their flesh. Then it seemed he was no more than ghost, living only a phantom life, underground, *below* life, cut-off, far away, loose and on the lightless rim of the world. Then he cried out, "O will you mock me, destroy me, ghost of light that I follow?" Those times he was tortured by his choice, he cursed his station, abused himself and finally blinded his eyes with his hands to put out the light. But there it was, shining, in his head, a miner's little lantern, going over the ground of his mind; and he could only follow it.

What put the blessing of the light upon him that turned his flesh to fire, that turned his eyes away from everything that would keep them from the path of the light? What serpent urged him to this record to get for himself this knowledge and this image which changed him into something that he could only be by himself, something which he wanted to give to others (what a mystery that what was his light became others' darkness) yet which seemed to destroy them or turn them away from him? Was the light, then, death? Was the light, then, his own image of himself which, given to others, stole their own self-image from them and left them him-imagined, without even the light to go after? What to proclaim out of this man's gesture, light or darkness?

Well, let me see how can I tell it, for I tell you he knew a most wonderful passing thing; and can I find tongue to shape it, I will leave something of us both behind, a shape of light in the darkness, a lighted shape of dust: a record.

"Why are you awatching out the kitchen window; what is there for you to see? Eat your supper and pay some 'tention to me. . . ."

"There is something live in the land, my wife Allie; and my eyes are awatching to see. But one eye is on you, my wife Allie; and one eye is watching through the window."

"You can't divide me with the outdoors; when your eye turns from me the light is taken from me and I am left in half a shadow; why do you turn the light from me?"

"I have an eye watching for the light, you must understand."

"Oh you are going to leave me again. When you leave me so cold and in my darkness, I cannot understand, Boney Benson; I cannot understand."

Lying connected to his wife in their moist bed, melted in their sweat and simmering in their sweet civet, he thought, "I am traveler home under the hill." Yet outside he would see a light, ground ghost; and he would turn back to himself and rally up himself, draw up and rise and dismember the joining to go to it. Often it would be only a lantern hanging back in the trees, with no hand to show for it; or sometimes just the light of the brooder in the henhouse; sometimes a glowing wad of fireflies along the ground, and sometimes a nightfire on the hill. In the end, after so much of this breaking away to see could it be this light, everything, every giving of himself, every sacrifice of himself only delivered him over and back to himself and his pursuit again. There was, finally, no escape.

Then one night at supper he surely saw it, and he saddled King and went after it. They followed all night long, finding nothing but what grew out of the ground or lay upon it, grass and creature. He returned at daybreak, after it disappeared.

"Oh where you agoing and it nightfall? Why are you leaving the suppertable so suddenly, you have golloped your food. Your supper will get cold and I will go cold. Where you agoing so suddenly?"

"I have seen it, I have seen it; and I am going to saddle my horse and follow it. Wait for me till I get back, my wife Allie."

"O do not saddle the purple horse, O do not ride the purple horse King. . . . Shall I keep the sweet potatoes warm in the oven?"

"I will never eat them, my wife Allie; or eat them cold. . . ."

So let us go with him a little ways, a ghost of the light, following him only with our eyes, so let us come sit here under the hill with him and he will tell us so we can tell it. Circle of insects round us, grasshoppers, caterpillars, eye like the pod of green peas, ripe bursting eye, pluckable. . . . They plucked out sweet old Gloucester's eyeballs and his poor houseless poverty came wild out of the hill, and in his skins led the blind old turned-out Somebody down the road to the cliff. Come let us hold us close to all this dream of dust, of these figures of dust and light, we are a radiant bowl of light and dust shaped by the stillness of his moment of telling. . . .

"I would not be mad as they say I am, poor houseless poverty, caved in the side of this hill, the road beyond with the foot of the traveler upon it, raising the dust at his heels, see him go, Old Somebody, holding to the highway. Breathed out of this dust, I will find the first things, late I will find them, last to the first things, come let us join to find the first beginning things, they are still, even yet, here in everything: say dust, say light, see what shall we call them. Old Ancestor, rib-sprung, old dusty one seared by the light, mixture of light and dust, come under this hill a moment, stay a moment . . . Old Somebody. We have the everlasting shed blood covenant upon our flesh.

"Walking one day I found a child let down from Heaven on a piece of string, standing in a meadow of bluebonnets and paintbrush, leashed out to me. This was my lost child and I told him what he did not know, left my words with him, our covenant, and laid this charge upon him: *speak of this little species that cannot speak for itself; be gesture; and use the light and follow it wherever it may lead you, and lead others to it. And though critics may mock you, lovers leave you and the whole world fall away from you . . . follow the light into the darkness where all vanishment comes back again.*

"I gave him, this errand boy, this runner and rider, the message and it rose and was delivered, but he was cut off and left earthbound and could not rise again to where he had dropped down from, but was dismembered and cast out, untied, to be a wanderer on roads of dirt . . . *behold I am he who sold you, bound in leathern thongs, to a new master; but o my brother! I beseech you remember not my sin against you and grant me this prayer. Bind me now hand and foot; beat me with stripes, shave my head and cast me into prison: make me suffer all I inflicted on you, and then perchance the Lord will have mercy and forget my great sin that I have committed against Him and against you!* Come on wild heart, my wild wild heart, come on; for there is another country and another language. I came into my life to find it a kind of darkness until I discovered the record of this little lantern, and I will die, too, with the little light in my hand, buried with the little light in the ground.

"Riding one night, I galloped upon a flock of shining night-people under shining trees; it was a festival of some large clan of blood-kin, they all had that strong *look* about them that told they were members of blood. They were beautifully dressed, in satins and pongees; and sashes of silk were hung from the delicate trees, fragile colored lanterns hung in the trees, the moon in the trees, too, like one of the lanterns; the breeze was alive, a soft trembling hand roving under and among the silks, all in a smooth pastoral place. The feast was laid out on the ground and covered with the most translucent veil of muslin, showing beneath it the fruit and the victuals, a heaped-up pile of riches. But keep the feast from the insect that was already coming down upon it, the flies and bees already hovered in a swarming circle around the edge, and the crawling things had trailed the festival and lay in hordes on the rim of the festival. Put it under glass, save it save it, this food and this flesh shining under the passing sun. The red and golden drums lie on the ground and the flutes and winds lie lipless, ungiven; and ungiven or given, the lips will pucker and the lungs will puncture and shrivel and fingers of flesh for drums will curl and cleave to bone. Yea dazzle me dazzle me! Round me like a wheel of stars. Flash the fireworks on me, blind my eyes, dazzle me. You are all so beautiful. 'We were on a picnic,' they would tell it, 'the whole flock of us, down by the sandbank at the river, on the Fourtha July. Suddenly in the woods, walking under the trees, was a figure; and someone whispered, "It's old Boney Benson." We watched him. Did he want to join us? He did not come any closer, but hovered on the edge of our picnic, across the bobwire fence, just looking to see. We were all, food and person, the whole picnic, in his eye. What did he want from us? *Him*—you know who—went to see what Boney Benson might want, *he* was not afraid of Boney Benson, even took him a biscuit and a drink of water; and when *he* tried to cross the bobwire fence *he* fell upon it and was caught and cut there. Boney Benson helped *him* off and went away—without the water, for the water was spilt; but *he* did not drop the biscuit and gave it safely to Boney Benson. The blood was on *his* trousers.'

"To us arrives the unanswerable at our door and cries *answer!* and will not stay or be there to hear when we open the door—nor can we ever give any answer, the unanswerable is unanswerable. Nor will the unnamable, always hovering over and round us for its name, be ever named. The patched webbed face of a ghost floats round us, hangs and hovers in our air lodged like a becalmed kite over us, moored to our hearts that try to send messages up the string to it. Dance my pretties, laugh; and on I go, on the road, the dust at my feet and you for a moment in the meadow, under the silken sashes, shining in the eye of the insect that has it all in the little mirror of his eye.

"In a grassy corner, humped upon a mossy rock, an old naked man bent over his geometric shape and measured with long forefinger and straddled legs of his compass the secret from his brain and his wild burning eye. He has measured the enigmatic arc, my pretties, he has found a figure for the distance between point and point, within the sharp corner of an angle he has found the little meaning; come let us slide into this tiny harbor of angle under the spread length of this old artificer's fingers, let us be measured and encompassed by this small compass scope, come on wild hearts, my wild wild hearts, come on, under the span of this naked old man's fingers, safe in the shape of his sweet brain of dust. Naked, no shoe for his foot, he has gone to his dark place to stay and meditate until he has his meaning.

"Horse of dreams, with a bowed down head and dust-shot eye, ride me away from this world of grief, come ride me ride me away. Till I have grieved myself free, at last; till I have sorrowed myself free. And then where we go it will not matter. We will carry our baby in our arms, we will have our trunk and the baby-buggy, that is all we will carry, and onto the road we will go, turned back into our lives that were stolen from us. Move here, move there, hide here, break out there; O will you mock me, destroy me, ghost of light that I follow?

"So what happened was this: we came onto the wide strange region lying under a nightfall sky. It was twilight, you understand, although good dark hadn't come yet. On our right was an orchard of wild fruit trees and the trees were full of white creatures, white, you understand. The pale early moon was the color of the creatures, fowl-like, and like it was of their feather, it seemed a white fowl rising from the far bush, the moon did, in the color of distance: blue. There stood the trees abloom with white creatures, only the glimmer of last daylight lingering over the roan-colored grasses; and in the background the scrawly trees were like marks scrawled on a dark wall.

"There were four of us, you understand, on horseback: the three Tilson boys and me, I was on King's back—he was going after it, too—and riding after it, what I had seen so many times I could but finally follow it. This is what we were going after, this gentle and curious light that was now following a straight path along the ground, and tumbling on as if it was a lighted ball of weed. And if I could tell you I would regale you with telling how this light had come up tattered out of the ground and wound itself into this ball and started rolling along. And if I could describe you it, I would do it, how this radiant object shed the most delicate and pure, clear illumination on little things in its path and along both sides; so that what it showed us who followed was the smallest detail of the world, the frail eternal life of the ground, the whiskers of a fieldmouse, the linked bones in the jointed feet of a hidden sleeping bird, a clear still white tincture of dew hanging like a fallen star on a blade of grass, a hairy worm on a stem like one lost eyebrow, the hued crescent of the shale of a sloughed snake like a small pale fallen rainbow.

"So following this ghostly little lamp of light, we came, of a sudden, into this unearthly landscape, the one I have told you about, with the white beings. We knew the country, you understand—our ancestors had broken it as wilderness and started all their seed there, my grandfathers and their fathers, me, all my blood-kin, children and children's children. We descendants thought we had measured and blazed it all. But there is always some unknown part of all that is known—and we had stumbled into it, following this light. I knew my ancestors had followed this light, it was that ancient a thing, this light; that they had ridden behind it, over branch and pasture, thicket and prairie, from supper till sunrise, when they saw it sink into the ground. There are the records to prove it, for these old men made records, stopping to put down what happened, even as I am doing: 'Around us were disorder, rancor, words gone sour in the mouth like persimmons; thoughts turned rotten in the mind, crops eaten, droughts and floods, poorly wives and an evil chance of children; but when we saw this light, we left the worst behind and followed to see what it was, that it might show us what our sorrow meant.'"

The record stopped here, there was never another word written. What had this old man seen or found that had stopped all words, that would not take words? What had happened to this old

Follower, so long gone? Had the light been his death, had he met with mishap or evil on the route of the light? Or had he not been able to put another word to all that he had seen and so *abandoned* the record to become the light? Think of that moment of *abandonment,* that moment of realization that spirit passes *beyond* its vain laboring to make flesh or word of what is beyond both and incapable of containing them wholly: he rose and vanished into that region, and there we must find him.

And now, after so much struggle and after so much following, I ask, *was he the light?* Does his cry, now before eyes on a lighted page, proclaim: *Will you follow the light that led me?* If from your bed or through your window, on a night of a good moon, you see a shape rise like a tatter from the ground and go along, saddle your horse and follow it and see where it will lead you.

A tilted gravestone marks this man and his proclaiming cry; and it is said, indeed, to this very day, in that town, that a light rises from it at nights and wanders over the countryside, beckoning after it a race of the road, a race of followers. What more to say. It goes *on,* as this teller and this listener do.

2. *The Message*

Call Boney Benson from his grave. Call him from the dirt, for some one of us must disturb him so that he will rise and wander over the ground of the mind until he is followed and defined and laid away again to rest.

Suddenly he comes back, rising, called for, to his name, swinging his lantern along the railroad track. With his return comes the image of a kite. It has come slowly, this slow-footed, late-arriving image of Boney Benson and the kite . . . wait for the coming back, as image waits, too.

In a town, once, there lived this Boney Benson. He worked at the depot and, like a skeleton-headed ghost in charge of the movement of the dead, flagged the midnight freight trains with a red lantern. One night, while you waited with your kin at the depot, the children in their sleepers, for the arrival of the ten-o-six, just to watch it for a thrill—you had all been riding on the highway to cool off (it was broiling August) and had come on back to park at the depot to watch the train come in—you saw him pushing a freight cart with a casket on it and saw him help some Negroes load it onto the baggage car. You saw him make the sign of the cross. People in the car whispered of someone lately died in the town—so this was why they had come to the depot—and you heard one of the menfolks say under his breath, "Good-bye, old Stacey," and it seemed the dead person was given over to the hands of Boney Benson. People in the car said "Old Boney Benson! Doesn't he look scarey; looks worse and worse ever time you see him"; and whispered his story beyond your hearing. You related him, again, to death and phantoms and thought him in some way and sorrowfully in charge of the dead who were moved where, in what direction, towards what graveyard or judgment, on the trains that rolled into the town out of blackness of night and went on ahead into swallowing blackness.

Whether he had a wife or family or other kinfolks in the town you never heard it said, and your only information came from conversations overheard—which makes you think how impoverished a servitude is childhood and how people talked about seemed only ghosts and that it is later, when we have our own eyes and language, that we reclaim these as flesh and blood people of earth, but only when they are ghosts, and too late. But they come back to take their lost flesh. Yet you heard enough said about him to render him a haunted man of bones, crossed by his own bony fingers, crucified on the gaunt cross of his own body, two sticks nailed together. At night he hovered over you in your nightmares, his crossed face, speaking of his life; but you did not ask a question.

Where did he live in the daytime, where did he sleep, who were his folks? On the days spent in the graveyard with the women kinfolks to clean the family plot and to plant camphor and crepe-myrtle trees and hoe the weeds, shape the graves of dead kin and put out poison for armadillos, grave robbers, you imagined him somewhere in the graveyard, nursing the dead.

It was late one March afternoon when you were flying a kite in the pasture that you looked up and saw Boney Benson coming down the train tracks, where he belonged, in your mind, as any train, as though that was the natural place for him to travel, and not the road or path. You watched him coming closer, in a steam of his own kicked-up dust; and when he got to where you were holding the string of your kite in the pasture, he switched off the tracks and crossed the pasture to you. You would not run; you waited; you were a kite's mooring and the kite was your responsibility in the sky and you could not abandon it or cut it adrift. He approached you ghostlike, like a dream you could have of him and so cry out, "Somebody! Somebody!" in the night until a hand touched and quietened you. Still, you were not afraid.

He stood over you, smelling of train and graveyard, as his image later hovered over you, as the kite itself hovered over you now, so long so limpbodied a man—as though he were pasted together, drawn loosely over the cross-sticks of his body, whittled arms; and he dangled there over you for a moment. Boney Benson looked up at the kite that hung over you in a gray steady wind, then down at you, and said, in his bony voice, "Have you sent a message up to it, Son?" You said no sir. And he said, "Well, then let's do it, Partner."

Now this was a kite built so carefully and with stern labor, made out of kindling wood and shoe-box tissue paper, the first built kite of yours that had ever flown: a miracle had happened, your construction had been removed a distance from you; you were no longer joined except by the most tenuous connection of thread: you the mooring on one end, on the other end the artifice, built of good stuff off the place, freed and lifted up into a life of its own, hovering over the place it had freed itself from and which had provided the materials to make it with.

Boney Benson took from his pocket a piece of barkish Indian Chief tablet paper written on in pencil and said, "Let me send the message." You gave him the tight string and stepped back—your kite was in his spidery hands. You looked up at the face of the kite, hovering over the world, and down a little to his, over you, too. It seemed both faces were in the air, lodged there over you, and his face was like the kite's: red papery face with sticks of bones. Boney Benson very carefully put the message on the kite string and it started going up. The message faltered, then moved slowly, climbing, climbing, stopped awhile as if to rest or as if afraid of so high an ascent, then went faster faster up to the kite and lay pressed close against the face of it by the wind as though there were a conversation—or the kite was reading the message.

Then the kite dived, in an instant, and began falling falling. Boney Benson started pulling in the slack. But the string fell all around him. You rushed up to help, but it was no use, the string was falling, coiling all over the pasture, looping and winding round you as though there were some runaway bobbin in heaven and all the thread was raveling, unwinding down upon you in the pasture; and the kite was crashing to the earth. You saw it falling far away at the end of the pasture and you saw it headed for a crooked tree.

But the message, like a kite itself, kept the air and began flying itself. You were, for a moment, Boney Benson and you, watching kite and message, one soaring and wafting and turning in the sunlight that suddenly broke through the March clouded sky, the other falling falling. The message went traveling on, now faster faster; and then the sun had its eyes on it and was reading Boney Benson's letter; then the wind took it for a moment and read it, Braille-like, with its soft lips; the message moved on out of the lighted zone of the sun and passed into the shadow of a cloud and if there was rain up there the rain must have had the message for a moment, too.

The message went on and on, through zones and fields of air; and again in a flash of sunlight you saw it like a silver mote, then lost it among a flight of birds, it like a bird itself; then finally, just as the kite fell broken across the branches of a tree, its knotted tail, made of an old quilt, looped over the limbs, far across at the edge of the pasture, you saw the message for the last time, going on, now itself like a kite, wafting, lowering, rising again, flashing in the shuttering light, over the town and then beyond it—on away into invisibility. Boney Benson finally said, looking down at you, "Excuse me for losing your kite, Son; I'll get you another one"; and you said, "Wonder where the message went . . . ?" and for an instant he bent in a gesture that would haunt you forever and uttered a deep, stifled cry, as though something had hit him in the pit of the stomach and mashed his breath out. And then he went on away, down the railroad tracks.

Now: what you saw, Boney Benson and you, was this: fallen kite and flying message, one free, one captive. You could tell about the kite, how its corpse lay hidden all summer among the leaves of the tree, leaf itself, with only you to know about it, secretly, as though it were a bird's nest, left by Boney Benson who never came again but vanished like the message; how the wind found it, though, even hidden, and rattled it to haunt you; and how in the autumn when all the leaves had been taken by the wind and flown away like pieces of paper or lay like fallen messages under the crossed tree or scattered like pages of lost letters over the pasture, blowing into yards, down the roads and the railroad track, slapped and pasted against wire fences to paper them like walls of leaves, the whitened bones of the kite's sticks hung like a glaring cross in the naked tree for all to see . . . until the sticks, even, finally disappeared into birds' or squirrels' nests or fell onto the ground and rotted into it. Thus it all vanished away into you, as into air and into ground, until one day it would be remade and told about, flown again. For what there is to tell about is *what was not seen* . . . and this is all your chore. What is not seen torments the eye as though eye were only a ball of glass in a socket, until the brain can build an image of what is unseen and give vision to the eye.

What happened to the message, the going-on part of the wreckage? Even then, you spent your days trying to account for it. Finally, you imagine, it frightened birds, slipped through the fingers of the wind that had once had it but could not have it again, fell, fell like a leaf. It fell over a landscape of fragile trees like hair, animals like broken curves in the fields, into the hush of afternoon where miraculous morning had happened and left the landscape dazed into afternoon and where tears of dew had dried, a weeping was over; and everything was stilled. Then the rain fell upon the message and made it quiet, and took its words away; or the sun drew up the words and mixed them into cloud and the message fell as gentle rain. Children with their parents in the fields may have looked up and said, "Yonder is something falling out of the sky, it's raining a piece of paper." But if there were some who saw, there were many more who did not see the falling message—so many things fall and no eye to follow them down, a solitary Newton watched an apple fall and who knows who saw the ruined wings of that old father's shape come down, on that terrible day?

What happened to the message? Upon a landscape of hushed

tumult and serenity, something was falling falling. It was no mote or vision in the eye of any who saw it flecking the sky and flashing, it was real and substantial as apple or winged son. The landscape was one of cows folded and horses cropping, of a few stones like sheep in the field, a smooth pastoral place where it seemed no violence could happen. Shimmering tresses of tree locks hung in the near distance, in the far distance some bare, scratchy trees looking like burrs in a meadow. In this landscape lay a little graveyard with graves and tilted gravestones, a gathered family; and this falling missile might have fallen among the graves.

What happened to the message, wherever it fell? It began a life of its own. Now having its own life, it could—and began to—attract life to it, involve itself in other life. A tree may have grown through it (later made a house) or a perpetual fern, eternally fertilizing itself; insects left trails and messages on it, rain melted its speech away—it was taken by all things, and finally mouldered into earth and spread into everything.

What did the message say on it? Sun knew it and rain knew it, wind knew it; but not you, you had to wait. "Why did you leave me, Boney Benson; why did you go away and it nightfall?" "When you come home we will all go into Mississippi to see can we find our kinfolks." "Many a beau have I let go, because I wanted you, because I wanted you. . . ." "I have read your letter and cried and cried; and read it and cried again." "No. 5 will arrive two-fifteen, on time, carrying mail and news"; "If, at nightfall, you see a shape of light traveling over the ground, saddle your horse and follow it, to see what it will show you. . . ."

What happened to the messenger? Where had he come from, before your time; where did he vanish away to? Imagine his room: bare, curtainless, crooked window shades streaked by rain because the windows had been left open; the smell of trains in it; a crucifix on the wall at the head of the bed. In his bed, on a thin sunken mattress, his long form under the covers, his dust-covered hightop shoes toeing out from under the bed, his Hamilton white-face railroadman's watch ticking on the little marble-top table. The closet door ajar, crooked on its hinges; within, his blue striped coveralls hung from a staple on the wall like his own hanged body. No photographs, no Bible, no Western stories, no hair oil; merely the room where he lay, ungiven to it, as if stopping over to rest, having arrived there on his way to not any particular where. But can a man's life be so bare, so unpossessed? Somewhere he had left something behind.

For years his gesture and his image haunted you, hung and hovered over you like a kite in the air around you, triangular face, bony, stretched papery skin of a kite, his face, swimming and dipping and bowing and rising and darting, looking down at you . . . his kite face . . . *send up a message!* You had built kite and kite had taken his message and delivered it. Now you must shape him, like kite, and send his message back to him. For out of a wreck something is left, freed, sent on to other hands, put into the world, leaving a ghost behind until ghost and flesh be brought together again and the whole thing vanish, accounted for, to its eternal hushedness.

What to proclaim out of it all? For years the message, scrap of paper bearing what words? had been falling falling over the unstilled landscape of your mind, with no place to land, no resting place, no one to receive the cry of the message. You were pondering and brooding over dust and light, the poverty of dirt, the little speck of light the dust draws to and hovers round. You thought of that king's son, wild in his skins, the traveler lost in the hill, his old kinsman blind on the road, the joining of father and son. You were full of this kind of thought and laboring with passion and sternness to shape dust and light and poor houseless poverty into some little lasting form, shaped out of dust but held together for a little while by the light you begged for. Every day the shape of a terrible thought or idea or memory rose up in you from some opened grave to claim your mind like a presence; it was a wrestling with some visitation of ghost. You fought it out upon another body, as though you thought flesh might appease or pacify the ghost; or upon your own, as if to chasten the ghost in your flesh. To be still! hands folded, mind resting like a fallen kite, its cry gone on, and take silence in the silencing of all flesh and let the ghost ride out of the flesh.

You, kite-maker and kite-flier, were in a great city where, following some shape—was it of light or of darkness?—you had wandered into an unreal, ghost-haunted territory, into a landscape of addict elations, hallucinations and obsessions, where it seemed you were a kite flying over the landscape—your gaze walked down the tight string that held you aloft, alienated you, separated you; and far far below you saw the fisted, gripped hand that held you—your only mooring to the ground, this vanished artificer. *Who will send the kite a message?* you cried; or can kite send *down* a message, though kite fall and lie broken and caught in a leafless tree like one torn leaf in a windless season? This cry was hidden in the thick and leafed and numberless cries of your brain, secret, lodged and hidden. You were in this city where men had lost speech and could not tell, where children had lost fathers, where childless men and womanless men searched for wife and child; homeless poverties were wild and aloose in the flumes of stone. Through holes in the walls between men, two eyes met, eye upon eye, seeing jungles in the eye, vines, a lion in the jungle, a tear. So this is what it has all led to, you thought, this ghost-grieved room where I sit, Hellstreet below, the odor of delicatessens, dogshit on the sidewalks, drunken men wheeling and calling in the street, the dirty yelling children (you sonofabitch you think you're a bigshot because you got a pack of cigarettes! motherfucker); the Cubans and the Portuguese sitting on the fire-plugs; the blown trash, the forlorn apartment houses; the caricature of a woods where human beings, moiling like insects, broke the tender night; and you wanting to make something tender and full of faith and simplicity in the midst of this tenderlessness and ugliness, this loveless, faithless, vile world of men and goods. To live in the veins until something deep deep within begins to open out and rise up, slowly slowly! It is in the veins that the purity lives and happens. It is all there, everything, the whole truth, the whole vision, in the veins, you thought. O grief! O lonely! Speech lies lodged under us like a river under slate; grief hangs over us like a becalmed kite: send messages up to it, down to it.

You thought of the messages ticking on the telegraphs at depots, of all the letters speaking in the mailbags and mailboxes, cries along the telephone wires, of all the people telling things, the whole world talking and telling and sending out messages; yet nobody could tell, the gesture was lost. For speech lay lodged under men like a river under slate, hung becalmed over them like a hovering kite in a windless season—send messages down to it, send messages up to it . . . try! try! The patched webbed face of a ghost floats round us, hangs lodged in our air over us, moored to our hearts that try to send messages up the string to it. *Proclaim it! Proclaim it!* But no message would rise.

Looking upon this world from your window, you saw the wind lift a scrap of paper from the dirty street and carry it high up into the air and close to your window—you could see that it was piece of a letter. *Boney Benson!* There was a cry, lifted from deep down in you up to your throat, that you could not utter. It was his cry, now covered up with dirt, that he had given to you and you had carried, long-since-silent cry the day you lost the kite and freed the message from his pocket. You turned and called out, man now and no longer child, speaker now and no longer listener, asking man's question, crying man's cry: *Boney Benson! what did the message say that day, what did the message say?* Cry cannot be left in throat or breast, unrisen and unfreed—put it into the air and let it go on, cried, freed, though falling wreckage follow and hang like ghost and ruin of cry all the long season: there is the fall and there is the rising. *Call Boney Benson from his grave!* Now Boney Benson was all your question and all your pain; and tell it.

His wife Allie had died with his unborn baby in her, as if the child had not wanted to be born—or had Boney Benson betrayed her in some way so that she would not give him his child? They said that in the last month the baby had suddenly risen in its mother's body as if climbing a tower, climbed up close to her heart and, rolled up in a ball and nestled there, it would not descend and come out into the broad world but died under the bell of her heart. They said how, as she lay dying, Allie Benson cried out to her phantom, gasping for the breath it was taking from her, "Go away, go away," and how, to try to breathe, she craned and stretched her neck and ducked and drew back her head as though she were nodding yes yes yes, clawing at her heart, at the assassin within her as if it were some kind of vampire creeping up the length of her. As she lay dying—and no one knew why, what was the matter with her, was it her heart, was she having a convulsion—the gathered kinswomen and the doctor, who finally came, tried to take the child from her, to save it at least; but they found the child had rolled away from the opening of its cave, like a ball, and had risen and tucked itself up close against her heart, to stay with her, it seemed; or as if to try to save her by giving her its breath; or perhaps to speak to her some urgent message through the blood, tolling the bell of her heart; but surely to take her life away. Thus they both died, mother and child, each taking the life of the other with him. Allie Benson died of strangled anguish and bewilderment and unearthly pain, in terror of her death, not knowing what her death was, whether it was Boney Benson's hands at her throat; in her terrible death's nightmare did she think he was strangling her to death for some blood vengeance or did she know it was this risen deathchild within her? Will anyone ever know? For she had not been able to make him out, this man her husband Boney Benson, and his mystery lived and thrived within her like some spreading, choking fungus, like some mysterious inner life she questioned every day: why he held himself apart from her, why he would suddenly leave her in the middle of love, why he would go off and come back, time and time again: and she could not understand, it grew and grew so that it was Boney Benson's mystery that grew within her, swelling her, and in the end would not come out into light of day but rose and perished, destroying her. This little murderer whose wet white rodent hands had seized her heart and clutched it till it choked and stopped, what was it, of what meaning was it that a child should murder its mother? They died together, then, Allie and child, and then Boney Benson buried them together in the graveyard where they lay, murderer within murdered, in a dirt grave.

Boney Benson turned against himself and blamed his Self for this ruin and loss—what did it mean? Had he been the agent of death, was he the murderer?—and after violent days of self-abuse he chastised himself by destroying his Self, in the wildest passion, in the grove of trees behind the house he and Allie had lived in. What he spoke out when he did this, what sermon he delivered to his Self no ear ever heard but ear of tree and wind and grass, and who can ever tell that, where no tongue is? He ran to Doctor Browder and cried, "See what I have done to myself!" Doctor Browder saw blood on Boney Benson's hands and when he looked to see he saw this terrible sight. But Boney Benson was doctored and healed and became a changed strange man; he changed into this tall, towery kind of a bony man, gone all to hair, they said, because his hair sprangled out like some Apache Plume bush, wild and cottony, and he seemed as stalky as a sugar-cane pole, and so gentle. He was an odd man to have in a town, in any place in this world. But he was gentle and harmless, for his harm was gone from him into a grave.

It was further said, by boys to each other when they were separated together in their own world and life by rivers or creeks or in gins or deep green ditches, where there hovered over them always the signal of the exulting boy's life, jumping up clear of the water, in swimming naked, they cried to each other, "Look what a stake I've got!" there was this excitement there was this pride, this swollen pride, this ready danger . . . it was further told by boys that Boney Benson buried his member in the grave. Surely he must have felt this was the only way to reach his lost child—through the way of its beginning and no other—the last, as the first, gift and sacrifice to give, it was no other's and no longer his own. He had knocked on Allie's breast and called to the child, after her death; he had laid his head on her heart and listened for sounds of it, but there was no other way to reach this child that he had given her, her death, made by him, his own artifice—of death. And certainly he said when he gave his Self to the grave, I will cry down to him with the cry of the cock and I will look upon him with the eye of the Old Ancestor, where he lies buried in his grave of her flesh of dust, our buried image that rose but would not come forth, seedling of the seed of my Self; I have given him myself through your rose of sweet flesh, I have delivered him my message through the underground tunnel of your sweet flesh. And now, he prayed, let my member turn to dust, he has no home but a house of dust, this poverty of dirt. He lay widened out over the dirt grave, imagining himself clasped to her, palm to palm, mouth to mouth, knee to knee; or thin as a line, narrow plank of flesh, he her light load; and when the curious and shamed and unbelieving people of the town came to look at the grave they saw this human shape mashed into the dirt like a butter print, or the dirt so scattered and roiled that an armadillo might have been there in the night.

The tale is told that the child was born in the grave, delivered itself of its tomb within tomb and, mole-like, began a life of its own underground, rising at nights when the Mexicans who lived in the Mexican houses round the edge of the graveyard were playing their mandolins and harmonicas and singing their passionated luted summer-heat songs in the pallid summer nights, to wander phantom over the countryside.

What rose from the grave to journey in the night time? People reported this light that seemed to rise like a ball from the grave of Allie Benson and her child and stray over the ground, as if it were some animal come out of its hole or cave at night to graze or cavort or wander, under a moon, in the night breeze, in the lunar stillness. It was the Mexicans who saw it at first from their windows and from their porches. Then night fishermen saw it along the river banks, and it was seen along the railroad tracks at night or in the woods by campers disturbed on their pallets. Boney Benson, hearing of this and knowing his own secret, came to hide in the graveyard at night to watch for this rising shape; and so it came to be known as Boney Benson's Light. This is the tale that was told.

At first he laid over the grave with his own hands and at night a piece of flat slate from the side of the river to hold down the phantom—and then under the moon the Mexicans could see him lying on the cold slab of slate, thigh against the rock, beating fists on the horizontal wall, knocking, calling down, finger-tips, lips, thighs upon the wall between him and his bereaved member.

So Boney Benson was this double man: railroadman at the depot, strange and shut-up swinging his lantern; and creature of his private room: when he opened his door to a dark room, closed it behind him and mashed the button to turn on the light, he burst into this possessed shape, haunted and spectral in a lighted box of a room, and then the light went out. He appeared at the graveyard on his horse. There his night search began; and when he saw this lighted shape rise from the grave he began to follow it, and this was his regular night-time journey, following this shape where it went.

The grave was seldom let alone or unvisited, it drew people to it to spy upon it. Three strong young men in their time of wildness that no house could hamper or hush had been hunting on their horses one night and they rode upon the grave to explore the gossip tale of Boney Benson's Light; and when their horses reared back and wailed and whinnied and their hound dogs bayed for death, cowering behind the bushes, the three young men looked to see why: the slate lid of the grave of Allie Benson and her ghostchild was broken open, there was a ragged hole in it and something had escaped. In their terror they sat fixed and gaping on their raring horses, when suddenly a figure of a man stepped out from behind the trees that circled the grave, and it was Boney Benson. "I have seen it, the light; it has risen and gone yonder. Will you follow it with me?" On their horses they went and followed, the three young men and Boney Benson.

The story, told first by the three young men, then on and on year after year by descendants and followers, kin and friend (they left the record, else how could we have known it?), is that the four followers on horseback rode and rode in the night, following the shape of light, until they came upon a field where all the little white children were, the gravechildren, misbegotten, wasted-faced, cat-sucked hair grown dank to their heels, fingernails long as spurs, wan-eyed and musty smelling, of the odor of wilted cemetery roses and mouldering zinnia stems, dressed in long loose-hanging little countrychild garments of faded no-color which hung limp upon them from the shoulders with only ragged holes for ragged arms; parentless, homeless, orphans of dirt, children of earth, musting among roots, in a graveyard kindergarten: pioneers! blood-kin! breakers of wilderness! homesteaders! Yet how even among these, one of them would not stay, not even among these; memberless, it orphaned itself even of orphans, and strayed away on; and they followed the light, Boney Benson and the three young men, on and on, on horseback, the hounds following, Boney Benson on his purple horse ahead and leading, all as quiet and passionate as men in love, going on away into the far night time, following the lighted shape, on away to the very rim of the world, it seemed. What they saw as they rode—was it a mockery or a blessing that grieved them or a vision that changed them or gave them a meaning of the haunted and bedeviled world they lived in? In a little glen they passed did they not see mother nursing child at laden breasts, father standing at a distance, leaning on a staff—they were resting and strengthening themselves, for they were on some journey, too; on a log did they not find woman and child, man under a tree where a lighted lantern hung; Madonnas in meadows, mothers among rocks, in caves; landscapes with martyrs, with hermits in hills and in trees, a husband leading back a back-turned wife from death, wings and limbs of a lost son falling from the sky; and once, in a broad grassy moonlit place two lovers on their backs, side touching side; and then the followers saw him turn, rise as if lifted on wings and light upon her like an insect on a flower, so aerily; and arms and legs winged and flared, he gathered over her in all grace and lightness, riding aloft her as if floating over her, and where he touched her closest he pierced her in such a whirring and bumbling and trembling that he welted and blazed her and left her stung; and the followers went on.

So they went on, in their wonder, losing the light betimes and Boney Benson crying out in his breast, *out, out of this darkness, where is the light?* and then, finding the light again, going on behind it, the May night all in them, the stars, the blue naked night, the full white lips of the young moon, the silver, the blue and the sweetness of the wind's limbs, gentle and delicate as a young girl's, all in them. So they went on, into a strange and uterine country under an astral light and saw in the darkling West the white star lowering toward the horizon, lying on the rind of heaven, and thought: tell us that flesh is a cold and boned cask that drops into whatever darkness lies below the rim, that flesh sets, as star does, into darkness and never rises in the burning East again nor burns the long night through, as star does.

Somewhere along the way, in this country, the three young men turned back, their passion wearied, saying, "Where you go we cannot follow any longer," but Boney Benson went on. He died, in another country, and was brought back to this graveyard to be buried next to the grave of his wife and child. But the record was made and kept and the light did not vanish. It continued to rise, you can still see it on any night, to this very day; and who will follow it to carry on the record?

Yet what to tell? What to proclaim out of it all? That messages of words travel into territory where there are no words, into that wordless region where there is only a kind of music, a wail, or a sigh, or a stifled cry: the gesture of the inexpressible, and they carry a message there to leave it. What we must say can be discovered, whispered, in the overbreath of what lies on a piece of paper, there is a music produced out somewhere, outside and over what is put down in words. Words can only carry us, on away, to what waits so splendidly and purely and overwhelmingly unspeakable, we are delivered to that. There lies the territory, the unuttering region we are led to, that region like the deep underwater zones that house the sunken gesture: a slowly undulating worm in the lower light, the winnowing curve of a root, the glister of a tiny slime-egg, the burst and glow and glimmer-out of ooze from which all seeds break—the first and forgotten source; and to conceive the world over again in the image of the life of this territory of unutterance is all worthy enterprise. There lies, pure and breathing, the fallen unread message, the unjoined member; there lies the imperishable record of what happened.

This is what you thought and this is what happened, on that terrible day in that accursed city when a cry long-ago-uttered rose and was given back; in that city that did not know that at all moments Icarus was falling, a watched apple dropping, Europa raped upon a wreathed Bull across an ignorant pasture, Orpheus leading back a lover who could be turned to stone by the look of his eyes, a piece of paper rising in a windy street, a ghost called back from the grave to take his name and his remembrance in a message that was given back.

Savata, My Fair Sister

All the rest of us in our family are dark; but Savata my sister is fair. Now Jesus, did you know, was himself a dark man. They say his hair was like lamb's wool and his feet like polished brass. Thank you Jesus.

Being fair-complected, my sister Savata has always felt outcast from the rest of us dark ones in the family. I saw this psychology of her early when it put her on the wrong track by driving her away to sing and dance in St. Louis. I wrote to her and said, Savata you are feeling apart; do not; you are blessed and set aside by Jesus. See it thataway; you are marked for special work for our Lord and Savior. Come on up here to Philadelphia where I am and work with Daddy Grace, he will put your fairness to uses of the Lord and His Name. Savata had a singing voice which Jesus blessed her with, thank you Jesus, I had not much of one but gave what I had of it to the Church.

Savata to my surprise came in her fairness to Philadelphia and lent her talent to Daddy Grace. He said he was just borrowing it for the Lord who would return it to her twofold. Well, Savata studied diction and delivery, she studied Hebrew (for we are Black Jews by ancestry), she changed her personality, got all of that baseness out of her system; and in time she got her preaching papers. There is a lot of money, oh a lot of money in God's Church. Savata, my fair sister, and I came to Brooklyn and established the Light of the World Holiness Church. She was ordained a Bishop and I was appointed by her to be her business manager. The Bishop Savata worked hard, Savata sang and Savata preached and I went door to door asking donations for our church. Savata grew more beautiful and more fair. She drew larger and larger crowds, more and more donations. People came from all over to hear and see such a fair Bishop. Many gave as much as $15 per Sunday. Then this little person appeared on our scene.

His name was Canaan Johnson and he was, I will have to admit, a smart thing. He knew Hebrew but was studying it even further; he was a teacher, black as the ace of spades, and asked Savata to set him up as a teacher of Hebrew to the members of the L.O.W.H.C. As we are the Black Jews by our ancestry, Savata announced to her congregation that Canaan Johnson would be at the disposal of them for $1.25 an hour as a teacher of Hebrew, which all must learn, to get the true tongue of Jesus, to be rightly saved. You can't be truly saved in just translation, Canaan Johnson announced to the congregation. Naturally they were all scrambling to him with their $1.25 an hour. Before I knew it Savata had not only taken him as a boarder into her house which the church bought for her as a Bishop's Lodgings, but had appointed *him* business manager of the Light of the World Holiness Church. The next thing we knew he had done disbursed $600 for a piano, $3000 for a pipe organ, and $100 for something we could never find out. I kept quiet (thank you Jesus) and withdrew from Savata's church. I put away my preaching papers and housecleaned for a living. Savata never made attempt once to get in touch with me. I sure had to pray hard to keep religion, I honestly tell you.

All while I was cleaning house, all while I was vacuuming and apolishing, I studied this situation and I was delivering one long livid sermon to Canaan Johnson, no doubt my masterpiece if it could have been heard. I would not go near to the church except to clean it on Saturdays. I owed this to the Lord and it was not for Savata and Canaan Johnson; it was my tithe. This is how I heard things. Savata had changed radically. She owned more and more possessions. She preached in a streamlined dress of silk and on it she wore a diamond star, I heard. It was her fairness's fault, I said. As we are the Black Jews, her difference became her curse, where she could have made it her blessing. Look how some other handicapped folks do—that Mordecai Blake, he scuffles himself, sitting down, all over the sidewalks of Great Neck in the name of the Church, and gets more contributions than a man with good legs awalking.

Time passed, with me housecleaning and tithing my time to the L.O.W.H.C. on Saturdays and hearing things and studying what to do. I kept my feelings to myself, thank you Jesus. Until one day I was told by the Lord to go visit Savata and to reason out with her, to try to help her. I went to her house in Brooklyn and what did I find but good Persian rugs on the floor, new slip covers on the furniture and I don't know what all else. Savata, I said, I hear you have a cluster of diamonds shape of the Star of David and a Persian lamb coat, added to all the rest of this display. Where Savata had before a deep voice for preaching and for singing, she now had a little pussy voice that made me sick at my stomach. She was put-on from head to toe, and it was the working of Mr. Canaan Johnson, believe you me. Savata, my fair sister, I said, your voice has done changed, your hair has changed in color toward the red side, I cannot believe you are my same sister. Let your sister look you over. Savata would not look me in the eye. You will not look your sister in the eye, I said, but you will scan *her* over to a T to see how stout she is because of her diabetes and to see the varicose veins in her legs from carrying too much weight. I am still in the service of the Lord, despite my personal appearance, I told her that. Savata said I ate too much cream things. To this I said right out, Savata let your sister see your diamonds and your Persian lamb.

Savata was stand-offish about it and said she did not display her private possessions openly. She said she wore them only around the house. This is around the house, I said, so let me see you in them. I hear tell you blind your congregation with the diamond cluster on Sundays—let it shed a little of its light on your poor sister. She purred and said Canaan Johnson would not like her to display her things openly. How close can you get, I queried her—in a room with your own flesh and blood kin? Savata prissed and said we had different fathers and I knew it. Now how uncharitable can you get?

Then I had to let go and tell Savata my true feelings, as the Lord had instructed me to if pressed, and for her good. I said,

Savata you are a Daughter of Babylon and you know what that is. That man Canaan Johnson is laying up all day studying up while you're out working. He's bound to get the best of you in the end, if he hasn't already. You're *paying* him to, I said. He is the Devil Incarnit. Will you please listen to your sister that you used to look for creesy-greens with in the marshes to make poke salad, that you walked barefooted with in the meadows, singing to Jesus. Remember your mother who raised you up under the apple trees. If you do not remember the days of your youth then may your tongue cleave to the roof of your mouth. We will discard the fact that you ran off to Montgomery and danced in the Sepia Revue of 1952 and remember only that I rescued you up to Philadelphia and saved your soul and put you on the right track. Do not backslide. Oh I told her. You are the fair one, I said, and you are marked off to do a special service by Jesus, and you are just having the wool pulled over your eyes by this studying man. He is smart, I grant you that, and knows Hebrew and studies up all day in his room; but he is studying up, at your expense, to leave you in the end; and pocket all your earnings in his pocket. Savata only whined back uh-huh in that ungodly Lana Turner voice. But I went on.

I said you must withdraw him as business manager of the church and reinstate me before all is lost to the Devil. I have had to go back to housecleaning because I have withdrawn myself from the Church. My papers are laying dormant in my bureau drawer, but they are up to date. You know I am overweight and have sugar-poisoning to boot. Savata my sister that the Lord blessed, I said, will you listen to me? But Savata stood calm and cold before me with her arms in a prissy position as if she was embracing herself . . . what that man Canaan Johnson had put into her, among other things, though he was very bright, granted. I got up to leave and said, Savata you are the fairest of us all and yet have the most talents: with the most talents come the most temptations, I know that. And I know that Daddy Grace promised your talent would be turned back onto you twofold if you gave it to the Lord, and that instead your temptation has been doubled on you—never mind. Listen to me, you have just that much more to preach about—more temptations. Do you think Jesus' disciples were spared temptations? Before I go, though, I would like to ask you one simple temptation and that is to have the courage to put on your lamb's wool coat for your diabetic sister and ex-business manager of the Light of the World Holiness Church to see you in it; and pin on your cluster of diamonds.

To my surprise she left the room and came back in her things. She stood before me in her coat that looked like they say the hair of Jesus was. I was impressed: she was a sight; almost, I thought, too physical to be a Bishop. Maybe I had put Savata on the wrong track. I made her take off her shoes and stockings and stand barefooted before me the way nature and God had made her, before Canaan Johnson shod her with brazen slippers. She did not have the legs for a Bishop, that was plain to see. I began to sing softly "Just As I Am Without One Plea." And to my joy—and thank you Jesus—I heard in a short time the sweet voice of Savata, pure and fair, singing the alto with me, standing barefooted with feet of polished brass and in her hair-of-Jesus Persian lamb and with her diamond cluster atwinkling. She looked like a Saint, her fair face aglow, the Jesus hair of the coat ashining and her cluster aburst with light, in that blessed moment; and I knew that she was still possible, despite her physical make-up, and that more than ever, even more than back in 1952 when she got off on the wrong track, it was my Divine God's business to save her back and steer her right again. The thing of it was, you had to lead Savata, show her where to go; she would run with the fox or chase with the hounds, either way, you just had to watch her all the time: a bad nature for a Bishop. Still, she had drawing power.

In suddenly walked Canaan Johnson with some deep book in his hand, and you could tell by the back of his head how he had been reading it, flat on his back. He had on a velvet smoking jacket. Savata stopped her singing and pursed her lips and said, *Ca-na-a-an;* but I went on . . . "Oh Lamb of Jesus I come, I come . . ."

Canaan Johnson sat down with his finger in his book and Savata sat down. When I finished singing, Canaan Johnson said, God bless you Ruby Drew for giving your voice to the Lord, and shot a glance at Savata. I said it is given free of charge to all who will hear it like the wind that doth blow, Canaan Johnson, I charge no fee for it; and looked him straight in his eye. If I should ask a price for what I give, I could have new slip covers too and a house with five rooms and a coat and a diamond cluster. The word of God, translated or no, does not reward us *all* with a velvet smoking jacket. I would be satisfied if it blessed me with just a pair of Denver heels on these old shoes. And if it would allow me a down payment of $5.00 on a refrigerator to save me from carrying ice up four flights to keep my husband's milk from souring. I am a Minister of the Gospel and have the papers to prove it.

Now, Ruby, he said in that voice, the source of your rancor is about the business manager of the Light of the World Holiness Church. This is obvious. The change has been hard on you but it has brought a great improvement in the Bishop Savata's church. Already the membership has been increased twofold and we are only beginning. It is a man's job to business manage a church.

I see what you mean, I said, snapping him and casting an eye over Savata who had put back on her boa boudoir slippers. You have disbursed $3000 of the church's funds for a pipe organ without one pipe organist to play it. The piano was ample enough, yet you had to replace it by a new one which you disbursed out $600 for from the funds of the church. You have robed my sister Savata in lamb's wool and displayed a diamond star cluster upon her breast and covered her furniture with new chintz and put down new rugs upon her floors, all in a new house that was disbursed for out of the church's funds, man's job or none.

For income-tax purposes, Canaan Johnson put in; but I cut right through that by asking him: as I am my sister's guardian, I have come here to ask what are your plans, Canaan Johnson, and how far are you going with this thing?

My plans are to serve the Lord through the instrument of Savata, he responded.

She is not your instrument, I said. You are playing with a Bishop of Jesus, camouflaging her to look like the Whore of Babylon, and all on the church's funds. In the hands of some men, natural God-made beauty is turned into a false idol. I said haven't you found yourself a good thing! Oh I know, I said. Behind all the downfalls of good great women stands an attractive man with presents and lies and private notions. Not a humpback, not a big-eared plain man or a serious settled type, but a jazzy, good-looking oily one with voice of a dove and tongue of a serpent . . .

You are so plainly after the Bishopric, Ruby Drew, Canaan

Johnson said, squinching his lashy eyes and fixing them right on me, that you are willing to libel someone. And to that I said, Bishopric or not, I have been instructed by the Lord to give up my housecleaning and return to the Church—to the Light of the World Holiness Church to be exact. The Lord and I are going to air out that church. You libel that.

Canaan Johnson became suddenly very crooked-looking and said with his oily mouth, Well Mrs. Airwick we'll see how far you'll go. Savata sat sparkling in her coat and said nothing. I rose and with the air of a Bishop removed myself from that house.

Before Savata my fair sister and Canaan Johnson knew it, they had themselves a lawsuit on their hands. I sued for the Bishopric and for everything that went with it, the house in Brooklyn complete with rugs and slip covers, the lamb's wool coat and the diamond cluster. As they were purchased with the Light of the World Holiness Church's funds, they belonged to it, was my plea. The congregation, one big choir that called "Bishop Savata!" like a bunch of birds on a fence, was seated in the courthouse at the proceedings, and they did not take more than one half hour to outdo me. Although I sat on the stand barefooted and all my God's darkness vested in a Bishop's robe and preached an exposé against possessions in the Lord's name that rocked that courthouse—I said that the Lord don't have no checking account, owns no precious stones, displays nothing but a heart of gold and the natural hair of his head which was like the wool of the lamb, just as nature made it—it fell upon deaf ears. I said that the Prince of Darkness had come to roost on the steeple of the L.O.W.H.C. But do you think one bit that they cared? They hurrayed Canaan Johnson. They didn't any longer know a good sermon from a bad, Savata and her business manager had corroded them to see only the beauty that perisheth, not the God's lasting truth. They hurrayed Savata and hurrayed Canaan Johnson like some King and Queen. Naturally they won, the court handed down a verdict in their favor. I even had to pay the lawsuit expenses. Well, I went on ahousecleaning, as you know.

Time passed, and you can guess what came to pass . . . just what anybody in their right mind would expect. It only takes time. Mr. Canaan Johnson took his leave one day, without one note or how-do-you-do. Savata sent for me and I found her in tears and a nervous pout. My first question was what did he get, where is the coat and where is the cluster of diamonds? Savata thanked God that she had locked the lamb's wool coat in her cedar-lined closet to keep the moths out of it. But Canaan Johnson got away with the diamonds, naturally. Never mind, I smoothed her, let the Devil take the Devil's own; you got the coat out of it. But when we went to her cedar-lined closet and unlocked it what did we find but a regular moth picnic, they had made a feast of the coat. What they left wasn't enough lamb's wool to cover a baldheaded man. I could have said hoard thou not up treasures on earth but I kept my tongue, thank you Jesus.

Savata had her nervous breakdown and gave two full weeks to it. After it was over, she was meek as a lamb. We deeded the house in Brooklyn over to the old folks of the Light of the World Holiness Church and it was called the House of the Saints. But the church membership fell off to a handful of the faithful. Most wouldn't stay after Canaan and Savata were gone. They went on off and formed them a glamour church of their own. I got out my preaching papers and took over, preparing to build that church up again, this time on solid ground.

Oh I could have made Savata my fair sister eat crow and plenty of it, but I kept God's mercy and suggested with charity, as becomes a Bishop, that Savata take over my housecleaning jobs for a while until she could get herself straight. That could be her penance.

And that's why I've come by here to speak to you, to tell you that Savata my fair sister will be replacing me every Thursday from now on. I figure while she's on her knees in her repentance she might as well bend over and move around a little with a mopping rag in her hand; and while she's walking the floor astudying her sins, it will do her no harm to push along a vacuum cleaner ahead of herself. Her repentance, joined to practical uses, will therefore earn back a little of what her wickedness lost. In that way, sin can pay a little—and it will show Savata how little: $1.10 an hour, to be exact.

So thank you for listening to my story that has introduced you to Savata, my fair sister and your new cleaning woman. And thank you Jesus.

The Faces of Blood Kindred

James came to stay in his cousin's house when his mother was taken to the hospital with arthritis. The boys were both fourteen. James was blond and faintly harelipped, and he stuttered. His cousin was brown and shy. They had not much in common beyond their mysterious cousinhood, a bond of nature which they instinctively respected; though James mocked his cousin's habits, complained that he worried too much about things and was afraid of adventure. James owned and loved a flock of bantams, fought the cocks secretly, and his pockets jingled with tin cockspurs. His hands even had pecked places on them from fighting cocks in Mexican town.

James' father had run away to St. Louis some years ago, and his mother Macel had gone to work as a seamstress in a dress factory in the city of Houston. Macel was blond and gay and good-natured, though the cousin's mother told his father that she had the Ganchion spitfire in her and had run her husband away and now was suffering for it with arthritis. When they went to the hospital to see Aunt Macel, the cousin looked at her hands drawn like pale claws against her breast and her stiffened legs braced down in splints. The cousin, white with commiseration, stood against the wall and gazed at her and saw her being tortured for abusing his uncle and driving him away from home and from his cousin James. James, when taken along by force, would stand at his mother's bedside and stare at her with a look of careless resignation. When she asked him questions he stammered incoherent answers.

James was this mysterious, wandering boy. He loved the woods at the edge of his cousin's neighborhood and would spend whole days there while his aunt called and searched for him by telephone. She would call the grandmother's house, talk to a number of little grandchildren who passed the phone from one to another and finally to the deaf old grandmother who could scarcely understand a word. But James was not there and no one had seen him. Once Fay, one of the young aunts living in the grandmother's house, called at midnight to say they had just discovered James sleeping under the fig trees in the back yard. Jock her husband had almost shot him before he had called out his name. Years later, when the cousin was in high school, he heard talk between his mother and father about Fay's hiding in the very same place while the police looked for her in the house—why, he did not know. At any rate, they had not found her.

He was a wild country boy brought to live in the city of Houston when his parents moved there from a little town down the road south. He said he wanted to be a cowboy, but it was too late for that; still, he wore boots and spurs. He hated the city, the schools, played away almost daily. The cousin admired James, thought him a daring hero. When he listened to his mother and father quarrel over James at night after they had gone to bed, his tenderness for him grew and grew. "He's like all the rest of them," his mother accused his father.

"They are my folks," the cousin's father said with dignity. "Macel is my sister."

"Then let some of the other folks take care of James. Let Fay. I simply cannot handle him."

Poor James, the cousin thought, poor homeless James. He has no friend but me.

One afternoon James suggested they go to see some Cornish fighting cocks on a farm at the edge of the city. The cousin did not tell his mother and they stole away against his conscience. They hitchhiked to the farm out on the highway to Conroe, and there was a rooster-like man sitting barefooted in a little shotgun house. He had rooster feet, thin and with spread-out toes, and feathery hair. His wife was fat and loose and was barefooted, too. She objected to the cousin being there and said, "Chuck, you'll get yourself in trouble." But Chuck asked the cousins to come out to his chicken yard to see his Cornish cocks.

In a pen were the brilliant birds, each in its own coop, some with white scars about their jewel eyes. Stretching out beyond the chicken pen was the flat, rainy marshland of South Texas over which a web of gray mist hung. The sad feeling of after-rain engulfed the cousin and, mixed with the sense of evil because of the fighting cocks and his guilt at having left home secretly, made him feel speechless and afraid. He would not go in the pen but stood outside and watched James and Chuck spar with the cocks and heard Chuck speak of their prowess. Then the cousin heard James ask the price of a big blue cock with stars on its breast. "Fifteen dollars," Chuck said, "and worth a lots more. He fights like a fiend." To the cousin's astonishment he heard James say he would take the blue one, and he saw him take some bills from his pocket and separate fifteen single ones. When they left they heard Chuck and his wife quarreling in the little house.

They went on away to the highway to thumb a ride, and James tucked the blue cock inside his lumberjacket and spoke very quietly to him with his stuttering lips against the cock's blinking and magnificent ruby eye.

"But where will we keep him?" the cousin asked. "We can't at my house."

"I know a place," James said. "This Cornish will make a lot of money."

"But I'm afraid," the cousin said.

"You're always 'f-f-fraid," James said with a tender, mocking smile. And then he whispered something else to the black tip that stuck out from his jacket like a spur of ebony.

A pickup truck stopped for them shortly and took them straight to the Houston Heights where James said they would get out. James said they were going to their grandmother's house.

Their grandmother and grandfather had moved to the city, into a big rotten house, from the railroad town of Palestine, Texas. They had brought a family of seven grown children and the married children's children. In time, the grandfather had vanished and no one seemed to care where. The house was like a big boarding house, people in every room, the grandmother rocking, deaf and humped and shriveled, in the dining room. There was the smell of mustiness all through the house, exactly the way the grandmother smelled. In the back yard were some fig trees dripping with purple figs, and under the trees was a secret place, a damp and musky cove. It was a hideaway known to the children of the house, to the blackbirds after the figs, and to the cats stalking the birds. James told his cousin that this was the place to hide with the Cornish cock. He told the cock that he would have to be quiet for one night and made a chucking sound to him.

The cousins arrived at the grandmother's house with its sagging wooden front porch and its curtainless windows where some of the shades were pulled down. The front door was always open and the screen door sagged half-open. In the dirt front yard, which was damp and where cans and papers were strewn, two of the grandchildren sat quietly together: they were Jack and Little Sister whose mother was divorced and living there with her mother. They seemed special to the cousin because they were Catholics and had that strangeness about them. Their father had insisted that they be brought up in his church, though he had run away and left them in it long ago; and now they seemed to the cousin to have been abandoned in it and could never change back. No one would take them to Mass, and if a priest appeared on the sidewalk, someone in the house would rush out and snatch at the children or gather them away and shout at the priest to mind his own business and go away, as if he were a kidnapper.

"Our mother is sick in bed," Jack said to James and the cousin as they passed him and Little Sister in the yard. Their mother, Beatrice, was a delicate and wild woman who could not find her way with men, and later, when the cousin was in college, she took her life. Not long after, Little Sister was killed in an automobile crash—it was said she was running away to Baton Rouge, Louisiana, to get married to a Catholic gambler. But Jack went on his way somewhere in the world, and the cousin never saw him again. Years later he heard that Jack had gone to a Trappist Monastery away in the North, but no one knew for sure. James grumbled at Jack and Little Sister and whispered, "If-f-f you tell anybody we were here, then a bear will come tonight and e-e-*eat* you up in bed." The two little alien Catholics, alone in a churchless house, looked sadly and silently at James and the cousin. They were constantly together and the cousin thought how they protected each other, asked for nothing in their orphan's world; they were not afraid. "My pore little Cathlicks," the grandmother would sometimes say over them when she saw them sleeping together on the sleeping-porch, as if they were cursed.

James and the cousin went around the house and into the back yard. Now it was almost dark. They crept stealthily, James with the Cornish cock nestled under his lumberjack. Once it cawed. Then James hushed it by stroking its neck and whispering to it.

Under the fig trees, in the cloying sweetness of the ripe fruit, James uncovered the Cornish cock. He pulled a fig and ate a bite of it, then gave a taste of it to the cock who snapped it fiercely. Before the cousins knew it he had leapt to the ground and, as if he were on springs, bounced up into a fig tree. The Cornish cock began at once to eat the figs. Jim murmured an oath and shook the tree. Figs fat and wet fell upon him and the cousin.

"Stop!" the cousin whispered. "You'll ruin Granny's figs."

"Shut up." James scowled. "You're always 'f-f-fraid."

The cousin picked up a rock from the ground and threw it into the tree. He must have hurled it with great force, greater than he knew he possessed, for in a flash there shuddered at his feet the dark leafy bunch of the Cornish cock. In a moment the feathers were still.

"I didn't mean to, I didn't mean to!" the cousin gasped in horror, and he backed farther and farther away, beyond the deep shadows of the fig trees. Standing away, he saw in the dark luscious grove the figure of James fall to the ground and kneel over his Cornish cock and clasp the tousled mass like a lover's head. He heard him sob softly; and the cousin backed away in anguish.

As he passed the curtainless windows of the dining room where the light was now on, he saw his old grandmother hunched in her chair, one leg folded under her, rocking gently and staring at nothing; and she seemed to him at that moment to be bearing the sorrow of everything—in her house, under the fig trees, in all the world. And then he heard the soft cries of Beatrice from her mysterious room, "Somebody help me, somebody go bring me a drink of water." He went on, past the chaos of the sleeping-porch that had so many beds and cots in it—for Beatrice's two children the little Catholics, for Fay's two, for his grandmother, for his grandfather who would not stay home, for Fay and for Jock the young seaman, her third husband, with tattoos and still wearing his sailor pants. He thought of Jock who cursed before everybody, was restless, would come and go or sprawl on the bed he and Fay slept in on the sleeping-porch with all the rest; and he remembered when he had stayed overnight in this house once how he had heard what he thought was Jock beating Fay in the night, crying out to her and panting, "you f . . ."; how Jock the sailor would lie on the bed in the daytime smoking and reading from a storage of battered *Western Stories* and *Romance Stories* magazines that were strewn under the bed, while Fay worked at the Palais Royale in town selling ladies' ready-to-wear, and the voice of Beatrice suddenly calling overall, "Somebody! Please help me, I am so sick." Once the cousin had gone into her sad room when no one else would and she had pled, startled to see him there, and with a stark gray face scarred by the delicate white cleft of her lip, "Please help your Aunt Bea get a little ease from this headache; reach under the mattress—don't tell anybody—your Aunt Bea has to have some rest from this pain—reach right yonder under the mattress and give her that little bottle. That's it. This is our secret, and you mustn't ever tell a soul." Within five years she was to die, and why should this beautiful Beatrice have to lie in a rest home, alone and none of her family ever coming to see her, until the home sent a message that she was dead? But he thought, hearing of her death, that if he had secretly helped ease her suffering, he had that to know, without ever telling—until he heard them say that she had died from taking too many pills from a hidden bottle.

The cousin walked away from the grandmother's house and went the long way home under the fresh evening sky, his fingers sticky with fig musk, leaving James and the dead cock under the fig trees. If he could one day save all his kindred from pain or help them to some hope! "I will, I will!" he promised. But what were they paying penance for? What was their wrong? Later he knew it bore the ancient name of lust. And as he walked on he saw, like a sparkling stone hurling toward him over the Natural Gas Reservoir, the first star break the heavens—who cast it?—and he wished he might die by it. When he approached the back door of his house, there was the benevolent figure of his mother in the kitchen fixing supper and he wondered how he would be able to tell her and his father where he had been and what had happened to James. "We went to the woods," he cried, "and James ran away." Later that night when James did not come back, his father telephoned the grandmother's house. But no one there had seen him.

The cousin cried himself to sleep that night, lonely and guilty, grieving for much more than he knew, but believing, in that faithful way of children, that in time he might know what it all meant, and that it was a matter of waiting, confused and watchful, until it came clear, as so much of everything promised to, in long time; and he dreamt of a blue rooster with stars on its breast sitting in a tree of bitter figs, crowing a doom of suffering over the house of his kinfolks.

James stayed away for three days and nights; and on the third night they had a long-distance call from James' father in St. Louis, saying that James had come there dirty and tired and stuttering. They had not seen each other for seven years.

Long later the cousin was in a large Midwestern city where some honor was being shown him. Suddenly in the crowded hall a face emerged from the gathering of strangers and moved toward him. It seemed the image of all his blood kin: was it that shadow-face that tracked and haunted him? It was James' face, and at that glance there glimmered over it some dreamlike umbrageous distortion of those long-ago boy's features, as if the cousin saw that face through a pane of colored glass or through currents of time that had deepened over it as it had sunk into its inheritance.

There was something James had to say, it was on his face; but what it was the cousin never knew, for someone pulled him round, his back to James, to shake his hand and congratulate him—someone of distinction. When he finally turned, heavy as stone, as if he were turning to look back into the face of his own secret sorrow, James was gone; and the cousins never met again.

But the look upon James' face that moment that night in a strange city where the cousin had come to passing recognition and had found a transient homage, bore the haunting question of ancestry; and though he thought he had at last found and cleared for himself something of identity, a particle of answer in the face of the world, had he set anything at peace, answered any speechless question, atoned for the blind failing, the outrage and the pain on the face of his blood kindred? That glance, struck like a blow against ancestral countenance, had left a scar of resemblance, ancient and unchanging through the generations, on the faces of the grandmother, of the aunts, the cousins, his own father and his father's father; and would mark his own face longer than the stamp of any stranger's honor that would change nothing.

Old Wildwood

On a soft morning in May, at the American Express in Rome, the grandson was handed a letter; and high up on the Spanish Steps he sat alone and opened the letter and read its news. It was in his mother's hand:

"Well, your grandaddy died two days ago and we had his funeral in the house in Charity. There were so many flowers, roses and gladiolas and every other kind, that the front porch was filled with them, twas a sight to see. Then we took him to the graveyard where all the rest are buried and added his grave, one more, to the rest.

"At the graveyard your father suddenly walked out and stood and said the Lord's Prayer over his daddy's grave, as none of the Methodists in the family would hear a Catholic priest say a Catholic prayer, nor the Catholics in the family allow a Methodist one; and your grandaddy was going to be left in his grave without one holy word of any kind. But both were there, priest and preacher, and I said what a shame that your poor old daddy has to go to earth without even 'Abide with Me' sung by a soloist. His own begotten children marrying without conscience into this church and that, confounding their children as to the nature of God, caused it all, and there it was to see, clear and shameful, at the graveyard. Then all of a sudden your two great aunts, my mother's and your grandmother's sweet old sisters, Ruby and Saxon Thompson, one blind and the other of such strutted ankles from Bright's Disease as could barely toddle, started singing 'Just As I Am Without One Plea,' and many joined in, it was so sweet and so sad and so peaceful to hear. Then we all walked away and left your grandaddy in his grave."

The grandson lifted his eyes from the letter and they saw an ancient foreign city of stone. So an old lost grandfather, an old man of timber, had left the world. He folded the letter and put it in his pocket. Then he leaned back and settled upon the pocked stone of the worn steps, supporting himself upon the opened palm of his hand. He rested a little, holding the letter, thinking how clear pictures of what had troubled his mind always came to him in some sudden, quiet ease of resting. He considered, as a man resting on stone, his grandfather.

Yes, he thought, the little old grandfather had the animal grace and solitary air of an old mariner about him, though he was a lumberman and purely of earth. His left leg was shorter than his right, and the left foot had some flaw in it that caused the shoe on it to curl upwards. The last time the grandson had seen his grandfather was the summer day when, home on leave from the Navy, and twenty-one, he had come out into the back yard in his shining officer's uniform to find his grandfather sitting there snowy-headed and holding his cap in his hand. Grandfather and grandson had embraced and the grandfather had wept. How so few years had changed him, the grandson had thought that afternoon: so little time had whitened his head and brought him to quick tears: and the grandson heard in his head the words of a long time back, spoken to him by his grandfather that night in Galveston, "Go over into Missi'ppi one day and see can you find your kinfolks . . ."

Where had the grandfather come from, that summer afternoon? Where had he been all these years? The grandson had scarcely thought of him. And now, suddenly, on that summer day of leave, he had heard his mother call to his father, "Your *daddy's* here," with an intonation of shame; and then his mother had come into his room and said, "Son, your grandaddy's here. Go out in the back yard and see your grandaddy."

When he had put on his uniform and stepped into the yard, there he saw the white-headed little man sitting on the bench. And there, resting on the grass and lying a little on its side as though it were a separate being, curled and dwarfed, was his grandfather's crooked foot, old disastrous companion.

The grandfather was an idler and had been run away from home, it was said, by his wife and children time and time again, and the last time for good; and where did he live and what did he do? Later, on the day of his visit and after he had gone away, the grandson's mother had confessed that she knew her husband went secretly to see his father somewhere in the city and to give him money the family had to do without. It was in a shabby little hotel on a street of houses of women and saloons that his father and his grandfather met and talked, father and son.

As he sat with his grandfather in the yard on the white bench under the camphor tree that summer, and now on this alien stone, the grandson remembered that the first time he had known his grandfather was on the trip to Galveston where they went to fish—the grandson was fourteen—and how lonesome he was there with this little old graying limping stranger who was his grandfather and who was wild somewhere that the grandson could not surmise, only fear. Who was this man tied to him by blood through his father and who, though he strongly resembled his father, seemed an alien, not even a friend. The grandfather had sat on the rocks and drunk whiskey while the grandson fished; and though he did not talk much, the grandson felt that there was a constant toil of figuring going on in the old man as he looked out over the brown Gulf water, his feet bare and his shoes on the rock, one crooked one by one good one. On the rock the boy gazed at the bad foot for a long, long time, more often than he watched the fishing line, as though the foot on the rock might be some odd creature he had brought up from the water and left on the rock to perish in the sun. At night he watched it too, curled on the cot in the moonlight as his grandfather slept, so that he came to know it well on both rock and cot and to think of it as a special kind of being in itself. There on the rock, as on the cot, the bad foot was the very naked shape of the shoe that concealed it. It seemed lifeless there on the rock, it was turned inwards toward the good foot as though to ask for pity from it or to caricature it. The good foot seemed proud and aloof and disdainful, virile and perfectly shaped.

On the rock, the grandfather was like a man of the sea, the

grandson thought, like a fisherman or a boat captain. His large Roman head with its bulging forehead characteristic of his children shone in the sun; and his wide face was too large for his small and rather delicate body, lending him a strangely noble bearing, classic and Bacchian. There was something deeply kind and tender in this old gentleman grandfather barefooted on the rock, drinking whiskey from the bottle. The grandson felt the man was often at the point of speaking to him of some serious thing but drank it all away again out of timidity or respect.

Each night they straggled back to their room in a cheap Gulf-front cabin full of flies and sand, and the grandson would help his grandfather into his cot where he would immediately fall to sleep. Then the grandson would lie for a long time watching his grandfather breathe, his graying curly hair tousled over his strutted forehead, and watching the sad foot that sometimes flinched on the sheet with fatigue, for it was a weak foot, he thought. Considering this man before him, the grandson thought how he might be a man of wood, grown in a wilderness of trees, as rude and native and unblazed as a wildwood tree. He held some wilderness in him, the very sap and seed of it. Then, half fearing the man, the grandson would fall asleep, with the thought and the image of the blighted foot worrying him. He was always afraid of his grandfather, no doubt because of the whiskey, but certainly for deeper, more mysterious reasons which he could not find out in this man who was yet so respectful to him.

One night after the grandfather had been drinking on the rock all day, he had drunk some more in the cabin and finally, sitting on the side of his cot, he had found the words he had to say to the grandson. He had spoken to him clearly and quietly and in such a kind of flowing song that the words might have been given him by another voice whispering him what to say.

"We all lived in Missi'ppi," was the way he began, quietly, to speak. "And in those days wasn't much there, only sawmills and wildwoods of good rich timber, uncut and unmarked, and lots of good Nigras to help with everything, wide airy houses and broad fields. It all seems now such a good day and time, though we didn't count it for much then. Your granny and I moved over out of Missi'ppi and into Texas, from one little mill town to another, me blazing timber and then cutting it, counting it in the railroad cars, your granny taking a new baby each time, seems like, but the same baby buggy for each—if we'd have named our children after the counties they were borned in, all twelve of them, counting the one that died in Conroe, you'd have a muster roll of half the counties of Texas—all borned in Texas; but not a one ever went back to Missi'ppi, nor cared. Twas all wildwood then, son, but so soon gone.

"I had such man's strength then, the kind that first my grandfather broke wilderness with into trail and clearing, hewed houses and towns out of timber with, the kind his grandsons used to break the rest. Why I fathered twelve children in the state of Texas and fed them on sweet milk and kidney beans and light bread and working twelve hours a day—mill and railroad—working Nigras and working myself and raising a family of barefooted towheads chasing the chickens and climbing the trees and carrying water, playing tree tag in the dirt yard stained with mulberries. Your granny wasn't deaf then, had better hearing than most, could hear the boll weevils in the cotton, could listen that well. We all slept all over the house, beds never made, always a baby squalling in the kitchen while your granny cooked, or eating dirt where it sat in the shade as your granny did the washing in the washpot on the fire with Nigras helping and singing, or riding the hip of one of the big girls or boys . . . my children grew up on each other's hips and you could never tell it now the way they live and treat each other.

"I didn't have any schooling, but my grandfather was a schoolteacher and broke clearing and built a log schoolhouse and taught in it—it still stands, I hear tell, in Tupolo—and lived to start a university in Stockton, Missi'ppi; was a Peabody and the Peabodys still live all over Missi'ppi, go in there and you'll find Peabodys all over Missi'ppi. You know there's a big bridge of steel over the Missi'ppi River at Meridian; that's a Peabody, kin to me and kin to you. Another one, John Bell, built a highway clean to the Louisiana line and starting at Jackson; that's some of your kinfolks, old John Bell, such a fine singing man, a good voice and pure black-headed Irishman with his temper in his eyes. Called him Cousin Jack, he was adopted, and just here in Galveston, to tell you the truth, I've been wondering again who from; I've wondered often about John Bell all these years, studied him time and again. When I came he was already in our family, running with the other children in the yard, seems like, when I first saw him, and we all called him Cousin Jack, and of all my family, brother and sister and even my own children, John Bell was the best friend ever in this world to me. Aw, John Bell's been heavy on my mind—John Bell! He was one to go to. Cousin Jack was not ascared of anything, brave everywhere he went and not ascared of hard work, spit on his hands and went right in. Went to work at fourteen and helped the family. Was a jolly man and full of some of the devil, too, and we raised a ruckus on Saturday nights when we was young men together, we'd dance till midnight, court the girls on the way home and come on home ourselves singing and in great spirits. John Bell! Fishing and singing on the river with a pint of bourbon in our hip pocket and a breath of it on the bait for good luck. But something always a little sad about John Bell, have never known what it could be. Maybe it was his being adopted. He knew that; they told him. But it was more than that. Then he married Nellie Clayton, your granny's niece, and I have never seen him again. He built a highway clean through the state of Missi'ppi and I always knew he would amount to something. Died in 1921, and now his children are all up and grown in Missi'ppi. They are some of the ones to look for. Find the Bells.

"Time came when all the tree country of East Texas was cut, seemed like no timber left, and new ways and new mills. I brought all my family to Houston, to work for the Southern Pacific. Some was married and even had babies of their own, but we stayed together, the whole kit and kaboodle of us, all around your granny. In the city of Houston we found one big old house and all lived in it. Then the family began to sunder apart, seemed like, with some going away to marry and then coming home again bringing husband or wife. I stayed away from home as much as I could, to have some peace from all the clamoring among my children. I never understood my children, son, could never make them out, my own children; children coming in and going out, half their children living there with this new husband and that, and the old husbands coming back to make a fuss, and one, Grace's, just staying on there, moved in and wouldn't ever leave, is still there to this day; and children from all husbands and wives playing all together in that house, with your granny deaf as a doornail and calling out to the children to mind, and wanting care, but would never leave and never will, she'll die in that house with all of them around her, abusing her, too, neither child nor grandchild minding her. I just left, son, and went to live in a boarding house. I'd go home on Sundays and on Easters and on Christmas, but not to stay. There's a time when a person can't help anything any more, anything. Still, they would come to me, one or another of my sons and daughters, but not to see how I was or to bring me anything, twas to borrow money from me. They never knew that I had lost my job with the S.P. because I drank a little whiskey.

"And I never went to any church, son, but I'm fifty years of age and I believe in the living God and practice the Golden Rule and I hope the Lord'll save me from my sins. But I never had anybody to go to, for help or comfort, and I want you to know your father didn't either, never had anybody to go to. But I want you to know you do, and I will tell you who and where so you will always know. I don't want you ever to know what it is not to have anybody to go to.

"So when you get to be a young man I hope you'll go over into Missi'ppi and see can you find your blood kinfolks. Tell them your grandaddy sent you there. Haven't been over there myself for thirty years, kept meaning to but just never did. Now I guess I never will. But you go, and when you go, tell them you are a Peabody's grandson. They're all there, all over there, all over Missi'ppi; look for the Peabodys and for the Claytons and look for the Bells . . ."

After the grandfather had finished his story, he sat still on his cot, looking down as if he might be regarding his bare crooked foot. The grandson did not speak or ask a question but he lay quietly thinking about it all, how melancholy and grand the history of relations was. Then, in a while, he heard his grandfather get up softly, put on his crooked shoe and the good one, and go out, thinking he was asleep. He has gone to find him John Bell, the grandson thought. The creaking of his bad shoe and the rhythm of his limp seemed to the grandson to repeat his grandfather's words: Peabodys and the Claytons and the Bells.

The grandson did not sleep while his grandfather was gone. He was afraid, for the tides of the Gulf were swelling against the sea wall below the cabin; yet he thought how he no longer feared his grandfather, for now that he had spoken to him so quietly and with such love he felt he was something of his own. He loved his grandfather. Yet now that he had been brought to love what he had feared, he was cruelly left alone in the whole world with this love, it seemed, and was that the way love worked?—with the unknown waters swelling and falling close to the bed where he lay with the loving story haunting him? There was so much more to it all, to the life of men and women, than he had known before he came to Galveston just to fish with his grandfather, so much in just a man barefooted on a rock and drinking whiskey in the sun, silent and dangerous and kin to him. And then the man had spoken and made a bond between them and brought a kind of nobility of forest, something like a shelter of grandness of trees over it all. The tree country! The grandson belonged to an old, illustrious bunch of people of timber with names he could now name, all a busy, honorable and worthy company of wilderness breakers and forest blazers, bridge builders and road makers, and teachers, Claytons and Peabodys and Bells, and the grandfather belonged to them, too, and it was he who had brought all the others home to him, his grandson. Yet the grandfather seemed an orphan. And now for the first time, the grandson felt the deep, free sadness of orphanage; and he knew he was orphaned, too. That was the cruel gift of his grandfather, he thought. The crooked foot! John Bell!

In this loneliness he knew, at some border where land turned into endless water, he felt himself to be the only one alive in this moment—where were all the rest?—in a land called Mississippi, called Texas, where? He was alone to do what he could do with it all and oh what to do would be some daring thing, told or performed on some shore where two ancient elements met, land and water, and touched each other and caused some violence of kinship between two orphans, and with heartbreak in it. What to do would have the quiet, promising dangerousness of his grandfather on the rock in it, it would have the grave and epic tone of his grandfather's ultimate telling on the side of the cot under one light globe in a mist of shoreflies in a sandy transient roof of revelation while the tide washed at the very feet of teller and listener. And what to do would have the feeling of myth and mystery that he felt as he had listened, as though when he listened he were a rock and the story he heard was water swelling and washing over generations and falling again, like the waters over the rock when the tide came in.

Suddenly he heard footsteps, and when the door opened quietly he saw his grandfather and a woman behind him. They came in the room and the woman whispered, "You didn't tell me that a kid was here."

"He's asleep, John Bell," the grandfather whispered.

Something began between the two, between the grandfather and the woman, and the grandson feigned sleep. But he watched through the lashes of his half-closed eyes as through an ambush of grass the odd grace of his grandfather struggling with the woman with whom he seemed to be swimming through water, and he heard his grandfather's low growl like a fierce dog on the cot, and he saw his grandfather's devil's foot treading and gently kicking, bare in the air, so close to him that he could have reached out to touch it. And then he knew that the foot had a very special beauty and grace of moment, a lovely secret performance hidden in it that had seemed a shame on his person and a flaw upon the rock. It had something, even, of a bird's movements in it. It was the crooked foot that was the source and the meaning of the strange and lovely and somehow delicate disaster on the bed; and it was that shape and movement that the grandson took for his own to remember.

John Bell!

The two people drank out of a bottle without saying a word, but they were celebrating something they had come through, as if they had succeeded in swimming, with each other's help, a laborious dangerous distance; and then they rose to leave the room together. But at the door, the grandfather called softly as he lifted the bottle once more to his mouth, "For John Bell . . . ," and the name rang deeply over the dark room like the tone of a bell upon the sea.

When they were gone, the grandson rose and looked out the window and saw the water with a horned moon over it and smelled the limey odors of shrimp, saw the delicate swaying starry lights of fishing boats; and there in the clear light of the moon he saw the rock he and his grandfather fished on. The tide was climbing over it and slipping back off it as if to cover it with a sighing embrace, like a body, as if to pull the rock, for a swelling moment, to its soft and caressing bosom of water; and there was a secret bathing of tenderness over the very world like a dark rock washed over with moonlit sea water and whiskey and tenderness and the mysteriousness of a grandfather, of an old story, an old ancestor of whom the grandson was afraid again. Now the grandfather seemed to the grandson to have been some old sea-being risen out of the waters to sit on a rock and to tell a tale in a stranger's room, and disappear. Would he ever come again to fish on the rock in the Gulf and to snore on the cot in the cabin? But as he looked at the world of rock and tide and moon, in the grandson's head the words of a pioneer sounded, quiet and plaintive and urgent: Go over into Missi'ppi when you get to be a young man and see can you find your kinfolks, son. Look for the Claytons and look for the Peabodys and look for the Bells, all in there, all over Missi'ppi . . . And the bell-rung deepness of a name called sounded in the dark room.

John Bell!

There in the room, even then, alone and with the wild lovely world he knew, tidewater and moonlight tenderly tormenting the rock outside, and inside the astonishing delicate performance tormenting the room, and the shape of the foot on both room and rock, the grandson thought how he would do, in his time, some work to bring about through an enduring rock-silence a secret performance with something, some rock-force, some tide-force, some lovely, hearty, fine wildwood wildwater thing always living in him through his ancestry and now brought to sense in him, that old gamy wilderness bequeathed him; how shaggy-headed, crooked-footed perfection would be what he would work for, some marvelous, reckless and imperfect loveliness, proclaiming about the ways of men in the world and all that befell them, all that glorified, all that damned them, clearing and covering over and clearing again, on and on and on.

He went back to his cot and lay upon his young back. Not to go to sleep! but to stay awake with it all, whatever, whatever it was, keeping the wilderness awake in this and many more rooms, breathing sea-wind and pinesap. Because—now he felt sure—the thing to do about it all and with it all would be in some performance of the senses after long silence and waiting—of the hair that would grow upon his chest like grass and of the nipples of his breast, of the wildwood in his seed and the sappy sweat of the crease of his loins, of the saltwater of his tears, the spit on his palms, the blistering of the blazer's ax-handle, all mortal stuff. To keep wilderness awake and wild and never sleeping, in many rooms in many places was his plan in Galveston, and the torment that lay ahead for him would come, and it would hold him wakeful through nights of bitter desire for more than he could ever name, but for some gentle, lovely and disastrous heartbreak of men and women in this world. And in that room that held the history of his grandfather, the little poem of his forebears and the gesture of the now beautiful swimming and soaring crooked foot, he knew for himself that there would be, or he would make them, secret rooms in his life holding, like a gymnasium, the odors of mortal exertion, of desperate tournament, a violent contest, a hardy, laborious chopping, manual and physical and involving the strength in his blistering hands and the muscles of his heaving back, all the blazer's work, the pioneer's blazing hand! Or places upon rocks of silence where an enigma lay in the sun, dry and orphaned and moribund until some blessed tide eventually rose and caressed it and took it to its breast as if to whisper, "Belong to me before I slide away," and what was silent and half-dead roused and showed its secret performance: that seemed to be the whole history of everything, the secret, possible performance in everything that was sliding, sliding away.

Finally, his breast aching and its secret that lived there unperformed, but with the trembling of some enormous coming thrill, the distant disclosure of some vision, even, of some glimmering company of humanity of his yearning with whom to perform some daring, lovely, heartbroken and disastrous history; and with terror of listener and sadness of teller, the grandson fell alone to sleep and never heard his grandfather come back to his cot, that night in Galveston.

Now they had buried the grandfather. Bury the good man of wilderness, he thought; bury in Texas dirt the crooked foot that never walked again on the ground of Missi'ppi where mine has never been set. And find him John Bell in the next world.

His hand upon which he had rested was aching and he relieved it of his weight and sat upon the solid slab of ancient Travertine stone. There, engraved in the palm of the hand he had leaned on, was the very mark and grain of the stone, as though his hand were stone. He would not have a hand of stone! He would carry a hand that could labor wood and build a house, trouble dirt and lay a highway, and blaze a trail through leaf and bramble; and a hand that could rot like wood and fall into dust.

And then the grandson thought how all the style and works of stone had so deeply troubled him in this ancient city, and how he had not clearly known until now that he loved wood best and belonged by his very secret woodsman's nature to old wildwood.

The Moss Rose

For Elisabeth Schnack

"Portulaca," the Third Avenue man said to him at the door of his shop when he asked the name of what he thought was a box of moss-rose plants for sale on the sidewalk.

"Aren't they moss roses?" he asked.

"Portulaca," the man said.

"Do they have orange and yellow and crimson blossoms?"

"That's right," the man said.

"And they aren't moss roses?"

"Portulaca," he said again.

He went on up Third Avenue saying the word to himself as he walked, so as not to forget it. *Portulaca.* "I guess that's what they call them up here," he said to himself.

He had grown up with them—*moss roses*—always in some flower bed, by a grave, by a pump where the ground was moist, in a hanging kettle on a porch. They were a part of another landscape, a flower illustration of many remembered scenes in another country. Here they were, on Third Avenue in New York City. Or were they the same—could they be? Oh, he thought, I guess people up here know and have this common little flower—why shouldn't they? But such a name as they've given it! *Portulaca.*

The El was quiet, the train was gone. Though the complicated and permanent-looking structure was there, soon it would be torn down. Third Avenue was quieter. People who had lived for years with the noise of the El interrupting their sleep and conversation and who had learned naturally to scream above it, still spoke in Third Avenue voices; but the train, the reason, was gone.

The children yelled in resounding voices on the sidewalks, though the noise over which they yelled had vanished; and he wondered if ever their voices would soften or modulate. No, they would go on through life yelling with powerful voices developed against the monster whose tracks they had been bred alongside. It would be the El going on through them; it was not really destroyed. They seemed the children of the El, and the tracks and platform had bred children who looked a little like them, curiously, as their parents did, so that their faces, bearing, physiognomy reflected the resisted force—as people who live in constant wind or on stony landscapes reflect the natural phenomenon which opposes them in daily life.

These Third Avenue people had the same vagabond, noisy air and quality that the ramshackle train and platform symbolized. The El had created a genus of humanity, almost as the plow had shaped his own; they looked as if they had performed some laborious job with the El, as an instrument of their daily bread, although it did not feed them or reward them with anything but noise and dirt. Still it shaped a style of life for them. Over the years a race had adapted itself to an inhuman presence and had learned, almost as if by imitating or mimicking it, a mode of life that enabled them to absorb it into their daily life, and to endure. They were a kind of grimly happy, sailorlike, reckless people, carefree, poor, tough and loud-mouthed, big-throated and hoarse-voiced. The old, who had lived so long with it, seemed very tired by it. They sat in their straight chairs on the sidewalks or on the steps of their buildings and conversed in loud voices—a gypsy breed with their Third Avenue dog, again his own special breed: a serene, somewhat sad, seasoned hound, resigned, fearless and friendly.

Portulaca, he said, walking along. Little moss rose. Well, he was homesick. But wasn't everyone? he consoled himself. By a certain time something, some structure, in every life is gone, and becomes a memory. But it has caused something: a change, an attitude, an aspect. It is the effect of what was, he thought, going on, that is the long-lastingness in us.

Thinking this, he looked up at the sides of the buildings and saw that the "Portulaca" grew here and there on the Third Avenue people's fire escapes. It was a rather common summer flower on Third Avenue! Well, the moss rose belongs to them, too, as it did to the old guard back home, he thought. Somehow the little moss rose was a part of any old order, any old, passing bunch, and it clung to those who represented the loss of old fixtures of everyday life, it was that faithful a friend. Now it seemed right that it grow along Third Avenue in boxes and pots on rusty and cluttered and bedraggled fire escapes, as it had in a house he knew once that was inhabited by a flock of raggle-taggle kinfolks, full of joy and knowing trouble and taggling and scrabbling along, a day at a time, toward a better day, surely, they avowed. So, in that old home far away, the moss rose used to look out on a train track, though the scarce train was an event when it chose to pass that way, as if it might be some curious animal out of the woods that had taken a daring path by the house. Still, something of the same configuration was here.

Portulaca! Little moss rose! he thought. The same patterns do exist all over the world, in cities and towns, wherever people live and arrange life around themselves, a bridge over a creek or a tunnel under a river, there is a way to manage. And a sudden sight of this human pattern in one place restores a lost recognition of it in another, far away, through an eternal image of a simple flower, in the hands and care of both; and in a moment's illumination there was in him the certain knowledge of unity forever working to stitch and tie, like a quilt, the human world into a simple shape of repetition and variation of what seems a meaningless and haphazard design whose whole was hostile to its parts and seemed set on disordering them.

He went back to the shop and told the man he would like to try a Portulaca plant. On his fire escape, just off Third Avenue, it would grow and bloom the fragile starlike blossoms of the moss rose he had loved so deeply in another place and would love here as well, though it might be a little different from the old one—something in the leaf, slight but different. Yet, everything changes, he thought, slowly it all changes. Do we resign ourselves to that? Is youth passing when we see this—the fierce battle of youth that would not accept change and loss? But there is always the relationship of sameness, too, in all things, which identifies the old ancestor: the *relatedness;* we'll cling to that, to that continuous stem around which only the adornments change, he thought. What if the leaf is a little different? The family is the same . . . the bloom is akin—Portulaca or moss rose. Though the El was gone and the house of kinfolk vanished, two beings as different as man and woman, he would water and tend and foster the old moss-rose family that was still going on.

Sitting on his fire escape, after planting the moss rose in a discarded roasting pan, he looked out through the grillwork of the fire escape and saw the gaunt white-headed man who resembled so much his grandfather in his small room across the courtyard through the Trees of Heaven, where he sat night and day, serene and waiting. Where was his home? Did he know a land where the moss rose bloomed? In his waiting, in his drab, monotonous loneliness, there was a memory living, surely. Who knew, one day it might freshen in him at the sight of something that lingered in the world out of his past, right in the neighborhood, just out of his window, and gladden him for an hour.

Squatting on the fire escape, he thought of his own dreams and hopes. As he sat with the little plant, gazing at it for a long time, a memory rose from it like a vapor, eluded him, and sank back into it. He sat patiently, to catch the memory that glimmered over the petals. What hummingbird remembrance, elusive and darting from his mind, still took its flavor, its bit of sweetness, from the moss rose? And then it came up clear and simple to him, the memory in the moss rose.

It was in the back yard of The Place, as it was called by all who lived there, long ago, under a cool shade tree in Texas. A clump of moss roses grew, without anybody asking it to, in the moist ground around the pump like ringlets of hair wreathed with red and orange and yellow blossoms. He had hung the bucket by its handle over the neck of the pump, and Jessy his small sister held one of his hands while he jacked the pump with the other. The chinaberry trees were still fresh before the sun would make them limp, the chickens were pert, the dew was still on everything, even the woodpile, and the sand in the road still cool. Their old Cherokee rose, that his grandmother had planted when she was a young woman in this house, was gay and blooming at every leaf and thorn, and frolicking all over the fence, down and up and around, locking itself and freeing itself—it would quieten down in the hot afternoon.

Over the squeaking of the pump, he heard a voice and a word . . . "star . . . star." He turned to Jessy and saw that she had picked one of the moss roses and offered it to him, a tiny red star, on the palm of her hand. The bloom was so wonderous and the gift so sudden that he had thought, at that moment, that all life might be something like this twinkling offering. When they went in, the bucket filled, and their mother asked what they had been doing, Jessy had answered, "Picking stars . . ."

Now the place was gone, the water dried up, no doubt, the moss rose finished. Jessy was dead these many years; moss roses grew around her small grave—unless they had been overcome by weeds; he had not gone back to that graveyard for a long time. Here on his fire escape (the landlady had once advertised it as a "renovated terrace") was a fragile remnant of that vanished world; he would tend it; it would no doubt bloom, in time. To find that simple joy again, what could he do to recapture it, to recapture what had been, long ago in the moss rose and in himself—that ready acceptance, that instantaneous belief, in that pure joy of morning, in one sweet summer, long ago at the water pump, holding his sister's tiny hand? All that had followed, as he had grown, dimmed and tarnished that small blinking star: error and disenchantment and loss.

I used to dream of a little fresh sunrise town like that one where we stood once, at the water pump, he said to himself, where I would be, as fixed upon the ground as the moss rose round the pump, rising in the early morning in vigor to my work and moving and living round it, drawing more and more life to it, through me. Instead, work and life seem to have withdrawn from me more and more, to have pushed life back from where it began, into cities and stone buildings, onto pavements, to have impoverished me even of memories that would save me despair, in a huge grassless city where no flowers bloom on the ground.

When the moss rose bloomed again for him, this time on a fire escape in a great city where he sat with gray streaks in his hair, he would be grateful for that. There might even grow another star to pick. So he would watch, day by day, for the flowers to appear, speaking patiently to himself, and again for the hundredth time, that some change was imperative round which to rebuild, out of which to call back the fullness of forgotten signs of love and visions of hope. Believe that it is right ahead, he said to himself, sitting with the plant on the fire escape. Start with one little plain, going-on thing to live around and to take up an old beginning from. Until slowly, slowly, hope and new life will grow and leaf out from it to many places and to many old forgotten promises.

The Armadillo Basket

Each spring the two sisters from Crockett would drive fifty miles to the little town of Charity for their annual work on the family plot in the Charity Cemetery. They would bring potted plants and ferns and seeds for old-maids and periwinkles. In the mornings they would ride from the old family house where their sister Laura lived—she had kept it all these years—to the graveyard at the edge of town. Then they would sit under the cypress trees around the big rectangle that held the generations: their father and mother Mary and William Starnes, the two Starnes grandparents, a memorial marker for their young brother, Son, killed in France in the world war and buried somewhere over there, and their baby sister who had died in the flu epidemic. Here they would talk about the early days when they were all in Charity, three generations living together in the wide family house, work in the dirt plot with spades and forks, and shape up the worn graves.

Laura would never go, said the dead were "gone somewhere else, now, and not in graves," and that their memory was alive in the house they had lived in. She was peculiar that way. She lived by superstitions and signs and omens. But Lucy and Mary knew that it was her feelings that kept her from the family graves; she could not bear it; Laura was the emotional one, holding to the past and still refusing to give it up. She kept it alive by living within it, in the old house where she moved about, day by day, as though all were still there. Lucy and Mary, modernized and flourishing somewhat in the growing town of progress, Crockett, Texas, and having fairly successful husbands, railroad men, chided Laura for her refusal to face the "reality of today"; but their reprovals had slowly weakened into an indulgence of her hidebound ways, which seemed to shame their change and was what they really wanted for themselves, and so they came to humor her. They felt, secretly, indeed, that Laura kept the world they had lost, she presided over it, saving it and protecting it within that house so that they could re-enter it every spring: there it was, as it had always been, waiting for them when they opened the front door with its frosted pane decorated with the fancy figure of a man riding a horse with frosty mane and flourishing frosty tail. The keeping of the graves, then, was *their* work, the honoring gesture toward what was gone, the tending of its dirt remains, though they would not admit it, even to themselves. They regarded it as a work of plain and practical duty, they declared. Laura, the spit image of her mother and the eldest of the family, living just as her mother had, as though she were continuing the life of her mother in this house, would not talk of it.

This morning they had started late, for Laura had suddenly said she would go with her sisters to the cemetery. She had started coiling up her hair into its knot on the back of her head, holding the hairpins in her mouth and saving the combed-out wisps of hair for the hair receiver on her dresser that still held the combings of her mother's hair and had been hers before. But an omen had happened on her dresser: her photograph of Mama, that had one eye eaten out by something in that cedar chest where it had been stored one winter, fell face down. Laura had got up from the dresser, in a kind of spell, and had gone back to the breezeway where Lucy and Mary were waiting, holding their breath, and said, "You all better go on, I've got some butterbeans to shell," and turned and walked back to her bedroom with a piece of her hair hanging down. "But why don't you pack your lunch in the old armadillo basket that Papa brought to Mama from San Antone the year they were married," she called out.

Lucy and Mary looked at each other and Lucy made the sucking sound with her tongue and teeth which meant "what a shame" and shook her head. Mary called back, "But you shell your butter-beans in that armadillo basket, Laura."

"I'll use my apron," Laura answered.

They packed the lunch in the basket and went off in the car. They drove along a little sadly, remarking here and there on old family houses they passed, how they were so run-down, and mentioning members that were still in them or had passed on. At the graveyard, they unloaded their tools and plants and the basket lunch and walked through the graves to the Starnes family plot. They sat down quietly on a stone.

Along the horizon some clouds were trying to gather, and occasionally they thought they heard a faint moan of thunder, far away. Yet it was still cool and so they sprang to their task of digging and planting and pruning.

"Mama's grave has surely gone to seed," one of them said. "It needs more dirt. Why we pay old Mr. Crocus twenty-five dollars a year, I don't know. He doesn't do a thing as far as I can see."

"But he's got so many graves to keep," the other explained. "And he *is* old and hobbly."

"We'll just have to keep coming up here every year to do it ourselves," the first concluded. "I'd rather do it anyway. Seems like it's our duty."

"I remember when I set this old canna lily out," Lucy said, pulling up a dry stick of a plant. "I had my hands full that summer; two of the children sick. But it looked so red and pretty, and Mama used to have hundreds of them all over the yard. Couldn't kill the old things then, and they do bloom year in and year out."

Lucy was cleaning away the lichen from the stone at the head of her mother's grave. "Poor old Mama—1874 to 1929. Seems only a few years ago. Died so quickly. I am sure it was cancer. You remember how her stomach bothered her all those last years. Yet she never said a word. Just went right on, day after day. I'm sure it was a cancer."

"And then poor old Papa. Lasted hardly a year after she went. Caught the flu in the sleet and rain and just gave up, to follow her," Mary said as she threw an old broken pot against the fence. "We ought to use metal pots, I think. These other pots just don't last."

"You know, I think the Jasper plot is the prettiest in here. It's the cedars that do it, always making shade. I hope you'll all keep me in the shade after I'm buried. It's awful to think of lying out under the glaring sun all day, or in the rain. And a cedar smells so good."

"Yes, it does."

"And I want a little something blooming all the time."

"I like little East Texas moss roses. Or maybe Shasta daisies in the summer."

"And a good big mound, kept all round and smooth. It would kill me to think my grave was flat or all run-down on one side like an old shoe. A person's folks should keep her grave looking nice as long as they have hands to do it."

Mary whined a little. They worked silently, shadowed by the certainty that they, too, would one day have a grave of their own to be kept.

"I remember when Mama used to bring us here. I remember the great big grasshoppers, how they'd fly like fat birds. The boys said they spat tobacco juice and that if it hit your eye, it'd put it out. And how they warned us not to drink out of the hydrants because the water was poisoned by the dead."

"I remember the old dried flowers scattered after a rain and their sick wet smell, like a morgue."

"And all the names and years on the stones."

"And the neat little graves of babies."

A sheath of silence slipped over the two, as close as a glove over the hand. They sat mute, remembering the dead little sister Mary Lou, a fragile little girl born into the epidemic when they were just young girls and died from it within the month.

"Well—the graves. We've a lot of work to do."

"Son . . ." Mary sadly called his name. "Remember the flag we hung in our window for him when he was over there? And how they burned Old Man Gloom in town by the Show, to keep up the spirit."

"Wonder what his life would have been like. He was just like Papa."

"I think it will rain. That would ruin everything."

They started throwing up fresh earth with their little spades. In the west, over a pack of little Negro shacks leaning against each other, a big mound of gray cloud was swelling and sliding up to the sun to obscure it. A muffled rumbling rolled through it like a faraway wagon over an old bridge.

Suddenly a weak, slack-faced little man stood out from a cypress tree and said, "Good day, ladies." It was Mr. Crocus.

"Oh, Mr. Crocus!" Lucy shouted and dropped her palmetto rake, a little frightened. "We are working again, you see."

"Yes, ma'am. It takes a lot of labor, you know, on these graves; and only one old man with a bad back to do it."

"I think the Charity Cemetery looks awful," Mary said. "I've never seen it so run-down."

"It's the rain, ma'am. Such a wet spring. And no one but me to do all the work. The days are gone when the politicians would throw their all-day meetings in the graveyard and the whole town would bring their lunch and weed the graves and listen to the speeches. Joe, my boy, used to help, but he's gone away now. Getting so many new dead, too. Seems like all Charity is dying. But we all have it to do. There's old Mr. Pollup down there in the corner; yet it seemed he would never go, and was ninety-four when he finally went." He spat tobacco juice into a scrubby hedge. Mary thought of the grasshoppers. "Died just last Tuesday. Big funeral. And the Leslie girl, laid up so long with the paralysis. Finally crept up to her heart. Sad thing, such a young girl. That's two, and now old Grandma Bailey tomorrow. Two niggers been digging all day over by the fence. They might quit any minute, get tired and go home and set on their porches. And if it rains we'll never finish in time."

"Poor old Grandma Bailey gone," Lucy said. "Laura told us. All the old ones going. Mama would have been the first to make pies for all the family, I know. She loved all the Baileys."

"Never know who's next," Mary declared.

A low drumming of thunder ran all through the west, over the Negro houses. A black barefoot woman stood on a porch of one of them and called to her children to come in.

"We haven't even eaten our lunch, Lucy," Mary complained.

"If it rains, I hope Laura closes all the windows, especially the big one by the bed with the counterpane Mama crocheted."

"Don't worry about that," Lucy said.

"Maybe that's not for us, that cloud," Mr. Crocus said, looking to the west. "They must be getting it in Conroe, I expect. Maybe we'll miss it. Lordy, I hope so. It'll be mud everywhere."

"It's awful, burying them in the rain," Lucy said solemnly. "We buried Papa that way."

The cloud had, in so little time, become so enormous and so low that it seemed the spire of Charity Christian Church, which was directly under it now, would stick up into it and burst it momentarily. It seemed to be reaching up to try to burst it.

Thunder, full-grown, cracked down upon Charity. Children shouted and ran about the Negro yards. The women were closing the windows and the wind began to ruffle the trees. In a silent second Lucy could hear the grating of the Negroes' spades against the abrasive earth, digging for Grandma Bailey.

And then a razored scythe of lightning ran quick through the cloud, there was a blast of thunder, and heavy drops of rain started falling and spattering on the stones. Lucy and Mary began to gather up their things.

"It's going to storm," Lucy cried.

The Negroes digging Grandma Bailey's grave stopped working and started trying to erect a canvas and old Mr. Crocus ran scurrying, his back bent. And shortly long strings of rain came down. It began to pour thick drafts of rain, cascades of rain. The women ran squealing to the car.

They sat inside the Ford coupé, after they had snapped the isinglass window flaps, puffing and looking wanly outside. After a few minutes they took the napkin off the basket and began to eat the lunch, silently. Through the streaming windows they saw the Negroes digging under the dripping canvas which bellied in the wind, but the rain was flooding down through its holes. Already there was mud on their feet. Mr. Crocus was not to be seen anywhere.

Lucy and Mary watched the rain washing over the graves and saw the rain melting down the humps of earth. The rain was falling in torrents over all the graveyard. The sky was all mist and water now, and the little Negro shacks were dreary and dripping, washed gray. They did not even look lived-in, except for the forlorn face of a Negro at a window in a shotgun house, looking out.

They sat eating their good lunch—which seemed wrong, since they had done so little work to make it taste good; but still it seemed the only thing to do. In a while, Lucy looked out and said in a sad watery voice, watching the rain flood over the graves, "The good Lord bless all the dead," as if she had to make up to somebody for enjoying such a good lunch of chicken and pickled peaches. Suddenly she spied an armadillo lying ridged like a big spotted conch under a crape-myrtle tree. She quickly opened the flap of her window and threw the stone of a pickled peach at him. "Shoo!" she shamed it.

And then, in the melancholy rain, the two sisters saw the armadillo shaggle hideously and as if under guilt, dragging its rat-like tail, into the family plot. They were both silent and appalled. In a moment Lucy burst from the car and ran in the rain toward the family graves, crying, "Sooey! sooey!" But the armadillo was nowhere to be seen. She came back, drenched, and sat wet in the car. The noon whistle whined from the sawmill. They could not eat any more of the lunch now, yet they did not want to go.

"When we're gone, it doesn't matter," Mary finally said, quietly. "Think of all the things that come at night to a person's grave. Can't afford to think of it. We're protected somewhere else. Hold to the living, that's what. Laura's right not to come. Let's go, Lucy, to see about Laura. She'll worry about us in the rain."

They started the car and went back through the mud and steady rain to the house. As they drove into the yard to put the car under the big shade tree, they could see that some neighbors were there, on the breezeway. When they got to the door they could not believe what Mrs. Larjen, the next-door neighbor, in her bonnet that shook on her small trembling head, was telling them, that when she had come over to see Laura a little while ago she had found her slumped over the butterbean shells in her apron, and that when Dr. Murray had got to the house he said she was dead.

Lucy and Mary found her laid out on her bed and the neighbor women already sitting around her who looked, in her fresh death, more like her mother than ever.

Rhody's Path

Sometimes several sudden events will happen together so as to make you believe they have a single meaning if twould only come clear. Surely happenings are lowered down upon us after a pattern of the Lord above.

Twas in the summer of one year; the time the Second Coming was prophesied over the land and the Revivalist came to Bailey's pasture to prove it; and the year of two memorable events. First was the plague of grasshoppers (twas the driest year in many an old memory, in East Texas); second was the Revival in the pasture across from the house.

Just even to mention the pestilence of hoppers makes you want to scratch all over. They came from over toward Grapeland like a promise of Revelations—all counted to the last as even the hairs of our head are numbered, so says the Bible and so said the Revivalist—making the driest noise in the world, if you have ever heard them. There were so many that they were all clusted together, just one working mass of living insects, wild with appetite and cutting down so fast you could not believe your eyes a whole field of crops. They hid the sun like a curtain and twas half-daylight all that day, the trees were alive with them and shredded of their leaves. We humans were locked in our houses, but the earth was the grasshopper's, he took over the world. It did truly seem a punishment, like the end of the world was upon us, as was prophesied.

Who should choose to come home to us that end of summer but Rhody, to visit, after a long time gone. She had been in New Orleans as well as in Dallas and up in Shreveport too, first married to her third husband in New Orleans, then in Dallas to run away from him in spite, and lastly in Shreveport to write him to go to the Devil and never lay eye on her again. We all think he was real ready to follow the law of that note. Then she come on home to tell us all this, and to rest.

Rhody arrived in a fuss and a fit, the way she is eternally, a born fidget, on the heels of the plague of hoppers. They had not been gone a day when she swept in like the scourge of pestilence. She came into our wasteland, scarce a leaf on a tree and crops just stalks, dust in the air. So had the Revivalist—as if they had arranged it together in Louisiana and the preacher had gone so far as to prophesy the Second Coming in Texas for Rhody's sake. She could make a man do such.

Already in the pasture across the railroad tracks and in front of the house, the Revivalist was raising his tent. We were all sitting on the front porch to watch, when we saw what we couldn't believe our eyes were telling us at first, but knew soon after by her same old walk, Rhody crossing the pasture with her grip in her hand. We watched her stop and set on her suitcase to pass conversation with the Revivalist—she never met a stranger in her life—and his helpers, and we waited for her to come on home across the tracks and through the gate. Mama and Papa and Idalou and some of the children stood at the gate and waited for her; but the bird dog Sam sat on the porch and waited there, barking. He was too old—Idalou said he was eighteen—to waste breath running to the gate to meet Rhody.

The hooded flagpole sitter was a part of it all. He had come in advance as an agent for the Revival and sat on the Mercantile Building as an advertisement for the Revival. He had been up there for three days when the grasshoppers come. Twas harder for him than for anyone, we all imagined. The old-timers said he had brought in the plague of hoppers as part of prophesy. They raised up to him a little tent and he sat under that; but it must have been terrible for him. Most thought he would volunteer to come on down, in the face of such adversity, but no sir, he stayed, and was admired for it. He couldn't sail down his leaflets that advertised the Revival, for the grasshoppers would have eaten those as fast as if they had been green leaves from a tree. But the town had already had leaflets enough that read, "The Day of Judgment Is at Hand, Repent of Your Sins for the Lord Cometh . . ."

The first night he was up twas a hot starry night. We all sat on the porch till late at night rocking and fanning and watching him. There he was over the town, a black statue that hardly seemed real.

When the Revivalist first appeared at the house to ask us for cool water, we invited him in on the back porch. He was a young man to be so stern a preacher, lean and nervous and full of his sermon. His bushy eyebrows met together—for jealousy, Idalou told us after he was gone, and uttered a warning against eyebrows that run together. He started right out to speak of our salvation as if it might earn him a drink of water, and of his own past sinful life in cities before he was redeemed. He wanted our redemption, the way he went on sermonizing, more than a cool drink of water; but water was easiest to provide him with and best at hand, as Aunt Idalou said after he had gone. He was a man ready to speak of his own frailties and Mama praised him for this. He wanted to make us all free and purged of man's wickedness, he said, and his black eyes burned under his joined eyebrows when he spoke of this. When he had left, one of the children—Son—helped him carry the pail of well water to the pasture, and then we all broke into sides about who would go to the Revival the next night and who would watch it from the front porch.

When Son came back he was trembling and told that the Revivalist had two diamond rattlesnakes in a cage, right in Bailey's pasture, and that he had shown him the snakes. Then he told us that the preacher was going to show how the Lord would cure him of snakebite as a demonstration of faith. He had converted and saved thousands through this example of the healing power of the Lord, saying his famous prayer as he was struck by this rattling spear, "Hand of God, reach down and help antidote the poison of the diamond rattler of Sin."

Rhody added that she had already found out all this when she came through the pasture and stopped to converse with Bro. Peters—she already knew his name where we hadn't. Then she added that the Revivalist and his company—a lady pianist and three men who were his stewards and helpers—were going to camp in Bailey's pasture during their three-day stay in town and that at the last meeting, the flagpole sitter himself was going to come down and give a testimonial. She further informed us that she had taken upon herself the courtesy to invite Bro. Peters and his lady pianist to eat supper with us that night. We were all both excited and scared. But Mama and Idalou began at once to plan the supper and went in to make the fire in the stove to cook it with.

Rhody was not much changed—a person like Rhody could never change, just add on—as she was burdened by something we could not name. We all noticed a limp in her right leg, and then she confessed she had arthritis in it, from the dampness of New Orleans, she said. Her face was the same beautiful one; she had always been the prettiest in the family, taking after Granny who had been, it was a legend that had photographic proof right on the wall, a very beautiful young woman. But Rhody's face was as if seen through a glass darkly, as the Bible says. More had happened to Rhody during the years away than she would ever tell us. "Some of the fandango is danced out in her," Aunt Idalou said, and now we would all see the change in Rhody that we all hoped and prayed for.

Rhody was thrilled by the sight of the flagpole sitter. She said she was just dying to meet him. She told us that this town had more excitement in it than any city she had been in—and that included several—and she was glad she had come on home. She unpacked her grip and took out some expensive things of pure silk her husbands had bought for her, and there were presents for us all. Then she put her grip in the pantry as though she was going to stay for a long time but no one asked her for how long. In the early days, Rhody had come and left so often that her feet had trod out her own little path through Bailey's pasture and we had named it Rhody's Path. It ran alongside the main path that cut straight through to town. We never used it, left it for her; but if she was gone a long time, Mama would say to one of us who was going to town, "Use Rhody's Path, the bitterweeds are taking it over, maybe that'll bring her home," the way mothers keep up their hopes for their children's return, though the weeds grow over and their beds are unused. Mama kept Rhody's room the way

Rhody had it before she left for the first time, and the same counterpane was always on the bed, fresh and clean, the big painted chalk figure of a collie was on the dresser, the fringed pillow a beau had given her with "Sweetheart" on it, and the framed picture of Mary Pickford autographed by her, "America's Sweetheart." "She's got sweetheart on the brain," Mama used to say. She carried sweetheart too far.

Anyway, the Revivalist took Rhody's Path to come to supper on. Around suppertime here came Bro. Peters and the lady pianist across Bailey's pasture on Rhody's Path, he tall and fast-walking, the little pianist trotting behind him like a little spitz to keep up with him. They came through the gate and onto the front porch where we all greeted them, and Rhody was putting on a few airs of city ways that made Idalou look at her as if she could stomp her toe. We were introduced to the pianist whose name was Elsie Wade, a little spinster type with freckled hands and birdlike movements of head. Miss Wade asked the Lord to bless this house and said that good Christians always gathered easily as if they were blood kin, which they were, Bro. Peters added; and we all went in the house, through the hall and onto the back porch. It was a late summer evening and the vines strung across the screen of the porch were nothing but strings after the grasshoppers had devoured them, but through the latticework of string we could see the distant figure of the flagpole sitter that the setting sun set aglow. Rhody kept wanting to talk about him. She said she thought he looked keen up there. Bro. Peters told that the flagpole sitter had been a drinking man, wild and in trouble in every county of Texas and Louisiana, until he was saved by a chance Revival Meeting in Diboll where he was sitting on the County Seat flagpole as a stunt for something or other. The night he came down to give himself to the Lord at the meeting brought wagonloads of people from far and wide, across creeks and gulleys to hear and see him, and many were saved. From that time on he gave his services to the Lord by way of the difficult and lonely task of sitting on a flagpole for three days and nights as a herald of the coming Revival. The flagpole sitter and the diamond rattlers were the most powerful agents of the Gospel and redemption from sin and literally brought thousands of converts into the fold, Bro. Peters told. Rhody said she was dying to meet him and Bro.

Peters assured her he would make the introduction personally on the last night of the Revival.

We sat down to a big supper for summertime: cold baking-powder biscuits, cold kidney beans, onions and beets in vinegar, sweet milk and buttermilk, fried chicken—there was nothing green in the garden left after the grasshoppers had taken their fill. Idalou told Bro. Peters and Miss Elsie Wade that she had fed the Devil with some good squash that she had rescued from the grasshoppers but burnt to a mash on the stove; and Bro. Peters said that the Devil liked good summer squash and if he couldn't acquire it through his agents of pestilence he would come by it on a too-hot stove—but that he was glad the Devil left the chicken; and all laughed, Rhody loudest of all.

Afterwards we went to the porch and while Idalou played the piano Son sang some solos, "Drink to Me Only," etc. But Rhody spoiled the singing by talking incessantly to the Revivalist. Then Elsie Wade applied her rolling Revival technique to the old piano that no one could talk over, not even Rhody, and made it sound like a different instrument, playing some rousing hymns which we all sang faintly because of our astonishment at the way such a slight little thing as she manhandled the piano as if it was a bull plow.

In the middle of one of the songs there was somebody at the front door, and when Idalou went she found it to be a man from Bro. Peters' outfit over in the pasture. He was anxious to speak to Bro. Peters. Idalou asked him in, but Bro. Peters, hearing the man's voice, was already in the hallway by the time the man entered. "Brother Peters!" he called. "One of the diamond rattlers is aloose from the cage." Bro. Peters ran out and Elsie Wade seemed very nervous, inventing a few furbelows on the treble keys as she looked back over her shoulder with a stiff pencil-like neck at the conversation at the front door. Her eyes were so small and glittering at that moment that she seemed like a fierce little bird that might peck a loose snake to death. Idalou invited her to wait in the house, though. "The diamond rattler is our most valuable property," Elsie Wade said, "next to the flagpole sitter."

All night long they were searching for the diamond rattler with their flashlights. We locked all the doors and stayed indoors and watched the lights from the windows. We started a bonfire in the front yard. There were fires in many places in the pasture. The bird dog Sam was astonished that we brought him in the house, but he would not stop barking; and Idalou said he would die of a heart attack before daylight if they didn't catch the valuable property of the viper, he was so old. It was a sinister night. At a certain hour we heard that the flagpole sitter had come down to help find the scourge of Sin. And then suddenly like a shot out of the blue Rhody jumped up and said she couldn't stand it any longer, that she was going out to help the poor Revivalist in his search for the diamond rattler. Everybody objected and Aunt Idalou said over her dead body, that Rhody's arthritis would hinder her if she had to run; but Rhody, being Rhody, went anyway. So there was that anxiousness added.

We all watched from the parlor window. In the light of the bonfire's flame we could see the eerie posse, darting here, kicking there, and we saw that the Revivalist carried a shotgun. The flagpole sitter had arrived in such a hurry and was so excited that he had not had time to take off his long black robe and hood that he wore on the flagpole, and his priestlike shape in the light of the fires was the most nightmarish of all. On went the search through the dark hours after midnight, and it seemed the Revivalist was looking for his Sin, like some penance, a dark hunter in the night searching for evil. And now Rhody was by his side to help him, as if it could be her sin, her evil, too. They seemed to search together.

We never knew, nor will, exactly what happened. When we heard the shot and saw flashlights centered on one spot, we knew they had found the snake; and when we saw them coming on Rhody's Path toward the house, the Revivalist carrying in his arms something like a drowned person, we knew it was Rhody. They came up on the porch, the Revivalist saying sternly, "Call the doctor, she was bitten on the hip by the diamond rattler and has fainted." He bit her bad leg.

They laid Rhody on the bed and Bro. Peters began saying his famous prayer asking the Lord to reach down and pluck the poison from his child. "The snake is killed—the flagpole sitter shot him," one of the men said.

It was Aunt Idalou who scarified the snakebite with a paring knife and saved the life of Rhody until the doctor got there.

Though she did it without open prayer, she prayed to herself as she worked on Rhody and used solid practical ways of salvation—including leaves of Spanish dagger plant in the front yard which Son ran and got, and hog lard. When the doctor got there he marveled at the cure and said there was little more to do except for Rhody to rest and lie prone for a few days. Idalou said she could count Rhody's prone days on one hand and Rhody commented that at least the snake had the common sense to strike her bad leg.

When the commotion was over and danger was passed, someone asked where the Revivalist was. He was nowhere to be found. In the early morning light, just breaking, we saw the pasture empty. There was no sign of anybody or anything except the guttering black remains of the bonfires. The flagpole on the Mercantile Building had nothing sitting on it. The whole Revival company had vanished like a dream . . . and had it all been one, the kind Rhody could bring down upon a place?

We hoped that would teach Rhody a lesson, but Aunt Idalou doubted it seriously. Anyway, Rhody stayed on with us till the very end of summer. Then one day there was that familiar scrambling in the pantry and it was Rhody getting her grip out. There was a mouse's nest in it. She packed it, saying she was going to Austin, to get her a job or take a beauty course she had seen advertised. When she had finished it, she told us, she might come back to Charity and open her a beauty parlor. We all doubted that, knowing she couldn't stay put for long in any one place, beauty or none.

We all kissed her good-bye and Aunt Idalou cried and asked the plain air what had branded her youngest child with some sign of restless wandering and when would she settle down to make a household as woman should; and we watched Rhody go on off, on the path across the pasture with her grip in her hand, going off to what, we all wondered.

"Well," Mama said, "she'll pull a fandango wherever she goes. But through some miracle or just plain common sense of somebody always around to protect her, with hog lard, or just good plain prayer, she'll survive and outlast us all who'll worry ourselves into our graves that Rhody will come to put flowers on, alive as ever." Rhody went out and took the world's risks and chances, but simple remedies of home and homefolks rescued and cured her, time and time again. She always had to touch home, set her wild foot on the path across the pasture that led back to the doorstep of the house, bringing to it across the pasture, from the great confused and mysterious world on the farther side, some sign of what had lately happened to her to lay it on the doorstep of home.

But with the world changing so fast and all old-time word and way paying so quickly away, she will have to correct *herself* in the world she errs in and by its means; or, in some way, by her own, on her own path, in the midst of her traveling. Surely we knew she needed all of us and had to touch us there, living on endurable and permanent, she thought, in that indestructible house where everything was always the way it had forever been and would never change, she imagined; where all, for her, was redeemed and put aright. Then, when she got something straight—what it was no one but Rhody ever knew—she'd gather her things and go off again.

"The sad thing is," Idalou said, rocking on the front porch looking at the empty pasture and the sad-looking path that Rhody took, "that years pass and all grow old and pass away, and this house will be slowly emptied of its tenants." Had Rhody ever considered this? And what would she do when all had gone and none to come home to?

But surely all of us who were listening to Idalou were thinking together that the path would remain, grown over and hidden by time, but drawn on the earth, the pasture was engraved with it like an indelible line; and Rhody's feet would be on it, time immemorial, coming and going, coming and going, child of the path in the pasture between home and homelessness, redemption and error. That was the way she had to go.

A People of Grass

He maundered about the city of Rome all day, misplaced. It was May, cold and dark and rainy, a bad spring, a cursed spring. Blossoms were late, crimped by cold and the pale touch of cold sun. He had left a cold room on whose worn floor of ancient tiles were sensual figures of faded crimson grapes and purple pears that stung bare feet with chill, and where a wan fire in a smoky fireplace did not warm naked flesh. Here in this room he had risen in cold dawns to the forlorn cry of swifts answering the toning of many bells; and through a window he saw the sunless dome of Saint Peter's that did not comfort.

In the late afternoon, a little before dusk, the skies cleared as he was walking through the Borghese Gardens; and suddenly before him, in a green clearing under great green trees, a flock of little girls from a convent were there playing and singing on the cold grass. Four white nuns watched over them. Here in the gardens in late pale sunlight there danced and whirled all these little girls. He went closer and lay on his stomach in the grass at the edge of the dancing green and watched them. Some who had fallen or rolled in the new grass had the stain of green on their pink dresses. Some wore earrings they had made out of grass buds, or bracelets and necklaces woven of grass and early poppies; and watching them as he lay in the grass, there cleared in his mind an old confusion of a faraway afternoon, in one Maytime.

It was a memory of a sunny May afternoon in Woodland Park

in faraway Texas with a soft wind in the great pine trees under which the school had made a clearing for the Grammar School May Fete. This was an enchanted day, and the brother's costume as the king of flowers was ready and his sister's as a poppy was finally made. The brother had a silver wand, a silver crown made of nothing but cardboard but dazzled over with silver paper, and the crown and wand lay waiting beyond his touch on top of the glass china closet that had been his grandmother's. (The brother kept the crown for many years, though the stars soon fell off and the silver burnished quickly; and lying there in the grass he wished that he might have it again, though it would change nothing.)

The sister's dress was a poppy, all of crepe paper, crimson and green, and for her head there was a little cap of an inverted poppy bloom with the green stem on it. Her costume lay spread on the bed in the extra bedroom that was to become her own when she was old enough to take it and no longer afraid to sleep away from the rest of the family. It was the most fragile dress, sewn with such distress by the mother who every day had spoken of the difficulty of it and how she thought she would never make it right if she had all her life to try. It did not last nearly so long as the brother's king's crown and his silver wand.

May Day seemed never to arrive but always hung at the edge of Thursday, until suddenly it was there, and there was the little family walking on the way to Woodland Park, the children in their costumes finally their own, holding hands and leading the way, the mother and father marching behind. The mother's eyes watched with a look of resignation the imperfect stem drooping on the sister's head as she walked carefully ahead. The brother could not see his crown, but he knew the sunshine was making it glisten, for he could see the way the silver wand, which he held very carefully as he walked, shone in the golden May Day light. The sister walked never so carefully in her life so as not to spoil her poppy dress, because her mother had warned her severely that the crepe paper would stretch out of shape or perhaps even "shatter," it was so ephemeral as any bloom, if she leapt or ran. The brother wondered how she could possibly dance the Maypole dance in it. She would have to do it very delicately.

At Woodland Park, a wide green slope on the banks of the

Chocolate Bayou, there was a resplendent May crowd standing and walking about. There were gay lemonade booths decorated with colored papers, kiosks with colored lanterns swinging in the breeze, tent-topped stands where ices were sold, rustling in layers of Dennison paper and flags of ribbons. In the middle of the park was the clearing and in the center of the clearing was the grand Maypole, tall and strong, with its blue and white paper streamers drawn down and held in place at its base, waiting for each dancer's hand to take its own. The wind was trilling the whole delicate construction and there was such a silken rustling sound of paper and leaves that the whole frail world seemed to be made of leaf and bloom, all trembling and shining in sunlight and wind. How one hoped that the Maypole dancers would do it right, as they had been instructed through so many days of practice in the school auditorium. They had only one chance. Everything had the feeling of extreme delicacy and momentariness on this transient afternoon, an expendable moment of May, that rain could fade and wilt, wind could tear and blow away.

The sister found her assembling group of friends who were flowers: roses, tulips, lilies, and a few difficult wisterias. The mothers had done a good job of making the costumes, under the teachers' guidance. They had spent two tedious weeks all sewing delicate stuff in one of the classrooms after school.

As the brother was the king of flowers, he had to stand alone at his place of entrance, for there was no queen of flowers . . . why, one did not know or had not even thought of. The brother's costume was only a black suit, but his very first to own, coat and trousers, and a white shirt and tie; and that in itself was enough to make it a special day. But it was the crown and the wand that made all the difference. His task would be to move among the folded girls, all in a crowd, and gently touch each of them with his wand and so bring them up to bloom, while the lovely but somehow so deeply sad music of "Welcome, Sweet Springtime" played out from the piano. He waited with thrilling fright. He was second on the program, since the first thing was the entrance and procession of the King and Queen of May with all their court.

It began, and a boy walked out stiffly from the crowd, took his place by the empty throne and blew a fanfare as clear as sunshine on his bugle. He blew it right, thank goodness, and for the first time; and so there was no danger of giggles among the flowers who had not been able to control themselves during rehearsals when the bugle blurted and made no fanfare whatsoever. After the perfect fanfare, everyone was very quiet and the piano began. The court entered the clearing. The brother began to have a throbbing headache and to feel deeply sick. Out came the flower girls, the littlest, throwing rose petals to make a path for the king and queen; but the jester who followed, all in bells and pointed paper, kicked up the petals, against admonitions in rehearsals, and this was the first wrong thing. Yet how could he avoid tromping the blossoms? The brother grew sicker. Then the princesses came, teased, then the princes, the dukes and duchesses, and finally the king and queen, whom the school had voted for. The piano was rolling out its coronation march when the brother ran behind it, the music bursting in his head, and vomited there behind the piano, holding the crown with both hands to keep it from falling. He thought he might die from sickness and fright. But he felt better, now, though shamed, and he went back to his place. Now the court was seated, and without mishap, looking like a whole garden of flowers, and there was great applause. A pause, and then the familiar melody of "Welcome, Sweet Springtime," which had haunted him ever since they had begun practicing, filled the air. Suddenly all the flowers ran out into the clearing and fell to the ground around the Maypole, finding their streamers.

Then in a moment of blindness and exaltation, the brother heard his cue of music and it was time for him to come in among the flowers. He did not know what he did, but he remembered only a feeling of deep sadness and loveliness as he entered the clearing and moved among the folded flowers, touching each with his silver wand and bringing each up to flowering, all the beautiful little girls who so long ago vanished to many places and none ever so wild and shy again as that afternoon in a golden park of pine trees and flowers; and the whole Maypole began to open out like an enormous paper parasol. The brother knew when he came to the poppy that was his sister, for in an instant he saw, as he lowered his wand, that green fault in the stem which his mother had been so grieved at not being able to make properly, though the other mothers had said it would do and not to worry about it; and in the last weeks it had become the anxiety of the household.

Once the mother even wept with despair over the stem and said, biting her lip and looking out the window, "I just cannot make it right"; and he had heard his mother and father speaking softly about it in the night. "It will be all right if you don't make it just perfect," the father had consoled her. "Children don't notice those little things." The brother and sister had been worried about the stem and wished, as they walked to school, that their mother could make it right. The brother even prayed for it at night, finishing his memorized prayer with "Lord help my mother make the poppy stem right." Then it was, at that instant, as he lowered his wand to touch it, that the little green stem seemed the fault in the household and a symbol of loving imperfection.

The brother touched with trembling wand the green stem on his sister's head, and he felt his sister shy at the glancing touch of it, saw her rise halfway as if in a spell and saw her trod a petal of her dress; and then he watched her stumble and fall, as if he had struck her with a burning rod.

He saw, in a mist of tears, a vision of his mother and his father and his sister and himself standing together in the clearing on the throne of May that was emptied of its royalty and where they had been brought to dock, ruiners of May, and the Maypole a twisted stalk of knotted paper behind them, casting shadow over them, his sister in her withered poppy dress and he in his suit with his burnished crown fallen down over his eyes like a blindfold and holding the silver wand that mocked him, his mother aggrieved and his father humbled; and he heard the thunderous laughter and soughing sigh, like a storm in the trees, of a vast crowd of May persons who, dressed in paper and leaves and petals, seemed to have come for a moment out of the trees and the grass and the rushes of the bayou that ran below the clearing, an assembly of judges and mockers and revelers, demoniacal and green and accusing. How cruel and how lovely was May, when everything was impetuous and passionate and merciless. And he could hear his mother's voice before the green jury, "I just could not make it right," and his father's, "We never had a chance, any of us, my mother and my father and my brothers and my sisters"; and the brother could feel his own wordless answer stirring in his depths where it would not for so long to come rise and be uttered.

The brother reeled back from his sister for a moment, but for some reason which he could not understand until many years later, until this moment when he lay in the grass of a foreign city on the rim of a little park where a crowd of orphan children played on the grass, he could not move himself to help his sister up. She had torn her frail paper dress; she was crying. The brother stood over his sister and his wand hung from his limp hand and dragged the ground and he began to cry, too, and there was a long interruption with the sister and brother crying, flower and king of flowers in the green clearing in the sunshine circled round by a world of faces, friend and stranger, all people of May, the music of "Welcome, Sweet Springtime" playing on, so very sorrowful now, it seemed a dirge of winter. Some of the flowers not yet brought to bloom by the wand could not restrain themselves from peeping up to see what had happened, and the whole garden was on the verge of shattering. In another minute a teacher had rushed out to help the sister up and motioned to the brother to go on. Yet he had not been able to help his sister come to flower, as he or nothing in this world could help his mother make the proper stem; and in that moment he knew certainly that no one ever could mend certain flaws, no mother's hands or brother's wand but some hand of God or wand of wind or rain, something like that, beyond the touch of human hands.

When the whole garden of flowers was in full perfect bloom, except for the blight of his sister whose dress was torn and one petal dragging behind her, and the Maypole opened out and trembling in the sunlight, the brother backed away from the clearing and into the crowd and found his way to hide behind the piano where he wept bitterly as it went on playing the sad springtime air. His throat ached, scorched with the lime of grief for his sister, for his mother, for this bitter time of May, and for his first suit and tie which seemed, then, to have something to do with some deep disaster of afternoon that even the crown and the wand could not alter or transform.

Behind the piano he wept bitterly in honor of more than he could know then. And he felt again as he had so many times before, already, in his very beginning life, that gentle blue visitation of a sense of tragic unfulfillment, a doom of incompleteness in his heritage, never quite brought to perfect bloom, as though its lighted way had been crossed by a shadow of error; and mis-touched, stumbling, bearing its flaw upon its brow and shying for the touch of a magical wand, it could not rise, but struggling to rise it tore its flesh and limped into its dance.

Now the flowers were standing in their circle round the unfurled Maypole and in another minute they were dancing the Maypole dance, and the sister was there. The brother saw his sister dancing round and round, weaving her blue ribbon in and out without one mistake, pale and innocent and melancholy in her torn dress, dragging along with her while she leapt, as if she were a little lame, the broken petal of the dress that seemed already to be withering, and upon her forehead the blighted stem drooped and bobbled, grotesque and mocking like a little green horn on her brow; and the brother saw, as the whole May Fete witnessed, that surely the sister was the serenest performer of all the Maypole dancers, an aerial creature wan from early failure, touched with some pale light, skipping and singing softly in a visionary moment of unearthly beauty; and he, like her, in those moments, felt touched, too, by that wand of delicate heartbreak held by the demon king that lives in May, that momentary month that would pass and never come again until the world and all its flowers and grass had been touched and brazed by the summer sun, burnt by the frosts of autumn and buried under winter . . . until the Maypole's ribbons of paper would fade and the poppy dress shatter, the wand tarnish and the cardboard crown moult its silver stars.

Then, there in the center of the green at the end of this hazardous performance, all the dancers gone away, stood the enduring Maypole woven and plaited without one mistake; and in the empty clearing there lay upon the mown grass of May the lost petal from the poppy dress.

Now he was watching and hearing the little girls in the Borghese Gardens, again; but after another moment he was standing, and then, looking back at them, he walked away, touching with the fingers that had long ago held the magic wand the stain of grass on his white trousers. Bitter grass! The bitter water of the fountains of this eternal city is surely for the watering of grass, he thought. Bitter love of God that suffers for this majestic perishability that the planting wind blows over and withers! Bitter May!

Bitter flesh, bearing upon it the ineradicable stain that tells the story of this oh great glory of flesh of grass!

In his alien room of ancient floor, round which the denouncing cry of the demon swifts whirled, he pondered the passing of early revelations, how they sink through the currents of years, their adornment dissolving away like petals of paper and pasted stars; and, at long last, shelled of embellishment and ungarnished, settle on the cold hard utter bottom and foundation of unalterable truth.

Zamour,
or
A Tale of Inheritance

For Dorothy Brett

It is said—and true—that Wylie Prescott became the richest man in one part of Texas because of the accident of inheritance. But few people know the circumstances of his coming to power and wealth. That is the tale to be told.

One time were two sisters in a faraway county of Texas called Red River County, and they had little black beards. Their names were Cheyney and Maroney Lester—they were not twins but close to being that—and even when they were just young girls of about fourteen they had begun to grow a sprouting of black beard.

The way it began was that Cheyney's beard started to show first and then Maroney's. Cheyney was very distraught and particularly as she felt she might fall into bad light with her sister Maroney, whom she worshiped. But Maroney came to her and said quietly, "Don't worry, dear sister Cheyney, this will make no difference between us—and besides, now I will tell you that for a long time I have noticed the same thing slowly happening to me." The two sisters embraced and vowed they would stay together for the rest of their lives. This bond was stronger than death, although death kept it, too, and a very beautiful one to see, endearing the Lester sisters to all Red River County.

Red River County was a wildwood in those days, neighbors far pieces apart, scattered along the wide red river and upon the red land. Rain would leave red puddles in the gullies, and red dust stained the water in stock tubs. It had a wildness to it, too, this county, and where it rose to hilly places there were rocks and trees of hard wood, there where the water of the red river could not soften it. It was a beautiful wilderness and plain simple folks lived in it, and until the time of this tale, very few ever left the county and practically none that would never come back to it. This was all in about nineteen-fifteen.

Now there was a younger sister in the Lester family, ten years younger than Maroney and Cheyney; and her name was Princis Lester. Princis Lester grew along with her sisters and never spoke one word about the difference between her own aspect and theirs, though she took notice of it at an early age. She came to regard it as just the way they were, and there was no talk about it. But when she reached the self-regarding age of eighteen, and as she was slender and beautiful and chestnut-haired where her sisters' hair was of the coldest black, and they plump as two biscuits, Princis considered point-blank for the first time the plight that had befallen her sisters and thought death more desirable.

She said to herself, if this were to happen to me, I would just kill myself, looking at her face very carefully in the mirror. She drew farther apart from her sisters, though she had never been close to them, for Cheyney and Maroney seemed to hang apart in space from her, two little hemispheres joined by this isthmus of hair. Anyway, times were changing and Princis was taking her start in a new time. There was a new commissary up a few miles on the riverbank, and there were gatherings of young and old here, giving the chance to farm people to dress up and look at each other and adding one more to the opportunities of Sunday church and family meetings up and down the valley.

Princis asked no questions of her sisters about what she considered a fatal infirmity—they might have been dwarfs or albinos from the way she regarded them. Still, they were sweet and gentle, laughing little creatures, her sisters; and in the autumn she listened to them laughing in the apple orchard in their nunlike felicity, and she watched out her window at them sitting in the apple trees like charming coons throwing down the fruit. What did they have that she didn't? she asked herself at the dresser. A beard, she answered herself directly. The beard seemed to make all the difference, even that of blessed happiness. But she liked them, they were so loving with her, their own young sister Princis, they never once looked closely at her face to see if there was the slightest trace of beard, they never once mentioned it; and if she had been their sister and that close kin to them, Princis might never have noticed their peculiarity after being with them for a little while, the way other more distant kinfolks seemed not to notice, coming once and a while on Sundays to visit in the afternoons. Eccentricities that take on price and preciosity in cities become humble matter of fact in country places among country folk.

She yearned to go away to a city, to get her a job or learn to be a beauty operator, or take a course in something, as so many others were doing. But she waited. She finished high school and then her mother and father died within a year. She stayed on at home until she was twenty-five, yearning to run away. There was such a distance between her and her sisters, one she felt she could never bridge, never as long as she lived—she could not cross that bridge of hair. The neighbors and cousins were miles down the road and there were few callers besides them. She waited on. At night as she sat by the light of the glass lamp while her sisters played the xylophone in the parlor, she would scout her face very carefully in her hand mirror. Sometimes she fell into a kind of trance before the face in the mirror as though it put her into a sleep. Then the whole world lay only in the oval pool of her mirror.

One time at the supper table, Princis suddenly cried out to her sisters, "Stop staring at me!" and left the table. Maroney said to her, "Why, Princis, our own beautiful little sister, we were not staring at you." But Princis put on her coat and went out the back door. It was drizzling and December. She walked in the orchard under the dripping fruitless trees. "This means I must run away," she told herself, "or I will end up by harming my two sisters who mean no harm to anyone."

What was that little cry she heard in the dark orchard, some animal or what? She walked softly toward the cry and saw two lovely burning lights. Those were its eyes. She went closer toward the lights, and it was a cat that leapt away from her. She pursued it. Up it went, scratching into a tree, where its eyes burned like some luminous fruit growing on the bare branches.

"Kitty!" she called. "If you are wet and cold, come to me. I am

Princis Lester and I will do you no harm. We can be friends with each other, if you will come on down."

She waited and watched the lights swinging through the tree. Then the cat came slowly down to where she stood and brushed a greeting against her. She picked him up, and he let her, and she felt how friendly his wet fur was to her hand, as though she had known it always. But its coat felt torn—it had been hounded by some animal.

Walking back toward the house with the cat, she said to it, "You have been lost in the cold rain and darkness. You had lost your way because you were nobody's cat and now you are mine; and what will I call you?"

In the house, Princis saw that the cat was a big black congenial male with cotton-eyes. She took off her new orange velveteen coat and wrapped him in it and took him into the parlor to show to her two sisters, and this would be an offering, too, to make up to them for what she had said at the supper table.

"Look here!" she said. "I have found a friend in the orchard."

Cheyney and Maroney ran delighted to Princis and the cat, whose head shone wet and black where it nestled in the orange velveteen. But the cat grumbled and spat at them and wanted to claw out to keep them away. Cheyney and Maroney drew back together, and Princis said, "He is just nervous," and took him into her room.

She sat down on her bed with the cat, dried him and brushed him with her hairbrush and said to him, "But what will I name you, because you are mine to keep." Some beautiful name, she thought. What beautiful names did she know? She could not think of any; but then suddenly a name breathed into her head, almost as though someone else were whispering her a name: Zamour! It was a lovely name she had seen on a poster nailed to a tree on the road and advertising a magician who would come to the commissary with a carnival that she never saw.

And so Zamour became Princis' own. He either stayed in her room behind closed doors or walked with Princis in the orchard where they had met. He stayed away from Cheyney and Maroney, never taking to them, and they, in their kind way, did not press themselves upon him but let him go his way under his own affections.

When Princis was thirty, she met at the commissary a young railroad man named Mr. Simpson. She spied upon him regularly at the commissary from then on. As each got to know when the other would come to buy supplies, each made a secret plan. She knew by his eyes that he would one day come to call on her, and she told Zamour about it, and that they would have to watch and wait for him to come. She and Zamour played a secret game together—"When Mr. Simpson Comes"—and they often sat together on the front-porch swing to watch for him or in her bedroom at night, with only the little blue glass lamp burning, playing the game of waiting for him maybe to come while Princis looked at her face in the hand mirror.

Though she never invited Mr. Simpson, she knew he would come. The night he came sure enough to call, her sisters were playing the xylophone in the parlor, "Beautiful Ohio," their favorite, over and over, such a music of gliding in a dream. Princis and Mr. Simpson sat in the hall on the hat-tree seat until the concert would be over and they could go into the parlor. But Cheyney and Maroney went on playing "Beautiful Ohio," their favorite, over and over, a music to rock a canoe or swing a seat in a Ferris wheel.

Mr. Simpson told Princis that he was an orphan from St. Louis, had no folks, and that he was being transferred to the city of Houston to work in the railroad yards there—he was a switchman—and Princis told him without catching a breath a word that might be used to sing "Beautiful Ohio" with: *elope:* that she would like to elope with him, a beautiful word that loped into her mouth out of the music and lovely enough, too, to name a cat by if she had not first found the gift of the lovely word Zamour nailed to a tree.

Mr. Simpson was so thrilled by Princis' generous offer that he took it, right there in the hall sitting on the seat of the hat tree that could have been the seat of a gondola they rocked in to the music whose glassy purlings sounded like a dripping and rippling of water to throb together upon and move a boat—toward all their future ahead. And so they eloped that very night, before the xylophone concert was ever over.

"Now we will have a chance to know each other," Mr. Simpson told her, "and we will make our future of a long time together until we are very old, when we will have my pension. That is why it is good to be a railroad man."

"And Zamour's future, too," Princis added. "For he will go with us."

Princis pinned a note on the hat tree saying, "I have eloped to Houston to get married and to make my future. Love, Princis."

Princis sent her sisters one postcard, showing a view of Houston looking north toward Red River County; and for many, many years there was no other word exchanged between them.

This was the time when people from small towns and farms were migrating to bigger towns and small cities, the time of change in Texas. Princis and Mr. Simpson moved into a small frame house in a neighborhood on Hines Street in Houston. The block of houses, called the Neighborhood by those living there, was inhabited by migrants from little towns, and a few were even from Red River County. These people had changed their style of living and slid into the pattern of the city. But oddly enough—for one would have thought she would be the first to change—Princis Lester did not alter, but from the day she settled there went on living as if she were still in Red River County. Something in Red River County kept her.

She did not dress up and catch the bus to spend all day in town, picking through Kress's or having a Coke and sandwich in a department store luncheonette, gazing at women to see if their purse and shoes matched; nor did she spend her afternoons in vaudeville matinées at the Prince Theatre that bubbled dazzling lights even in the daytime; nor shop in Serve-Yourself Piggly Wigglys: she had a charge account at a little grocery store nearby where the man whom she knew personally reached up to the top shelf with a clamping stick to get her a box of Quaker Oats. "Whenever I get homesick for Red River County," one of the neighbors said, "which is less and less—it's all so changed, not like it used to be there—I just go look in Mrs. Simpson's house and feel I've been home to Red River County right on Hines Street in Houston. Why does she harbor home and past?"

When Princis raised the windows in her little house, she put sticks there to hold them up until Mr. Simpson explained to her that windows held up by themselves in the city of Houston. She had her Singer sewing machine and she pumped the pedal to make her print dresses with country flowers on them; she made her own sunbonnets and wore them in the Neighborhood and even in the house or when she swung on the front porch, like her sisters. She put her crocheted counterpane on the bed and her doilies, turned under her own hand, on the dresser and on the arms of the upholstered chairs to protect them.

Princis Lester's Houston behavior was an uncalculated change, among other changes, which at first surprised Mr. Simpson and then pained him literally to death. Princis kept herself from Mr. Simpson, and this took him by such surprise that he could not understand. She had shown him such a yielding eye at the commissary and in the hall under the hat tree. Still, for a while it was an excitement and a challenge to such a man as he, and he pacified himself by thinking about all Princis could give him, all the newly broken wilderness of future awaiting them both, when she was through her waiting. She turned, within the very first year, back toward her ancestry, and this in a world turning toward the other direction, so that such a new world could not support the change —it gave no ground to build upon, she might as well have made a house of mosquito netting; and against what weather could such a flimsy dwelling protect her? Princis became, in the Neighborhood, a curio left behind by a diminishing race, the last of the little country women, as if that race were finishing in her in a little house on a street in a city.

She seemed the last carrier of the bred-up aspects of a played-out species of large ears, small neat heads, faces no bigger than a coffee cup, dainty claws of hands with which to shell pea and bean, to cup a chick, to gather eggs one at a time and not to break any, to hang out small washings, dip one dipper of well water but not to draw a bucketful. When old Mrs. Graves first spied Princis Lester from her two-story boarding house across the street that once, when she and Mr. Graves first came to it from Benburnett County, was their home full of their seven children, she said to old Mr. Graves, sitting in his cane-back rocker in the one room they now lived in, "That new little woman in the Neighborhood will come to change and we will see her do it. Where are all the fine country women that once came to the Neighborhood, where have they all gone in the world? Something has changed them all away." The Graves house had been the grand house of the whole street which ran fifteen blocks between grammar school at one end and junior high at the other. On a corner, it claimed two lots, one a wide space of trees and with a small greenhouse, a chicken yard in the back. It had even had awnings. Now the cars of the boarders were parked under the trees and there was no grass there, only a sort of soiled dirt from drippings of cars; some blown-out tires were lying around, and on Sundays some boarders washed their cars there. The greenhouse was a wreck of glass, roof caved in and the stalks of perished flowers still in it. In summer, though, trumpet vines covered the ruin. But in winter it was ugly to see. The servants' quarters were now rented to a woman from California who, at her age, was studying piano. Some nights it seemed she was trying to show off by playing the "March Slav" so loud for all the Neighborhood to hear.

Though Princis Lester stayed Red River County, Mr. Simpson took to ways of the Neighborhood and drew away from the house and from Princis. He was not a waiting man and he had waited beyond his capacity. Now it seemed to him that he had made a bad bargain at the commissary in Red River County, and he used these words one night to tell Princis Lester so. He started bowling two nights a week with the Hines Street Team while the wives sat in the boxes at the bowling alley and had their beer and cigarettes, yelling when the team made good strikes; or he went to baseball games and wrestling matches, or played dominoes in town somewhere; and he wanted Venetian blinds. More and more Princis was alone, except for one other thing she brought from Red River County and that was her friend Zamour.

In the evenings Princis Lester, in her straight-down country dress falling like a sack down her body, would stand on the front porch or walk up and down the sidewalk on Hines Street in the twilight and call to Zamour to come in. "Zamour! Zamour!" she would call, in a sweet song, until Zamour, plain country cat, would come dallying in on his delicate high hind legs and too-short front ones, so that he seemed to be coming down a ladder to his destination. Sometimes Mr. Framer, one of the neighbors and a policeman, when he was off duty sitting on his front porch cooling off with his bare feet cocked up on the banister, would mimic her and whistle back an insinuating whistle, until his wife,

Mercel, came out of the house smoking her cigarette to tell him he ought to be ashamed. They were Rockport County people who drank their homebrew and fished on the jetties at Galveston on Sundays. They painted all the flowerpots red on their front porch and made a garden in their back yard with painted Roman-art bullfrogs standing on the rim of a fish pool, a goose, and a little elf sitting on a toadstool. Their garden was of city mode, azaleas and camellias; but there was always one row of onions and one of bell peppers and a little greens.

Time passed and Princis withdrew more and more from the city and from the Neighborhood. She would not answer the knock of visiting ladies from the houses in the block, and one in particular, a Christian woman from the Neighborhood church who said she brought greetings from the Married Couples' Class, and had a bob with a permanent wave in it. No one saw Princis Lester any more, walking in her sunbonnet to the grocery store in the late afternoons with Zamour following her and the two of them having their conversation. She and Zamour kept indoors. Neighbors watched her forlorn-looking house through their windows, ferns on the porch burnt up from lack of water, newspapers and circulars in yellow drifts on the porch. They wondered if she was sick or not. The men on the bowling team knew that Mr. Simpson had moved to the Railroadmen's boarding house in town and told their wives.

Then one afternoon there was suddenly the announcement of Zamour on the sidewalk, and sure enough at twilight the Neighborhood heard the call "Zamour! Zamour!"; and something was broken, like a long drought. They saw Princis walking up and down the sidewalk again. Her some sort of confinement was over, it was probably out of embarrassment or mourning at the flight of Mr. Simpson. Month after month, they followed this single daily appearance of Princis Lester at twilight, with only the calling of Zamour to let the Neighborhood know she was there, and her total silence and absence the rest of the time. "I think that's why she calls the cat so long and so sadly," one of the neighbor women said, "to let us know she is still there. For how else would we ever know, if it were not for the sign of the cat?" "And when she does come out, to call the cat," another said, "she looks white as a ghost. But that's because of the heavy powder she wears on her face, as if she'd fallen into the flour bin. Still, that's the old Red River County way: all caked powder, an inch thick, and no rouge."

One day Mr. Simpson fell very ill and was taken to the Southern Pacific Hospital. He lay there month after month, still a young man and sinking ever so slowly toward his death because of drinking. Princis Lester talked once to the doctors who came and made her let them in by crying out that it was a death message—and she said at the door, "About who, my sisters?" The doctors told her that her husband must have been drinking all his life, for he had a cancer of the spleen from it. Did she know? they asked her. "No," she said to them. "I never knew Mr. Simpson that well."

Princis would not go to see Mr. Simpson at the hospital. She wrote a postcard to Red River County—but not to her sisters—and asked her cousin, a twenty-year-old boy named Wylie Prescott, to come and try to get him some kind of job in the city and stay in her house until Mr. Simpson could die. He came—he was from the Prescott branch of the family, kin some way to her, her mother's younger brother's son, she remembered; and he had very little to say, or Princis heard little of what he said. She did not even ask him about Red River County. He took the back bedroom to have for his, though he never seemed to be in it.

The young cousin began a secretive life, the city provided him this opportunity, and he got a job driving a large dusty truck which he parked on Hines Street in front of the house at night. He made his own secret life right away, or found it; and sometimes in the humid evenings, now, the Neighborhood would see Princis and Zamour sitting in the swing on the front porch and the cousin on the front steps playing his guitar. The Neighborhood, living their ways, would all be in their houses: the Catholics on the corner in theirs, the one who had the big tomboy named Sis, in theirs; those in the rotting two-story Graves house in theirs—all the roomers in their hot lighted rooms, their cars parked in front of the house and their radios on at different stations—while the decrepit owners, Mr. and Mrs. Graves, sat pushed back into one room they lived in, with pictures of their seven children and their wives and children on the walls. The yards had been watered and the mosquitos had come, suppers were over, the oleanders were fragrant, and there was the sound of accelerating night traffic on the close boulevards. Tree frogs were in the trees, for there usually had been no rain for three months, and their song was as if the dry leaves were sighing. Then Princis Lester would stroll up and down the sidewalk, ghostly in her thick face powder, arms folded as if it were chilly, her felt houseshoes on, with bonbons of fuzz on the toe, calling, "Zamour! Zamour!" and there was the faint strumming of her cousin's guitar accompanying her little cat call.

It was her cousin Wylie Prescott who came in late one night and saw something, after sitting in his truck in front of the house with Mercel Framer, with whom he had become good friends, playing poker and drinking beer with her to keep her company because Mr. Framer the policeman had night duty. What the cousin saw was Princis Lester sitting in her bedroom by the low light of a little lamp, gazing like a statue into a mirror she held in her hand. Zamour was sitting on her shoulder watching and poised as if to catch a bird in the mirror. They did not even hear him come in. He watched Princis and Zamour, then shut the door very quietly and went on peeping through the crack. There she and Zamour sat, frozen in a spell of gazing. He went on to bed, thinking, "As long as they don't mess with my playparties I won't bother theirs."

When Mr. Simpson finally died, Wylie Prescott disappeared, so far as the Neighborhood could make out, for the truck was gone and no sign of him. Princis Lester took Zamour in out of the Neighborhood for good and they kept together in the little house very quietly, to wait for Mr. Simpson's pension. Every morning at five-thirty the faint click of the alarm clock, turned off now but still set at the hour when Mr. Simpson used to get up to go to the railroad yards, was like a little ghost living on in the clock. "Mr. Simpson is still living in that big ticking clock," she told Zamour. "But when his pension comes, we're going back to Red River County." She played a game with Zamour, to wait for the pension. "When we go back to Red River County, what shall we take with us?" Princis named things first—she would take this, and she would take that; what would Zamour take? Zamour did not seem to want to take anything, only looked up at her through his cotton-eyes, arched his back for her to put her fingers in his fur, and rubbed against her legs, shimmering up his tail. They had grown so close.

Most of the time Zamour had been so much like a person, a beautiful, loyal, and loving person, that Princis had forgotten that he was just a mortal cat, and she talked to him, did nice things for him, making plans for him in Red River County. "We'll plant a little garden and have us some okra in it, have our cow, and there'll be a shade tree for us, when Mr. Simpson's pension comes and we go back to Red River County"; and she would run her fingers through his fur until Zamour would stretch himself long and electric under her caress. But when she would come upon him sprawled on the bed, involved in his frank bestial sleep, mouth gaping and wild teeth bared in his cat snore, she realized, passing to another room, that Zamour was just a dumb beast and could play no game with her, speak no conversation. "Why go back to Red River County at all?" she asked herself despondently. "He is no one to be with." Then was when she was so very lonely that she wished to see her sisters. She wrote a little letter to them and said, "Do not be surprised but I am coming back to the house in Red River County when Mr. Simpson's pension comes."

Her sisters were still there in the old house. There had been a few postcards exchanged during Mr. Simpson's illness and upon his death. What would they think when they saw her coming through the gate to the house, carrying Zamour and her suitcase? Or would she surprise them, come at night without their expecting her, walk up the road hearing their xylophone music which they had played together for years, hymns and sacred songs and some songs out of their girlhood, but most of all "Beautiful Ohio," their best one. People passing the old house on the hill at night would hear the sounds of the xylophone and used to say, "Those are the sweet bearded Lester Sisters." She would open the door, the music would stop, and Cheyney and Maroney would run to her in their delicate bracelets of beard that seemed to hang from the tips of their ears and loop round their chins, and take her back; and the three of them would live the rest of their lives together there in Red River County.

But no . . . she could not. They were of another tribe, it seemed to her, almost as if they were of another color and language; they had their own ways, their own world—she was an alien there. There would always be the question in her mind, did they love her or did they mock her. It would only mean another waiting with the face mirror, to see if it would come to her, and with them waiting and watching, too—she was sure they would wait and watch, for how could they help it? I am not like them, I am not like them, she told herself; they make me feel so lonely and unusual . . . and she could not go back to them. She and Zamour would find a little cottage of their own near her sisters and they would live happily there on the pension. She would go to see her sisters once in a while, as the other kinfolks did, be nice with them, listen to their music, accepting their difference, as she had when she was young. The pension was what to wait for.

It was so long, her waiting. Now she and Zamour mostly sat in the upholstered chair in the living room facing the front door, waiting for the deliverer of the pension. She made a nice place of waiting there. She and Zamour would not go out for anything, for fear of missing the person who would come. Every morning as soon as the click of the shut-off alarm sounded in Mr. Simpson's clock, she would rise in a nervous haste and rush to her waiting place and begin to wait. Sometimes she fell asleep in the chair, waiting, forgetting everything but the waiting, and wake in the morning still in the chair; and go on waiting there. The chair took her shape, as if it were her body, and Zamour, who sat in his place on the back of the chair as if on her shoulder, had grown so nervous that in his waiting he had clawed it to its stuffing of straw and clotted cotton. But Princis had not heard or seen this. In the Neighborhood there was a wedding once, and Mercel Framer was shot at by her husband early one morning when he came home off night duty to find her in a parked truck with a stranger in front of his house, causing some scandal and commotion on Hines Street; and a baby of the Catholic family in the corner house had died—the funeral was held in the house and the cars were parked as far as the front of Princis' house. But she went on waiting, bridelike, in her chair, and never had a single notion of birth or death or scandal beyond this sensual embrace of the chair and the longing for the knock on the door as if a bridegroom would be there to come in and take her so full of anxiety and saved rapture. If she had to get up from the chair for a moment, the chair seemed to carry on the waiting for her, though it clung to her and was loath to let her go, they were so locked together. But she would instruct Zamour to keep his place and take over until she got back—and she came back to the chair panting, as if in desire, to plug herself savagely into it and be fitted tightly, shuffling henlike in it until she settled in a satisfaction on this nest of waiting.

If there was a knock on the door she would grow rigid and whisper to Zamour, "That's Mr. Simpson's pension, there they are"; and go to the door with a welcome ready—just to find a salesman of Real Silk Hosiery or Avon Products who, looking at her, stepped back as if frightened and went away. When the delivery boy had brought the groceries the last time—how long past?—and told her she could not charge them any more because they did not believe at the store that the pension would ever come, he stood away from her and stared at her. "They all must think I am crazy," she said to Zamour, and considered herself for a moment, then added, "because my face must show the secret waiting"; and went back to the chair.

Still the pension would not come, and she waited and she waited. What it was or how much, she could not guess; but the pension was what all railroad people talked about and waited for, and when it came, one beautiful morning, everything would be all right. How it would come or who would bring it she was not sure, though she imagined some man from the Government looking like Mr. Simpson in the commissary, when he was so fresh and full, arriving on her porch calling her name and as she opened her front door handing to her, as tenderly as though it were some of Mr. Simpson's clothes, a package with the pension in it.

One afternoon of the long time a rain storm began, and a neighbor knocked on her door to try to tell her there would be a Gulf hurricane in the night. When Princis spied the neighbor through the curtains she did not break her connection with the chair but sat firmly clasped by it and would not answer nor listen, seeing that it was no one bringing the pension. But the neighbor knocked and knocked until Princis went to pull back the curtain and glare at the woman to say "Give me my pension!" and Princis saw the woman draw back in some kind of astonishment and run away into the Neighborhood. "The Neighborhood is trying to keep the pension from us," Princis told Zamour.

The rain fell harder, and in a time the rain began to fall here and there in the room. She did not care. But the rain began to fall upon her waiting place, upon her and upon Zamour and upon the good chair. "They are trying to flood us out, before the pension comes," she said. She went to get the mosquito bar she had brought from Red River County and stretched it, between two chairs, over the upholstered chair, the way children make a play-tent; and over the mosquito bar she put a faded cherry-colored chenille bedspread she had made many years ago, just to make the tent-top safe. "This will preserve us from the Neighborhood," she told Zamour.

But where was Zamour? He had suddenly escaped the back of the chair in a wet panic. She managed to catch him, brought him back and wrapped him in her old orange velveteen coat with only his wet head showing; and huddled in the Chair under the tent, nursing Zamour, she went on waiting. The water was falling, everywhere now there was the dripping and streaming of water. She began to sing "Beautiful Ohio," but in the middle of the song she spied her favorite ice-blue glass lamp that she had had all these years, and she crawled out of the tent, leaving Zamour in his swathing and rescued the lamp. It was so dark. Would the lamp yet burn? She plugged it in the socket near the tent, and yes, it still glimmered pale snowy light that made her warm and glad. She brought it into the little tent. She took up "Beautiful Ohio" again, right where she had left off. The tent began to leak wine-colored water and she remembered that old sweet red water in the gullies of home when the summer rains came. There is my home, she remembered.

The wind rose and the rain poured down; and after dark, her blue lamp miraculously burning, a portion of the roof over the living room where she and Zamour sat, lifted and was gone. "What is the Neighborhood doing to destroy us?" she cried to Zamour. "They are tearing our house down and turning the Gulf of Mexico upon our heads." And she remembered the leering face at her window of the woman who had come with some threat and warning to her. "Still," she spoke firmly, "they cannot keep our pension from us. We will wait here." Through her mind went the question, "What else is there of mine to save in under this tent from the destruction of the Neighborhood?" She thought of the cherished things she had possessed so long, to take back to Red River County in the game she had played with Zamour: the golden thimble—no, let it go; Maroney, her eldest sister, had mailed it to her parcel-post as a wedding present. The alarm clock with Mr. Simpson getting up in the morning in it: no. The little setting hen of milk glass who sat on her savings of dimes and nickels and pennies—she would get her, for she had been one of the things in this house to wait with her, waiting so brightly on her milk-glass nest full of savings. She found the glass setting hen and brought her back into the tent. The savings were dry, thanks to the way the little hen sat tight over the next part.

Now the water was deep on the floor and the tent was sagging and dripping. Still the lamp burned. One other thing she suddenly thought of and that was her face mirror that was willed to her by her grandmother, it was bronze and had green mold in the crevices, but on the back were the figures of two shy lovers under a tree. She had forgotten the mirror for so long during all this waiting for the pension. She waded through Red River and found it, feeling it out in the darkness, where it had always been, in the dresser drawer, and waded back to the tent with it, her hand sliding at once into the intimacy on the handle which she had worn by clasping it so long. It felt as familiar as a part of her body. "If the pension would come," she begged.

As she got to the tent with the mirror, Zamour turned suddenly fierce and leapt at her like a tiger. She could not catch him, screaming, "Zamour! Zamour!" and Zamour bounded through the water into the darkness. She flounced through the waters of the darkness after him and she could hear him wailing and tearing at the wallpaper and knocking over the furniture. Had Zamour lost his mind, after all she had done to try to keep them both patient? No, cats hate water, she thought. I must pacify Zamour. She cornered him where he had run and leapt, on top of their tent, and in the pale light of the lamp beneath she saw Zamour's face wild and daring her to reach out to him. She reached out, murmuring, "Zamour, Zamour, it is just water"; and as she put out her wet hands, the mirror clasped in one of them, Zamour attacked her and clawed her face, and fled. She cried out and began to weep, fell back onto the floor of water, holding up the mirror to keep from breaking it, and she lay there crying, "O Lord," and buried her bruised face in her hands.

But what did she feel there on her wounded face, was it blood, was it water, and was it fur like the very coat of Zamour? She crawled on her hands and knees, the face mirror still in her hand, into the tent, muttering, "Lord, don't let the light of the little glass lamp go out"; and by the light of the lamp she held up the bronze mirror and saw in it her bearded face, and it bleeding, and the mirror cracked. Accompanying the watery sounds in her house she heard the low gurgling of Zamour somewhere in the dark drenched wilderness, like the sounds of a whimpering baby. She called out, "Zamour! Zamour! do not cry; come back to our tent, I am Princis, remember me; I will do you no harm." But Zamour would not come, he only wailed and sobbed his forlorn watery sounds of fear and alienation in the darkness. She humped under the ruined tent, in the sodden chair, and quietened. Then she whispered, "It is here, it has come, what is mine. Cheyney and Maroney, my two sisters of Red River County, I can come home to you now." And then the light of the lamp went out.

She sat in her chair under the tent in the wilderness. In her lost darkness, she tried to make up her life again like a bed disturbed by a restless sleep. What had led her to where she was, waiting for a pension that would never come? She could not name herself any answers—she would salvage Zamour.

She crawled out of her tent on hands and knees and the tent of gauze and chenille fell upon her like a net. She crawled on, dragging the tent, and hunted through the swamp for Zamour, ever so quietly. She might have been the quietest beaver. She saw two gleams—those were his eyes. She oared herself closer, closer, ever so softly. What was this lost and trackless territory she crawled through, it was like a jungle slough, it was not any place she had ever known, neither sea nor land, but a border-shore of neither water nor earth, a shallows where two continents divided. Zamour, Zamour, her heart begged as she waggled closer to his burning eyes, but her lips could not utter his name. Zamour, Zamour, something deep in her whimpered and bleated, as if it were cold, as though retrieving Zamour he might warm her like a collar of fur.

On her knees, she reached out to the two low gloamings and

were they coals of fire that burnt her to the quick, or were they the eyes of a rattlesnake whose fangs struck her at her face? and she bouldered back, then reared up, bearlike, scrawling and pawing with her hands and arms to claw this fiend away. She heard the crashing of objects Zamour collided with as he escaped her. Was this wildcat clawing the world down upon her? She heard him making a sound that was familiar to her, somewhere, it was a ripping to pieces; and then she heard the burst of glass and the sound of spilling coins; and she remembered her lost waiting place with the chair and the lamp and the setting hen. Which way was this place, to go back to? Where was the light, where was the face mirror? Over there, she thought, still on her haunches. No . . . over here. And then she knew they were forever lost. She had no way, no sign to go by.

She lifted up, feeling now so light, like a buoy, and rising from her knees she sank again, at rest, like stone into the shallows where she was, another waiting place, as if she might from that moment on be a permanent mossy rock in these reefs and tides—of what geography? She breathed. It was all over. She gave it all up then. The tent was hanging from her as though she would carry it forever like a coat of hair. "I give up the lamp and the mirror and Zamour, and even the pension. I give up even the last thing," she said to herself; and, giving it all up to the last thing, she rested and settled, being this rock of nobody, no one she had ever known, renouncing all the definitions, the landmarks, the signs she had gone by to get to this nowhere in this dark bog of debris, on this lightless floor of the mud of her accepted eternity.

But what was that little cry? She found out two lights burning in the faraway distance. Some mercy ship is coming on some channel, she thought; what are those two mercy lights? It was an indestructible sign, lighting her memory back to an orchard on a frosty night and the sound of a cry and the glimmer of two eyes in a tree, and the meeting of two friends. *Zamour!* What was that watery music played out by the rain's hammering drops on broken glass but the tinkling little hammerstrikes of the xylophone . . . and oh her two sisters! She would survive in this dark world she sat in, she would start from there. For it was hers to begin with, to make her own. Something of her own had come to her and there was this to begin with: she was the sister of her two sisters,

Cheyney and Maroney Lester and their own blood. If this darkness ever lifted and the waters ran away, if there was enough light to go by, she would try to find her sisters; and if there was no light she would go by darkness, rising out of these waters, and find her sisters wherever they were in this night waterworld and arrive there, steering herself home, to join them, crying, "See, I am your sister, Princis Lester." They would take her in, be so glad, there would be no more watching, no more waiting, *for they were sisters*. And they would live together in a home of warm felicity.

But Zamour uttered a kind of witch's cry again, from somewhere, somewhere, as if to call her to his claws again; and Princis Lester cried out in the darkness, "Zamour! I give up even you." What time of night was it, because there was suddenly a bright light shining upon her and could there be a voice she heard saying, "Arise, shine; for thy light has come." Who, what had come for her? There were voices and knockings at the front door. They called her name. Why could she not answer? Then they beat upon her door and called her name, "Mrs. Simpson! Mrs. Simpson! Let us in!"

"My name is Princis Lester," she murmured, "sister to my two sisters in Red River County."

Then, how many of them there were, she could not tell—she had not dreamt there were so many survivors in the world—but enough to pound and kick against her door, calling her name louder and louder. She would not answer a thing, she could not move, until a loud strong voice called:

"Mrs. Simpson! Let us in! *Your husband's pension has come!*"

And at that call that echoed through the darkness, she began a lumbering crawl. Shaggy and dripping she buffaloed through the water, slowly slowly, dragging the immense weight of herself and the ragged tent over what seemed sharp rocks and broken shell of a sea floor, across the gravel and shale of the widest shore, slowly slowly toward the light; and found the door. Rising to her knees with her last gasp of strength, she pawed open the door and ogled into the dimming light and the blurring faces of what shining company of bright humanity that looked first like the young face of Mr. Simpson in the commissary, then like the faces, ringleted with hair, of her two sisters; and then there were no faces but it could be the guttering light of Zamour's eyes. "Hanh?" she murmured, with a look of mercy and salvation in her terrible tilted face; and this was how the Neighborhood caught her. Hanging from her as though it were the frazzled coat of a hounded animal was the rag of the chenille and mosquito-bar tent. A black shape shot through the door and into the Neighborhood, and it was Zamour.

That was quite some years ago; and for some years, quite a few, Princis Lester was in the Home, in the county seat of Red River County, resting. She could not tell anyone there what happened, or had no mind to—who knew which? She prinked her beard that wreathed her face like a ruff of titian down and took deep pride in it, it was her one interest. She seemed to be dozing at peace in it, something safe in a nest. There was a purity about her that everyone admired. She was the cherished one of the Home, quietly gleeful, considerate of others, craving no favors but getting them in abundance. She had a peculiarly enviable quality that made the others there long to be like her, even down to the beard. Some said, "What does Princis Lester have that the rest of us don't, to make her so . . ." and they could not find a word to put to her to describe how she was; and another would answer, "A beard." One or two came to her at first, before they knew her, and said, "Listen here, Princis Lester . . ." and mentioned barbering or miracle creams that would burn a beard away; but in time they could not imagine Princis Lester any other way: take her beard away and she would no more have been Princis Lester of Red River County than any of them if they had hung a false beard about their face and said, "I am Princis Lester." It has, they said, to be in your heredity.

Princis' sisters came to see her regularly during their lifetime—it was a precious sight to see them chuckling and softly crooning together—and they would pat each other through long, smiling conversations. Then the time came for the two sisters to die, they were chosen almost at the same time, which seemed right—Cheyney first, then Maroney right after; and they lay buried side by side in Red River County. Oil was discovered on the land where the Lester house once stood, called, now, the Prescott Lease and a very rich strike. Princis Lester still sat like a memorial hedge in the Home, up at Winona, very very old and still, but living her life on.

The pension? It came, finally, after all the red tape of officials and signatures. Amounting to about twenty-eight dollars a month for a switchman with not too many years' service, it waited for years in a file marked "unclaimed" until Princis Lester might one day have her mind to claim it with, until it was clear that she would never find mind for the pension; and so it waited to go to her nearest of kin, her cousin, Wylie Prescott, when she passed on, along with her few personal possessions.

Zamour lived out of doors in the Neighborhood for a long time, a renegade, like the black ghost of Princis Lester. He would not take up with anyone, but he would eat out of anybody's saucer or come up to be petted in a kind of suspicious, faithless way. He showed no trust in anyone, that was plain to see, considering all day long, as he seemed to, what we humans do to poor animal kind. Some of the neighbors, whenever they could lure him, tried to ask him what happened in that little house where he lived so long with Princis Lester, he seemed so close to speaking sometimes. But of course he had no tongue to speak with, he was dumb beast and so there was no story to be had from him. His poor cat brain held the secret. One day the Neighborhood saw him walking away, tail in the air as if a balloon were tied to it—Princis Lester might have been beside him and speaking to him as they walked to the grocery store, for Zamour had that old dalliance in his gait. They saw him go on away, to somewhere; and he was never seen again in the Neighborhood.

Time passed, and with it Princis Lester, laid by her sisters to make three graves in Red River County. "Those are the graves of the bearded Lester Sisters," visitors to the cemetery remarked to each other. It was time for the next generation, and out of it rose the figure of Wylie Prescott to take his inheritance.

Wylie Prescott became a big figure of his generation in Texas, oil king and cotton king, cattle king and lumber king, and something important in the Legislature. He married a girl from a prominent old lumber family of Trinity County and added her inheritance to his. They had a daughter named Cleo and when she was sixteen took her to France and bought up a boatload of old, expensive antiques. While in France, Mr. Prescott went so hog-wild over French chateaux that he bought a whole one and had it moved, piece by piece, from Normandy to Houston, where it was put right back together again exactly as it had looked in some early century. It occupied a huge estate of many wooded acres, and Houston people drove by on Sundays and pointed at its towers topping the trees, telling each other that it was a French chateau from France. In it were all the French tapestries and coppers and cloisonnés, and among these were a once broken but now mended milk-glass setting hen, a golden thimble, and a cracked hand mirror, left behind to Wylie Prescott, heir to all Zamour's and Princis' waiting, with this tale hidden in them for no one ever to know, and Wylie Prescott's secret.

Though Cleo Prescott never asked questions about these old-time Texas relics that were now quite sought after as antiques, she showed more of a fondness for them than for any of the valuable French antiques; and when she fondled them, Wylie Prescott would warn her never to look in a cracked mirror because, according to the superstition, it would bring a curse of bad luck to women.

And that is the tale of Princis Lester and Zamour and the inheritance that followed them.

The Geranium

Since the two people in the house had not looked for any kind of signs, since they had not looked at anything outside themselves, brooding through the long winter, they could not know that something magical had come upon the geranium after long waiting.

The man in the house had wearied and waited. Often he felt himself only a rooted stalk in this house. Often he had wanted to die, having nothing but his own self, rising and falling in its anxiety and anguishes. He wished lately for any new thing, anything bright and unused and freshly made, not tampered with or mauled by the mind or the relentless clutch and seizure of the senses. He had known, like a calendar, that the new time was coming: he had heard the Lenten bells, and on Ash Wednesday he had seen the people returning down the roads, bent in some new kind of humility. But he waited with fear, even terror, for how could he bear the sudden thrust of it, the enormous burst of sweetness and gentleness upon him after the failure of the winter? He did not feel prepared, he had not been made ready. He could not bear a blade of grass, he thought, nor the sight of the thawed river across the yard that would, surely and irresistibly, crawl one day, like a reborn serpent, out of its frozen sheath.

Something between the man and his wife had gone stale and bloodless in the winter. They did not come to each other with any burning union; each stayed away to each, alien and suspicious and cunning, frightened to be touched, rankling at the approaches and the trespasses of each other. They had gone tired and rotten inside.

Because she had lost him somewhere in the long, sunless time, the woman in the house was wanting to take to herself anything vigorous and having surprise in it, anything to catch her up and bind her tightly to her place again. She had fallen loose and molty and not quick to any promise or challenge. Yet she defended herself against any signs of what she might be yearning for.

The whole house had the coldness and the lightlessness of languor in it. All the books seemed read and exhausted of being used. The stoves were scarred and sooted from long winter burning. There was nothing in the yard but stubble and bare boughs or the white burial of snow.

But on a night in late March there was a kind of equinoctial turmoil in the world. It began in the afternoon with the triumphant entrance of a clattering wind that blew upon the earth and shined it like a chamois. At dusk the first rain came, sweet and cleansing; then scrawny snow fell, regretting the rain, like an emptying of the last few flakes of winter. In the earth and heavens there was the pitiful, almost embarrassing yearning and striving, turning and trial of an adolescent toward a vague and dubious call to fulfillment. There was clearly an agitation abroad, some kind of labor.

They sat at supper and resisted. They had had the wind at their doors and at their windows like something alien knocking to get in, and there had been the nervous rattle of trees and panes.

"If it is going to freeze again, I had better cover the pump," he said, and rose and went to the well.

She went on eating. Let him cover the pump, the well has gone dry, she thought.

After a while he came back and stood at the door. His hair was blown down and his face looked washed and bright. She thought him a stranger for a moment and she was frightened a little.

"Come outside by the well, Miriam," he said.

She got up and went outside with him, wondering what he had there at the well for her.

They stood, apart, in the terrible stirring of the world outside. She would not venture to the well with him, but stood away, by a tree. He stood by the well with a faint arabesque of tenderness in his body. The unbearable scent of new rain seeped in the yard, and there was a quivering change shimmering over the well and toiling in the tree. Suddenly something had come. The old blood was trying to thaw like all the rivers in the land; there was a kind of sloughing time upon the world, a kind of shedding of old scabbiness, and they did not want it yet they were dumbly calling to it; they cared and did not care, were not sure, were troubled and uncertain. They stood apart, one under the tree, the other by the well. The smell of the washed earth seemed to turn them, "Turn, turn . . ."

Finally she said, "I'm cold and the supper will get cold."

They went into the house.

When they sat again, in a kind of shyness, they did not know what to do with each other. Their forks trembled in their hands and clattered faintly on the plates.

While she was washing the dishes, he suddenly looked at the window and saw a surprise there, like a gift left secretly.

"Look, Miriam," he called softly. "The geranium by the window is going to bloom."

She did not want to look yet, it had come too suddenly, without warning; and she stood over the dishpan not wanting to see anything, not wanting to go humble and bend to anything. But she took her hands dripping from the water and moved them with an infinitely subtle gesture of tenderness toward the geranium pot, as if she wanted to hold it a moment like someone beloved returned. For she saw, deep in the shadowy crevice between two limbs of the geranium, a cluster of little hairy pods gathered round together and covered with a frail green membrane. Slowly and ever so patiently, through a long, blossomless time, the geranium had waited by the window; and now it showed upon its body the sign of the change that had happened within itself.

He was watching her. But something called back her soiled hands to the water and she drowned them in the water again.

She stood with her hands hidden in the water as if she were trying to wash some stain from them, to cleanse them of some blight. Then she wanted it, willed it, and she looked again. There she saw it, the timid hesitancy of the beginning bloom, and she knew, now, that the same sign was in him. She saw him standing by the geranium, he was a little like new, himself, and she did not want to look him in the eyes, straight. But she looked again, this time trembling and defiant, and she saw the undeniable signal, the little, folded crimson annunciation, like a small horn to blow a reveille.

They had come through; and whatever it was that was stirring the earth outside had come into their house and, who knew, might come into them on the morrow, like a slow turning, like the bridegroom forth from his chamber and the bride out of her closet.

She went on washing the dishes, putting down a cup or a plate to be dried by him. And finally she said, as if she wanted to make an oblation to it, "Give the geranium a little water, Jim."

He felt as if she were unfolding, yielding ever so slightly to him. And when he sprinkled the water on the geranium she felt as if he were anointing her, and the blood in her hands quickened a little as she turned them round and round in the ablution of the water.

The Horse and the Day Moth

In Memory of Margo Jones

The waked dreamer was sitting on the side of his bed, head in his hands and staring at the floor, remembering his daydream and trying to order it, thinking how we see so much, know so much and yet are able to shape and tell so little of it all and that so slowly and with such pain. It was a hot summer afternoon in the great city.

Suddenly in the hot afternoon stillness and yet in his dream he heard a shouting and calling of voices. "Hey! Whoa! Whoa!" and, immediately following, the sound of hoofs on the brick street outside. He ran to his window and saw in his street the shape of a fierce and galloping horse, head in the air and tail flying, as though it had loped out of his mind. Leaning out his window he watched the runaway horse, here in the street of a great city, rushing and snorting, sometimes on the sidewalk, sometimes in the street. Children were fleeing but a running crowd was following the horse. Then he heard the sirens of police cars. As he watched the wild horse loping down the street—leaning farther and farther out the window and away from his room that held the dream, though really more and more into the dream he had had—he saw, finally, at the far end of the street, a policeman leap out to seize and capture the runaway horse. Then he saw the crowds close in around the captive animal, in the glaring sun, far at the end of his street; and he went back to his bed and sat on the side of it again. Suddenly there was the sense of the day moth again.

Sitting on his bed, as though he could not leave the place where the dream had happened and where it still lived, he remembered another horse. It was one winter afternoon in the city when he was walking, in winter rain, on the edge of Central Park where all the horse-drawn carriages were, that he saw a crowd formed around something. He went to see. In the middle of the circle of people there lay a horse that had just fallen dead. The carriage, which was still bound to him, was overturned and lay on its side too as if it were a permanent member of the horse, in life and death. The police were already there, the driver of the carriage was standing back from the disaster in dumfoundedness, and the rain was falling on the huge, black, oily side of the animal and trickling down his belly. Suddenly the question had cracked in his head like a pain: But what can any of us do when some large fragment of life falls dead in the street for all to see? He thought of equestrian statues in plazas, and it was for a moment as though a stone horse had fallen whole among a crowd of walking people, and who was to remove and raise it again? He noticed, he remembered, that some of the crowd stood there looking as though they were suffering some large loss of their own, as though a memory had dropped down or a hope had gone dead in broad daylight for the world to see, and who or what was to remove it or raise it again?

The crowd stood quietly under umbrellas or huddled in overcoats. There are these moments in great cities when not even the stone bastions of buildings seem defensible but might too fall into an avenue. A newcomer would arrive, asking, "What's happened, what's happen—" and stop cold when he saw, over a shoulder or through an opening in the crowd, the still pile of black animal on the wet pavement. The horse's head was stretched upward and its teeth were bared as if it were neighing and its mane lay wet over its neck. It seemed twice as large as any animal, this horse, in its death. The buildings around seemed smaller. He had turned and walked away. Where to go, how to be? he wondered.

As he walked away there flashed in his mind a little scene of two summers back, in a garden in Texas in the summertime, when he had gone home for a visit with his mother, who was very ill and would have perhaps no other summer ever beyond this one. She was able to sit in the garden and so they sat under the afternoon trees in a wooden porch swing hung from the branches. She was speaking of flowers flourishing in the garden under her own hand. There was the sound of a hammer in the background, and he thought how always in the summertime there had been the sound of an unseen, remote carpentry in this neighborhood of small, clean wooden houses, some repair going on, someone mending his house in the fair days before winter came. His mother was naming the flowers to him again for the hundredth time, speaking of their eccentricities, of their hardships under the sun or too much rain, of the "perennials," of this one "that turned out to be white though I bought it for a red"; and how the grandchildren in their games had run through the round flower bed "but, anyway, the seeds came up in their footprints." "The flowering garlic has already run up seed, and it so early," and he looked to see it sure enough speared on top with its own seed as though it were at that moment "running up" seed as he looked at it.

It was a sad time and yet a very serene time and, feeling this, he got up to go look at the Louisiana daisies that had been brought many years before from Shreveport when an aunt came from there to visit and that were purple beyond any purple. He saw this: on a blossom there lighted, out of nowhere and as if out of his mind, in a gentle glee, a little lion-faced butterfly the size of a bee. There was a shagginess about this moth—it was, really, a little day moth—a mongrel quality it was; and yet it had a fierce face of lions and leopards and was the color of those. This was the kind one had always been able to catch easily, they were so tame. Here was this little thing, still in the world and still over these flowers, waiting for pinched fingers to catch. One had somehow thought they had all vanished, this scrubby, ordinary little race of butterfly! He easily caught the day moth, easily as ever. This creature is still with us, he had thought, in a kind of loyalty that made him think that all that had been before was still the same and would always be. So neither of them, prey nor captor, had changed through the years. He held it for a moment, like an aching greeting, then let it go. Sure enough, there it was, on his finger tips as before, the faery gilt of the day moth's tiny wings. He kept it on his fingers all afternoon, though visitors came and though there was much talk about many things; all afternoon he was aware of himself holding his fingers as though they had been burned, thumb and middle finger that had caught for an instant the quietly immortal little day moth. He was instinctively preserving the touch there, the delicate burn and stain of the day moth's wings shining in broad afternoon sunlight. Toward the end of the afternoon, around darkening, his mother had said it was time to go in the house, and he took her hand and helped her in. It had been the first time he had touched anything with the stained hand that had held the moth.

It was as small and simple a happening as that which he remembered, this quiet little scene that lighted up, inexplicably, in his mind as he walked away that day from the great dead animal, down Fifty-seventh Street, in the rain. How in the world did the horse and the day moth find each other in him, and what had brought them together? He had wondered then and wondered now again, sitting on his bed. Would anyone ever know the relationships between objects seen, now and then, between moments and sights, disparate and antithetical as they seemed? At the river he had stood in Sutton Place, and looked at the rain on the water and thought again: But what is there to do, seeing these sights of summer and winter, in the rain or sunshine, but to let the mind relate them to each other for its own secret reasons, to carry horse and butterfly within oneself, through many seasons, until they find each other and reveal a meaning to their carrier? But what had brought them together in him, their meeting place? he had wondered at the river.

As he sat on his bed, close to where the dream had happened, he thought how that day of the dead horse had been filled with the sense of enormous objects falling, like buildings into streets, bridges into rivers and statues into plazas, until the little memory of the day moth had ended it with the sense of fragile flights and glimmers of small risings and flutterings. For he had walked, fugitive, out of this room of giant disorder, of violence, as though Cain had lived there, where the weight of his secret life was heavy as fallen stone and nothing, nothing would rise out of it, or who would raise it again; though he knew the fragility of his violence and the delicacy of his ferocity. But he saw, now in his room, that a balance was struggling, that a shape from outside, in the world, and inside, in a dream, was at work. There is a link, he knew again now, between the happenings of the daily world and the dreaming mind that holds its hidden images. It was as though life were unfolding on either side of a partition, a wall.

Now he held the dream as close as another body in his bed; and now there was a joining, as in love. We cannot believe, he thought, how all things work together toward some ultimate clear meaning, we cannot believe. Human life is at once in a conspiracy to prove us of small or no end, and a conspiracy of incidents and images to lead us to a beginning again. There is the constant, gentle and steadfast urging of the small, loyal friendliness, the pure benevolence of some little Beginningness that lies waiting in us all to be taken up like a rescued lover and lead us to a human courage and a human meaning. The rest is death: murder (self or other), betrayal, violence and cruelty, vengeance and crimes of fear. But the little Beginningness is in all of us, waiting.

In his dream he had seen his mother standing half in the doorway of the house, in darkling light, in the attitude of an early photograph he knew of her, her hair bobbed and graying, for she was so ill, even then, calling out to him and his sister in the yard where they had drawn a hopscotch in the dirt: "Come on in now, it's darkening." And when they had gone in, he and his sister, they had found the house filled with the darkening and no answer to the call but the low, gentle, echoing cry, "Come on in now, it's darkening."

Now all in his room there was the hovering presence of the day moth.

There Are Ravens to Feed Us

This was in a bleak stone apartment building in New York City, where he had come. All winter—it was a rainy one, and day after day gray and thick—the family below him cursed one another. He could be waked early in the lower tumult that seemed, for a moment as he woke, to be continuation of his unhappy dreams. What contention there was between the members of this family below he never knew—some deep resentment one member had against another, some awful secret among them all. There seemed no resolution or pacification of this hidden strife.

What had happened to these people? He heard ringing accusations, warnings of reprisals, threats of vengeance. This one voice, that of an older man (was he the father?), said it was going to leave, was going to pack its bags and get the hell away; this other voice, a woman's, young and shrill (the daughter's?), said it despised all the rest of the family and would be glad when it could move to an apartment of its own; and still another, that of a young man (the son?), declared that all life was filled with liars and cheats and wished it could cross the ocean to another country, any country, and die; or get on a long train and travel away, forever. Finally, the oldest voice of all, a flat old woman's (the grandmother's surely), delivered over the other voices declarations of doom and godlessness and hopelessness, said its long, tired life would never end in peace.

At noon each day there seemed to be a kind of truce, for silence hung over the cursed family below him. Then there was not a sound. Perhaps they had murdered each other and all lay dead and quietened. But around three o'clock the strife began again and rose in the sunless air of the deep and desert chasm between his building and the next so that the echo in this hellish canyon between two brick sides of buildings where windows opened out onto a bleak damp hole was like that of damned souls. Then the city seemed breathless and suffocating, without mercy or hope, and was he placed here to live out an eternity of hatred and accusation and self-doubt on the rim of a pit of despair from which hollow voices wailed and resounded? His work desk was fixed against a little window that opened onto the chasm, and the savage attacks from below rose and echoed into his room and hung over him as if to mock his work. He tried hanging double folds of blankets at the window to seal out the sound, but this only created a more sinister echo of muted crying and clashing and shrieking of voices. Once he spoke to tenants who lived below the damned family, wanting to find some sharer of his haunted days and nights. But to his surprise they said they heard nothing but an occasional scraping of chairs or the traffic of feet, that was all.

One day it was so unbearable that he was filled with despair and left his room in the morning. He walked the streets in the rain and sat in the park in the rain, looking at human faces as if he had forgotten there was any humanity left in a race of haters and accusers. Away from his tormented room, he saw that his nights and early mornings, when he lay in his bed and heard from the pit the hollow rising and falling catcalls and oaths and slanders uttered by members of this shadow-family against each other, had seemed an evil nightmare, a relentless obsessional vision of the human race clashing on an endless desolate plain of eternity where there was no hope. Was it his own internal dream of despair, and was he guilty of the sin of despair? What was his crime against humanity, what was his sin against hope that this doom rose up from the forlorn shaft between brick walls and resounded through his window and cursed his room? Were there voices at all, except those of his own inner selves of fear and distrust and bitterness? Did such a family live below him at all? He had never seen them, though he had embodied and costumed their voices and created living people out of them. He walked and walked. Then at midafternoon, full of self-doubt and carrying the guilt of the whole vision, he determined to return to the apartment house, walk up the stair very slowly, stop by the door of the apartment below his, listen for the voices, then rise to his room and sit by the window to listen again.

He approached his apartment house from the opposite side of the street, for he feared it and came toward it suspiciously. As he walked along the other side, looking toward his haunted building, something beautiful was happening to the building. There, standing on the steps of it, was a bright gathering of young people dressed in spring colors. It was a wedding! There were bridesmaids in pale and delicate rose and violet colors, they were holding bouquets of lilies-of-the-valley and violets and irises. They stood on the steps like a vision of loveliness and purity against the background of the ugly and haunted apartment building that had housed his torment. He stood and watched. Then the bridesmaids moved from the steps to the sidewalk and there followed beautiful young men in white coats and forget-me-nots in their lapels. They joined the bridesmaids. Now some little doll-like girls holding enormous bunches of flowers came out the door and stood on the steps for a moment, then joined the bridal party on the sidewalk. And last there came like a white vision the blessed figure of the bride. She stood on the steps of his building and for a moment the ugly stone was transformed as if a vision had touched it. From the windows above, hands appeared and scattered down blossoms and petals. The haunted stone building that had entombed him prisoner of violence had opened and had freed this pure and lovely happening like a redemption of darkness and grief. Was it the beginning of a change in everything for him, for the world? Was this the difficult and verily impossible-seeming miracle wrought at last, at so long last? Might it be the beginning of something new, of change toward better, toward hope?

After large limousines had opened their doors and received the wedding and borne it away, he crossed the street and ascended the steps. There were petals of flowers lying there. Inside, as he began to walk up the four dark flights of shabby stairs where he had once imagined shapes of terror lurking and expected to encounter at each turning some face or figure of anguish and doom, he saw here and there on the stairs the petal of a rose, the blossom of an anemone. He approached the apartment of hate and heard not one sound from it. Had they gone away, if ever they had existed, the accursed family? When he passed their door he saw a wreath of white flowers fixed there. Now he knew that the beautiful wedding had come from the house of violence.

He went into his room where the very air seemed becalmed and he opened his little window and listened and felt peace over the chasm that had held despair. Then he sat at his desk and began to prepare himself for some day that would soon come for him, an event of glad tidings, some fulfillment of wish, reward, a day or a night of beautiful sensation, some abstract gladness, some sight of loveliness, the sunshine lying upon his floor, the birds of spring lighting the Trees of Heaven beyond his back window, and the air and light of springtime filling the winter chasm of despair.

Tenant in the Garden

In Memory of Spud Johnson

To this little town in Napa Valley came this little old printer named Mr. Stevens, and he was about fifty at the time. He had been appointed to teach printing in the junior high school.

Mr. Stevens had been a printer and a bookbinder in the Southwest most of his life and had never taught school before. He was a frail, doll-like man with such a faint voice. He had lived his life in the Southwest, quietly and meagerly, working at his little hand press and in his small shop and taking care of his old sister until she died. After her death he felt the need of a trip and a change. So he put his sleeping bag and his camp stove in his little car and drove along carefully towards San Francisco, pitching his camp at nightfall in a grove or a desert on the highway. When he got into Northern California, he liked it so much that he decided to live around there for a while; but he would have to have a job. When he heard of the dire need for print-shop teachers in the public schools of California, he filled out his application and was hired at once and sent to Napa.

He found two rooms in the half-story of a house belonging to a kindly old lady who lived alone except, she stated, for visits of her brother from Petaluma on weekends. This brother was, she added, an ex-sea captain who was now a part-time minister in the church. The first weekend sure enough brought the Bishop Jack, as he was called, in from Petaluma. Bishop Jack rose at 5:00 A.M. with a burst of composite sacred and maritime song—it was a hymn sung in an ohoho mariner style, resounding in the half-story where he and Mr. Stevens slept, and rousing the whole household. At such an enforced early breakfast as they had to come down to, Bishop Jack presided, fresh as the morning dew and full of spiritual energy. He gave a short sermon on God's world in the freshness of morn while the bacon and eggs were frying and went on to the subject of the church militant when they sat down to eat them. Then he announced he had retired from his church in Petaluma and from all churches and had come home to his sweet sister's house where he would live for the rest of his long life, fishing and praying and singing. This meant that Mr. Stevens would have to leave, though he was invited to remain on in this warm household of good Christian fellowship.

A few days later, Mr. Stevens found in the garden of a large, old-fashioned house exactly where he wanted to live. It was a playhouse of an earlier style with one little room, a tiny porch with two columns, and one small step. There was a gable and, in it, two eye-sized dormer windows. Mr. Stevens prevailed upon the lady who inhabited the big house to rent him the playhouse. At first she would not hear of it; but when Mr. Stevens told her he had brought with him the furnishings of his kerosene camp stove and tiny oil lamp and his sleeping bag, she had a vision of how nice it would be and was won over, feeling the need of company, anyway. She did not say yes at once but, "wait a minute", and ran, in her great strides, into her big house. In a moment she came out again and was by Mr. Stevens' side saying, as she handed him some faded dotted swiss curtains that were lacking a number of dots from old age and many launderings. "Here . . . for the windows! They belong to the playhouse." This was her verbal contract with the tenant of the playhouse.

The big lady who owned the playhouse but lived in the big house was Mrs. Algood, a large Swedish woman with big feet and a big head with abundant hair. She had been living alone since her husband died and her daughter for whom the playhouse had been built, had married young and moved to the Valley of the Moon. "My daughter Sybil played all her childhood in this little house," she told Mr. Stevens in her cool Swedish lilt of voice, "almost right up until she moved to the Valley of the Moon—though, during her last years, when she had shot up into a tall, thin girl, she had to stoop over to get inside. Then she met this logger from up in Oregon and could not see anything but him. They eloped, without even telling me, to the Valley of the Moon. I have not written her one letter since."

Now at night there was a yellow light illuminating the playhouse. It was autumn and frost came on the panes and the fallen leaves gathered on the idyll porch of the little house. Sheltered by a large eucalyptus tree, Mr. Stevens sat in his house and heard the cones drop. A squirrel sat on the porch and sometimes on the roof. Rain fell a few times and gave him a cozy feeling. Children in the neighborhood saw the lighted playhouse. When Mr. Stevens would blow out his kerosene lamp and slide into his sleeping bag, zippering himself up into it like a mummy or papoose, he felt safe and hidden and warm in his peaceful dwelling.

But in printing class there was no peace and little safety. The boys were rough and chased each other around the shop. They printed vulgar words and did not like Mr. Stevens and would ridicule him. They seemed to want to chip off pieces of him like a little clay kewpie, by throwing chalk and spit wads at him when his back was turned. As his voice was so small, Mr. Stevens could not even raise it above the clanking of the manual printing presses, much less above the ruckus of his students; and so pandemonium reigned. He had been used to living quietly in some small space or other, in his small workshop with the hand press or in his little bed-sitting room with the tiny wood stove on two animal-like legs and with two little eyes upon which sat a dainty copper teakettle and a cupsized saucepan. Here he had sat at his table and bound small books with cloth, gingham prints with flowers, and done no harm to anyone. Why had he taken this job that had cruelly brought him out into the open world where he seemed to cause strife and antagonism just by being the way he was? He was meant to sit quietly some place, alone. He was happiest that way. His sister had known that, and she was the only one who had.

Other teachers felt disdainful of him and spoke to him of "discipline" in the classroom. But he simply did not have the voice for it. The students called him names, disliked him because he was piddling and funny-looking, whispered that he looked and acted like an old, bald-headed woman and that his wizened face was like a mummy's. His voice grew fainter and fainter. He would come home, in the afternoons, hoarse and trembling and exhausted. Then he would sit still on the front porch, resting and despondent and wondering what to do. He wished he could run away and go back to his peaceful valley in New Mexico. But his nature was stoic and long-suffering and he would not quit.

One day, about a month after he had been there, he suddenly walked out of the print shop and left the riot to take its own course. He walked calmly across the schoolyard and towards home. When he looked back, he saw the stacked heads of the boys at the window, watching him, quiet and dumbfounded. He walked on.

At home in the playhouse, he pulled the dotted swiss curtains across the windows and closed the front door. Then he stuffed his little pipe, put it in his mouth and lit it, and got into his sleeping bag and zipped himself up safe in it, leaving his arms free.

Mrs. Algood came out of her big house and knocked at the playhouse door and called why was he hiding in there. He told her to come in, in a hoarse whisper. When she found him in his sleeping bag, smoking, she felt very sorry for him.

"I have quit my teaching job," he told her calmly.

"Well," Mrs. Algood said to him, "I will sit here with you for a while so you won't be too lonesome."

In a while there was the noise of people. Mrs. Algood looked out the tiny window to see the printing class coming across the garden to the playhouse.

"A bunch of boys are coming to call on you," Mrs. Algood told Mr. Stevens.

When the class came to the little gate and stood there, Mr. Stevens got out of his sleeping bag and went out on the porch. All the boys yelled and shouted. Mr. Stevens sat down on the step and puffed his little pipe.

"We heard that you lived in a playhouse and came to see if we could believe our eyes," one boy said.

"Old baldheaded woman!" yelled another.

Mrs. Algood came out of the playhouse and stood there, humped over. A boy yelled, "He has a wife, a giant for a wife!"

"You bunch of boys get out of my garden or I'll call the police and the truant officer. You are acting like a bunch of scallywags; why are you not all in school?" She shook her fingers at them.

"Because the teacher left us—in the middle of the period," a boy said, shaking his finger back at her. "You better call the truant officer after him."

"And we followed him," another said.

"Yeah, and look where we found him hiding. In a girl's playhouse." All the boys laughed.

"He lives here," Mrs. Algood said. "The playhouse is his home, and good enough as any."

"Not where we come from," a big red boy said. "He ought to be in the nut house."

Mr. Stevens got up and stood leaning against the little white column on the porch. Mrs. Algood stooped like a pained giant under the low roof. She and Mr. Stevens stood together there and dared the mob. One boy suddenly threw a rock at the window and it crashed through. But Mrs. Algood and Mr. Stevens did not budge.

Suddenly across the garden came some of the neighbors who lingered in the background under the trees in their house dresses and house shoes. Then came the Principal of the school, speeding up in his car. He got out and slammed the door and came running across the garden. The boys quieted down and parted to let the Principal pass through them to the gate. He was round and plump and red in the face.

"Now what is all this?" he cried. No one would tell him.

"Why is the print-shop class standing here, two blocks from school, and it eleven o'clock in the morning, and its teacher standing casually on the porch of a doll house, smoking a pipe?" he roared. "Have I lost my mind?" The Principal's face was crimson with rage.

"Because Mr. Stevens resides here and has quit his job," Mrs. Algood said. "And I am the proprietress and landlady of this property and house and can order you away or call the police if you do not hold your horses."

One of the boys called out, "He ran away from print shop in the middle of class. We all followed him here."

"What is the trouble, Mr. Stevens?" the approaching Principal asked, a little quieter and wiping his glasses, the way he did when he sat at his desk and had a culprit before him in his office.

But Mr. Stevens' voice was completely gone now, and he could say nothing.

"He has lost his voice yelling at his class of hoodlums," Mrs. Algood said.

The Principal ordered the boys back to school and at once, and they moved away, whispering to each other and looking back. Then the Principal opened the gate and went upon the porch where he stooped.

"Sit down," Mrs. Algood said, "Mr. Principal. You'll break your back trying to stand up."

The Principal sat down on the step, completely covering it. The neighbors went away, talking to each other. Mrs. Algood asked would they like some coffee and said she would get some. In a moment she came back with coffee in a play set of painted china cups and saucers, a painted coffeepot on a tin tray.

"This is the set that goes with the house," she said, "and not a one broken over all the years since my daughter married the logger and left to go live in the Valley of the Moon." And she poured and passed round the coffee. They had it on the front porch.

"I am J. P. Sandifer, the Principal of Valley High," the Principal said, sipping his coffee.

"Glad to meet you," Mrs. Algood said, drinking hers.

A neighbor woman next door was watching them from her window and suddenly called back into her house, "Mama, come here right this minute if you want to see something." Presently a little old gray lady was at the window and the woman said to her, "To my name and soul, Mama, look out there at what is happening on the porch of Mrs. Algood's playhouse." The old lady saw a little bald-headed man, a giant woman and a pumpkin shaped man all having a tea party on the front porch of the playhouse. She gazed and gazed and did not speak. The daughter said, "I'm so mixed up today. I don't know whether to call the police or go join the party."

"Why don't you go practice on your grand?" the old lady said.

Mr. Sandifer told Mr. Stevens he would call again the next morning before school to speak with him, seeing as how his voice might be restored to him by then, with a little rest and quiet. He advised the print-shop teacher to stay away from school for a few days and to rest his voice. He then said good-by to Mrs. Algood, thanked her for the coffee and left.

"Never mind," Mrs. Algood told Mr. Stevens. "There is nothing the school can do to you but ask you to resign, and that would be a good thing. You must never go back to Valley High. You are welcome to live here as long as you like. If worst came to worst, you could put a printing press in my basement, next to the washing machine. We could work side by side. In the meantime, why don't you get back into your sleeping bag and take a little rest."

"Thank you," Mr. Stevens mouthed.

Late in the afternoon, at visiting time, a visitor appeared at the little gate, and it was the little old gray lady from next door. She had her sunbonnet on, and carried her walking stick and she called Hello! at the gate and then stepped through it. She rapped on the porch with her stick and Mr. Stevens came to the door.

"How do you do," she said. "I am Mrs. Pace from next door. Seen you through my window, living in this playhouse, and have come to pay you a visit." Mr. Stevens went into the house and brought out a child's rocking chair and the little old lady sat down in it and began to rock. "I have watched this little house from my window, which is right across there through the shrubs, for many a year," she said, "and nothing in it since the mean little girl grew up so tall and married and went to live in the Valley of the Moon. I am very glad that you have moved in. It's nice to see your light at night." Mr. Stevens nodded to her and puffed his little pipe.

"I came to live with my son Fritz a long time ago, so long I can't remember when," she said, rocking in the chair, "but I do know it was when my husband died in Red River County, far away from here. Agnese is my son Fritz's wife and she loves a grand piano more than anything ever in this world. As a result, my son Fritz is saddled with paying out a grand piano for most of his working life and then off his old-age pension after that, I guess: a grand piano is hung around Fritz's neck like a millstone. It is so big that they had to tear the door down to get it in the house. Now they want to move to another house that's big enough to hold the grand, but cannot afford to move the piano, so must live where the piano is, which just about fills the living room. Agnese can't have any children, so she takes it out on a grand. At first she said she would teach to pay for it, but never one student did she even try to get.

She will begin to play the grand after supper. You will hear it. Right after supper she will sit down to her grand and she will play. First it will be 'The Turkish March.' She always begins with that."

Mr. Stevens nodded and puffed his little pipe, and Mrs. Pace rocked and rested a little. Then she sang out a song:

"We lived—'twas a long time ago—my husband and me, in red dirt country. 'Twas Red River County. . . . far away from here. We rode a red road to town in red dust in the summer, and came home in the moonlight on a red road.

"The sweet waters of Red River, sweet as wine," she said. "Sometimes I would give anything in the world to go live back in Red River County again. But guess I will never see it again in all my life. Where do you come from?" she asked Mr. Stevens.

Mr. Stevens lipped that he was from New Mexico.

"I would not like New Mexico. I would like only Red River County," Mrs. Pace said, stubbornly, clenching her lips. "I just came to pay you a visit," she said, rocking, "and mainly to tell you about Red River County. I never get to visit anybody anymore because my daughtern-law Agnese says I'm not to go out of the house account of my swollen ankles. But I know I am strong as an ox. When she went into town to pay on the grand piano—she won't send it by mail, takes cash and hands it in person to the music store—I put on my bonnet in a hurry and sneaked over here to pay you a little visit and to speak of Red River County."

"I'm glad you came," Mr. Stevens whispered.

"And now I must go, for tonight is my night to set the table. Me and my son Fritz take turns, and if ever we miss our turn my daughtern-law Agnese loses her temper. She has an ugly mouth when she is mad. I must go and get my bonnet off before she comes back from playing on the grand."

Mrs. Pace got up slowly and went on back to the house next door.

In an hour or so, near dusk, a group of men got out of an automobile that had driven up on the street in front of the playhouse. Mr. Stevens was still sitting there, smoking and rocking. The men, three of them, came across the garden and stopped at the gate to the playhouse.

"Are you Mr. Stevens?" one of the men asked.

Mr. Stevens nodded yes.

"We have to talk to you," he said. The three men came through the gate to the porch of the playhouse. They stood there, looking sternly at Mr. Stevens.

"We are from the city rent commission and have come to advise you that you are breaking the law by inhabiting what is not a fit dwelling but a playhouse. This is no rent house. There is no running water, no sanitation; and you will be fined and put in Napa Jail if you do not vacate the playhouse at once. We will not leave until you do. Where is the proprietor of this house?"

Mrs. Algood had already come out of her house when she saw the portent of the three officials arriving. She said to the men, "Mr. Stevens cannot speak for he has lost his voice trying to teach print shop in Valley High. But he has done nothing wrong; it is my playhouse which I have rented to him and I demand to know the trouble he is in. Mr. Stevens has done nothing wrong. He is a kindly man and wouldn't hurt a fly, quiet as Sunday."

"He will have to leave the playhouse at once," the man said, "and we are here to evict him. The house is not habitable and does not meet the requirements of the city pertaining to dwellings."

The neighbors were coming out of their houses again and some were already standing at the edge of the garden, listening and whispering to each other. And then suddenly the whole neighborhood seemed to be at each other's throat and one of the officials of the town had to come back and ask the group to either be quiet or go to their houses.

In the midst of all this, Mr. Stevens was very quietly doing something inside the playhouse; and in a little while he came out with his sleeping bag rolled up and under his arm, his camp stove and suitcase in the other hand. Then, the officials glaring at him and the neighborhood standing in the yard watching every step he took, Mr. Stevens walked past them with his possessions to his little car parked in front. The boys of print shop began to whistle and yell, "'Ray! 'Ray!" and the neighbors all mumbled to one another. Then Mr. Stevens got in his car and shuffled to get himself in a comfortable driving position, as though he were going to drive a long, long way. Suddenly he heard the rolling sounds of "The Turkish March" being played on the grand piano in the house next door. He looked at the back window and there was old Mrs. Pace waving to him. Then he started his car and drove away.

The three officials went into the playhouse, looked around it, came out and closed the door, casting an official and warning glance at Mrs. Algood, who could say nothing. The Principal was saying to one of the men of the neighborhood that he did not know what he would do for another print-shop teacher, they were so scarce. And if you finally found one, he turned out to be a misfit. He said he guessed he would have to drop print shop from the curriculum and add another Broadening and Finding course for students at Valley High.

After the officials had got in their official car and driven away, the neighbors went back to their houses and Mrs. Pace looked for a long time at the empty playhouse under the trees.

In her house, Mrs. Algood said to herself, sitting down at her table, "I'll write him a letter. He seemed so homeless. He never said anything about it, and couldn't abide sentiment—I saw that. Still, he seemed to be looking for a small space to live in and just be himself, with his few things. The people of the neighborhood don't like that, though, won't stand for a person being the way his is if it's a little different from their own way. He was already a good neighbor to me and might have made a good one for the rest of the neighborhood that's changed so much from what it used to be. If they'd have let him stay, he might have brought the neighborhood back to a few good homemaking ways it has lost or forgotten, if they'd have given him the chance—despite there was no running water in the playhouse."

She wondered what kind of community he had lived in before he came to Napa. Now she realized she had never asked him, she had been so busy trying to make him comfortable in the playhouse and had had so much to tell him. She didn't even know where to send a letter. She felt a deep sadness about Mr. Stevens. This feeling was stronger, even, than her resentment of the neighborhood and her anger towards the boys of print shop.

She would go out to the playhouse and take down the dotted swiss curtains, fold them neatly and put them back in her old goods box. On the little porch in the darkening dusk she felt sharply the sadness of Mr. Stevens; his warm, real presence was still there. Now she knew a little more about the sadness she felt:

it came from his silence. He had spoken so little while he was living in the playhouse. Of course he had lost his voice, which was small to begin with and stunned by the shock of print shop—but he was by nature the quietest, sweetest-natured little person she had ever known.

"The Turkish March" was resounding from the grand piano next door—it was that time of day—and Mrs. Algood opened the playhouse door, stooping into the playhouse, feeling Mr. Stevens' presence in the dusk light as strongly as if he were still there.

But there was someone there, and it was old Mrs. Pace rocking in the rocking chair in the early twilight. Mrs. Algood was shocked and a little frightened, but in the half-light Mrs. Pace looked so much like Mr. Stevens in the rocking chair that she did not scream, but for some cloudy reason embraced Mrs. Pace and said, "You scared me to death; I thought it was him!"—the very first words that she had spoken to the old lady in many a year.

"You mean the little neighbor man," Mrs. Pace answered. "No, it's me and I've slipped through the window of my room without my daughtern-law Agnese knowing it. It is so nice and peaceful in here and quite a feeling of home that the little old man left."

"Well, you are welcome to come here whenever you can sneak out, I guess," Mrs. Algood said to her, laughing a little hysterically. "You may replace Mr. Stevens. But you must be careful climbing through your window."

"Fact is, I'm stronger than anyone thinks," she said, rocking and looking around. "And if you want to know the truth of it, I have been coming in here for a long time to rock and be peaceful and think about Red River County—usually at this hour; and never a soul knew it, not even the Law or the Principal at Valley High. Now that you have found out, I hope you will come and join me and never tell Agnese. We could have lots of conversations during the hour Agnese practices the piano. That is the perfect time because she has such a fit thrown over her by the grand that she will not think of calling the Police as she did after Mr. Stevens."

Mrs. Algood was astonished at first, the same way she had been when Mr. Stevens had told her he would like to live in the playhouse. But then, as before, she relented and saw how nice it was to have again the living warmth of some human in the little house.

"I'll leave the dotted swiss curtains up," she said, "and put a piece of cardboard over the broken window until it can be fixed." After a moment she added, "And you and I will be more careful. We will have to do it by stealth—your tenancy, as the Law Officer called it. I never knew I had such a good thing in the little old playhouse of Sybil's; and all because of Mr. Stevens. I had thought it had become just a souvenir because of Sybil's growing up. You are about the size of Sybil before she shot up so tall," Mrs. Algood said, sizing up Mrs. Pace.

"Well," Mrs. Pace said, "you have me to thank for realizing a special place in the playhouse long before anyone ever heard of a Mr. Stevens, nice as he was."

In a day or so, the little widow lady down the street and her minister brother, the Bishop Jack, came at twilight to call, out of curiosity over the notoriety of the playhouse and to question after the fortunes of Mr. Stevens, and they found Mrs. Algood and Mrs. Pace having a conversation inside the playhouse. They were invited in, and though the Bishop Jack had to bow to get in, his sister slipped in without the slightest trouble, as if the house had been made for her. On the same afternoon, an old maiden lady of the neighborhood, named Miss Stokes, came and knocked on pretext of asking if she could rent the playhouse for a Millinery Shop. She offered to electrify it and pipe in water so as to satisfy the city regulations. But Mrs. Algood, who was speaking to Miss Stokes for the first time in how long, said that while she could not bring herself to make a place of business out of a little homestead, she could be persuaded, seeing as how natural circumstances had led to it, to make it a social gathering place; and invited Miss Stokes to join. That was the beginning of quite a few gatherings in the playhouse. For many twilights during that long autumn there was conversation galore, a game of Fortytwo in the failing light, flirtatious sermonizings by the Bishop Jack, with "The Turkish March" playing in the background, and no one ever reporting to the Police.

"Everybody's looking for a meeting place," the Bishop Jack psalmized, "and there has always been a sacrificing pioneer at the beginning, like little old Mr. Stevens." He had his eye on Miss Stokes.

This was back in 1940 and the neighborhood still talks about the autumn Mr. Stevens came and left, and how the playhouse got its start from that—though, to the last, old Mrs. Pace claimed the honor of finding it first. But no one heard of Mr. Stevens again.

The Thief Coyote

People in the river valley were aroused one late autumn afternoon when someone saw a red coyote running down the road to Cranestown with a turkey from Coopers' farm in his mouth. Since not only his turkeys but sheep and calves and chickens of other farms were imperiled, a posse was quickly organized by Mark Coopers, who had a way of calling men of Cranestown together at the slightest augury of what might be, in his mind, disaster or peril to everyone, especially himself. A posse was quickly organized to try to track the robber down.

Mark Coopers, who had more turkeys to lose than anyone else had sheep or calves or chickens to give up to the thief, and who, moreover, wanted some large enterprise to put himself to, went down to the hermit Lazamian's cabin and told Franz Lazamian about it. He sent his son, Jim, who was gathering pecans in the nut grove, across to the Hansons. Jim found Sam Hanson by his barn and told him to be at his father's house in an hour, ready to go out after the coyote.

A little before four, Hanson came. "Who saw it?" he asked Mrs. Coopers.

"Several people in Cranestown. And I heard the turkeys gobbling. We could put out a trap, I think."

"It's no use doing that," Mark Coopers answered, coming in with his boots to put on. "We just have to kill the coyote if we can. Once he's been here and tasted the bird, he'll come back with several more of his gang. There'd just be a big feast."

"Then who else is coming?" Hanson asked. "I've got hay to put up."

"The hermit Lazamian is," Mark answered, pulling on a boot. "And we'll take Jim. Then we can gather some more, probably Pete Jackson anyway, at the store."

The young man Jim was sitting on the divan, dangling his cap between his spread legs, looking at the floor.

Lazamian came a little after four, quietly came in and stood looking to see what was in the Coopers' living room, and the posse was ready. Mrs. Coopers gave them a bucket of coffee and some rolls she had been baking, and they started, Coopers carrying the bucket and Lazamian the bag of sweet-rolls. Every man had a shotgun except Jim, who carried an aiglette of a rope coiled round his shoulder.

It was getting colder and something in the late autumn daylight brought out green and yellow in the hillsides, made a deep yellow poetic flowering bush flare up and look like gold streaked in the meadows and running up the flanks of hills. The air was snowy and voices made smoke in it. It was the time for nuts to fall, and the first snow might be coming any day. The women of Rogue River Valley had been for some time canning peaches and apricots and stewing apples. The Michaelmas Daisies had already gone away, and the fire of the Broom blazed on the slopes and roadsides.

At the store, Pete Jackson said all right he would come, but he grumbled because he had to leave the new Kalamazoo Pride stove he was warm by. He put a pint of whiskey in his rear pocket. Some other men sitting around would not come for such a crazy thing as hunting a coyote.

Walking down the road in the new wind, the men talked about the thief.

"I figure we'll go down to Rogue River, then follow it along a while. Then when it gets dark . . ."

"And that's only an hour or so off," Hanson interrupted.

". . . we'll loop back around and come up Chapman's Hill," Coopers continued. "If we don't find him by the river, we'll get him in the hill. A reward to the man who gets him."

Something in the air, or the coming dusk, when men want to be home; or discomfort, or the wrongness in going away from one's house on an expedition at the end of day when all things should be coming back, turned the men querulous. But Coopers the leader was leading them on, with the image of conquest in his head.

"Let's all have a drink to begin with," Jackson said; and he passed the bottle secretly through the group like a profane whispering in the ear, because of the young Jim. Lazamian shook his head negatively when the bottle came to him.

"We've got to be alert," Coopers said, "watching every bush and thicket."

They got to the river, flowing swiftly along, carrying rafts of weed and brush which had dropped in it. Suddenly a cracking sound broke the quiet. Every man but Jim started. But it was Jim eating a pecan. Coopers was angry.

"Stop cracking those infernal nuts!" he shouted. "How many you got?"

"A few in my pocket," Jim answered.

"Then throw 'em out. Here, give 'em to me!"

Jim handed his father a handful and Coopers flung them into the river.

They went on. Jackson took another gulp of whiskey.

Lazamian was just going along. He was frail and had a mystic face, pointed at the chin and forehead. He went silently and softly along, no harm to anyone. No one in the group knew nor would know whether he liked going along after the coyote. All they knew was all anyone knew about Lazamian the hermit: that he was apparently serenely ready when someone came to him for a thing to be given or done—yet his life showed that within it there was always something held back for something yet to come. He went silently and softly along, with occasionally a disturbed hop in his gait. He might have been going for some sure treasure, or, with such a face, on a pilgrimage to a distant cross.

Hanson was a heavy Swede, going roughly and noisily. He and Coopers led; Jackson, who was just a follower good to have, was second, as though faltering a little, like a lame man; and behind Jackson was Lazamian, drifting along. Jim, still counting pecans in his mind, was last, a kind of conscripted follower. When chunks of dead moss or pieces of bark would fall, the group would start, wait, look cunningly about, then go on.

The hunted thief lay where, no one knew, but warmly snugged in some cove or lair, red and fierce by his river which he knew; tired perhaps, but no longer hungry, and so resting.

There was a green moon, gleaming like a cat's eye, already in the sky, swimming in an iridescent film. It was quite dark now and a little snow was beginning to come. "Autumn is really gone," someone said. Not a living creature jumped or ran or rustled. There was only the pelt of cones and the seed of trees, the slough of summer, on the rogue water. The serenity that can be in waiting was there in the rogue woods; the river went quickly along, aloof in its river-world, understanding as only rivers and woods can understand season and change and not betraying them. It purled softly except when it came upon rocks, and then it gurgled a little and went on.

"We'll stop here," Coopers said, "by this flat rock and heat our coffee and eat the sweet-rolls that Mary baked. Then we'll go on."

They started a fire and it lept up like a yellow and red rag, and the men came round it and put out cold hands to it. Then they put the coffee bucket over it and all sat down close.

"Wonder where the robber is?" Jackson asked.

"If you ask me, I'd say he was a hundred miles from here. And probably running farther away every minute. I never heard of chasing a coyote like this," Hanson grumbled.

"No," Coopers informed them. "I'd say he's got a pack of thieves like himself around here close, near the treasure at Cranestown. Traps don't work. Listen for a cry like a woman's, then we'll go to the cry and find our thief."

"But who saw him?" Lazamian asked quietly, the first time he had spoken anything.

"My birds," Coopers said, quick to set him aright and anyone else there who might be suffering a doubt in his mind. "My turkeys went crazy about two this afternoon. And then somebody in the town reported it to the store that they saw a red coyote running right through Main Street with piece of a turkey in his mouth. The store rang up my wife and she came running to tell me in the field. That's when I sent the boy Jim, pecan picking, to Hanson, and I went to get Lazamian."

"I'm cold," Jackson said. The stove in the store was laughing and glowing in his mind, merry and bright as it squatted on its little iron haunches.

And then, to brighten the moment, Coopers began a lewd tale about somebody in Cranestown. This livened up the group, and the fire quickened and made wanton shapes and mirages. Jackson and Hanson told stories in their turn, waiting for the coffee to get hot. Jim did not know what to do. He backed off a little from the others and sat in the shadow to himself, and from there he watched his own secret vision in the fire which the men's stories tried to shame. Lazamian just drew in the dirt with a stick. Jackson passed the bottle around, for this was whiskey talk and he felt something at last was going to be good.

Just then came a sound like twigs breaking under foot, such as an animal's foot makes as it goes over the ground. Everyone leaped up, but Coopers came up so anxiously that he kicked over the bucket of coffee and spilled it on the ground. There was a hiss from the fire, whose light was lowered, and a general rush.

But it was no coyote, only Jim cracking a pecan which he had saved back in his pocket with one other.

Coopers was savage. He ran over to Jim and struck him across the face with his hand, shouting, "Goddam it, Jim, you've lost our coffee with those infernal nuts! I thought I threw 'em all in Rogue River!"

Jim hunched under the blow, sat a moment, and then got up to go away farther. He felt one hard lone nut in the bottom of the sack of his pocket like a little stone. He clutched it tightly. "The pecans," he thought, "lie all on the ground waiting for me to come to gather them." And he thought, all in a moment, about picking up pecans all day long in the grove where it was quiet and the world was his own, no one to bother him and come talking about things. He had his own plan. He had planned to get ten croaker-sacks by nightfall if it hadn't been for the coyote. Then his father had called him in to send him to Hanson's place to tell Hanson about the thief. Other boys around Cranestown had made some little fun of him because he picked pecans instead of killing hogs and branding cattle, and this seemed to hurt him more now than it ever had. Why should he care about a coyote that had stolen a turkey or that people said had stolen a turkey? He only wanted right now to be back in the pecan grove, holding at least his own plan shaped in his head. For he had kept a restless watch on things, too, even as his father had—there was some shape to this watchfulness, some shape in what he watched. Beyond this, all around him, lay a huge roiled and anxious shapelessness, the impulsive doings of disquieted and suspicious men, hunts to kill, plots to gain, plans to trick to glory or increase.

But he knew where his own plan lay and how it was shaped. What right had men to force their shapelessness upon him? For he had, in some way, already made up his mind, alone in grove and orchard, that his real and loving work was to collect quietly what the earth had made and had fallen, yielded to him upon the ground, and store away a quiet gathering-up of small, dirt-grown morsels and meats. Why must men make him feel sly like a thief?

Now everyone was angry because of the spilled coffee, except Lazamian, who didn't seem to mind at all.

"You'd think you wanted the coyote not to be killed! To eat all your father's birds!" Coopers bawled to Jim in the shadow.

Jim gripped the little nut tightly and kept quiet.

"Well, we can all eat the sweet-rolls that Mary baked, anyway," Hanson suggested.

"And wash 'em down with what little is left of this bottle," Jackson said.

They gathered again around the dampened fire. Some spirit in them, like the fire, had been dampened. Lazamian brought over a piece of sweet-roll to Jim, who sat away by the river bank, and silently handed it to him.

"I think we ought to go back," Jackson said, after a time. "We'll never get the robber tonight. Go back and try a trap."

Coopers was angry and tired, now. "I told you we'll never get him with a trap. Next it'll be a lamb, then a calf, then more of my birds. We'll all be feeding a whole coyote pack all winter if we don't get this one and hang him on a fence-post. We've got to teach them not to come down to Cranestown, and this will do it. Now let's go on." Coopers realized they had sat too long by the fire.

They were getting up from the fire when Lazamian spoke for the second time during the expedition.

"But are we sure there was a thief?"

Jim trembled a little where he sat to himself in the darkness by the river.

"As sure as you can be of what eyes tell you!" Coopers yelled, stomping out the fire.

"Have you counted your turkeys?" Jackson asked, looking Coopers straight in the eye and daring him a little. There was something about a fire being put out on a cold night he did not like.

There was a portentous wait. A kind of petty mutiny was in Jackson and Hanson, and they were wondering if they could count on Lazamian, who had suddenly spoken for them. They were all standing, looking hard at Coopers. Coopers was tired of trying to convince the fainthearted hunters and he made a desperate speech.

"Listen, you cowards," he said firmly. "I told you my wife heard the birds making a commotion. Something was after them. All right. And then the store said somebody saw the robber coyote with the turkey . . . All right?"

But Hanson was tired of all this, and he spoke out definitively,

"Well, I'm cold as hell, and right now I don't care a hoot about turkeys or coyotes or anything but being in out of this cold. It's beginning to appear to me that this is a damfool stunt, like most of your others. In thirty minutes if there's no coyote, I'm turning back, and the devil with the rest of you."

A raw wind was coming down over them and it made the flames of the fire suddenly leap up and crack like a whip. What was in the fire that made it so sensitive to men's feelings?

"And the same for me," Jackson the follower said, meaning it, "and for the hermit Lazamian, too!"

The wind rasped the trees and the place where the men were suddenly went lonely and stark. The fire was dying again. By the river Jim was bearing the clash of the men against his father. He looked towards the fire-shadow to see his father standing alone on one side of the fire and the men divided against his father on the other; he saw his father's big face glowering in the fire's glimmering light and he heard him say, in a patronizing voice, weak now and not convincing, almost like an aside, "A reward to the man who gets the thief coyote." But not a word was returned from the three dissenters standing together across the low flame from Coopers. Sides had been taken; the men led out here by a phantom thief to this fire-lit region on the edge of all that seemed unreal and ghostly appeared to Jim to be isolated from the living world and turned upon each other. He suddenly wanted more than anything in the world to be gathering pecans in the sun, alone and counting the nuts and no men quarreling around him. Those across the fire from Mark Coopers were sure now that there was no coyote. The biting wind, the darkness and the loneliness of the place by the river, the first snow, the lost coffee, made them want to be home, within walls, after a hot supper.

Then a crackling sound like something moving came from the river; then quiet; then another sound; then a heavy noise of movement, stealthy but measured. There was a pause within Coopers so that he might be sure of the sound, then he took his gun. At last, he thought, this may be the coyote, come just in time. The kill will prove it to these turncoats, or at least, if the noise is something else, a shot fired will shake them and reassure them and draw them back to me. But he was sure it was the coyote, now. He was poised with his gun. The men were fixed and silent.

Towards the river Coopers saw a crouched shape, and in a twinkling he raised his gun and fired there. The others jumped, the wide resounding reality of the burst restored them to Coopers' cause for the moment, they thought he might be right after all. Jackson shouted, "Did you get him?" and all of them ran to the river surely expecting to find the shot coyote. Lazamian reached into the flame and pulled out a burning stick for a light and came with the flare. They saw for a magical instant the limp and folded shape of a coyote lying over the snowy leaves. But when the hand of Lazamian touched the shape and the light he held was lowered to show the features of the captive, there was the figure of Jim lying on the ground with a string of blood beginning over his eye and curling down his cheek.

They came back early the next morning through the frozen trance of snow that had fallen all night, bearing the wounded Jim from the river. They had walked all night trying to find their way out of the woods they had thought they knew so well. Early people of the valley who saw the little procession thought Jim had been bitten by a snake or injured in some way in the hill.

"Those are Coopers and his men who went after the thief

coyote," a man told others in front of the store, waiting for it to open up. "Something has happened to the boy Jim."

Jim lay slung over the shoulders of Coopers like a sack of something soft, feathered with snow. Coopers was shambling along, stern and stonefaced.

"Run get Doctor Marvin and tell him Jim Coopers has been shot by a gun on Rogue River!" Jackson called to them. "Tell him to come quickly to Coopers' house!"

Through the town as the procession marched along, this one and that one saw Mark Coopers marching grave and stupid with his son thrown over his right shoulder, his son's hands hanging down dangling as if they were trying to catch at his father's legs or pick something out of his rear pockets, and his hair was strewn down like weed. Behind were Hanson, tired and whiskered, with a stare in his face; and Lazamian, who moved dumbly along like a puppet. Jackson was running ahead in a kind of terrified gambol, shouting to half-asleep people to get Doctor Marvin. Dock and wild buckwheat were in the men's hair and burrs and thistles clove to their lumberjacks. Some people joined the train and marched along its sides or followed behind, whispering.

And when a kind of idiot old man of Cranestown, a man named Old Torrence Reeves, whom everyone mocked, came ambling curious and sidewise like a crab up to Lazamian in the march and asked, "What's the trouble with Jim Coopers?" Lazamian said the third thing he had uttered since yesterday when the expedition left Coopers' house to hunt the thief coyote.

"He was just cracking a pecan by Rogue River."

Old Torrence Reeves thought this a crazy reason for a boy to be hung dead over his father's shoulder, judged the world idiot, standing with his crooked mouth open, and did not follow.

As the posse approached Coopers' place, crowded with followers and stragglers and mourners, Mrs. Coopers came out on the porch and looked down the road to see the group marching up to her house. She thought her husband was carrying triumphantly the coyote over his shoulder. But something in the way it was carried and something in the movement of the people in the procession made her think the burden was not beast but human. And when she ran out to her gate and looked carefully, she saw it was no coyote thief but her son, Jim.

But what had been prepared in her mind to shout to the men when they victoriously returned, tired and hungry, she cried out anyway, hoping it could not be Jim over her husband's shoulder, in the way people try to fool themselves out of sudden incredible disaster, trying to speak a falsehood that might change the impossible truth.

"I've got a big hot breakfast with pancakes ready!"

"Call Doctor Marvin!" Jackson cried. "Call Doctor Marvin!" And then Mrs. Coopers crumpled down at the gate and the procession had to go around her to get through.

Some of the crowd moved into the house, some stood in the yard, still wondering what had happened, and a few women were over Mrs. Coopers on the ground. And just as Lazamian sat down on the steps, very tired, to think about it all, he heard someone in the crowd say, "But has anybody told them that the thief coyote they went so far afield to catch has been right here tormenting the Coopers' place all night long, in the pecan grove?"

It was then that Lazamian was sure he saw, within the oval frame of his eye, the fleeting vision of a coyote leaping across the Coopers' field towards the pecan grove with a turkey in his mouth.

The Enchanted Nurse

To remind you of love, halt within us and waiting to be started, that little Beginningness that lies waiting in us all, I have to tell the story of beginning together: how the meeting and coming together of two human beings is a rescue; and how lovelessness is a perishing. To remind you of love and to recall to you its history, I speak of all this, if you will listen to me, this tale that lives within my senses as if it were an odor smelt or the feel of a hand, the echo of a voice in the ear.

Now I speak at the end of a long time, and as someone old, for I am an old man sitting in a small room in a boardinghouse . . . it all comes to this, in the end, one voice in one small room telling what happened in many places and at many times in the broad world. The town is named Port Angeles, in the state of Washington, where I have come home, and it is a little town on the Strait: a landing-town where the ferry that crosses the Sound has stopped for many years. The time of the telling is early afternoon, about two.

Before darkening I shall have finished, it will take just the heart of an afternoon, and one of broad bright sunlight today, to tell what took so long to take shape. I have got it all straight and simple by thinking about it many many years.

My body is vanished, almost, so how shall I describe myself to you? I feel as though I were only eye and ear and breath, and I speak of what I have seen and heard: my eyes and ears are in my mouth that tells: I have died and gone away elsewhere. In my face, if you could see it, you would find all the tracks of thoughts—deep ruts where they have, being sometime heavy like a loaded wagon, borne down their wheels deep into my flesh, and wheel-shapes where they have spun around within their spoked prisons of themselves. You would find places in my face where thoughts have quarreled with themselves and struggled, disturbing the flesh; graves of pain and gravestones of grief, and hope that ended in grief; little flags and pennants of joy, craters of sorrow; and a wide bountiful field of my blisses. You would see, if you looked closely, crosses for suffering deaths of people who have died in my face. It is, then, this tracked and populated face, the landscape of my life: look at it like a map and you will discover the countries where I have lived. One of these countries is named Love.

Love, then, is the marrow of my story . . . I speak in language of the bone, which, it is said and I know well, is slower to mend even than the heart. So consider my voice the voice of a Nurse, a witness and servant to healing and repair. That has been my life-long job. Old nurses, superannuated and the healing out of their hands, take it to their mind and there nurse over again all that was sick and wounded and needed help toward healing and see, later, so much more of the mending process and what was mended, than then. My name is Curran.

Now old minds take a crooked way, so let me. It is the old mind that shapes best, in the end, so let it get there in its tarrying, studying way, as an old man crosses the fields—he gets there, and ready to tell of every little long-lived thing he has seen. Young tellers, full of passion and of a restless tongue, go too quickly and too hotly, often passing over the beautiful quiet little signs of things that are always there, on their way, which an old traveler knows to look for.

In the days of The War there was in London a young man who was serving as what the profession calls a Physiotherapist. He worked with broken and afflicted limbs. He knew the bone. This young American nurse had come to St. Bartholomew's Hospital in London to finish his special studies when the war broke out. As you will see, this young man was myself. As Bart's, that ancient mending place, was in the danger area of the city of London, the orthopedic ward was removed fifty miles away to the little town of St. Albans, which St. Augustine founded—and you know all about him—and housed in what was once a grand old country mansion. The house had many gables and tented roofs with vanes and finials and steeples crested with iron pennants and iron birds hovering over or lit on them; it was three stories high, each story full of wide rooms whose walls had been pulled down to make long wide wards; and the great house was crowned with a round turret jeweled with little precious windows. On the top of the turret was a thin fierce spire upon which the figure of a rearing and strutted cock rose in the wind as if to trouble the air.

On the second floor of this converted mansion was a big barny room so crammed with cots that the wounded who lay side by side upon them could touch each other. It was on this floor that the wounded of Dunkirk were put to be mended, I might tell you, and here many of them perished. This ward was a delicate world where men, rescued from great damage and out of violence, were suspended from wooden frames by cords and wires, hanging on frail netlike looms that were hourly manipulated by shuttles and purchases to keep them mobile. It was a world of fragile weaving and knitting, the laid-out broken body of a broken army. After the slow retreat through water and cold and darkness, under fire, these frail males had joined each other, so silently and so alone, as before, in this long slow march back, toward regeneration. Here, in this rude room, this simple long room of cot and patient, there was going on the most delicate and careful and imperceptible knitting of tissue, the slow stitching of frail threads of bone, the minute work of marrow and blood, remaking life out of its own substance. Here, men who had staggered exhausted and crippled and through water to this high, removed place—we had rescued them out of a flood—observed their wound as something so much greater than themselves but something they could bear and something which had a life of its own, quite apart from their own process of life, from their own human fictions and fantasies. If you came suddenly to the door of this room, it might appear to you to be another kind of battlefield, with little white tents in rows and men half billeted in them, for the damaged limbs had to be protected by rooflike coverings. And then, on second look, you would be sure that it was a room of quiet and delicate work, of weaving and stitching, as if some intricate lace were being woven on long rows of wooden looms, because the men were strung upon these wooden frames as if they were figures being woven on the threads of looms by the nurses who stood over them manipulating them; or it might be a world of spider architecture.

At the end of the War the casualties of Dunkirk were moved back up to London, to Bart's, but St. Albans continued to be used as a hospital for the lamed and crippled. I stayed on there, to continue my work as an Orthopedic Therapist. The ward changed; it had another populace. This time there were several children in it, all boys of course, for it was a male ward; and we had a variety of patients. But the life, the inner life, of the ward was the same.

Beginning in about September, it rains and rains and rains in England. It does not stop until around March, and if it goes on, which rarely happens, there is a flood in low places. It was a day of slow rain when Chris, the young American, was delivered to the ward. He had had a severe damage to his right leg from a fall in Europe, in Rome; and he had managed to struggle back to London with his two companions, a young man and woman. When he arrived in London he found, at Bart's, that his leg was no longer of any use to him unless he had an operation on the bone. Bart's sent him out to us at St. Albans, and we performed the operation on his leg.

On a day of slow rain this Chris was delivered to the ward. He was in the company of, or I should say supported by, this young man and woman, for they were helping him along, each holding him under an arm, both very handsome, the girl greeneyed and fair, the young man dark and darkeyed. It was his face that struck me when I first saw it, for it was of such a dark mysterious look; and yet it had in it some animal ferocity. These, I knew at once, were not ordinary people and not from this country. They were, you could tell it, strangers.

It was an awkward time to receive a patient, for it was recreation hour and all the ambulatory patients were on the floor, either on crutches or in wheelchairs; but this young man was badly in need of bed and care. His friends—or deliverers—left him in my care and disappeared after embracing him. Suddenly the dark young man came back and asked me when the operation on "my friend" would take place; and I looked on the schedule and told him tomorrow morning at nine. "The young lady and I will be here," he said, and left. So I had this stranger in my care, and so it all began.

"I am Curran," I said to him, "and if you will come with me I'll lead you to your place." We maundered through the traffic of recreation hour, the wireless was booming with music, men were calling at each other, nurses were giggling and running about, patients with great white plaster legs or sitting in wheelchairs or hanging onto a crutch were playing billiards on the huge table in the center of the room. There was such a whirling traffic of runaway wheelchairs that Chris cowered against the wall for fear of being run down, and then I knew how wounded he was, for the deeply wounded are so vulnerable to the wounded and protect themselves from each other. I knew he was thinking how he was, already, one of this lame and confined company. We found his cot and Chris sat down on it. I asked him how his leg was, and I remember he said it beautifully, "glittering with pain" . . . was the way he put it; and I knew that he had an idea, a conception of his injury.

At that moment Bobby broke loose from the circle of rushing wheelchair traffic round the billiards table and skidded his little wheelchair alongside the table. He leapt in one springing leap onto the billiards table and the cues went up at once all around the table, like spears in the air, as if to threaten him who was so dangerous. In another flash, Bobby, quite like a very young and skinny unfeathered bird, was hopping and bouncing about on the butts of his joints which were like cypress knees, in the middle of the table. Cries of "Now Bobby! now Bobby! off Bob!" went up from all the billiards players; and I had to go over, calling "Bobby! Bobby!" With one bolt Bobby was off again and into his wheelchair, and in another instant he was whirling away again, amuck among the cots, skidding up to the strung and balanced patients terrified that they might be unhung. Cries of "Bobby! Bobby!" from all the beds and billiards players and nurses sounded again, as if from that many parents. A nurse was chasing him now, and when he caught him and threatened to take him back to his cot, which had four high sides to it like a little pen, Bobby burst into screams and tears and whirled away again. Chris turned to me as he sat on his cot and asked who Bobby was. "He's been here since he was born, this is his home; he won't last long," I told him. "That's why we humor him. He was born without legs and has a knot on his spine."

Now a nurse had put Bobby into his pen and Bobby's screams had settled to a low, unbroken mewling from his prison. Often one of the men on the floor would go over to the child and speak softly to him, reason with him or pacify him, but it was as though Bobby could not hear them, as though he were in another world and he knew what it was, and he could not hear what his friends who loved him were trying to say to him, for what could they say that would help him, anyway? I saw Chris hunch down onto his cot as if to hide away from this motherless, womanless, doomed child.

I fetched Chris his supper but he would not eat it. Now the ward had changed into something very quiet, as though the tides were over, and there had settled over it, recreation and supper being past, a kind of docility and a sadness, as upon the twilight sea: men fell to sleep or read or lay remembering or hoping or planning. Chris was still sitting on the side of his cot, in a kind of trance the way animals are when they are brought into a strange room: they wait to get their animal sense of the place. Chris was reluctant to commit himself fully to the ward; but I told him to get into bed for I had to prepare him for the operation tomorrow. Suddenly the lights went down, it was darkening time, and Chris lay very still in his cot. Then the voice of one of the nurses in the low light spoke out the evening prayer, "Lighten our darkness, we beseech thee, O Lord; and by thy great mercy defend us from all the perils and dangers of this night . . ." I saw that Chris's head was turned away toward the window that held the night like a dark ocean in its panes.

Now in the settled quietness the noises of the farther room became audible . . . a kind of profound stirring as though one heard it from depths. Then in the darkness a voice from one of the cots whispered across to Chris, "America, where do you come from?" But Chris did not answer. In a moment he asked me in a low lost voice, "Tell me what is in that other room?"

"The critically ill," I said. Then the terrible ordeal going on in the other room, the deep suffocating sounds, the low cries, sounded again. Now that the ward was quiet, the sounds of the other room made it a profound reality. There was one low, steady cry that kept sounding and sounding like the call of one frail bird in a deep woods. Chris was listening to it as though it were calling to him.

"Who is it?" he asked me.

"A man who fell from a high roof and shattered his limbs. He is in very great pain. So you see, you are not so badly off. Now try to go to sleep, for I shall have to wake you several times during the night to prepare you."

Suddenly Bobby began to cry, first it was a whimper, then catching sobs, then a wail that seemed to stab Chris. "Nurse! Nurse! I am falling!" A nurse came soft-footedly to him and whispered "Shhh Bobby! Shhh! . . . you are having a dream . . ." Bobby's cry softened to small sobs, and Chris rose to his elbow and watched the nurse rub Bobby's back and quieten him and tuck him in again; then Chris sank down again, thinking, I knew, of the Rome he had fallen in and of Europe that had wounded him and stricken him. In a moment I said to him, "Bobby dreams, as many of the legless do, of his lost limbs and that he is walking. His dream is that he is walking and in peril of falling . . ." And then Chris fell asleep under the sedation I had given him.

I sat watching him and thinking about him, the mystery of him. And then, in the quietness, against the low moan from the next room, the voice of little Lord Bottle, as we came to call him because his habit was to call, too frequently, "Nurse, the bottle, the bottle!"—he could not control his animal functions—pierced our quiet and disturbed Chris: *"And the Lord said unto Cain, where is Abel thy brother? And he said, I know not: Am I my brother's keeper? And he said, What hast thou done? The voice of thy brother's blood crieth unto me from the ground."*

Lord Bottle was our intrepid little preacher, the child of Evangelist parents who had obsessed him with prayers and hymns with which he plagued the ward until we could, by force, stop his mouth. *"And now art thou cursed from the earth, which hath opened her mouth to receive thy brother's blood from thy hand: When thou tillest the ground, it shall not henceforth yield unto thee her strength; a fugitive and a vagabond shalt thou be in the earth."* Would no nurse come to stop him? I waited, fearing to leave Chris.

"And Cain said unto the Lord, my punishment is greater than I can bear. Behold, thou hast driven me out this day from the face of the earth: and from thy face shall I be hid; and I shall be a fugitive and a vagabond in the earth; and it shall come to pass, that every one that findeth me shall slay me." The ward was stirring in its sleep, but no nurse seemed to be coming. They were all in the Critical Room, busy with the perishing whose deep sighs of exhaustion were the moaning undertone of Lord Bottle's long pronouncement. *"And the Lord said unto him, therefore whosoever slayeth Cain, vengeance shall be taken on him sevenfold. And the Lord set a mark upon Cain, lest any finding him should kill him. And Cain went out from the presence of the Lord, and dwelt in the land of . . ."* and then mercifully and abruptly the mouth of Lord Bottle was hushed by the hand of a nurse who had finally got to him. "Bottle! Bottle!" the little preacher called to the nurse who was with him now.

"Go to sleep, Chris," I said. "I will tell you about the little preacher tomorrow; go to sleep"; and when I put my hand on his belly to pacify him I felt him shuddering with quiet weeping and watched him, finally, fade away again into the sleep I had brought him to.

During the night I prepared him three times for the operation. Each time he woke in a kind of trance, turning to me to say a name I could not clearly hear, but once I clearly heard him whisper "Cain!" and I knew it was the word the little preacher had put into his drugged brain to make a dream, the way dreams borrow to make their substance. Early in the morning he asked me where I lived and I told him in the little turret. He asked me what I saw from there and I said the whole far countryside. Could he sometime, when he was better, go up and look out at England from the turret? And I said yes, I will show it to you when you are able. Then who was his doctor? And I told him his doctor's name and that he had met him around midnight when he had come in to see about him.

"But did I talk to my doctor, then?" Chris asked me.

"You gave him a good and clear accounting of yourself," I said. "And the doctor promised you, when you asked him, that you would leave St. Albans with a good strong leg." Chris fell to sleep again.

The next morning—a fair day, the rain had stopped—they performed the operation on Chris and brought him back around noon. I need to tell you that there was a very good chance that Chris might never have his leg again, he had so abused it after he had wounded it, either not caring or thinking he could heal himself, in time. He was a very depleted young man when he came into the hospital, for he and his companions had traveled all over Europe and he had fallen in the very middle of the journey; and because he was so used up by some farther expenditure of energy which we did not know about but observed the signs of: some deep-lived anxiety, some deeply-searching secret of his, he rose faintly from the anesthetic like a leaf turned ever so delicately by a slight breath and then sank into a dead coma of exhaustion, as though he had withdrawn from us all. The whole right half of his body was stricken—somehow the injury and the operation had now affected the other parts of his body, and we feared that he might die.

I was assigned to this body—for where was Chris?—that swooned before me for how long I do not remember; there seemed no accounting of days. We raised the little tent over him and laced him onto the apparatus which we called "the loom." My job was to keep his body mobile. Each hour I worked with the still, spread-out body, beginning with the head that rolled like an infant's in the hands, then the breast and torso, limp as rope, the limber loins, and then the delicate, mending limb. All during those days I watched and worked over Chris, wondering "Who can you be and what in the world has happened to you that you would will to remove yourself from the living world?"

His two friends had appeared again the morning of the operation and they had waited in the corridor of the ward until Chris was brought down from the operating room. When we had put Chris on his cot, the two were given permission to come in the ward and sit by his cot to wait for him to wake. I noticed at first that they seemed to be quarreling and that out of the quarrel they reached an agreement, a hostile agreement of some kind, to the effect that each refused to come in to Chris with the other and that each would come alone to him. They finished their quarrel with the words, like some terrible finality drawn over the whole situation—which of them the pronouncement came from I did not know—"If he dies, you helped kill him."

But when Chris came to, for those several minutes, the two were suddenly standing by his side as though the quarrel had meant nothing, and I saw Chris look at the young man and young woman with half a look of threatening and half of love and then pass on away into his death of sleep. There was something between these three. The friends had brought, this time, the few personal effects of Chris's and I took them for him. In a few minutes, they left. They did not ever appear again. They had delivered him here, to me, it seemed, and had vanished, leaving his few possessions with me. These consisted of a little packet of photographs of Venice, all that beautiful naked race of people standing along the rims and on the rooftops of buildings and palaces, upon spires and colonnades; a large photograph of the three companions standing in the ruins of Rome, and one picture of the three standing together before the David of Michelangelo in Florence, Chris in the center under the loins of David, the girl and boy on either side. Some one of them had written under the picture the words, "*I would not see thy new day, David. For thy wisdom is the wisdom of the subtle, and behind thy passion lies prudence. And naked thou will not go into the fire. Yea, go thou forth, and let me die. . . . Yet my heart yearns hot over thee, as over a tender quick child.*" There were also letters, opened and unopened, a little silver box with words inscribed: "On silver, on clocks, on flesh, on water." Inside was a delicate gold ring with three stones, two bits of burning ruby and a tiny sparkling diamond in the center. The only other thing was a hide-bound notebook on whose pages I saw what must have been notes, ideas, what? put down by Chris. I put all these objects under the little tent we had raised over the patient, but I put the ring on his finger. It moved me to see the little relics and tokens of his expatriated life close to him, all he possessed, apparently, in the Old World, against his wounded and sleeping body, in that physical intimacy one loves to keep with the few, small objects he cherishes. Chris no longer lived in his body, I thought; it had been removed from him, or he from it, drawn up and away. Under his tent there was only the place of the mind and the memory and desire; the rest, bone and flesh, was in other hands. I had only the stricken body to work with . . . but soon there came into my charge all other.

I did not know what was in Chris's mind, but I could imagine; and I could finally name what he put into *my* mind. Was it the idea of Europe and how it seemed Europe had struck him a blow and halted him. What was the meaning of this crippling? Here he was, healing among strangers. He would return to his country, home, hobbling from the wound, as though he had suffered a blow, expatriation, bearing the wound of history, of ruins, and, above all, of a secret personal failure, a failure of self, perhaps, which none of us could know. And he would always bear and carry the long white scar of it, on his leg. Would he speak to himself, over and over, the words I myself heard within my own head: "I tried to walk too far afield too soon and too quickly. I fell. I left work undone in my own fields—and where I was struck down so early. This wound reminds me of the fields of my beginnings which I abandoned and betrayed because there was a murderer hiding, ambushed, in them: my own brother, my own people. But what I fled at home I found waiting for me abroad, to bring me home again: the killer, the crippler is everywhere." Why, I thought to myself, sitting by my patient's side, cannot I go home, why cannot I return until something in this foreign land heals me and gives me the courage to *go back?*

He hung, before me, footlong, in a hurtling shape, his right leg extended and toes pointed, like a dancer, his left leg bent at the knee and foot turned outward, as though, falling, he had been caught in a net by me who nursed and manipulated his body to bring it to move again. Every hour I would manipulate the strings and wires by means of little wooden shuttles and the body of the youth would hunch and fall as the loom gently creaked and his body made forced mechanical movements which his body seemed to resist fiercely. What strange powerful *resisting* life was in this apparently resigned body before me?

It *was* as though he had fallen, this figure, and as though we had caught him, here in this hospital and on this ward for the crippled, in this net upon which we had him stretched and fastened. We have rescued him, to put him back together again, I thought. The damage of the fall I could tell, for I could measure that by what I saw and worked with. The rest, what he fell from, where he fell, the distance of the fall and the damage of *that* I had to measure by what I could not see or the fallen fully tell. Yet it is just this mysterious and invisible record which really tells the tale. What is broken, shattered, we put back together again in this mending place; we assist the knitting of the bone and the stitching of the tissue; this is a place of rehabilitation. The process, briefly, is to elevate and hold still the afflicted member and wait until it finds its reality and its function again. It must find itself what it has lost or been bereft of, and by its own means. So much for the crippled limbs of men. But these are places of the mind, too; for the mind, unhalted, runs on or runs back, and does its piecing, its regeneration, too. The relation of limb to mind is interesting, for limbs can lead a man in one direction while his mind is going in another: a man seen going down the sidewalk or the street is going one way, where his good legs take him and his arms, as though they were oars, row him. But who knows where his mind is traveling? In this place, then, where the limbs are of no earthly use, there is the traveling of the mind. Consider the many crossings and recrossings of the little rescue boat of the mind, from one shore to another, landing at islands perilous and benevolent, met by people on the shore or by none upon the lonely wastes and beaches. Look at all these little rescue boats of beds in this my ward. You know who is the invisible Boatsman.

Though the body of my patient, Chris, traveled some ways when I forced it by means of the mechanical apparatus I controlled, its journey was a wooden, mindless, heartless one, like that of a wooden Image on wheels and pulled by ropes. My patient's propelling power was behind and above, unseen. He would not go where any wood or line led him, but where he *had* to go. You see already the dangers that I know, who might be moving him where he was *not* going—the selfsame dangers that befall a man who tells a tale of someone. Now you begin to see the responsibilities of a nurse.

There is something dreadful among us, I thought as I worked my loom with Chris upon it, a figure over the city we live in, to remind us; a shape in the streets following us; a ghost in the room we sleep and eat in, to remind us . . . a creature within us that could murder or keep life. No one can cure us of this murderer but ourselves, we cure ourselves and through love. We keep life by love, and by rescuing the perishing lovelorn, crossing over to show and to remind them of the healing of love.

The comatose Chris, in his state of profound insensibility, was on my mind every minute. I soon became obsessed with him. The danger was to *identify* myself with him—a nurse must not, finally, *care*, who cares and does not care. During those days we went on such a long journey, he and I, through more countries than I can ever tell you, though I can tell you some, and this is my purpose, will you believe it. They said I was a kind of sorcerer and that I used witchcraft; but you must judge, when I am through, what witchcraft I used. (As for my own life, some other time I will tell you it—there is a lot to tell.)

As I wove Chris as though I were remaking him, this putting together into a hale unhalted whole again became for me the only reality. Everything else was unreal: I had no words, no eyes for, no responses to anything outside this place where he was, in my charge, and where I sat or stood beside him. My work with him became a work of love, the mark of a good nurse. During the work of love, I lost my sense of relationship to the world around me; this work was the only reality and it drew all things to it. I lived for and through the mysterious process going on within this reconstruction which began with me by being manual and mechanical, using only my hands and my professional knowledge, and grew to be a whole experience involving all of me—and what happened was this: something in *me* was restored, Chris was bringing together lost parts of me. There was this mysterious double action, this marvelous reciprocity, the way we human beings work upon each other. My daily responsibilities beyond this work fell into desuetude; my living-place in the turret was like a violent man's, since I was never there to keep it in order, the way rooms seem to fall to pieces without a human being in them. My friendships were neglected. I would not leave Chris night nor day, except to rest for an hour in the Lounge; and then he and I would be joined, even there, in my dreaming, and our dialogue would go on uninterrupted. Other nurses criticized me, but the doctor praised me. It was, then, a love-work, this nursing. But as there are storytellers who will tell you that they never let themselves get into a story they tell, so there are nurses who will say they have never suffered their patient's pain or healed a part of themselves in the patient's healing—but find me them! There is the marriage of pain and pain, of healing and healing.

Once, on my way to the Lounge to sleep for an hour, I saw, at the turning of the corridor and at the head of the stairs beyond, what I was sure was the figure of Chris, dressed in white and holding a tiny white little baby in a blanket. With him were an old old man and woman, countryfolk. They were all very quiet and somber, as in a vision, and I saw that the baby was dead and that the young man who held it was not Chris, of course, but an Interne delivering the dead infant to the morgue. He turned to me and asked me if I would go with him and the old people to the morgue. We went, and in the morgue we laid the cold little corpse out on a stone slab, for the old ones to look at. They were its grandparents. "It would have had Cornelia's nose," the old woman said, as if she were relieved. They were not moved by this little death, but quarreled over the expense of burying the infant; their daughter could not afford it, they could not, either—and why should they? The Interne and I told them that the hospital would bury it and the two old people turned and left. We stood, the Interne and I, together with the little homeless death in our charge.

When I returned to Chris, it was as though he knew about it all. It was in this way that the shape of my patient—regard the word—became the living object to which everything that happened was related.

I am speaking of a connection, woven, as of threads and veins and vessels, through which human beings may communicate and tell each other everything. I have had a lot of patients in my time, and I have learned from all of them—something about myself—as I nursed them; many times, in the end, I saw that *I* was nursed back, brought back to something lost sight or sense of. But Chris was the best patient I ever had. Sometimes I sit here on sunny days watching the lapping waters of the crested Sound and think how I have had and tended a number of very fine and remarkable people in my time, but . . . *remember Chris?* And I remember how I have died with some and have been brought back to life with others, but . . . *remember Chris?* Always, in the end, no matter how many patients I go over again and nurse back in my memory, it is the same, in the end . . . *remember Chris?* We are this way, and therefore, bound together. We brought each other back, and I wonder if he knows or will ever know it, to tell it? If he would one day find me! or I see him, as I thought to have seen him this morning: suddenly at the landing I was sure I saw him walking off the Ferry onto this Strait, come to tell me what I tell you. But no, not yet, it is not his time.

The Rescue

It was the second day of Chris' coma, and the rains had begun again, this time torrential. I began to work round the heart of Chris.

As our hospital was situated in a low place, by noon the waters had begun to rise. It was as though Chris and I were safe in a dry cove under a waterfall. I began to manipulate the loom—the strings and wires and little wooden shuttles that would bring his body to move again—this time in the area of his breast, for his heart was struggling. We were in that territory, where our conversation went on. Now it seemed that the working of the loom was the turning of a wheel that caused the flooding of a memory and could bring, through struggle, rescue from it.

Was it error that I took my subject so to myself? Did hallucination or vision, out of lonely judgment, follow: I can only put down what happened.

By nightfall, the waters of the flood had risen already to the level of the second floor, where we were, and we knew the night would be a perilous one, because the rains still poured down upon us. We began to make plans for evacuation to the third and topmost floor if that should become necessary. Chris hung above the level of the water, dry and safe, coming slowly to life on the loom I worked. All the earth seemed covered with water and my weaving movements were like the rowing of a boat with my patient as my passenger.

We should have known a flood was coming, because for a whole week before the rains all the animals knew it was coming. You never heard so many bullfrogs in all Kingdom; crickets and treefrogs, too were calling and sobbing all night long; and scrootch-owls scrootching. And all during the first night of Chris' coma one lone frog sobbed and sobbed outside below his window, like a human voice, as I worked the loom round Chris' head. The zoo, a mile away, was unhappy and troubled, the nervous horses stamped and snorted their heads, the cats called and the elephants sounded their baleful trumpets. It was a disturbed night. The men's wounds augured bad weather, too, and so I was reminded again of the connection between animal and human wounding. It had been so dry. The very land cracked and was like an old face—if you have ever noticed an old face, how it is like the ground. But never you mind, the drouth was broken, and then some, and for a long time.

The first rain was green rain, if you've ever seen it; but the whole world, trees and houses and grass, seemed yellow. It was going to be a catastrophe, and we should have known it. The limbs of the patients knew it, where the patients did not. But the animals had known it first. They always do, yet it is said they have no minds.

By nightfall we began the evacuation to the top floor. The children were first, and the little Preacher, Lord Bottle, was preaching passionately in his sleep as we carried him up, crying out between exhortations, "Nurse, Nurse, bottle! bottle!" and of course this sermon, a special one for us all, rising out of the extraordinary circumstances, touched on The Flood. The ambulatory patients went in a slow line on their crutches, complaining of their wound, and because of the fragility of the patients, the removal took hours, as they moved like sleepwalkers, and many of them were half-asleep or under their nighttime sedation. It was all very quiet and trancelike, without the slightest confusion or panic, as though we were acting out some prophecy; there was the rhythm and spell of dreamlike dancing about it all, as though each man carried a tune in his head to keep time to. The only sound was that of the thundering rain like the rolling of many deep waves. We decided to move Chris among the last, and so while he was waiting for his turn, I worked very hard round his heart to make it strong enough to move him, navigating his wooden bed with the tent over it as if it were a boat and I rowing him through the waters, a long ways.

As I looked out the window onto the turbulent waters of the rising flood where we had searchlights to watch the rising level, I never before or after saw such a sight. Animals began floating by, because the zoo was wrecked and all the animals aloose. Nurses and Internes and what patients could help stood on the second story gallery and quietly, as if in a dream, snatched to salvation every living animal they could lay hands on. They threw lifelines into the teeming waters and never knew what might be brought in: the big front room at the far end of the second floor was like a menagerie—this was where they led the animals that came in as though they were welcome and in the utmost pacification. In came the lions and the giraffes, the elephants and the hippopotamuses, the whole benevolent kingdom; and now the hospital seemed to move, like the heart of Chris, to be riding along on the crest of the flood with all this strange cargo and population, this sanctuary. We knew there must be gigantic destruction all outside, since the remnants and wreckage of it rode and bobbled past us through the light of the searchlights. Still they came in as they were rescued out of the waters, all the peaceful animals, birds and even marvelous snakes who did not even show their wicked tongues, they were so grateful it seemed; and little blinking monkeys were brought in, sheep, every kind of animal you can imagine. And as they were led through the ward, they were mingled with the quiet and benign procession of the delicate wounded men, they all went out together.

Pretty soon we began to see people floating by and they were pulled in, too, when they could be caught. The waters kept rising and rising and the torrent falling, the way a fall causes a rise. One man that was saved and brought into our sanctuary—coming by holding on to a floating door that seemed, in the searchlight, to be a door of light—when he was snatched in and dried off, said he saw rafts floating and got on one, saw two eyes, said "who's on this raft with me," and twas a bear. He got off in a hurry. Said he saw another raft and got on it and there was a great big snake. He said he got off quick. "Well," his rescuers said, "they're both in there, in the other room, the bear and the snake; we saved them."

And he did not say a word, the rescued man. Another, a woman, told us that the Italians were all in the trees in the dark, calling *Io morirò! Io morirò!*

How the building stood I'll never know. Occasionally it shuddered with the stiff twisting of the waters, but otherwise it rode them as lightly as a buoy. Yet it was filled with all this humanity and life. More people were pulled in. Children who had lost their parents but hoped to find them upstairs in this sanctuary, delicate old men holding to their breast a little hen or cock like a drop of feathers, or a drenched staring old cat under their arms; two wilted little nuns looking as though all the starch had been rinsed out of them, wearing their habits like drenched wings; and so many more.

With all the quiet suffering and the dumbshow traffic of the crippled, the drowning and the washing away, all I could really think of was what was poor Chris dreaming through it all, in his other country, alone through it all. He is the only safe one, really, I thought, for he is up above and over and clear of all this washing water down below him. I kept a watch on him to see if he might make some sign to say that he was coming down from his coma that raised him above it all; but there was not yet any sign, he was closed up in his dry tent. I worked round his heart until the time to move him away in his bed to the third floor. Once, I turned to see a huge and hideous hippo coming through the window, he had been helped out of the flood, and someone said he is the ugliest creature God created. But one of the refugees, a little old bent gray man who had just been brought up saved, said, "These creatures are the most sensitive and delicate of all. Do not let them hear you speak of their repugnance, for they live among men only through love, and if they sense that they are ridiculed, they will die." The gentle hippo went on his way, led by someone, to the menagerie in the far room. But soon, because it was feared that the second story would be engulfed, the animals were moved up the stairs. We heard the ghostly sounds of the great hooves and clawed feet on the steps. When I navigated Chris in his bed into the large wide third-floor sanctuary, I saw a lovely sight: the patients were in one end, quiet and at rest, and at the other end of the room the large beautiful family of animals, every kind, was gathered together, some lying, some sitting, some standing licking themselves dry or resting or licking others dry—there was the clean odor of wet fur—the whole company of the sanctuary had made friends and there was a harmony and a good-will among all that household, the peaceable kingdom.

We rode through the flood for days and days, no one knew how long. I certainly don't remember. Everybody helped with the preparation of food and with the housekeeping, and the household of animal and wounded flourished.

We rode the flood, and I waited for some sign from Chris. But he rode it like a buoy, rocking as I rolled him gently from side to side upon the loom I worked. As I tended his notebook, too, I left Chris to look into it for another sign to go by.

I found some pages written in Venice, for "Venice," and a date, were signed down at the end of the writing. What I read rose up into my head like a cry of Proteus out of the waters and sank back again. Something was rescued by Chris, in Venice, I saw, and again, there in the ward:

The Wounding of My Ancestry

I think of my grandmother's house in the city where she had moved, and she has given me the money in a little black purse and the list to buy at the store, the same things: a loaf of Wonderbread with the colored glasses inside the wrapper and postcard pictures of fishes and birds to be looked at through them; and a fifteen cent soup bone. I can hear her deaf woman's flat voice crying "Why don't any of my children ever come to see me?" as she sat in her rocking chair with one leg folded under her, the guitar like a baby across her lap. In the next room, but not the one where Beatrice lay moaning with her headache that never seemed to let her alone and for which they had scarred her beautiful face by operations to try to find the source of her misery, I can hear my grandmother sing "I'll Be No Stranger There" as she played the guitar; and looking at the wreck of the sleepingporch with so many beds and cots—for Beatrice's two children, for Fay's two, for me, for my grandmother, for my grandfather who would not stay home, for Fay and for Jock, I think of the plight of the kitchen with the boiler of kidney beans on the stove and the roaches running, the dripping faucet that stained the sink rust-colored, and of the backyard where the fig trees smell rotten and the damp weeds steam in the hot sun, and the pervading odor of Natural Gas sours the air.

Then I hear Beatrice's voice calling me, flat like her mother's, as though she too were deaf, but she was so very beautiful, blond silken hair that fell in locks around her enormous blue eyes . . . and her scarred face round which she wore a veil, as if she were masked, even in bed—I see her blue eyes peeping over the edge of the veil as if it were a wall, and the broken shape of mouth when she drew deep breaths of pain, the trembling of the veil when she cried out. "Chris, please Chris, come to your Aunt Beatrice, she is so sick."

I go into her sad room where her husband had not set foot for many months, he had disappeared, though Aunt Fay's, her third, was around the house all the time, having no job nor seeming to want any, and he was a young Seaman with tattoos and still wearing his Seaman's pants, Jock was his name, he cursed and was restless, would come and go or lie on the bed he and Fay slept in on the sleepingporch with all the rest, smoking and reading from a storage of battered Western and Romance Stories magazines under the bed. "Please help your Aunt Beatrice get a little ease from this headache; reach under the mattress here—don't tell anybody, Chris, your Aunt Beatrice has to have some rest from this pain—reach right here under the mattress and give me that little bottle. That's it. This is our secret, Chris, and you must never tell anybody."

Why should this beautiful Beatrice have to die in a Rest Home, alone and none of her family ever coming to see her until they sent a message that she was dead? But I thought, then, that if I had, secretly, helped ease her suffering, I had that to know, without telling—until I heard them say that she had died from taking too much medicine from a hidden bottle, and where did she get it and who gave it to her?

Now we are riding, at midnight or later, my grandmother and I in the old car I went to college in, as fast as I can drive it, my little old gasping grandmother no bigger than a hen huddled in the seat beside me, clucking and clutching at my knee, moaning "Hurry, hurry, Chris, your grandmother is dying; God will bless you for this. That none of my children would come to me when I called" (she had called so many times), "and that my grandson came to take me where I can die in peace, the Lord will bless him. Hurry, hurry, Chris, your grandmother is choking to death. You go on to college, Chris, and don't let them make you go to work, you get your college education and you won't be like the rest of them. . . ." The rain was still falling as it had been for a week, it was Spring, and the charity hospital was on the banks of the bayou which had overflowed and flooded the road: the hospital seemed to be rising on the water and floating like a huge lighted ship. When the waters came to the running board of the car, it stalled and could go no farther, and I took the light little shrugged up shape in my arms and carried her through knee-deep water, reaching the hospital.

We went in the emergency entrance and found water on the floor; but the charity patients, some Mexicans, some Negroes, some poor countryfolk, were sitting or lying on the benches waiting for the Nurses. My grandmother kept choking and gasping "tell them to hurry, Chris." They finally carried her to a ward, I helping. While they got her to bed, I sat in the waiting room hearing the rain and going from time to time to the window to look out on the rising flood of the bayou. I saw animals in distress, floating and swimming, and one of the Nurses told me that the polluted waters of the bayou had caused a sickness, a kind of plague, for the water supply of the surrounding section of the city had been contaminated, and did my grandmother have the sickness? "No," I answered, "she is just very old and worn out from trying to die so many times." And when I turned and said, "Please let her die," the Nurse answered that she had died, calling to Beatrice.

I put this down because I have suddenly remembered it here in this city built on water, and because tonight as I was going up the magnificent stairway to the Princess Galvana's dinner party I suddenly smelled the odor of kidney beans cooking and I heard my grandmother's voice crying "Hurry, Chris, hurry, your grandmother is dying," and I felt compelled to turn back and go away. But for what reason? I reasoned with myself, and so went on. At dinner I overturned my wine glass three times, embarrassing even the butler running with napkins, the third time. Several Americans were there: Lady A, though, was the only one I knew; a beautiful harelipped woman artist, and a fortyish, effeminate litterateur who kept speaking of the prizes some committee, of which he was Chairman, was going to bestow shortly. Lady A kept being called to the telephone in the next room, returning the last time to say, "Paris—I'm afraid we're going to run into war over oil in Persia."

Venice, 19 . .

Following these pages put down in Venice were more, directly following; and they were signed "Rome."

The Marvelous Ones

The act was a marvel. It was one of perfect grace and balance and imperiled order. The bodies of The Three were clothed entirely in the purest white garments like another layer of their skin and tight as their own flesh, though they seemed somehow *beyond* nudity. The muscles of the two men, and particularly those of Marvello, who was powerful yet lithe, and the gentle liquid quiver of their buttocks, swelled and sank and tightened with the erotic grace of male passion. Their thighs and loins and bellies surrounded, as if to insulate, that dangerous engine whose language The Act seemed to be, the hub and shaft which turned the wheel of this marvelous machinery.

The two men, in the act, drew near each other upon the wire in a gradually increasing ferocity of pressing, their torsos hunching and relaxing and hunching again as they balanced themselves aloft; and then the girl, a crystal and stellar creature, would slide down between them, delicately fitting as the blade of a sword; and together, in an overwhelmingly exciting climax, the two young men would fit against her almost as if they were molding themselves around her voluptuous form—it was marvelous the way their bodies fitted into one magnificent white body of flesh—and move, like a machine, to lift her up as though they had ejected her from the cleaving opening between their one body which their two bodies had made. For a moment, then, she had slipped from above where she perched on a rod both of them held, into the cove of their two bodies, had merged into their bodies so that what one saw was one male-female body, a dazzlingly sensual androgynous being; and in another moment, the single androgyne was writhing and hunching and flexing, and in the next moment, the female part of this momentarily created being was thrust upward out of them as though having been suddenly created out of that moment of fierce and turbulent work and borne into the world of air above them. She, as if newly created and pure as that, hovered in the air above the two men, quivering and beatified; and then down into the erotic male machine she slid again. What was it we were watching? Something we almost dared not look upon, yet a sight from which we could not turn our eyes. It was clear that The Three existed in a violently sensual relationship, yet what we saw was the spiritual manifestation of it. It was the silence of it all that thrilled and terrified us, this act of "Gli Maravigliosi," "The Marvelous Ones" in the Roman Carnival.

The Three flexed and shimmered in a pale moss-blue light that was cast upon them from somewhere above; their act was an engine of all order and exquisitely wrought relationships; and when they were still, in the shape they finally made and held, their fury and energy spent—how long? it seemed timeless—there was a residual quality of purity, of peace, of chastity about them. It was a marvel to behold. Outside, in the stalls of the sideshows were the huge beasts, the monsters and the misshapen, and on the platforms were the dishonest bodies of mountebanks; and beyond these the disorder of the town; and farther beyond, the chaos of the human world. But here, under this was pale light in this tent within a tent, was the beautiful shape of order wrought through sensual work. These three seemed to have been struggling not only *with* the bodies of each other—for this is what they had to work with toward that ultimate *bodiless* shape they achieved, so that it was, finally, the shape of an *idea*—but *against* the bodies of each other, in some tension, some resistance. Yet through it all they came to this serene shape of clean, of purified order. Something unclean was purified in us who watched, something imperfect was made, for the moment of watching, flawless: we would hold the memory of this to go by, if we could keep to it, outside this tent, in the sideshows where we watched the twistings and grovelings of animals and freaks, in the town and beyond in the world where we struggled within ourselves and in the daily world. One could not destroy the vision of the *gesture* of The Three, though he could not describe the shape of the gesture—was it that of a cross, the strong Marvello as the beam and the young man and young woman as the slender crosspieces, for at the overwhelming climax, in the shape they finally made and held so timelessly, Marvello held the two aloft. Was it the shape of a weathervane as the two birdlike creatures turned in the air around the swiveling cock-body of Marvello; was it a finial shape on the top of a stunning tower of a human body? There was no describing it. Through my American mind kept running the little nursery rhyme *This is the house that Jack built*. But the gesture of this made shape was put into the minds of all onlookers, as if under a small glass dome, where it would hang, like the gesture itself, to pacify to order or torment to disorder.

Afterward, all of us spent and quietened and relieved of some tension, of some yearning and craving within ourselves, we tried to buy photographs of the Marvelous Ones to keep as a reminder; but there were none to be had, nor had any ever been made, we came to understand. In fact, the audience was searched for cameras before the performance began. There was to be no recording of this indescribable gesture but that which no man could prohibit, and many wished they could, the senses. That, I knew, was the truth of The Three, that they had created for us the kind of experience that lives in one's senses. How many live in our loins, in our eyes, in our ears and lips! But many agents could destroy this sensual recording or mutilate it beyond recognition: the devilish mirrors within ourselves that distort into pantomime and caricature, that betrayal of the senses, that sensual deception we all use so well to wither away what lives in our senses, the betrayal of the gesture. Yet one knew that the spirit, honest and pure and just, holds the rod and walks the wire upon which the flesh performs, the spirit's work. I knew that we all only wanted and searched for something to be true to, some small sensual image which our minds could hold like a hand an object through which we could be true to the spiritual choices we had made and struggled to keep; and something through which we could love our human world and, particularly, the beloved we would, each of us, one day find and keep to and do our work with, perilously balancing.

Rome, 19 . .

We rode the flood, this strange company, and we seemed to flourish. But a woman we had rescued fell in love, it was reported, with a bird, a splendid imperial Swan; and one young rescued man, who grew restless and impatient, escaped from the sanctuary (we did not try to stop him, every man did as he pleased) by means of wings he made for himself out of feathers of some of the birds and out of plaster of Paris used for the casts of broken limbs. We saw him sail for a moment and then fall into the flood. And there was a sullen man who had some hidden feeling in him which we could not understand, and in the days that followed we watched him rankle and knew that he felt malice toward someone of the company. One night he tried to murder another man who, so far as we could make out, had not committed one unseemly act.

In time, groups were formed, certain of the refugees emerged as leaders with causes and others became their followers, there was dissension between the groups; and so we saw that we had the same race of men as had existed before the flood. For awhile we thought we might be beginning a new world. There seemed no other that had not been destroyed by the catastrophe of water, and we seemed the only humanity surviving. But soon we saw that in the sanctuary there was going to be the same world over again.

There was a report that a stranger in a boat had done a heroic job of rescuing people from houses and trees and rooftops. It was now known that he had brought people and animals in his boat, and even some few precious objects which he thought worthy of saving back from the destruction of the water. Who was this rescuer? He was searched for among the company, but no one like him was to be found. Then had he drowned, this rescuer, had he lost his life in the rescue? The people he had saved tried to describe him, but each description, vague and undetailed, contradicted the other, and in the end we had no more than a sense of the rescuer. Some said they had seen him somewhere before, but they did not know where.

We knew we were safe, so long as the building survived, what with the animals who know more about the catastrophes of nature than we humans. In time, they would know what to do; they would leave when it was time and safe, so we depended on the animals.

During the flood, I worked round the heart of Chris; and as I did my work in this country of him, I imagined a sad and lovely tale to see if it might speak for him and for this region of his mysterious world that lay in my claim as though I had seized or conquered it and now ruled it like an emperor. Given as much as I had read from him, my imagination began to collaborate with him; and hearing as much as I had heard from him, from that voice beneath his body, the human cry of that face which I heard as I looked at him, I began to try to speak with it or to speak to it, or to answer it. I began to create, or to *re-create* a world for this body to live in. This face of flesh and bone was yet a face of earth, like the ground and what composes it: clay, quarry, dirt; and like what grows in the ground: weed, grass, leaf. But we all of us know that something, some power, can bring this flesh of clay and grass beyond its common substance into a race of legendary people, a people of larger-than-human stature and bearing, and then deliver it back to what withers and dies, or stays forever. A man who makes such a being raises him to a triumphant sense of self through this very gesture. It is this gesture which pervades and surrounds and emanates from what is created or made up. This is the hand, the inventing hand which, as if in great danger itself (and you see the danger), had seized out of pandemonium this ordered image, had snatched it out, whole and safe and undamaged from chaos to give it; the hand is safe, we know, but it quickly obliterates its gesture of salvation or any attention to its own heroic act and withdraws itself, leaving only the rescued image which has, now, taken on a *sense of its rescuer*, and adds that to its own meaning. It is this quality of the *marvel* of which I speak. I think you see the process of this construction out of a destruction, the way repair works: your object and subject (for they are one) seems at once about to disintegrate and yet to order itself out of its fragments with astonishing simplicity and through the means of one simple shape or form as the center around which the whole design clusters and from which it takes its larger shape. In the end, this simple, residual shape seems to have been seized at the verge of disintegration and rescued back into order. After one has been in the company of his subject for awhile, his subject seems to have been saved from his unutterable peril and to have been rescued from his disturbed intensities and passions aloft into a permanent and liberated air of grace, informed with his own sense of what he has been rescued from. For this subject is, finally, one who has suffered through, together with his creator and savior, what has happened to him, what he carries within himself, his terrible and beautiful vision which he has had no fear of showing; and he has arrived at this permanent instant of integration at which his creator sees him there in his now fearless and indestructible totality of *himself*. The subject has not been surrealized or intellectualized or psychoanalyzed. To look at your invented or to live with him for awhile is to have to submit to the processes at work within him, for he shows you an active, dynamic experience of a growing, searching, suffering process, and to come through with him, in the end. This was my objective with my patient.

Now we were both, Chris and I, in great danger and in that perilous and delicate balance of which I have spoken. In the service of the idea of Chris, I saw how my idea had taken on a moral reality all its own, speaking for itself, beyond me and independent of me, and it began to add to my invention. What I felt I had rescued, or was rescuing, had taken on the sense of its rescuer and added that to itself.

But would my idea ever walk on two feet and go its own way, or would it end the ghost of an idea, and forever an invalid, to whom my ghostly voice would call out, "*Be* my idea of you!" I began my collaboration with him . . .

Tapioca Surprise

Before the rainstorm broke on the little town that unusual autumn afternoon, the whole world seemed to turn apple green, as if it were sick, and not a thing stirred, no leaf or limb or anything. And then, in the green stillness that was like the sick town holding its breath, there descended upon the telephone wires in front of Opal Ducharm's house a flock of blackbirds to sit all in a quiet row there. "Blackbirds at even', misery and grievin'," Mrs. Ducharm recited at her window, where she happened to be to watch Mrs. Sangley across the street. Rentha Sangley had just appeared on her porch with her head and face swaddled in an ostentatious bandage, so that she looked like some nun, and she was sweeping the leaves in the still moment before the storm would break. The whole town seemed to be waiting, except Rentha Sangley, who was showing off her bandage to the neighborhood to try to get sympathy.

And then it turned very dark and a little wind started and Mrs. Ducharm saw Rentha Sangley go in her house. The blackbirds flurried and broke their pattern, and they left the telephone wire swinging. The leaves, some of them big and tough as hides, began rolling and flying; and one leaf rushed in through the door Mrs. Opal Ducharm opened, and lay still on her rug. She slammed the door and stared at the leaf and recited, sensitive to omens, "Leaf on the floor, trouble galore . . ." and picked up the leaf.

Now big raindrops slapped on the sidewalks, and right away

there was a steady colorless pour. This meant, without one doubt, that The Paradisers—of which Opal Ducharm was President—could not meet on the high school football field to practice their special number. And that they would have to miss another time of practicing for when the Grand Paradiser, Hester Shrift, would come next week to review the performance of their Fife and Drum Corps that was so renowned throughout the very state . . . and because of her, since she had organized and trained Paradisers all over the country. "You blackbirds, you leaf. This is what you were telling me, and maybe even more," Opal Ducharm said, going right to her phone. She did have a feeling of everything all wrong and ominous, the way she sometimes did.

She tried her phone again. No, it still would not work! But thank goodness Maudie Rickett had called in time—she was the last to get through before the phone had gone deaf on the other end, when the sky had first begun to gather and threaten. "Maudie," Opal had said, "We'll all come on, in spite of if it rains, to my house and see what we can drum up—socially. It's necessary to the morale of the organization to *assemble*—in *some* way—despite *natural* interferences. You call your list and tell it of the change." And then she had started calling her list—for even the President had a list—when of all things this deafness smote the other end of her phone. She couldn't get a person to answer, no one said a thing. Now how could that be? Then she tried, hung up and tried again, but she could never get anyone, not even Central.

Of all times to have this unusual thing happen to the phone! She would just have to run across to Rentha Sangley's and use her phone. This would also be an excellent chance to find out the meaning of her big bandage, what kind of accident or trouble had beset her *this* time. She ran through rain and flying leaves and knocked on Rentha Sangley's door, using not her knuckles but the special knocker that was a woodpecker carved by Mr. Sangley before he passed.

Rentha Sangley appeared. It seemed her eyes were the only unbandaged thing left upon her face. "I saw your bandage from my window, and *what* happened to you, your poor thing?" But before Mrs. Sangley could get a word out edgewise through the wrappings, Opal Ducharm put first things first and said, "Rentha, honey, could I use your phone in an emergency?"

"It was a little cyst," Rentha said, showing Opal the phone. "I could have had bloodpoison or a cancer, and lucky to have neither." She walked painfully but proudly under the burden of the bandage, almost as if she were wearing a new big hat. "Dr. Post cut it out yesterday, using a little chloroform on me."

But Opal Ducharm already had Central on the phone and she was explaining the crazy condition of her phone—which was more serious than any cyst cut out. "I'll run right home, honey," she said to the telephone operator, whom she knew personally. "I'm across the street at Rentha Sangley's and you try ringing me at home. This is an emergency."

"I do hope you'll be healed up soon, Rentha," Opal commiserated, and went for the door. "I have to hurry now to my phone."

"Oh I'll be all right," she said, weakly and with a pained face. And then she bellowed towards the kitchen, "Grandma Sangley you stay out of my hard sauce!"

"How is Grandma Sangley?" Opal Ducharm asked, opening the door.

"Into everything. And me encumbered like this . . ."

But Opal was already running down the steps and out into the rain. I just hope all the ladies will know not to go to the football field but to come to my house, she said to herself, running.

As she opened her door she heard the thrilling sound of her phone ringing. This must be the operator. She ran and answered, but there was nothing. Opal Ducharm said hello again. Still no response from the other end. Yet there was the feeling of somebody there, like somebody hiding in a house and not answering your call. What a kind of a phone to have! she declared. And today of all days. Then she said into the phone:

"Now honey, don't you say a word because I can't hear you, you'll be just wasting your sweet breath. You may be that little operator I just talked to over at Rentha Sangley's phone but I can't tell, I mean how could I?; and you may be a Paradiser and if you are, then this phone is broken on your end, I don't know why, but just listen to me, this is for *you*. This is Opal Ducharm, President of the Paradisers, Unit No. 22, as you know, and since it's just pouring down bullfrogs, as you *know*, we cannot practice for our special performance for the Grand Paradiser Hester Shrift at the high school football field but will convene at my house for a get-together instead. Don't talk, don't talk! I can hear your little clicking but don't try to talk, honey, because I can't hear you. Just listen to me. We have to *postpone* because of this downpour. Just come on straight to my house instead of to the football field. *And call your list.* Do you hear? *Call your list* and tell it of the change." She waited, but there was not a sound, not even the little clicking, and so she banged down the receiver and was so unnerved she wanted to cry. But the phone rang again, and again there was no sound. She went through her speech again. This happened over and over, and each time she told again the story of the meeting at her house until she was hoarse. I just hope some word has got through to the Paradisers, she said.

To calm herself and to forget her anxiety, she stood at the door and called Sister, her sweet cat. Sister arrived miraculously, the way she always did, out of silence and nowhere, tail high in the air, and brushing against everything, dawdling to torment Opal. She seized her and squeezed her harder than she meant, until Sister's claws came out of her; and then she kissed Sister's purple ears. She sat down with her and felt a claw in her thigh. "Why sweet Sister," she said, "you act like you despise me." And then she spoke a long whispered confidence to her and felt the claw loosen. Opal was hungry. But she would wait for the Tapioca. Still, at this moment, she did not know which she loved more: Tapioca or Sister.

And then it was four o'clock and time for the meeting—and rain rain rain.

But the usually expert machinery of the list-calling did not work so smoothly and everyone was confused. There were some women at the football field, drenched in the rain, and some no place at all, so far as the callers could make out, for no one answered any place that was called. The result was only a fragment of Paradisers at Opal Ducharm's house, twelve women out of twenty-eight . . . two lonely squads. "We'll just have a little social," Opal Ducharm said, trying to make the most of a bad situation—which was one of the tenets of the Paradisers—for they had a whole philosophy of life; they did not just blow fife and beat drum. "Anyway I *feel* like a relaxin' social," Opal said. "But one word," she added. "Be sure to get your dresses in shape. We will all, of course, wear our white formals. With white corsages. This must, as you know, be perfect for the Grand Paradiser."

The ladies all sat around talking about their troubles and afflictions, the way they loved to do. Opal Ducharm went to her kitchen and started preparing refreshments, which was this time Tapioca. She could hear Moselle Lessups telling about her dentist, Dr. Gore, who was all the scandal in the town because he had been discovered practicing without a license. "He *knows* his profession," she was declaring, "and I don't care *what* they say about his certificate, whether it's forged or not. He can tell you what every tooth in your head is up to. And in a fascinatin' way. And holds a little mirror up so you can see his work in progress. Some people don't like to see, just want to close their eyes till it's all over. But if you *know,* it helps, *I* think."

"'You see, Mrs. Lessups,' Dr. Gore showed me in the little tooth mirror, 'a big molar is pushin some little ones away from it. It found the vacancy left by the tooth you had pulled out and it has tried to lean over into this vacant place. Do you understand?' he says. "Yes," I said . . . "but . . ." 'We can't have that big old molar doin this to all those other little teeth,' he says, 'can we?', with such a tenderness and real interest and affection for the teeth. "But what will we do?" I says. 'Pull it right out,' he says. 'It's no good to you,' he says, just as though he suddenly despised my big molar. 'It's just crowdin all those other smaller ones and jammin them all together in too little a space.' "Well," I says, "Dr. Gore, I don't want all my good teeth pushed to the front like old Boney Vinson's down at the Station!" I says and laughed. "But use deadening because you know how nervous I am."

The ladies listened and wagged their heads.

Then Paradiser Clover Sugrew gave one of her imitations that quietened the room down for a few minutes until Mrs. Mack McCutcheon burst up from her chair over everybody and went off into one of her exaggerations that nobody could stop—you just had to let her go on through with it to the end, like a rock that suddenly, for no good reason, started falling down a hill. It was about her Napropath for her nervous headaches.

"It is caused by one little nerve!" she cried, before anybody hardly knew what the score was, "made like a . . . oh, we all have it, you have it and I have, this little nerve . . . let's see, what's its name, never *can* remember it, ought to, it's the cause of all my misery, ought to know it better'n my own name—aw shoot, can't think of its name now . . . but *any*way, this little ever-what-it-is nerve just stops working—on my Junction Board . . . which is situated right back here at the bottom of my neck and right between my shoulders. Don't look so *morbid,* you all, you all have one too, we all have, all have a Junction Board so don't look so morbid. Anyway . . . imagine your Junction Board as like a switchboard—this is what the Napropath tells me—all the nerves are there, they are all there, switchin on, switchin off, pluggin in calls to the brain. Well, when *it* stops workin—'why, please tell me,' I asked my Napropath; and he shrugged his shoulders to say, 'That's the mystery, Mrs. McCutcheon; now drop your chin;' when *it* stops, then (wouldn't you know), two *other* nerves—the, let's see—oh don't know their names either. *Anyway*—we've all got these, too—these two nerves runnin down your chest on either side—*then* the headache starts. But the most *peculiar* thing is that I have a *tramp nerve*. It just wanders around, can never tell where it'll be next—aren't our bodies a miracle? The good Lord made such a masterpiece when he made these bodies, works of art, a mystery for all to behold . . . . ."

Mrs. Mack McCutcheon stopped abruptly and what came in over her dead silence was Mrs. Randall's voice saying, "all I said was 'I never in my life!' and turned and walked right out of Neiman-Marcuses with me a new hat on."

As Mrs. Randall was the one who had money and drove to Dallas to buy all her clothes, the subject of her exclamation was urgently important to the other ladies. They listened to her. She was telling about the little male milliner in Neiman-Marcuses. "I tell you I never in my life heard anybody be able to talk about a hat the way he does. He said, 'This is *your* hat, Mrs. Randall, I knew it the moment I put it on your head. This hat is a nice statement on your head. Not sayin too much, just enough. Just the right kind of a statement for you to make goin down the street—not a shriek, not a sigh, but a good-size, sure and strong positive yes!, Mrs. Randall.' How he can talk about a hat, that Lucien Silvero, brought in by Neiman-Marcuses from New York!"

Opal Ducharm was whipping her cream for the Tapioca Surprise and listening when she could to all the stories that were like a stitching party in her living room. Then she put her bowl of firm cream on the table and turned to the bowls of Tapioca looking very special, ready for the cream.

A noise was behind her and she turned round to find Sister the cat upon the table over her cream. She could not clap her hands fast enough, however, to stop Sister from dragging her tongue across the top. Then she cried, softly so the ladies could not hear, "Shoo, you Sister!" and Sister sprang away and ran to sit by the door, where she casually began cleaning her face and whiskers. "You hateful Sister!" Opal whispered as she smoothed over the little rut left by the cat's tongue. "Now you go outdoors!"—and she opened the door for the cat.

Opal Ducharm put the cream on the Tapioca, it looked so delicious, and then she stood at her kitchen door with the tray and said with real charm, "Surprise, Paradisers!"; and all the conversation stopped. The ladies loved the surprise refreshments at the meetings, and all tried to be original.

The surprise was passed round and admired, and all the Paradisers crooned with delight. And then they all started in on it.

When Opal Ducharm went to the kitchen to get her bowl, she spied through her window what looked like a sprawled cat in the driveway. She ran out to Sister and found her truly dead and not sleeping or playing possum. Sister was lying over on her side, drawn long and limp; and her paws were thrust out from her as if she had died trying to hold away whatever kind of death had taken her. Round her black lips were speckles of whipcream and some was still hanging on her whiskers. And then Opal saw the whole picture in a flash. "Poisoned by the cream!" she gasped. Just like those fifty-four people that got bacteria in the banana cream pie at the Houston cafeteria. She rushed up the steps through the door and as she ran she was beholding the image of twelve Paradisers lying flung down like the cat, poisoned dead: Ora Stevens, Moselle Lessups, Clover Sugrew, and all the others, drawn out and limp on her living room floor, all the fifes and drums stilled forever. She flew to the living room, flung out her hands and cried, "Stop the Surprise! Stop! Stop! It is deadly poison and has just killed the cat!" and knocked flying to the floor a spoonful that Esther Borglund was just about to devour. And then she told the bewildered Paradisers about her discovery of the cat, dead in the driveway with the cream on her whiskers and how earlier she had caught Sister with her tongue in the bowl of cream. The ladies were stunned, but Opal shouted, "Get your purses and we'll all run to Victory Hospital just around the corner, that's the quickest thing;" and to Myrtle Dubuque who was already on the phone she yelled "Myrtle that phone's dead, too, dead as Sister and dead as we'll all be if we don't hurry hurry . . . ."; and they all rushed out. By grace, the Paradiser Lieutenant was there—it was Johnny Sue Redundo—and with her whistle, which she blew at once and, as if by magic, organized rout into loose squads which lurched without their usual and State-renowned precision, but as valiantly as they could, towards Victory Hospital.

At Victory Hospital the Head Registered Nurse, Viola Privins, was doing all she knew to keep the ladies calm until Dr. Sam Berry could help them—applying cold towels, taking pulses, giving antidotes. Mrs. Cairns had a thermometer in her mouth and many of the ladies had hypos for shock. Cots were put up in the hall by the Emergency Room like the time of the Flu epidemic, but most of the ladies were just too sick to lie down. In fact, the ladies were getting sicker and sicker; some thought they were ready to have a convulsion; and Mrs. Randall, the sickest of all, kept seeing her face writhing and going purple in her mirror. (She had just gobbled up most of her dish of Tapioca, she loved it so.) One Paradiser fainted, and the fattest—it was Ora Starnes—had to be laid out her full length and weight in the Emergency Room, where she was brought to with a cold cloth and ammonia. But when she opened her eyes upon a nurse helping in a stabbed and bleeding derelict, she snuffed out again quick as a candle and hogged the only emergency table.

There was the question as to who should go in to the stomach pump first, since there was only one pump. Some said the officers should go, others suggested alphabetical order, Mrs. Lessups insisted that those who ate the most should go, and Leta Cratz said the sanest thing of all when she shouted, "The sickest should be first—Mrs. Randall is nearly dyin!"

In the midst of all this pandemonium, Myrtle Dubuque, the secretary of the Paradisers and elected that because she was so calm all the time, was moving up and down among the Paradisers, patting them and saying, "Honey, be calm!" She was as steady as if she were taking down the minutes of a rowdy business meeting.

Finally Opal Ducharm, the President, took hold of the situation and reminded all that the motto of the Paradisers was Charity, Unselfishness and Service—and went in first to the pump, which had just arrived with Dr. Berry, with exemplary dignity even in pain. This inspired others to self-effacement except Sarah Galt (who was only a probationary member anyway) who said she was not going to wait any longer and was going to call her personal family physician.

The ladies started going in to Dr. Berry, one by one, and he was efficient and sweet with each patient. But you can imagine what confusion little Victory Hospital was in. It was just the time for the patients' supper but not a one got it. Everything was delayed, compresses, pulses, pills and bedpans; and red lights begged from most every room. But there was no nurse to answer. "This would be the worst tragedy in the town since the time the grandstand collapsed at the May Fete," a little student nurse, Lucy Bird, said. Mrs. Laura Vance, the richest woman in the town and in Victory Hospital for one of her rest cures, put on her Japanese Kimona (from her actual trip to Japan) and came out to assist. But by this time half the town was there. "What is it?" somebody asked Lew Tully who was in, again, for a drying out. "Beats me, but from what I can tell, somebody tried to poison and then rape twelve Paradisers."

"Why'd he want to poison 'em?"

"Why'd he want to rape 'em?" answered Lew.

Paradisers came running in who, in spite of the expert machinery of the list-calling, could not be reached when there was important official information about the organization to be relayed, but had immediately heard, without the slightest difficulty of being reached, of the tragedy of the Tapioca. But most of them were of no help at all, they just got in the way; and Myra Pugh got a hypo she didn't merit, in the scramble. Volunteers came from all over, even Jack the Ant Killer was there—why, nobody knew, but he thought he could help; and Mack Sims of the Valley Gold Dairy was there because he had sold the cream and was afraid the Paradisers might get out an injunction against him for poisoning them, especially if anybody died. Some husbands came, but not Jock Ducharm, this was his day in Bewley, selling his product; and anyway those who did come just got in the way, except Mr. Cairns, a real businessman with sense, who immediately called Honey Grove Hospital, twenty miles away, for their stomach pump, and it was coming by ambulance immediately. A reporter from *The Bee* came in and Opal Ducharm appointed Grace Kunsy to act as temporary publicity chairman since the regular one, Ora Starnes, was just too sick to say one word for the papers.

By the time several of the ladies had survived the ordeal of the stomach pump and were standing around or lying on the cots, feeling saved and relieved, if languorous, the panic began to subside a little, and it appeared that the women would all come through. Opal Ducharm was complaining that there should be more stomach pumps in a hospital this size and that the Paradisers should have a Bazaar to raise funds for these. She put it on the agenda for the next meeting.

So no one died, and with the help of the volunteers, it was finally over, every stomach was purged, and about nine o'clock that night Dr. Sam Berry pronounced them all out of danger. The women were told to rest for a while, but not a one would stay at Victory Hospital. Mrs. Delancy, the smoker of the group, had another cigarette, and they all went home.

Poor Opal Ducharm, of course, felt the sting of the near-tragedy most severely, for it seemed her fault, and yet it couldn't be. She got home weak and exhausted.

"It just makes me sick, I declare to my soul," she was saying to herself as she opened the door, when there was Jock, her husband. "And where in the name of the Savior have you been?" she yelled, knowing perfectly well that it was his day in Bewley.

"I just got in about twenty minutes ago, Opal. You know today was my day to go to Bewley."

And when Opal saw that Jock was not going to be sympathetic, this was going to be too much. But then he never did care anything about the Paradisers, wouldn't even become an Auxiliary, and wear the special tie-clasp, like the other husbands, but bowled instead. "If they want me in the Auxiliary let 'em meet another night besides Tuesdays. That's my bowling night," he said. This was a source of great hurt and shame to Opal who, after all, *was* the President.

"Well you shouldn't have gone to Bewley today! You missed something near-fatal. You could have helped, which you never do, so never mind."

"Helped what?"

"I had to have my stomach pumped, that's all. But never mind."

"You know I sell my product in Bewley on Tuesdays, Opal. And what did you swallow, for Christ's sakes?"

"Something poisoned. But never mind."

"Well Opal, we'll get back to the poison in a minute, but what I'm trying to tell you is that Sister is dead."

"Oh don't remind me of that because she was poisoned too!"

"Poisoned? Well I don't know about you, Opal, but that damned cat wasn't poisoned. What I'm trying to tell you is that Ruta Tanner just left here. She came to tell you that when she drove in the driveway during your meeting she believes she hit a cat. She felt a thud and saw something lying on its side in the driveway. Now how much closer can you get to the fact that she ran over Sister and killed her?"

"Oh to my Savior!" Opal wailed. "But why didn't Ruta come in here and tell me? It would have saved us all from so much suffering!"

"She said she was too upset to come in and disturb the meeting with such bad news. And especially seeing as how, since she's on probation for drilling drunk under the influence of martinis at the Thanksgiving Special March, she felt too humiliated to come in on a meeting. If you ask me, she's been hitting the gin like a bat outta hell since you all expelled her—or whatever the hell you did. She said to tell you that she tried to call you from Pig Stand No. 2 but your 'phone wouldn't work. Anyways, I called her a dumb hit-and-run-driver and said I was going to sue her and that lounge-lizard husband of hers with the beer-belly. I don't want to get mixed up in it, lemme alone. I've been in Bewley all day tryin to sell my product to a bunch of numbskulls."

"Oh where is poor Sister now?" Opal shrieked and tore at the divan which Sister's claws had already shredded in places.

"I just put her in an A&P shopping bag and will bury her directly. What else can I do, for God's sake? If you don't get hold of yourself you're going to have to have more than your stomach pumped. Your brains, for Christsakes. Anyway," he said, under his breath as he went to the refrigerator to get a beer, "there'll be less cat hair all over everything in the house . . . . *including* my blue suit which by now *looks* like Sister. I was about ready to give it to her."

Opal Ducharm could have been humiliated by this comment, but she was now going through such various feelings that she didn't know which to settle for. At first she felt elated because nobody was poisoned, and then she thought of Sister killed and was heart-broken. She started to call the poor exhausted women all pumped half to death for nothing, but she remembered her dead phone and felt rage. Then she really got just plain fed-up with the whole thing and in a second decided to eliminate every feeling but one, her appetite, and started for the kitchen.

"Well," she said. "I know what *I'm* going right to the icebox and do. That's eat me a good big helping of that Tapioca. There's an awful lot left and I didn't even get to taste of it."

And from the refrigerator she drew out a finger wrapped with whipcream and smacked it up with a brave tongue in a kind of toast to the killed cat and to the whole affair, and, bringing a mound of the good Tapioca, came in and sat down by Jock.

"When I've quieted down and can stand to recall it, I'll tell you the whole terrible thing," she advised Jock.

"Whenever you're ready," Jock said. "Shall I wait—or bury the cat?"

Bridge of Music, River of Sand

Do you remember the bridge that we crossed over the river to get to Riverside? And if you looked over yonder you saw the railroad trestle? High and narrow? Well that's what he jumped off of. Into a nothing river. "River"! I could laugh. I can spit more than runs in that dry bed. In some places is just a little damp, but that's it. That's your grand and rolling river: a damp spot. That's your remains of the grand old Trinity. Where can so much water go? I at least wish they'd do something about it. But what can they do? What can anybody do? You can't replace a *river*.

Anyway, if there'd been water, maybe he'd have made it, the naked diver. As it was, diving into the river as though there were water in it, he went head first into moist sand and drove into it like an arrow into flesh and was found in a position of somebody on their knees, headless, bent over looking for something. Looking for where the river vanished to? I was driving across the old river bridge when I said to myself, wait a minute I believe I see something. I almost ran into the bridge railing. I felt a chill come over me.

What I did was when I got off the bridge to draw my car off to the side of the road and get out and run down the river bank around a rattlesnake that seemed to be placed there as a deterrent (the banks are crawling with them in July), and down; and what I came upon was a kind of avenue that the river had made and paved with gleaming white sand, wide and grand and empty. I crossed this ghostly thoroughfare of the river halfway, and when I got closer, my Lord Jesus God Almighty damn if I didn't see that it was half a naked human body in what would have been midstream were there water. I was scared to death. What ought I to do? Try to pull it out? I was scared to touch it. It was a heat-stunned afternoon. The July heat throbbed. The blue, steaming air waved like a veil. The feeling of something missing haunted me: it was the lost life of the river—something so powerful that it had haunted the countryside for miles around; you could feel it a long time before you came to it. In a landscape that was unnatural—flowing water was missing—everything else seemed unnatural. The river's vegetation was thin and starved-looking; it lived on the edge of sand instead of water; it seemed out of place.

If only I hadn't taken the old bridge. I was already open to a fine of five thousand dollars for driving across it, according to the sign, and I understood why. (Over yonder arched the shining new bridge. There was no traffic on it.) The flapping of loose boards and the quaking of the iron beams was terrifying. I almost panicked in the middle when the whole construction swayed and made such a sound of crackling and clanking. I was surprised the feeble structure hadn't more than a sign to prohibit passage over it—it should have been barricaded. At any rate, it was when I was in the middle of this rocking vehicle that seemed like some mad carnival ride that I saw the naked figure diving from the old railroad trestle. It was as though the diver were making a flamboyant leap into the deep river below—until to my horror I realized that the river was dry. I dared not stop my car and so I maneuvered my way on, mechanical with terror, enchanted by the melodies that rose from the instruments of the melodious bridge that played like some orchestra of xylophones and drums and cellos as I moved over it. Who would have known that the dead bridge, condemned and closed away from human touch, had such music in it? I was on the nother side now. Behind me the music was quieter now, lowering into something like chime sounds and harness sounds and wagons; it shook like bells and tolled like soft, deep gongs.

His hands must have cut through the wet sand, carving a path for his head and shoulders. He was sunk up to his mid-waist and had fallen to a kneeling position: a figure on its knees with its head buried in the sand, as if it had decided not to look at the world any more. And then the figure began to sink as if someone underground were pulling it under. Slowly the stomach, lean and hairy, vanished; then the loins, thighs. The river, which had swallowed half this body, now seemed to be eating the rest of it. For a while the feet lay, soles up, on the sand. And then they went down, arched like a dancer's.

Who was the man drowned in a dry river? eaten by a dry river? devoured by sand? How would I explain, describe what had happened? I'd be judged to be out of my senses. And why would I tell somebody—the police or—anybody? There was nothing to be done, the diver was gone, the naked leaper was swallowed up. Unless somebody had pushed him over the bridge and he'd assumed a diving position to try to save himself. But what evidence was there? Well, I *had* to report what I'd seen, what I'd witnessed. Witness? To what? Would anybody believe me? There was no evidence anywhere. Well, I'd look, I'd search for evidence. I'd go up on the railroad trestle.

I climbed up. The trestle was perilously narrow and high. I could see a long ways out over Texas, green and steaming in July. I could see the scar of the river, I could see the healed-looking patches that were the orphaned bottomlands. I could see the tornado-shaped funnel of bilious smoke that twisted out of the mill in Riverside, enriching the owner and poisoning him, his family and his neighbors. And I could see the old bridge which I'd just passed over and still trembling under my touch, arching perfect and precious, golden in the sunlight. The music I had wrought out of it was now stilled except, it seemed, for a low, deep hum that rose from it. It seemed impossible that a train could move on these narrow tracks now grown over with weeds. As I walked, grasshoppers flared up in the dry heat.

I saw no footprints in the weeds, no sign of anybody having walked on the trestle—unless they walked on the rails or the ties. Where were the man's clothes? Unless he'd left them on the bank and run out naked onto the trestle. This meant searching on both sides of the trestle—Christ, what was I caught up in? It could also mean that he was a suicide, my mind went on dogging me; or insane; it could also mean that nobody else was involved. Or it could mean that I was suffering a kind of bridge madness, or the vision that sometimes comes from going home again, of going back to places haunted by deep feeling?

Had anyone ever told me the story of a man jumping into the river from the trestle? Could this be some tormented spirit doomed forever to re-enact his suicide? And if so, must he continue it, now that the river was gone? This thought struck me as rather pitiful.

How high the trestle was! It made me giddy to look down at the riverbed. I tried to find the spot where the diver had hit the dry river. There was absolutely no sign. The mouth of sand that had sucked him down before my very eyes had closed and sealed itself. The story was over, so far as I was concerned. Whatever had happened would be my secret. I had to give it up, let it go. You can understand that I had no choice, that that was the only thing I could do.

That was the summer I was making a sentimental trip through home regions, after fifteen years away. The bridge over the beloved old river had been one of my most touching memories—an object that hung in my memory of childhood like a precious ornament. It was a fragile creation, of iron and wood, and so poetically arched, so slender, half a bracelet (the other half underground) through which the green river ran. The superstructure was made more for a minaret than a bridge. From a distance it looked like an ornate pier, in Brighton or early Santa Monica; or, in the summer heat haze, a palace tower, a creation of gold. Closer, of course, it was an iron and wooden bridge of unusual beauty, shape and design. It had always been an imperfect bridge, awry from the start. It had been built wrong—an engineering mistake: the ascent was too steep and the descent too sharp. But its beauty endured. And despite its irregularity, traffic had used the bridge at Riverside, without serious mishap, for many years. It was just an uncomfortable trip, and always somewhat disturbing, this awkward, surprising and somehow mysterious crossing.

Some real things happened on this practical, if magical, device for crossing water. For one thing, since it swayed, my mother, in our childhood days, would refuse to ride across it. She would remove herself from the auto and walk across, holding onto the railing, while my father, cursing, drove the rest of us across. My sister and I peered back at the small figure of our mother laboring darkly and utterly alone on the infernal contraption which was her torment. I remember my father getting out of the car, on the other side, waiting at the side of the road, looking toward the bridge, watching my mother's creeping progress. When she arrived, pale, she declared, as she did each time, "I vow to the Lord if my sister Sarah didn't live in Riverside I'd never to my soul come near this place." "Well you could lie down in the back seat, put the cotton in your ears that you always bring, and never know it, as I keep telling you," said my father. "I'd still know it," my mother came back. "I'd still know we was on this infernal bridge." "Well then take the goddam train from Palestine. Train trestle's flat." And, getting in the car and slamming the door, "Or stay home and just *write* to your damned sister Sarah. Married to a horse's ass, anyway."

"Mama," said my sister, trying to pacify the situation. "Tell us about the time you almost drowned in the river and Daddy had to jump in and pull you out."

"Well, it was just right over yonder. We'd been fishing all morning, and . . ."

"Aw for Christ's sake," my father said.

On the other side of the bridge, after a crossing of hazards and challenges, there was nothing more than a plain little town of mud streets and weather-faded shacks. The town of poor people lived around an ugly mill that puffed out like talcum something called Fuller's Earth over it. This substance lay on rooftops, on the ground and in lungs. It smelled sour and bit the eyes.

As I drove away toward that town, haunted by the vision of the leaping man and now so shaken in my very spirit, lost to fact but brought to some odd truth which I could not yet clear for myself, I saw in the mirror the still image of the river bridge that had such hidden music in it, girdling the ghost of what it had been created for, that lost river that held in its bosom of sand the diving figure of the trestle that I was sure I had seen. I was coming in to Riverside and already the stinging fumes of the mill brought tears to my eyes.

Figure Over the Town

In the town of my beginning I saw this masked figure sitting aloft. It was never explained to me by my elders, who were thrilled and disturbed by the figure too, who it was, except that he was called Flagpole Moody. The days and nights he sat aloft were counted on calendars in the kitchens of small houses and in troubled minds, for Flagpole Moody fed the fancy of an isolated small town of practical folk whose day's work was hard and real.

Since the night he was pointed out to me from the roof of the little shed where my father sheltered grain and plowing and planting implements, his shape has never left me; in many critical experiences of my life it has suddenly appeared before me, so that I have come to see that it is a dominating emblem of my life, as often a lost lover is, or the figure of a parent, or the symbol of a faith, as the scallop shell was for so many at one time, or the Cross.

It was in the time of a war I could not understand, being so very young, that my father came to me at darkening, in the beginning wintertime, and said, "Come with me to the Patch, Son, for I want to show you something."

The Patch, which I often dream about, was a mysterious fenced-in plot of ground, about half an acre, where I never intruded. I often stood at the gate or fence and looked in through the hexagonal lenses of the chicken wire and saw how strange this little territory was, and wondered what it was for. There was the shed in it where implements and grain were stored, but nothing was ever planted nor any animal pastured here; nothing, not even grass or weed, grew here; it was just plain common ground.

This late afternoon my father took me into the Patch and led me to the shed and hoisted me up to the roof. He waited a moment while I looked around at all the world we lived in and had forgotten was so wide and housed so many in dwellings quite like ours. (Later, when my grandfather, my father's father, took me across the road and railroad tracks into a large pasture—so great I had thought it, from the window of our house, the whole world—where a little circus had been set up as if by magic the night before, and raised me to the broad back of a sleepy elephant, I saw the same sight and recalled not only the night I stood on the roof of the shed, but also what I had seen from there, that haunting image, and thought I saw it again, this time on the lightning rod of our house . . . but no, it was, as always, the crowing cock that stood there, eternally strutting out his breast and at the break of crowing.)

My father waited, and when he saw that I had steadied myself, he said, "Well, Son, what is it that you see over there, by the Methodist church?"

I was speechless and could only gaze; and then I finally said to him, not moving, "Something is sitting on the flagpole on top of a building."

"It is just a man," my father said, "and his name is Flagpole Moody. He is going to sit up there for as long as he can stand it."

When we came into the house, I heard my father say to my mother, lightly, "I showed Son Flagpole Moody and I think it scared him a little." And I heard my mother say, "It seems a foolish stunt, and I think maybe children shouldn't see it."

All that night Flagpole Moody was on my mind. When it began raining, in the very deepest night, I worried about him in the rain, and I went to my window and looked out to see if I could see him. When it lightninged, I saw that he was safe and dry under a little tent he had raised over himself. Later I had a terrible dream about him, that he was falling, falling, and when I called out in my nightmare, my parents came to me and patted me back to sleep, never knowing that I would dream of him again.

He stayed and stayed up there, the flagpole sitter, hooded (why would he not show his face?), and when we were in town and walked under him, I would not look up as they told me to; but once, when we stood across the street from the building where he was perched, I looked up and saw how high he was in the air, and he waved down at me with his cap in his hand.

Everywhere there was the talk of the war, but where it was or what it was I did not know. It seemed only some huge appetite that craved all our sugar and begged from the town its goods, so that people seemed paled and impoverished by it, and it made life gloomy—that was the word. One night we went into the town to watch them burn Old Man Gloom, a monstrous straw man with a sour, turned-down look on his face and dressed even to the point of having a hat—it was the Ku Klux Klan who lit him afire—and above, in the light of the flames, we saw Flagpole Moody waving his cap to us. He had been up eighteen days.

He kept staying up there. More and more the talk was about him, with the feeling of the war beneath all the talk. People began to get restless about Flagpole Moody and to want him to come on down. "It seems morbid," I remember my mother saying. What at first had been a thrill and an excitement—the whole town was there every other day when the provisions basket was raised up to him, and the contributions were extravagant: fresh pies and cakes, milk, little presents, and so forth—became an everyday sight; there he seemed ignored and forgotten by the town except for me, who kept a constant, secret watch on him; then, finally, the town became disturbed by him, for he seemed to be going on and on; he seemed an intruder now. Who could feel unlooked at or unhovered over in his house with this figure over everything? (It was discovered that Flagpole was spying on the town through binoculars.) There was an agitation to bring him down and the city council met to this end.

There had been some irregularity in the town which had been laid to the general lawlessness and demoralizing effect of the war: robberies; the disappearance of a beautiful young girl, Sarah Nichols (but it was said she ran away to find someone in the war); and one Negro shot in the woods, which could have been the work of the Ku Klux Klan. The question at the city-council meeting was, "Who gave Flagpole Moody permission to go up there?" No one seemed to know; the merchants said it was not for advertising, or at least no one of them had arranged it, though after he was up, many of them tried to use him to advertise their products—Egg Lay or Red Goose shoes or Have a Coke at Robbins Pharmacy—and why not? The Chamber of Commerce had not brought him, nor the Women's Club; maybe the Ku Klux had, to warn and tame the Negroes, who were especially in awe of Flagpole Moody; but the Klan was as innocent as all the others, it said. The pastor was reminded of the time a bird had built a nest on the church steeple, a huge foreign bird that had delighted all the congregation as well as given him subject matter for several sermons; he told how the congregation came out on the grounds to adore the bird, which in time became suddenly savage and swooped to pluck the feathers from women's Sunday hats and was finally brought down by the fire department, which found the nest full of rats and mice, half devoured, and no eggs at all—this last fact the subject of another series of sermons by the pastor, drawing as he did his topics from real life.

As the flagpole sitter had come to be regarded as a defacement of the landscape, an unsightly object, a tramp, it was suggested that the Ku Klux Klan build a fire in the square and ride round it on their horses and in their sheets, firing their guns into the air, as they did in their public demonstrations against immorality, to force Flagpole down. If this failed, it was suggested someone should be sent up on a firemen's ladder to reason with Flagpole. He was regarded now as a *danger* to the town, and more, as a kind of criminal. (At first he had been admired and respected for his courage, and desired, even: many women had been intoxicated by him, sending up, in the provisions basket, love notes and photographs of themselves, which Flagpole had read and then sailed down for anyone to pick up and read, to the embarrassment of this woman and that. There had been a number of local exposures.)

The town was ready for any kind of miracle or sensation, obviously. A fanatical religious group took Flagpole Moody for the Second Coming. The old man called Old Man Nay, who lived on the edge of the town in a boarded-up house and sat at the one open window with his shotgun in his lap, watching for the Devil, unnailed his door and appeared in the square to announce that he had seen a light playing around Flagpole at night and that Flagpole was some phantom representative of the Devil and should be banished by a raising of the Cross; but others explained that what Old Man Nay saw was St. Elmo's fire, a natural phenomenon. Whatever was given a fantastical meaning by some was explained away by others as of natural cause. What was right? Who was to believe what?

An evangelist who called himself "The Christian Jew" had, at the beginning, requested of Flagpole Moody, by a letter in the basket, the dropping of leaflets. A sample was pinned to the letter. The leaflet, printed in red ink, said in huge letters across the top: WARNING! YOU ARE IN GREAT DANGER! Below was a long message to sinners. If Flagpole would drop these messages upon the town, he would be aiding in the salvation of the wicked. "The Judgments of God are soon to be poured upon the Earth! Prepare to meet God before it is too late! Where will you spend Eternity? What can you do to be saved? How shall we escape if we neglect so great salvation! (Heb. 2:3)."

But there was no reply from Flagpole, which was evidence enough for the Christian Jew to know that Flagpole was on the Devil's side. He held meetings at night in the square, with his little group of followers passing out the leaflets.

"Lower Cain!" he bellowed. "You sinners standing on the street corner running a long tongue about your neighbors; you show-going, card-playing, jazz-dancing brothers—God love your soul—you are a tribe of sinners and you know it and God knows it, but He loves you and wants you to come into His tabernacle and give up your hearts that are laden with wickedness. If you look in the Bible, if you will turn to the chapter of Isaiah, you will find there about the fallen angel, Lucifer was his name, and how his clothing was sewn of emeralds and sapphires, for he was very beautiful; but friends, my sin-loving friends, that didn't make any difference. 'How art thou fallen from Heaven, O Lucifer, son of the morning!' the Bible reads. And it says there that the Devil will walk amongst us and that the Devil will sit on the rooftops; and I tell you we must unite together to drive Satan from the top of the world. Listen to me and read my message, for I was the rottenest man in this world until I heard the voice of God. I drank, I ran with women, I sought after the thrills of the flesh . . . and I admonish you that the past scenes of earth *shall be remembered in Hell.*"

The old maid, Miss Hazel Bright, who had had one lover long

ago, a cowboy named Rolfe Sanderson who had gone away and never returned, told that Flagpole was Rolfe come back, and she wrote notes of poetic longing to put in the provisions basket. Everybody used Flagpole Moody for his own purpose, and so he, sitting away from it all, apparently serene in his own dream and idea of himself, became the lost lover to the lovelorn, the saint to the seekers of salvation, the scapegoat of the guilty, the damned to those who were lost.

The town went on tormenting him; they could not let him alone. They wished him to be their own dream or hope or lost illusion, or they wished him to be what destroyed hope and illusion. They wanted something they could get their hands on; they wanted someone to ease the dark misgiving in themselves, to take to their deepest bosom, into the farthest cave of themselves where they would take no other if he would come and be for them alone. They plagued him with love letters, and when he would not acknowledge these professions of love, they wrote him messages of hate. They told him their secrets, and when he would not show himself to be overwhelmed, they accused him of keeping secrets of his own. They professed to be willing to follow him, leaving everything behind, but when he would not answer "Come," they told him how they wished he would fall and knock his brains out. They could not make up their minds and they tried to destroy him because he had made up his, whatever it was he had made his mind up to.

Merchants tormented him with proposals and offers—would he wear a Stetson hat all one day, tip and wave it to the people below? Would he hold, just for fifteen minutes every hour, a streamer with words on it proclaiming the goodness of their bread, or allow balloons, spelling out the name of something that ought to be bought, to be floated from the flagpole? Would he throw down Life Savers? Many a man, and most, would have done it, would have supplied an understandable reason for his behavior, pacifying the general observer, and in the general observer's own terms (or the general observer would not have it), and so send him away undisturbed, with the feeling that all the world was really just as he was, cheating a little here, disguising a little there. (Everybody was, after all, alike, so where the pain, and why?)

But Flagpole Moody gave no answer. Apparently he had nothing to sell, wanted to make no fortune, to play no jokes or tricks; apparently he wanted just to be let alone to do his job. But because he was so different, they would not let him alone until they could, by whatever means, make him quite like themselves, or cause him, at least, to recognize them and pay *them* some attention. Was he camping up there for the fun of it? If so, why would he not let them all share in it? Maybe he was there for the pure devilment of it, like a cat calm on a chimney top. Or for some very crazy and not-to-be-tolerated reason of his own (which everyone tried to make out, hating secrets as people do who want everything in the clear, where they can attack it and feel moral dudgeon against it).

Was it Cray McCreery up there? Had somebody made him another bet? One time Cray had walked barefooted to the next town, eighteen miles, because of a lost bet. But no, Cray McCreery was found, as usual, in the Domino Parlor. Had any crazy people escaped from the asylum? They were counted and found to be all in. The mind reader, Madame Fritzie, was importuned: There seemed, she said, to be a dark woman in the picture; that was all she contributed: "I see a dark woman . . ." And as she had admonished so many in the town with her recurring vision of a dark woman, there was either an army of dark women tormenting the minds of men and women in the world, or only one, which was Madame Fritzie herself. She could have made a fortune out of the whole affair if she had had her wits about her. More than one Ouija board was put questions to, but the answers were either indistinguishable or not to the point.

Dogs howled and bayed at night and sometimes in the afternoons; hens crowed; the sudden death of children was laid to the evil power of Flagpole Moody over the town.

A masked buffoon came to a party dressed as Flagpole Moody and caused increasing uneasiness among the guests until three of the men at the party, deciding to take subtle action rather than force the stranger to unmask, reported to the police by telephone. The police told them to unmask him by force and they were coming. When the police arrived they found the stranger was Marcus Peters, a past president of the Lions Club and a practical joker with the biggest belly laugh in town, and everybody would have known all along who the impostor was if he had only laughed.

A new language evolved in the town: "You're crazy as Moody," "cold as a flagpole sitter's ——," "go sit on a flagpole" and other phrases of that sort.

In that day and time there flourished, even in that little town, a group of sensitive and intellectual people, poets and artists and whatnot, who thought themselves quite mad and gay—and quite lost, too, though they would turn their lostness to a good thing. These advanced people needed an object upon which to hinge their loose and floating cause, and they chose Flagpole Moody to draw attention, which they so craved, to themselves. They exalted him with some high, esoteric meaning that they alone understood, and they developed a whole style of poetry, music and painting, the echoes of which are still heard, around the symbol of Flagpole Moody. They wrote, and read aloud to meetings, critical explanations of the Theory of Aloftness.

Only Mrs. T. Trevor Sanderson was bored with it all, shambling restlessly about the hospital in her Japanese kimono, her spotted hands (liver trouble, the doctors said) spread like fat lizards on the knolls of her hips. She was there again for one of her rest cures, because her oil-money worries were wearing her to death, and now the Catholic Church was pursuing her with zeal to convert her—for her money, so she said. Still, there was something to the Catholic Church; you couldn't get around that, she said, turning her spotted hands to show them yellow underneath, like a lizard's belly; and she gave a golden windowpane illustrating *The Temptation of St. Anthony* to St. Mary's Church, but would do no more than that.

There were many little felonies and even big offenses of undetermined origin in the police records of the town, and Flagpole was a stimulus to the fresh inspection of unsolved crimes. He drew suspicions up to him and absorbed them like a filter, as though he might purify the town of wickedness. If only he would send down some response to what had gone up to him. But he would not budge; and now he no longer even waved to the people below as he had during the first good days. Flagpole Moody had utterly withdrawn from everybody. What the town finally decided was to put a searchlight on him at night, to keep watch on him.

With the searchlight on the flagpole sitter, the whole thing took a turn, became an excuse for a ribald attitude. When a little wartime carnival came to the town, it was invited to install itself in the square, and a bazaar was added to it by the town. The spirit of Flagpole had to be admired, it was admitted; for after a day and night of shunning the gaiety and the mockery of it all, he showed his good nature and good sportsmanship—even his daring—by participating! He began to do what looked like acrobatic stunts, as though he were an attraction of the carnival.

And what did the people do, after a while, but turn against him again and say he was, as they had said at first, a sensationalist? Still, I loved it that he had become active; that it was not a static, fastidious, precious and Olympian show, that Flagpole did not take on a self-righteous or pompous or persecuted air, although my secret conception of him was still a tragic one. I was proud that my idea fought back—otherwise he was like Old Man Gloom, a shape of straw and sawdust in man's clothing, and let them burn him, if only gloom stood among the executioners, watching its own effigy and blowing on the flames. I know now that what I saw was the conflict of an idea with a society; and I am sure that the idea was bred by the society—raised up there, even, by the society—in short, society was in the flagpole sitter and he was in the society of the town.

There was, at the little carnival, one concession called "Ring Flagpole's Bell." It invited customers to try to strike a bell at the top of a tall pole resembling his—and with a replica of him on top—by hitting a little platform with a rubber-headed sledgehammer; this would drive a metal disk up toward the bell. There was another concession where people could throw darts at a target resembling a figure on a pole. The Ferris wheel was put so close to Flagpole that when its passengers reached the top they could almost, for a magical instant, reach over and touch his body. Going round and round, it was as if one were soaring up to him only to fall away, down, from him; to have him and to lose him; and it was all felt in a marvelous whirling sensation in the stomach that made this experience the most vaunted of the show.

This must have tantalized Flagpole, and perhaps it seemed to him that all the beautiful and desirable people in the world rose and fell around him, offering themselves to him only to withdraw untaken and ungiven, a flashing wheel of faces, eyes, lips and sometimes tongues stuck out at him and sometimes a thigh shown, offering sex, and then burning away. His sky at night was filled with voluptuous images, and often he must have imagined the faces of those he had once loved and possessed, turning round and round his head to torment him. But there were men on the wheel who made profane signs to him, and women who thumbed their noses.

Soon Flagpole raised his tent again and hid himself from his tormentors. What specifically caused his withdrawal was the attempt of a drunken young man to shoot him. This young man, named Maury, rode a motorcycle around the town at all hours and loved the meaner streets and the women who gave him ease, especially the fat ones, his mania. One night he stood at the hotel window and watched the figure on the pole, who seemed to flash on and off, real and then unreal, with the light of the electric sign beneath the window. He took deep drags of his cigarette and blew the smoke out toward Flagpole; then he blew smoke rings as if to lasso Flagpole with them, or as if his figure were a pin he could hoop with the rings of smoke. "You silly bastard, do you like what you see?" he had muttered, and "Where have I seen you before?" between his half-clenched teeth, and then he had fired the pistol. Flagpole turned away then, once and for all.

But he had not turned away from me. I, the silent observer, watching from my window or from any high place I could secretly climb to, witnessed all this conflict and the tumult of the town. One night in my dreaming of Flagpole Moody—it happened every night, this dream, and in the afternoons when I took my nap, and the dreaming had gone on so long that it seemed, finally, as if he and I were friends, that he came down secretly to a rendezvous with me in the little pasture, and it was only years later that I would know what all our conversations had been about—that night in my dream the people of the town came to me and said, "Son, we have chosen you to go up the flagpole to Flagpole Moody and tell him to come down."

In my dream they led me, with cheers and honors, to the top of the building and stood below while I shinnied up the pole. A great black bird was circling over Flagpole's tent. As I went up the pole I noticed crowded avenues of ants coming and going along the pole. And when I went into the tent, I found Flagpole gone. The tent was as if a tornado had swept through the whole inside of it. There were piles of rotten food; shreds of letters torn and retorn, as small as flakes of snow; photographs pinned to the walls of the tent were marked and scrawled over so that they looked like photographs of fiends and monsters; corpses and drifts of feathers of dead birds that had flown at night into the tent and gone so wild with fright that they had beaten themselves to death against the sides. And over it all was the vicious traffic of insects that had found the remains, in the way insects sense what human beings have left, and come from miles away.

What would I tell them below, those who were now crying up to me, "What does he say, what does Flagpole Moody say?" And there were whistles and an increasingly thunderous chant of "Bring him down! Bring him down! Bring him down!" What would I tell them? I was glad he had gone; but I would not tell them that—yet. In the tent I found one little thing that had not been touched or changed by Flagpole; a piece of paper with printed words, and across the top the huge red words: WARNING! YOU ARE IN GREAT DANGER!

Then, in my dream, I went to the flap of the tent and stuck out my head. There was a searchlight upon me through which fell a delicate curtain of light rain; and through the lighted curtain of rain that made the people seem far, far below, under shimmering and jeweled veils, I shouted down to the multitude, which was dead quiet now, "He is not here! Flagpole Moody is not here!"

There was no sound from the crowd, which had not, at first, heard what I said. They waited; then one voice bellowed up, "Tell him to come down!" And others joined this voice until, again, the crowd was roaring, "Tell him that we will not harm him; only tell him he has to come down!" Then I waved down at them to be quiet, in Flagpole Moody's gesture of salute, as he had waved down at people on the sidewalks and streets. Again they hushed to hear me. Again I said, this time in a voice that was not mine, but large and round and resounding, "Flagpole Moody is not here. His place is empty."

And then, in my magnificent dream, I closed the flap of the tent and settled down to make Flagpole Moody's place my own, to drive out the insects, to erase the marks on the photographs, and to piece together, with infinite and patient care, the fragments of the letters to see what they told. It would take me a very long time, this putting together again what had been torn into pieces, but I would have a very long time to give to it, and I was at the source of the mystery, removed and secure from the chaos of the world below that could not make up its mind and tried to keep me from making up my own.

My dream ended here, or was broken, by the hand of my mother shaking me to morning; and when I went to eat breakfast I heard them saying in the kitchen that Flagpole Moody had signaled early, at dawn, around six o'clock, that he wanted to come down; that he had come down in his own time, and that he had come down very, very tired, after forty days and nights, the length of the Flood. I did not tell my dream, for I had no power of telling then, but I knew that I had a story to one day shape around the marvel and mystery that ended in a dream and began in the world that was to be mine.